NARROWS GATE

NARROWS GATE

A Novel by
JIM FUSILLI

PUBLISHED BY

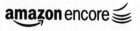

Published by AmazonEncore
P.O. Box 400818
Las Vegas, NV 89140

ISBN-13: 9781612181370
ISBN-10: 1612181376

To my parents,
Narrows Gate born and raised.

CAST OF CHARACTERS

NARROWS GATE

Sal Benno

Leo Bell

William "Bebe" Rosiglino, aka Bill Marsala

Hennie Rosiglino, mother of Bebe Rosiglino

Vincenzo Rosiglino, father of Bebe Rosiglino

Vito and Gemma Benno, proprietors of Benno's Salumeria, Sal's uncle and aunt

Abramo Bell, Leo's father

Father Gregory, pastor of St. Francis of Assisi Church

NARROWS GATE CREW

Fortunato Spaletti, aka Frankie Fortune, *caporegime* for New Jersey

Domenico Mistretta, aka Mimmo, responsible to Fortune for Narrows Gate

Boo Chiasso, soldier assigned to Mimmo

Fat Tutti, soldier assigned to Mimmo

Freddie Pop, associate

FARCOLINI ORGANIZATION

Carlo Farcolini, *capo famiglia* or undisputed boss. Consolidated the New York–New Jersey crime organizations. Aligned with the Sicilian Mafia.

Cy Geller, South Florida–based consigliere. Former head of Jewish mob in New York.

Anthony Corini, *sotto capo* who oversees the Farcolini relationships with government, business, entertainment and other so-called legitimate enterprises. Long-time Farcolini associate.

Bruno Gigenti, *sotto capo* responsible for traditional criminal activities in New York and New Jersey. Joined Farcolini after the hit on Nunzio Patti, his former boss.

Sigmund Baumstein, aka **Ziggy Baum**, reports to Corini. Charged with expanding gambling and entertainment activities to Las Vegas.

Eugenio Zamarella, Bruno Gigenti's hit man

Fredo Pellizzari, soldier and driver to Bruno Gigenti

Gus Uccello, aka **Gus the Boss**, deceased

Nunzio Patti, deceased

BEBE'S WORLD

Rosa Mistretta Rosiglino, Bebe's wife; Mimmo's niece; mother to Bebe's son, Bill Jr.

Nino Terrasini, Bebe's pianist and bodyguard

Phil Klein, Bebe's manager

Rico Enna, executive at talent agency owned by Anthony Corini and Klein's boss

Eleanor Ree, internationally renowned Hollywood actress and Bebe's mistress

Guy Simon, musician and Ree's ex-husband

Captain Bridges, proprietor of radio's *Captain Bridges' Amateur Hour*

U.S. MILITARY & GOVERNMENT

Maj. Henry Landis, head of the Army's Psychoanalytic Field Unit

Lt. Charles Tyler, Army liaison to the Psych Field Unit and, in the post-war years, the Senate Criminal Investigation Committee

Sen. Alvin Dunney (D, SC), head of the Senate Criminal Investigation Committee

PROLOGUE

One late-spring day in 1928, Carlo Farcolini invited his boss to lunch. "Too much tension between us," he explained to Gus Uccello, hat in hand. "People have been telling you wrong. I want to make clear my point of view."

Uccello agreed to a formal sit, pleased his underling had bowed. Farcolini ran a tight ship over in Jersey and delivering the heroin in hatboxes was a stroke of genius. But his ideas were too modern, too American. Next, this guy will have us in bed with the niggers.

Farcolini suggested a little place Uccello liked, way out in Coney Island. To Uccello's mind, no bodyguard was required. The old rules were clear: Gus the Boss couldn't be touched. Farcolini would be held liable if the unimaginable occurred.

Farcolini brought the car around to Mulberry Street. He held open the door when Uccello appeared.

Uccello enjoyed the ride, the fresh air, the scent of the ocean. A pleasant day, no? He said it reminded him of the Tirreno off Capo Gallo.

Farcolini knew there was no way this Mustache Pete could see the pie was too small and cut too thin. Uccello hadn't considered the possibilities in the new country. Meanwhile, we got guys hijacking each other, paying the cops to arrest each other—we're killing each other over who's going to run the labor rackets, the piers, gambling, the whores. We look like petty thieves. We appear incapable.

In the restaurant, Uccello put on a typical display: shoveling down the antipasti, *pappardelle* with a lamb ragu, a whole roasted chicken with lemon and *caccociulli*, Gus the Boss sucking the bones. All the while, Farcolini picked at mussels in wine, braised escarole on the side, some fresh-baked bread, sipping a homemade red while Uccello wielded his fork like a weapon.

"So," Gus the Boss said finally, as the last plate was cleared. "You think we should go in with the Jews…"

Eavesdropping, the restaurant owner signaled to his mother-in-law, who tottered over to offer a ricotta cheesecake made in her kitchen upstairs—just for Signor Uccello. The tiny 80-year-old woman smiled seductively, a withered angel. "I bring it down," she said.

"Go now," Uccello replied with a gluttonous grin, waving his finger in the air.

With that, the owner excused himself to escort the old widow upstairs. "Unless you want I bring the coffee first…"

"I'll do it," Farcolini said.

Eager to be served by his subordinate, Uccello nodded.

Sitting across Surf Avenue in a boosted car, Frankie Fortune saw the owner and his mother-in-law depart.

Four doors opened in unison: Fortune, Anthony Corini, Sigmund Baumstein and Domenico Mistretta stepped onto the street.

Farcolini pushed back from the table, scraping his chair on the terrazzo.

Seconds later, Uccello took the first of 22 rounds to the face and chest, rattling in his seat like he was being electrocuted. He fell back with a gruesome thud.

Twenty-two rounds, meaning only two shots missed.

Later, when they saw the story in the *Daily News*, they teased Mistretta, who they called Mimmo, claiming he'd put a pair in the Franklin stove.

Meanwhile, Farcolini walked the streets of Little Italy with Cy Geller, the head of the Jewish mob, at his side. Farcolini had secured permission from Uccello's rival, Nunzio Patti, for the hit after Farcolini had shown him the stupidity of Sicilian crews at cross-purposes. Patti was amenable to working with Geller and the Jews; and, having pledged to Farcolini the waterfront on both sides of the Hudson in exchange for a bigger slice of the heroin trade, he felt secure. Now Nunzio Patti sat on top of the mountain. Once he learned everything Farcolini knew, he'd turn him into mulch, his half-Jew crew too. He'd give the assignment to Bruno Gigenti, who was built like a buffalo and had no qualms about putting a rival down.

Four months later, Farcolini met his new boss in a lounge at the Hotel Commodore and told him that an agent for the Internal Revenue Service intended to pay him a surprise visit. Patti ran a legitimate carting company from an office in the Graybar Building next to the Grand Central Terminal. "The books are clean," Patti said. "I got no cause to worry."

"The muscle," Farcolini reminded him. "You got men on probation."

Patti looked hard across the table, remembering Uccello in Coney Island, the grisly photo in the *Daily Mirror*.

"*Convenienza*," Farcolini said, meaning propriety. Then he added that the Treasury men would arrive at 11 o'clock. "Maybe you want your lawyer there."

"No, I'll act surprised," Patti said. He was thinking Farcolini might look like a droopy-eyed caveman, but the son of a bitch made the trains run right.

Next day, a few minutes after 11, Patti's secretary buzzed Sigmund Baumstein into the inner office. In Farcolini's crew, Baumstein was known as Ziggy Baum. Normally a flashy dresser, Baum wore a conservative suit and tie for the assignment.

When the real T-men arrived at noon, they found Patti with his carotid artery severed, and Baum gone. The secretary was gone, too. Through the beveled glass, she'd seen Baum's shadow do its work. The cops located her four days later in Poughkeepsie. When they asked her to describe Patti's killer, she said, trembling, "Jewish."

Back in New York City, the cops waited, expecting to find Cy Geller's gangsters dead on their doorstep, Sicilians taking their revenge. When nothing happened, they understood an alliance had been formed. This, they knew, was not good. Somebody on the dago side had made the smart move.

His power consolidated, Farcolini established as his deputies Anthony Corini and Bruno Gigenti, the latter a brutal Patti ally whose services he'd secured before the hit. Given his choice of domain, Cy Geller selected Miami, a key port for heroin coming through Cuba. From the West Coast, Ziggy Baum would report to Corini, who would serve as Farcolini's deputy in matters of government and legitimate businesses, such as entertainment and the press. Jersey was given to Frankie Fortune, with Gigenti turning over his Hudson County crew, which in turn was assigned to Mimmo to run out of a candy store in downtown Narrows Gate, close to the piers, close to the trains, close to two tunnels into the city. In return, Gigenti got extra points on liquor, narcotics, gambling and prostitution. New York was his to rule, particularly the piers, trucking and unions. Fortune reported directly to Farcolini, as did Corini and Gigenti, who took over Uccello's old storefront in Little Italy as his headquarters.

And so Carlo Farcolini had in place his syndicate, the one he'd envisioned several years ago while he recovered from a beating Uccello had authorized. Properly organized and populated by men of appropriate temperament, Farcolini saw no reason why it couldn't run the rackets in the United States for the remainder of the century.

The week before Christmas 1931, Vito Benno found his 8-year-old nephew sitting on the floor behind his grocery store's counter. The plump, curly-haired boy held an old Beretta semiautomatic in his lap.

Startled, Vito kept an eye on his customers, women bundled in scarves and heavy coats who crowded the shop, hefting tins, studying dry goods. Cured meats and cheese hung on hooks.

"I told you I don't want you near the gun," he whispered in Sicilian.

The boy held onto it, flexing his little trigger finger. "That cop Maguire," he replied softly. "He hits your arm, your leg, with the nightstick."

"Sal—"

"He's coming now, right? For his money."

Vito held out his hand. "Salvatore, give me the gun."

"No."

Vito Benno was thin, a little hunched in his posture, bronzed even in winter, a touch of snow in his black hair. By nature, he was mild in manner, reasoned, unhurried. But now his mind was gripped with dread. His nephew was usually carefree, always eager to please, never a moment's trouble. Now he was saying he could shoot a cop.

"What kind of trouble are you looking for?" Vito said.

"Nobody puts an eight-year-old in jail."

"Sal, don't make me—"

"You grab the gun from me now, the thing could go off."

The bell rang over the front door. Cold air rushed in.

A sinister voice sang, "Oh, Vito. Vito."

Maguire the cop, the scourge of Polk Street. He was intent on removing immigrant slime from Narrows Gate. The Irish, to his mind, having arrived several decades ago and winning the fight for survival, owned the mile-square town, save this overcrowded, stink-riddled patch. Empowered by the rat-eyed Mimmo and his band of thugs, the *guappos* were itching to take over, preparing to push uptown, to soil streets trod by the righteous, the honorable. Maguire swore to all he held holy that he would never allow that to happen. Having his way with them, their bones battered and their money gone, soon they'd sail back home. All would be as God intended.

Maguire shook the light snow off the shoulders of his navy coat, his nightstick posed in prominent display.

Vito's patrons scurried to the door, leaving the warmth of the stove the boy stoked not an hour ago.

"I'm waiting," Maguire said.

The shopkeeper toddled around the counter, wiping his hands on his apron.

Gun in his fist, Salvatore Benno spun to his knees.

In halting English, Vito Benno said, "I'm sorry, but maybe next week. Next week before Christmas—"

"Ah, but you recall I told you Christmas arrives a wee bit early this year, Vito."

Cowering, his head bowed, Benno said, "Yes, but I must have my, my…The money from customers…I don't have the money from…Not now."

When the last of Benno's patrons fled to Polk, Maguire turned. The broad grin falling from his face, he swung the nightstick. The blow struck bone hard on the side of the shopkeeper's leg. Maguire then thrust the stick's butt end into Benno's midsection. He collapsed in a heap.

Salvatore Benno raised the gun. Now, he thought. Jesus Christ, shoot him now.

"The honey, Benno," the cop said as he stared down, his jaw twitching, spittle on his lip. "The fuckin' honey…"

"A minute, please," Vito said meekly, his hands shaking. Struggling to his knees, he sent a furtive glance toward the case, hoping to catch his nephew's eye.

Thinking the shopkeeper was looking to where he kept his cash, Maguire bent at the waist and peered past jugs of olives and platters of breaded cutlets. He saw Salvatore Benno staring at him.

"On your knees too, eh?" the cop said.

The gun was hidden from view. But the boy still had his finger on the trigger.

Maguire returned upright.

Shoot the son of a bitch, Sal Benno told himself, quivering as he tried to focus his rage. Put one between his balls. Drop the man who shames us where we live.

Vito limped around the counter. In Sicilian, he said softly, "Put the gun on the floor. Sal, please…"

Looking up, Sal Benno saw a deep sadness in his uncle's eyes. He understood: Maguire's brutal arrogance the man could take. But his nephew resorting to crime, no.

"Vito, I'm not standing for one of your games," Maguire said impatiently. "I'd just as soon see this foul place empty." He turned his back to survey the shop. "God, the stench of it…"

The boy clenched his teeth. He closed one eye. Trembling, he lifted the gun.

Then he slumped and put it on the wooden floor. Slowly he got up, the knees and the rump of his pants sprinkled with sawdust. As he walked away, he muttered in Sicilian, "I'm you, I go see somebody."

Vito Benno reached under his apron and fished a roll of bills out of his pocket. Maguire took it without a word. He left, though not before spitting on the floor as Sal Benno watched, his eyes teary in angry defeat.

Leo Bell drowsed in his room, a book on his chest, his father asleep down the hall. He turned to the clock on the nightstand. Another half hour and it's 1932. Horns will honk, whistles will blow, church bells will chime. The uptown Irish will bang spoons on the bottoms of pots and pans. Happy New Year! And then what? Everything's the same. Last year, this year, a page on a calendar, and what changes? Unless you make a move, not a goddamned thing.

His hands clasped under his head, Bell stared at the ceiling. Earlier in the week, he toyed with the idea of a New Year's resolution. He could be a better son, helping around the house while his father worked dawn to dusk on Manhattan's Lower West Side. Though he was an excellent student, maybe he could overcome his shyness and be more helpful. Maybe he could find a way to share his secret with his best friend, Salvatore Benno.

He lifted the book. Jack London, a man who had been places and had seen things, held the black earth in the palm of his hand, felt the ocean's salt on his cheeks. Over the hiss of steam heat, Bell heard a familiar rattle: the sound of tiny stones flung against the downstairs parlor window.

Outside, Benno shivered on the brownstone steps. Perched on the back of his head, his fedora seemed to float above his curly black hair.

In his robe and slippers, Bell went down to the door and stuck his head into the night air.

"I want you should see something," Benno said. He shuffled, his fingers tucked under his arms.

Bell opened the door. "Get in here."

"No. Hurry," Benno insisted.

"Where are we going?"

"We got twenty minutes. *Andiamo*," Benno replied, clapping his hands.

Soon they were in Church Square Park, which separated Narrows Gate, the Italians to the south, the Irish to the north. Snow mounds lined the concrete paths that cleaved the grass, and icicles clung to groping tree branches. The park was empty. Maybe a half-mile to the east, the Hudson River was frozen. A full moon hovered above the New York skyline.

"My uncle, he was going to see Mimmo," Benno said, "but I told him no, don't. Go higher. See Frankie Fortune. The shop-keepers, they all went."

Though he wore gloves, Bell blew onto his hands.

"See, a thing like this, you're going to need a big OK."

"A thing like what?" Bell asked.

Benno pointed to the steeple above St. Matthew the Apostle, the cathedral-like redbrick church to the west of the park. "Watch," he said.

"Watch what?" The tip of Bell's long, thin nose was already numb. "Sal, what are we talking about over here?"

"Watch," Benno repeated.

Bell removed his glasses, huffed on them, rubbed his handkerchief on the lens.

One late September morning three years ago, Sal Benno, a charmer even in kindergarten, entered the schoolyard at St. Francis of Assisi and saw somebody he'd never seen before, not in his uncle's store, not on Polk Street, not nowhere. The kid was tall for his age and had a serious expression on his face. Also, a dimple in his chin.

"Who are you?" Benno said in Sicilian.

"Leo Bell," the boy replied, his eyes steady.

"Bell?"

The new boy hesitated. His father had warned him of this. Don't talk about your name, where you came from, who you are. If you have to, remember the story.

"Leonardo Bell," the boy said.

Father Gregory watched the other kids running, shouting, playing. The rotund priest resembled an overgrown kid himself, his haircut from under a bowl, pink cheeks, sandals. He had a lip-gnawing purposefulness that downtown mothers hoped would also emerge in their sons. For most of them, the priest was the only native-born American adult they knew.

"Where are you from?" Benno asked.

Again, Bell remembered his father's admonition. "Irpino, Italy."

Benno frowned.

"I am Italian," Bell added in English.

x

Benno's English was pretty good, so he went along. "You don't sound Italian."

Bell didn't waver. He'd rehearsed with his father, who considered keeping him out of school an extra year so his accent would diminish, but the boy was precocious. At age three, he could read in his native language, and now he picked out whole sentences from the *Daily News*. He was steady, mature even, and in that demeanor his father believed he saw the boy was carrying the burden of his mother's death.

"Anyway, that's no good around here," Benno told him.

"Italian is no good?" Bell said plainly.

"We're Sicilian."

Bell didn't understand the difference. As bright as he was— and in the coming years, the Franciscan nuns would advise his father to skip him ahead at least one grade—he didn't know the Sicilians considered their island a nation separate from Italy, even if the Italians didn't. This was common knowledge in downtown Narrows Gate.

At that moment, Mother Maria appeared, clanging the school bell, calling the children to order.

Benno reached up and threw his arm around his new friend's shoulder. "Don't worry about nothing," he said in English.

They walked together toward the line for the kindergarten class. Benno went to the front: He was the shortest boy. Bell, seeing how it was done, stood near the rear.

Benno looked back and winked.

Bell smiled in relief.

Benno and Bell. They were inseparable from that moment. From age five, they knew: you don't find a friend like this twice and you don't ask why something so true takes hold.

Now, with the prospect of welcoming 1932 with frozen feet, Bell said, "Sally, I'm looking but I'm seeing nothing."

"Oh no?" Benno said triumphantly. He pointed toward the church.

At that moment, high on a ledge that surrounded the base of the spire, two men appeared, lit by thick moonlight. One man, the taller of the two, carried a bundle on his shoulder. The other, brutish and with the demeanor of a man in charge, peered to the street far below.

"Who is that?" Bell asked. He wondered if a stiff wind would send the two men off the ledge and onto the picket fence that surrounded the church.

"I don't know the names," Benno replied. "But the bundle? It's Maguire. The cop Maguire."

Bell turned. "The dirty cop?"

Benno held up his hand. "Are you gonna watch or you gonna talk?"

Up on the ledge, Maguire kicked frantically.

Struggling, the taller man turned to his stoic partner, who nodded.

The body dropped. A rope around its neck, it snapped back and began to bob.

"Whoa," uttered Leo Bell, amazed.

Soon Maguire's body swung like a pendulum.

"Would you look at that," Benno said in wonder. "How come the head don't come off?"

As the cop dangled limp and lifeless, the two men paused to admire their work. The short, brawny one was Bruno Gigenti, who came to Farcolini's crew as an outsider, having been with Patti before he had his throat opened by a Jew. From his perch on the spire, he could see the piers on both sides of the river. Even on New Year's Eve, ships were being offloaded, each piece of freight swollen with a tariff, part of which would end up in his pocket.

Gigenti had been asked to address the issue with the crooked cop, the request coming from the top. He was glad to do so, seeing as he felt a distance between himself and Don Carlo.

With a nod, he told his associate to move on. He shimmied to the bell tower, climbed back inside and dusted his hands before he shoved them into his coat pockets.

In the empty park, Bell said, "We should go, too."

Benno shook his head, his hat bobbling. "I want to be here when the bells ring."

"And when the cops come?"

"Hey, I'm down here. He's up there."

"Sally..."

Benno continued to stare up at Maguire's body, satisfaction in his dark eyes.

The Irish woke up shaken. Most of them knew Maguire was for shit, but this affront couldn't stand. There were implications.

Councilmen from uptown descended upon the mayor's office. "My constituents are outraged," they said. The police chief listened carefully and pledged a thorough investigation. Downtown would be turned on its head until the killers were exposed. The chief rested his hand on the butt of his gun for emphasis.

"They shouldn't be allowed past Church Square," said one councilman.

"What I'd like to know is who's next?" asked another. "Maybe we all find ourselves up on St. Matty's."

"It's that Farcolini," a third said. "This is well-known. You wouldn't be surprised to learn there's those who think he's got a grip on this office, the same as he has on the piers, the truckers, the nightclubs..."

The mayor looked at the jowly men who filled the room, their tweed vests straining to cover their stomachs, the reek of self-preservation rising from the bloat. "We've got one rogue cop dead and you want to go to war," he said. "Isn't it true some of you in this room thought Michael Maguire a low sort? Isn't that why you insisted he be assigned Polk Street?"

Shifting in their seats, the councilmen muttered uncomfortably.

The mayor continued. "If you'd like to bring your protest directly to Mr. Farcolini, I'm sure it can be arranged. Any takers?" He looked at each man, who responded with silence. "You go back to your folks and tell them the chief has this on highest priority. Tell them you insisted and we've heard."

Over coffee and a crumb cake, the mayor told the police chief that nothing could be done. Surely, it was Farcolini via Fortune, Mimmo and their men at the candy store. One could say they were protecting their constituents, too.

But, the mayor added, the raw fact of the matter was that the numbers of Italians had swollen to 6,100 adults—and Hennie Rosiglino had registered them all to vote.

"We go after them and we're all out of a job," the mayor explained.

The police chief suggested a solution: Hennie would get Fortune and Mimmo to kick in to pay for the funeral. The chief would deliver the money personally to the Maguires, saying it came from a widows and orphans fund.

"Next time we find a floater in the river," the chief said, "we'll squeeze a bullet in his head and say he was the man who put down Maguire."

"Good thinking," the mayor allowed.

PART ONE

CHAPTER ONE

Back in 1923, when he was 8 years old, Bebe Rosiglino found himself in trouble. Two classmates, Sonny and Ray-Ray, had cooked up a scheme: They'd steal a basket of peaches from Garemoli's cart and sell them over by the piers. They asked Bebe to distract the bowlegged Sicilian by taunting his horse.

Bebe readily agreed. Friends had been impossible to come by. Since the day he was born, his mother, Hennie, had spoiled him rotten. Her sisters did too, kissing him sloppy, their flabby arms pressing him to their bosoms. Hennie's love came in waves: One day she thought he was heaven-sent—my "beautiful boy," hence the nickname Bebe. The next day, he was a bum, good for nothing. A mistake. Get out of my sight.

Instead of hugs and kisses, Hennie gave him what the other downtown boys couldn't afford: Buster Browns, Little Lord Fauntleroy suits, new knickers, butterfly-collar shirts, a fedora, garish jewelry. She bought him a bicycle and a baseball mitt, and the little boy with jug-handle ears sat on the porch, savoring ice cream with jimmies from a sugar cone—all of which guaranteed him a daily ass pounding he took like a suckling torn from the tit, wailing, frantic, rejected again. His father Vincenzo had been a boxer, so had his brothers Rocco and Lou. Toughs nobody fucked with but, as Hennie pointed out, everybody could outsmart. They tried to teach Bebe to at least throw one back—you never know, it could land. But what's the point? A fly hit harder.

3

As far as the peach-stealing scheme went, everything was smooth until Sonny shoved Garemoli and the old man stumbled and fell. Suddenly, the agitated horse—named Tony, like Tom Mix's in the pictures—reared high, upset the cart and bolted free. Hurdling along Polk Street, it trampled a half-dozen screaming people, breaking an elderly woman's arm and upending a baby carriage. After crashing through the front window of Albini the Tailor's, it raced out to the street, glass jutting out of its torso, skidding on the cobblestone, falling, getting back up. The neighborhood in terror, Pete the Butcher trailed the frothing horse with clothesline he struggled to turn into a lasso. Finally, a cop shot the horse dead, its blood running to the gutter. A crowd gathered but peeled back, sickened.

Soon a lawyer from City Hall walked toward the Rosiglino home, which was on the border of Church Square Park. As neighbors watched, the lawyer said, "Hennie, I hate to be the one to bear the news, but we got Bebe at the station and…"

In front of the mayor and his secretary, Hennie beat Bebe until his ears bled, her screams and curse words ricocheting down the halls. Pulling her off was like wrestling a bear. Finally, they shouldered her into the men's room.

Later, the desk sergeant said, "Ooh, she's lethal, that one."

The mayor replied, "If I'm her husband, I blow my brains out twice daily."

Sonny and Ray-Ray laid the thing on Bebe, a Sicilian after all, and the mayor agreed. Hennie would make good for Garemoli's dead horse and the old widow's broken arm, even though everybody knew the scrawny, insufferable kid hadn't the wit for the scheme. Sonny and Ray-Ray were Irish. Their fathers wore suits to work and rode a bus to Newark.

Sitting lights-out in his room, welts throbbing, Bebe sobbed. Outside, the world continued without him: the flow of traffic, his classmates' voices in Church Square, the Jew with his pots and pans, the rush of industry at the piers, the trains at the Lackawanna Station; in the old neighborhood, under the scent of frying peppers, Sicilians sang the old songs. Crouched on his bed, he reviewed the walk home from City Hall: his mother shoving and shouting at him, women leaning meaty arms on apartment window ledges to stare down, little kids on the sidewalk laughing when they passed. Everybody knew Bebe had fucked up, two Irish kids playing him for a stooge. Bebe tried to explain to his mother, he tried to say, "Mama, I—" He told her he didn't plan it and he was sorry the horse broke free and she'd been embarrassed—*humiliated*—by what had happened. He was sorry. He was.

Alone in his room, he asked himself how could he ever get his mother to love him. Even before this, she didn't. He knew that. She didn't. And all he wanted to do was please her. He would trade all the hugs and kisses his *nonni*, aunts and cousins gave him for a word of kindness from his mother.

Instead, he got "I can't stand the sight of you. Go away. Go." Tossing him into the living room, she said, "Having you ruined my life, you know that? *Ruined* it."

He'd heard it before. He was a waste, good for nothing. A bum in the making. It'd be a blessing she should never have to see him again.

Coming home from the Hook & Ladder, Vincenzo asked for his son, his tired voice dripping with trepidation. "*Dove è Bebe?*" he said as he slid out of his suspenders.

"Fuck Bebe," Hennie replied.

A few minutes later, his father tried again. "He's gotta eat, no?"

"Fuck him. I don't care if he starves to death."

"Hennie…"

"I curse the day he was born. I swear to God I do."

Bebe worked on it throughout the night and waited until Hennie left the house in the morning. His Aunt Rosalie made peppers and eggs, the bread fresh from Dommie's and snuck it upstairs. She told him his mother said he had to stay in his room; for how long, who knows? "Bebe, what you done…" she said, shaking the back of her hand. "*Madonna mio…*" Squeezing his cheeks, she kissed him cute on his olive-oiled lips.

He dressed in pressed short pants and a striped T-shirt. When he heard Rosalie doing the dishes, he opened his bedroom window, climbed out and, shimmying along the edge, used the toothing-stone as a ladder. When he reached the ground, he scampered, hopped a fence, and soon he was crossing Buchanan Avenue, heading up toward Elysian Fields, which overlooked the piers and the Manhattan skyline.

Shortly after 10 o'clock, with little kids toddling around on the merry-go-round and slides in the playground behind him, Bebe jimmied through the park's tall, fleur-de-lis guardrails and stood on a slate ledge above a rocky slope to River Road some 40 feet below. From his perch, he could see to New York City—the spire of Trinity Church, the Woolworth Building, the gilded dome of the Pulitzer Building. On the river, tugs nudged an ocean liner into position to head toward the Atlantic. Freighters crowded the busy piers, and men who knew his family pushed dollies stacked with cargo. Now and then, a car motoring along River Road fell behind a truck groaning to the Holland Tunnel. Seagulls circled at eye level.

A breeze rippling his dark hair, Bebe took a long look at the puffy clouds and then gazed down at his Buster Browns. Then, without regret, he stepped from the ledge like the air could hold his weight.

He plummeted to the soft earth below, landing on the soles of his feet, jarred but uninjured. But then he tumbled head over heels, just missing a tree that craned toward the river. Rolling over, he was turned sideways and, as he built surprising speed, his lower body slammed into a mossy rock jutting from the incline. The blow fractured his right femur, but he kept tumbling. Finally, he tore through the muck at the curb and landed on River Road. A Model T truck slammed on its brakes to avoid hitting him.

"For fuck's sake, boy, what's wrong with you—" Then the nut-nosed Irishman popped from the cab and saw Bebe's thighbone poking through his skin.

"Oh, Jesus!" he shouted, hopping in place, waving frantically. "I'll go get help." He ran off, ignoring the blare of horns by drivers who hadn't seen the boy in the road. Syrupy blood clotted on the asphalt.

After the ambulance took Bebe to St. Patrick's, the cops wandered around Elysian Fields and then called down the detectives, who tried to verify the driver's claim that he hadn't run over Hennie Rosiglino's son, that the kid appeared in the road already broken.

Seven people said Bebe jumped.

"Like he could fly?" a cop asked.

"Like he wanted it to look like he tried to kill himself," replied Mrs. Matuschek, who'd brought her three kids to the park.

"But just *try*, not *do*?" the detective asked with a frown.

"Well, he didn't throw himself on his head, if that's what you mean."

Hennie wavered between hysteria and fury. By the time Bebe came out of surgery, she insisted the driver be charged, even though she was told he'd done nothing but stop his load from crushing her son.

The mayor came to offer comfort and reason, passing along the irrefutable testimony reported by the detectives. But Hennie was resolute. She wouldn't be seen as the reason for Bebe's stunt. Everybody knew she adored her beautiful boy.

She turned to Vincenzo, teary eyed in his blue Hook & Ladder uniform, his face a rag of worry.

"Get Carlo," she told him.

For once, Hennie knew less than she thought. Carlo Farcolini was born in Vallelunga, Sicily, on the same block and was baptized in the same church as Vincenzo Rosiglino's late father, Guillermo. Vincenzo didn't know this, but Farcolini did and, before Bebe was born, he employed Vincenzo, his *paesano,* as a truck driver running bootleg whiskey from the Narrows Gate docks to speakeasies throughout North Jersey. When Vincenzo was pinched by the cops, he kept his mouth shut and took the 18-month hit, as Farcolini knew a man from northwest Sicily would. He had Mimmo deliver $1,000 to Vincenzo's wife, a brassy bigmouth he couldn't tolerate.

To Farcolini's mind, he and the Rosiglinos were even. So now, years later, when Mimmo called to tell him Hennie wanted a meeting, at first Farcolini waved it off. But then, recalling Vincenzo as a stand-up guy, he agreed to her request.

Tossing the mayor's name around, Hennie had Bebe put in a private room in the adult ward at St. Patrick's. When Farcolini, Frankie Fortune and Mimmo arrived, the room overflowed with Bebe's aunts and cousins, a few of the *Siciliani,* plus the flowers the police chief had sent.

"Mimmo," said Fortune, as Farcolini waited in the hospital corridor with forbearance, looking down at his shoes, hands stuffed in his pockets.

Mimmo went in and cleared everybody out, leaving Vincenzo, Hennie and Bebe, his damaged leg in traction, the bone shoved back in place, stitches and the swollen thigh yellow and purple. In the bottle on the hook was some kind of pain relief and Bebe looked stupid and content.

Farcolini and Fortune entered and Mimmo shut the door behind them. The streetlights cast ghostly shadows into the room. Thick windows muted the conviviality in the park below. Vincenzo rose to greet his former patron. Farcolini took his hands as Vincenzo kissed his cheeks. When Vincenzo offered his chair, Farcolini, raising his hand, said no.

From the other side of the bed, Hennie explained in Sicilian, "Carlo, they ran over my son."

Frankie Fortune answered in English. "So?"

Through his haze, Bebe believed Fortune was the best-looking man he'd ever seen, a regular Adonis.

Farcolini stared at the injured boy.

"Like he was nothing, they ran him over," Hennie continued. "A mutt in the street."

Mimmo had told Farcolini what happened. Fortune knew too—sources in the police department and at the *Jersey Observer* confirming Mimmo's report.

"As I understand it, the driver saved the boy," Fortune said.

"After he hit him," she insisted.

"Not so," he replied.

Hennie raised her voice. "He fell and—"

"He did not." Fortune again. The measure of respect that remained in his demeanor was in deference to Vincenzo.

"You owe us," she said. "My husband—"

Farcolini turned and dismissed her with a withering gaze. Then he leaned in, cupped Bebe's chin in his hand, patted his cheek. The boy returned his smile.

As he turned, Farcolini said, "Vincenzo."

Rosiglino nodded in appreciation.

Fortune rapped a knuckle on the door.

Mimmo opened it. "Safe," he said. Nuns and nurses had cleared out.

The three men left, Fortune squeezing Vincenzo's steely bicep as he passed.

"**D**river Cleared in Waterfront Mishap." The headline in the morning's *Jersey Observer*. The write-up explained that William Rosiglino, the lively young son of Vincenzo Rosiglino, a member of Hook & Ladder Company Number 5, and his wife, Henrietta, tumbled onto River Road while playing near Elysian Fields. The brave boy suffered a terrifying injury without complaint and was recovering at St. Patrick's Hospital.

"In a private room," Hennie told the Irish newspaper in her fist. "None but the best for my beautiful boy."

Later that day, Mimmo delivered a radio to the kid at St. Patrick's Hospital.

"You speak Sicilian?" he panted. The fuckin' radio weighed almost as much as he did.

Bebe said, "*Si.*"

A nun at the window watched as Mimmo wiped his damp brow. Physical labor took its toll. In addition to sun-sensitive eyes, he had flat feet that slapped the ground like somebody threw down fish.

In Sicilian, he said, "From your Uncle Carlo. This."

"OK," Bebe said. "Thanks."

Two in the morning, Indian summer 1930, the neighborhood graveyard silent. Hennie was blowing smoke toward the moon, sambuca in the teacup as she sat on her stoop, shoes off, cajoling anybody who passed by, busting balls if they asked a favor. The Irish, they saw she thought herself the queen of the neighborhood, this gasbag, this Depression-proof fixer, friend to the mayor, friend to Mimmo and the rest of his crew at the God-forsaken end of the town. It pissed them off no end.

For the past few weeks, Hennie was slapped sideways by a troubled mind. No way she could figure what her son was going to do when he grew up and what kind of *ciuccio* he'd be after she died or had a stroke that sent her drooling. Now 15 years old, Bebe was gangly, as graceful as a drunk on a ladder, dopey looking with those ears and slow to catch on. What a package. The kid got fired from the Avalon Theater, McSquinty telling her, "Hennie, he can't make change. He don't know which end of the broom to push."

Over dinner, she said, "Bebe, let me ask one question: Is your head empty or is there something going on?"

Twirling spaghetti on a spoon, he said, "I'm supposed to clean bubblegum off the bottom of seats? Me?"

"You're too good to scrape gum?"

"That's a job for bums."

"So what's a job for you? Tell me, Bebe. If you got an idea, share it, for Christ's sake."

After the Avalon told him to get lost, Hennie sent him to the *Jersey Observer*, a guy who worked at the Hook & Ladder offering to intervene. The first night, Bebe was over by the presses for maybe 10 minutes: all he had to do was keep the linotype machine lubricated, but he tripped and banged his head, type flying out of the magazine, the front page ruined. Worse, he fell on the operator and the guy's wrist broke.

Bebe walked home along Polk Street, his head hanging, slacks covered in grease. Everybody saw clear that he'd fucked up again. Too bad Hennie taught the kid to treat the neighborhood like it was a sewer. Somebody might've thrown him a kind word.

For his part, Bebe could've sat on the curb and cried. His mother was right: He was a first-class clown. Everything he touched turned to failure. OK, the Avalon was a shit job, but the *Observer*, Jesus, Bebe went in trying. He wanted to succeed, to make his mother proud. He wanted to belong. They gave him a locker and the boss seemed all right. The guys in gray overalls and paper hats moved like they were parts in the machines. He tried to do exactly what he was told—all the clanging, grinding, the lubricant's scent, the slippery oilcan in his hand. He tried to concentrate, but his mind drifted, ideas were interrupted. Then catastrophe and soon he was facing the long walk home.

Now, a couple of weeks later, sitting out there in front of her house, Hennie was thinking, What am I going to do with this kid? A car passed, somebody she didn't recognize, and then silence returned. She flicked a cigarette toward the curb.

And then she heard it.

Upstairs in his room, Bebe was singing.

Hennie leaned back to listen hard. At first, she doubted it was him. Bebe's voice was sweet, feathery sort of, wasn't it? He could carry a tune, but not enough so they let him sing "Ave Maria" at a solemn High Mass, everybody looking at him impressed, looking at her. But this voice, the one she was hearing now, was a man's voice, not only deeper but richer. It held its tone, to her amateur ears. It had personality. It's Bebe and, my hand to God, it ain't half bad.

By now, Hennie was huffing up the stairs, ignoring Vincenzo asleep on the sofa. Up another flight, she knocked on Bebe's door.

He stood there in his boxers and undershirt. She could count his ribs he's so skinny.

"Do that again," she said as she stepped into the room.

"What?" Bebe thought he was in trouble, even if he didn't know what he'd done.

"Sing."

"Ah, for Christ's sakes, Ma—"

"Come on. I heard you. Come on."

Bebe hesitated. Maybe five years ago, Hennie dressed him up in a sailor's suit and a little Charlie Chaplin cane and had him sing for coins at Chatterbox, telling him, "Fuck the choirmaster, you've got talent, real talent, you go sing, Bebe. Show 'em, that's right." In the bar, Bebe saw the rolling eyes, the grimaces, felt the dull pats on his back. Feeney's crowd gave him money to get lost. But his mother was proud.

"Go ahead," she added now, sitting on the edge of his bed.

Bebe took a breath. Then he started in, snapping his fingers, doing it with pep, the words flying out like tommy-gun fire.

"Wait. Hold on," Hennie said. "What's that?"

Bebe flushed with embarrassment. "All right, Ma. This I don't need at two in the morning."

"No, do it nice and easy. Like before."

"Like when?"

"Bebe, three fuckin' minutes ago. Come on."

He tried to remember. Three minutes ago, he was changing his slacks on their hangers to make sure there were no wrinkles; lemons and rosemary sprigs were in his closet so his clothes smelled good. Three minutes ago, he was thinking the world could go to hell. He was wishing he had a friend.

Bebe began to hum the same tune—"You're the Cream in My Coffee"—and then he started in singing soft, letting the notes come out puffy to waft above his head.

Hennie looked at him in amazement.

His eyes closed. Bebe kept singing, the cloud-notes now floating around his bedroom. "You will always be my necessity. I'd be lost without you..." He swayed, opened his hands at his sides, tilted his head just right.

"Beautiful," said Hennie when he finished. She labored to hoist off the bed. "Beautiful."

Bebe studied her face for a hint of sarcasm. None.

"You can do that again?" she asked.

He nodded.

"Who showed you to sing like that? You know, with the charm."

Bebe didn't know. He liked to make it up. Take the melody and go a little bit slower, maybe listen to the words and find how to tell the story gentle, like he was whispering down some girl's neck. He shrugged. Then he threw a thumb toward the radio in the corner, the one Carlo Farcolini had given him years ago. "There's all sorts of singers, but they sound the same."

Hennie said, "Don't do nothing till you hear from me."

The next day, she intercepted Nino Terrasini as he was leaving the Venus Pencil factory, his shift done, and now, after he'd washed up, he was walking through Church Square Park over to the Union Club where he played piano to make a few extra bucks. He was also in a combo called the Hudson Four. Hennie heard they showed promise.

Terrasini was a good-looking Sicilian, his hair coal black; his eyes, too. He walked tall, like America had put steel in his spine. He was 18 and dated a Polish girl up in Weehawken, her father a successful purveyor of smoked meats. The girl meant Terrasini planned to get out of Narrows Gate. Maybe he could use a boost.

"Nino," said Hennie. She was on a bench, waiting. She patted the wood. "Sit."

Terrasini was a friendly guy, so he sat.

She offered him a cigarette, but he took out one of his own.

"Tell me about the Hudson Four," she said.

Terrasini nodded. "There's these three guys."

"Three? Then why the Hudson Four?"

"I'm the fourth," he replied. "They sing, the three."

The kids had begun to leave the park, rushing, running, screaming, shoving as they headed home. When the day shift ended at the factories, shipyards and piers in Narrows Gate, it was time for dinner.

"They sing good?" she asked.

Terrasini shrugged. "*Mezzo-mezzo.*"

"Who's the weak spot?"

He pondered. "I would say Vinnie."

"Vinnie?"

"Patroni. Vinnie Patroni."

"Who is he?"

"Who is he? He sings in the Hudson Four."

"Nino, come on."

"He's like anybody else. He works at the five-and-dime."

"His father?"

"Dead."

Ah, thought Hennie. Patroni's a nobody. "Here's what you do," she said, turning to face Terrasini. "You dump this Patroni. In comes Bebe."

"Bebe?" Terrasini smiled. "He's a kid."

"Don't worry. He'll have his working papers."

"No, I mean, who wants to see a kid singing?"

"You take him in, Nino, and you tell me what you need."

Leaning an elbow on the back rail, Terrasini tilted toward her. Like everybody else in Narrows Gate, he knew Hennie was a fixer. "For one, I need to get out of the Union Club. I'm lucky I take in two bucks a night in tips."

"You sign a contract?"

Terrasini said no.

She took the cigarette off her lip. "So what's the problem?"

"Two dollars is two—"

"You play the Blue Onyx."

"Mimmo's joint?"

Hennie nodded.

"I don't know..." he said warily.

"Don't be cute. Mimmo's not stocking the crew with piano players."

She's right, thought Terrasini. Some imbecile makes a move the Farcolinis don't agree, they don't ask for a lullaby.

"But you go slow," Hennie said. "Your job is to take care of Bebe. Ease him in. You understand me?"

Terrasini looked over her head to the pencil factory. "If I had a car, the Hudson Four could work all over," he said.

"Like Weehawken."

"You can't take a public-address system on a bus."

This one is smarter than he looks, Hennie thought as she agreed to his terms. She'd ask Mimmo to get someone to boost him a car. If Terrasini went back on his word and let Bebe struggle, the cops would find the old plates hidden in the trunk and nail him for grand theft auto.

Then she went to work, the new Hudson Four in the papers almost every day as they played school dances all over the county, private parties as far south as Asbury Park, and dinner clubs, mostly as relief for experienced acts. She found them a weekly gig singing on the radio in Elizabeth, a free advertisement that produced more opportunities to hone their material. Any palm needed greasing, Hennie came across, and soon the emcees were introducing the group by saying Billy Rosiglino and the Hudson Four.

Terrasini had a pretty good idea where this thing was headed, and he didn't mind. Growing up in Narrows Gate, he saw Bebe as an ass wipe, but he had to hand it to him. The kid was working his bones off. OK, so Hennie was knocking on doors and making telephone calls, turning smart, leathery music business guys mushy with phony charm; if you knew her in Narrows Gate you would piss yourself laughing.

But it was Bebe, too. He took singing lessons, diction lessons, went to dancing school so he could hide the limp from the leg he broke as a kid. By now he could read music as good as Terrasini, who took piano lessons starting at age 4. He'd rehearse from daybreak until well past midnight. Tell Bebe something once and he never forgot. And gracious? Always sir, ma'am, always by name, always asking after the family. After a while, Hennie didn't have to tell him to send flowers with a thank-you note.

All the "Bebe this, Bebe that" caused a rift in the group. The other two guys asked Terrasini for a private meet.

From the minute Terrasini picked them up, they started bitching, making Bebe's minor failings into a reason to set him on fire. They accused him of hijacking the group, ignoring the fact that he put in about a hundred times the effort they did developing his talents.

After Terrasini drove up and down Hudson Boulevard listening to this crap, one of the guys said, "What do you think?"

"We're working, right?" he replied. "Who gives a shit the emcee says his name?"

The other two continued to protest.

"Excuse me," Terrasini said. "Are we making three, four times a week what we made with Patroni? Are we playing bigger rooms, the radio? Plus the broads. Are you kidding me? As far as I'm concerned, you should kiss Bebe's ass."

The two howled in derision.

"We should kick his ass, the little fuck," said the one in the backseat.

Terrasini looked in the rearview. "One, nobody touches Bebe. Two, you feel things suck so bad, maybe you ought to think about quitting."

"Why should *we* quit?" said the guy in the passenger seat.

"Because it's Bebe's group," Terrasini said. "Or ain't you noticed?"

The two guys scoffed. But soon there was silence in the car.

For the next few weeks, it got worse for Bebe, the two guys busting his balls relentless and Bebe, no threat, had to take it. They flushed his cufflinks down the toilet, hid his slacks, soiled his shoes. They told Terrasini to drive off and leave him behind, which he would not do. In rehearsal, they altered the harmony on "Shine On, Harvest Moon" or "I Found a Million Dollar Baby (In a Five-and-Ten Cent Store)," leaving Bebe confused, struggling to find his note as they fell to laughter.

Bebe kept his mouth shut and suffered their bullshit. Terrasini waited—sooner or later, Bebe's going to tell Hennie and she'll go to Mimmo, right? But Bebe said nothing and then one day the two sons of bitches tore his favorite jacket up the back, laughing when Bebe tried to put it on, the thing coming apart. Feeling like he could burst into tears, Bebe ran out of the room. Terrasini grabbed one guy by the lapels, his fist cocked and quivering. "The next guy who lays a hand on him deals with me," he said as he threw the guy down. "And I hope to hell it's soon."

The one problem with Bebe, if you could call it a problem, was the girls. They took notice, this kid with his picture in the papers, and when they came to the show, they saw he had these sparkling blue eyes. They wanted to take the gawky kid in their arms and hold him and kiss his cheek, run their fingers through his hair, purr at him. They waited at the stage door. They were kids like him and they didn't think anything of standing out there in the rain, the snow, the summer heat. They didn't think it was unseemly. They were bubbly inside. "Billy!" they'd squeal. "Billy!" And Bebe dove in.

And in no time he figured out their innocent passion was a thing he could use. He'd look at the crowd of hopping girls, bouncing on their toes, clapping their hands, and he'd pick one. Maybe she wasn't 14 or 15 years old. She's 16 and, though she's still got one foot back in childhood, she's ready. Soon she's in the backseat with Bebe, who's telling her he spotted her from the stage, that she's got a special something—he had an instinct for what the girl prized in her appearance: her eyes, nose, lips, hair, figure, legs. But he understood that part of his charm was she wanted to mother him. So he went in pure. It's all sweetness in the backseat, tender whispers. He hesitates but takes her hand and soon they kiss and kiss again. He runs his thumb along her neck; his hand falls to her thigh. She had no intention, not really, but now she's alive with electricity. Nothing like this has ever happened before. She is melting. She moans. Bebe tells her, "I knew it would be someone like you," and soon her skirt is up, her panties down and Bebe's in.

This happened two or three times a week, and pretty soon Bebe's got a bounce in his step and he don't give a shit what the other two singers in the Hudson Four think. In the world he's living in, nobody can touch him. The music and the girls put him in a golden place. His needs are fulfilled.

CHAPTER TWO

There came a point when Sal Benno saw this school thing wasn't going to work out too good. The proof: No matter how hard he pushed his face into the books, nothing stuck. Meanwhile, Leo Bell sat in the classroom and everything the teachers said he understood and pretty soon he knew more than they did. Whenever a teacher asked a question and nobody stuck up their hand, she went, "Leonardo…" and Leo stood and gently explained it to the rest of the class in such a way that nobody was angry with him, nobody was jealous, but nobody wanted to be his friend neither, he's like another adult hanging around.

Bell tipped Benno on where to find the answers for their homework, which accounted for his decent grades. "This could be cheating," Bell said as they studied side by side in the back of Benno's Salumeria, their books on the butcher block.

"Let's say no," Benno replied. As a hedge, Benno confessed each week to Father Gregory, who threw him a few extra Hail Marys to make him feel better. The portly priest had a pretty good idea the boy was going to end up behind the counter at his uncle's store, so if he could add and subtract he'd be fine. Salvatore Benno wasn't the type to put his thumb on the scale to harm the neighbors. He was loyal, firm in his opinions—the kind of kid who stuck up for the weakest in the schoolyard. When Father Gregory came by Benno's to pick up the package they put together for him and the nuns, he made sure to tell them Sal was a good boy; tell his mother, Giovanna, not to worry.

But Vito Benno was concerned. Sal was kind and happy, and it was better all of a sudden when he came around, as different in the room as when somebody lights a candle at night. But he could not forget the incident with Maguire and the gun and how his nephew was willing to come to his aid regardless of consequences. He knew there were forces in the neighborhood that could take advantage of that kind of loyalty. Vito Benno saw the kids at the candy store looking at Mimmo in his smoky sunglasses, bossing a crew; watching as Frankie Fortune rolled up in a shiny new car, the suits he wore, the way he don't give a shit. He heard the way the kids whispered the names Farcolini, Corini, Gigenti—men who were legends, Sicilians who took shit from nobody, the cops didn't push them around. They liked that, the kids. They saw their fathers working endless hours for next to nothing; they lived in a box, three to a bed, the pipes dripped, there's rats. What are they going to think? What choice would they make?

So Vito prayed the boy stayed good, trying to think of a way to protect him. He owed it to his sister. Once Giovanna had her own glow. She was sweet and fragile, but gullible, and now she was broken by what happened: the man she thought was her future husband taking off like a thief in the night. Now she worked a sewing machine up in Union, looking old before her time, and everybody in the neighborhood shook their heads in sadness, remembering when she was young and full of hope.

One rainy Saturday afternoon, Benno and Bell were sitting in the back of the store, sharing a chicken Aunt Gemma had fried in olive oil, adding red pepper flakes and fresh lemon juice. They were eating off wax paper, two kids deep in the unspoken warmth of friendship. Bell was looking for a napkin, the grease from the chicken coating his fingers, and Benno offered him the hem of his apron. Their bellies full from the chicken, fried potatoes and escarole, Benno went out to the store to get a paper bag for the legs, a meal in themselves for Bell and his father. Bell swept the breadcrumbs off the butcher block into his palm and went looking for the trash. When he looked up, he saw Enzo Paolo approaching Vito and Gemma. The cop had his five-corner hat in his hands, rainwater dripping from the brim.

Bell heard Gemma scream. Then a plate crashed to the floor.

Bell darted from the back room.

On the floor, a shattered jug. Olives rolled across the sawdust.

Gemma wailed. Hurrying, Vito led her to a stack of boxes so she could sit. Dark-skinned widows who had been shopping, dressed in black as if the tragedy were preordained, rushed around her, ancient brows furrowed in concern.

When Bell arrived, he saw Benno's face had gone blank except for a trembling at the lips and the corner of his eyes.

"My mother's…" Benno said in Sicilian, his voice hollow. "My mother. They found her…She's dead."

"Sal," Bell said. "I'm—Ah, Sal." He took his friend by the arms, holding him as if he feared he would fall.

"My mother…" Benno muttered again.

Gemma howled again, her scream an unearthly siren. She beat her fist against her chest.

"I didn't do nothing for her," Benno said as he shook his head. "Nothing."

The widows were crying as well, twining their rosary beads around knobby fingers. They knew Giovanna Benno as a girl, slight, pretty, who'd blossomed nice. They remembered when her long black hair shone in the sun; she used to brush it 100 times a day, Gemma once reported. Giovanna walked on her toes, happy until that charmer Zitani did her awful.

Father Gregory burst through the doorway, his robe damp with mist. "*Vito, il mio Dio. Ciò è impossibile.*"

Vito pointed him toward his nephew.

"Salvatore." The priest was sweating, his round face knit with panic. In the confessional, he had learned from the boy that he'd pointed a gun at Maguire the cop. Now this—the kind of blow that can confuse a child, maybe even drive him away from the church before he had the means to confront a crisis of faith. Father Gregory draped his arm over the boy's shoulder and looked hard into his eyes.

"Salvatore…"

"I'm all right, Father," Benno said plainly.

Bell interrupted. "Sally, don't," he said. "Nobody here wants a hero."

Benno slumped. "Because of me, she had no chance. None."

"Sal, no," the priest moaned. "No. The opposite is true. If not for you…"

"She loved you, your mother," added Bell, who'd always thought of Giovanna Benno as a living ghost.

The priest rubbed Benno's back. "Leo's right. Your mother loved you. You can't doubt this."

Benno began to nod slowly. Finally, a tear fell to the floor.

Seeing Benno like that, Bell fought back tears of his own. It's true his friend's mother had been a sorry thing who could barely raise a smile, her pride stolen. But for more than a decade Sal had heard her voice, felt her touch. He had memories.

"Sal, maybe you go over to your aunt," Father Gregory suggested.

Bell looked across the room. The crying women surrounded Gemma, who pressed her handkerchief against her eyes. Meanwhile, Antonio the Barber was talking to Vito. Other shop owners and neighbors were gathering outside.

Soon Sal was holding his aunt, who let out another cry as she accepted his embrace. Bell watched as the women closed around them, reaching to stroke Sal, their happy neighborhood boy.

The barber trailing, Vito Benno came over. The priest shook his hand and offered his condolences.

"You heard what Enzo said?" Vito asked in Sicilian.

The priest told him no.

"She fell under the trolley. The wheels…"

Bell saw his friend's uncle give the priest a knowing glance.

"She fell," Vito Benno repeated. "Slipped and fell."

Bell heard himself say, "It's raining."

"Yes," Father Gregory said. "The tracks were wet." He shook the shop owner's hand again. "Come to the rectory to arrange the service."

Vito Benno said he would.

Antonio the Barber pulled out a bottle of bootleg rye he'd bought from Mimmo's boys, Narrows Gate awash with illegal liquor. He poured four glasses, handing one to the man who lost his sister to despair, another to the priest and one to Bell, composed, stalwart, no longer a boy.

"*A Giovanna*," the barber said as he raised a glass.

Bell said, "*A Giovanna*."

The glasses clinked.

Bell brought Sal home for the night. Though the elder Bell had purchased the brownstone on Third Street and had two tenants, he and his son lived a humble existence in meager rooms that lacked a woman's eye for what a home needed.

Still stunned and confused, Benno was struck by the weighty silence in the apartment. He could've used some noise to block his thoughts. Every week there were funerals at St. Francis. You heard the bells in the classroom, you could smell the incense, then here comes the casket. People died: old, young, sick, accidents, killed tripping and falling under trolley wheels. It happens. You shrugged when you heard that the crew chained up a guy and threw him off a bridge, blew another guy's brains out the top of his head. After a while, you thought it's nothing, somebody dying. But it ain't nothing.

"Salvatore," said Mr. Bell. "Come. Sit." He was small man, bald right down the center of his head, a little belly, always wearing a vest that matched his slacks, a watch on a gold chain. He was older than the other parents at St. Francis, maybe past 50. Giovanna Benno had been 28.

Benno hopped into the chair and settled next to Mr. Bell. Benno expected he would say something poem-like with "thou arts" and "knowests" about dying, going to heaven, Jesus is standing there, his arms open, understanding on his bearded, Sicilian-looking face. Already, Benno took some comfort in that, maybe his mother found a little bit of peace.

"This is a raw deal you got," Mr. Bell explained.

"I know. But it's OK."

"No, OK it's not. Not by any stretch of the imagination."

Bell watched from the doorway as his father dropped his hand on Benno's shoulder. "A raw deal," Mr. Bell repeated. "I didn't have the pleasure of knowing your mother, but I am told she was a good woman. She loved you."

Benno shrugged.

"No? So you're thinking you can be safe from sadness by fooling yourself?"

"No," Benno said in mild protest. But he was thinking, Mr. Bell can read minds?

"Your mother is with you always. This you must never forget. And always you must make her proud." Mr. Bell rose. "You and Leo, you share this situation now," he said. "Neither mother is here. So you help each other in this objective—to make your mothers proud. All right?" Mr. Bell offered Benno his right hand as if to seal an agreement.

Benno shook it. "Sure," he said. "All right, Mr. Bell. You got it."

Later, while Leo slept next to him, Benno stared at the ceiling with an arm and a leg hanging off the single bed, Mr. Bell snoring down the hall. He thought about the day, his aunt wailing, the olives in the sawdust, Father Gregory, Mr. Bell telling him his mother is with him always.

But what was she wearing this morning when she left the house? What's the last thing she said to him? What did he say to her? Benno couldn't remember. In his mind, last week was this morning; this morning was three months ago. There was his mother on Christmas day or watching him diving off a pier into the Hudson, a wan smile on her face for a fleeting moment. He could see her hands, thin, her fingers rubbed raw from work. Then it all disappeared.

Jesus, thought Sal Benno, I'm an orphan.

Nobody in Narrows Gate who knew Bebe personally would admit it, but in November 1935, the whole town was sitting around the radio when the Hudson Four got their shot on *Captain Bridges' Amateur Hour*, which was sent across the country via the CBS

Network. Hennie hustled and noodged to get the quartet on the program, knowing they'd reach more people in one night than if they played a thousand nightclubs. Finally, Bridges relented and gave them an audition, which they nailed, Bebe singing lead on their jazzy barbershop version of "Shine." Afterward, Hennie snuggled up to Bridges and said, "Now, Captain, you're not going to hit the gong while my son is singing." From behind his desk, Bridges smiled wicked, raising a fat cigar to his lips. Hennie went back to Narrows Gate wondering whether she had finally come up against somebody she couldn't outsmart. Bridges had America's number-one radio program and he didn't get there by luck. Maybe he was setting Bebe up. Maybe he had a hard-on for small-town Sicilians. Already he butchered the name Rosiglino when he tried to pronounce it. As she counted down the days to the appearance, she saw the Captain with a charcoal heart, as a Southern sadist. She was wondering if it was time to see Mimmo, maybe he makes a cornice fall off a building when Bridges takes a walk on Fifth Avenue, it just misses, maybe it squashes his dog and he learns quick.

Usually when she went to a show by the Hudson Four, Hennie rode in the backseat with her son, with Nino Terrasini driving. But on the afternoon prior to the Bridges broadcast, she hired a car just for her and Bebe. A big black Ford pulled up in front of the house and the neighborhood came out, the Irish in knots over whether to snub Bebe or claim him as an adopted son. Hennie and Bebe descended into the fading November eve like it was prom night, Bebe in a white dinner jacket, a red boutonnière in the lapel, razor crease in his slacks; Hennie wore a fox stole and waved like a queen, savoring the moment. Revenge was some sweet nectar, huh?

"Bebe, listen to me," Hennie said as the car eased from the hydrant.

Like I haven't been, Bebe thought.

"This is your shot. You hear me? *Your* shot."

Bebe was holding a circular makeup mirror, studying his teeth. Grooming mattered, even on radio. Look sharp, feel sharp.

"He asks about the Hudson Four, you answer. You."

He snapped the mirror shut.

"You say your name. Say 'Billy,' not 'Bill.' You're a kid."

Bebe bristled when he was reminded he was the youngest of the Hudson Four. But not now. He saw her point. Youth was an advantage. He was the innocent newcomer, the boy on the way up. So far, they were on the same beam.

"When you're singing 'Shine,' you step out. Make little asides. You know, when all of you sing 'Cause my hair is curly,' sing something before the next verse."

"Like what?"

"I don't know what. Think of something. What would Crosby do?"

"He'd go 'bub-bub boo-boo.'"

"Then go 'bub-bub boo-boo.'"

Actually, in the version he cut with the Mills Brothers, Crosby commented on what the guy sang, adding a bit to the lyric: "Yeah, that's some bush on his head," and the like. The Hudson Four tried it in rehearsal and the other two singers hated it, mostly because it put Bebe out front even further.

The big Ford approached the gaping mouth of the Lincoln Tunnel and then they were on the Manhattan side, buildings piercing the clouds, and heading crosstown for the Loew's where Captain Bridges broadcast before an audience. Hennie was thinking the crowd ought to be satisfied they got a free ticket to see a big-time show, but no. They had to groan and boo, egging on the Captain to pick up his mallet, slam the golden gong and get some *zoticone* booted off the air, a career over before it began.

"What are you going to do if he gongs you?" Hennie asked as the car navigated toward 42nd Street and Times Square.

"He's not going to gong me," Bebe replied. "Maybe he gongs the Hudson Four. But he's not going to gong me."

A bear of an opera singer with a handkerchief and little feet got to finish his number and the monkeys in the audience cheered like they knew Pagliacci from Bozo. In the box they gave her above stage left, Hennie dropped her chin on her hand, her elbow on the velvet rail. Fidgeting, she dug for another cigarette. She stood, she sat. The Captain hadn't gonged anybody yet.

The announcer was selling the new Chrysler Imperial Airflow. On the opposite side of the stage, out of sight to the audience, the Hudson Four gathered, ready to appear.

Next, the orchestra played a little fanfare. "And now, ladies and gentlemen," the announcer intoned, "here's America's favorite talent scout, Captain Bridges!"

When the applause faded, Bridges spun the clacking Wheel of Chance and went into his "around and around she goes" spiel, like he left it to fate to choose who'd appear next. Already Bebe and the other two singers were standing at a microphone, those two dumpy *ciuccios* looking like bus boys, Bebe shining like gold, that smile, and too bad America can't see those eyes on the radio. Terrasini was seated at the piano, the stage manager creeping away on tiptoes, careful to avoid the stream of cables.

Hennie was electric with nerves. Stomach acid was burning a hole in her throat.

"And now," said the Captain, reading from index cards, "we'll have the Hudson Four, a group of good-looking boys from over in Narrows Gate, New Jersey."

Across the river in Narrows Gate, people who were hunched around the radio turned to look at each other, flush with a swelling of civic pride. They'd been acknowledged on the air for something other than a body found on Observer Road, splayed on the piers, spread-eagle in the Hudson.

"Who's going to speak for the group?" the Captain asked.

Leaning against the rail, Hennie mouthed the words, "I will, Captain Bridges. I'm Billy."

"I will," a chipper Bebe Rosiglino said. "I'm Billy and we're looking for a job. How about it, Captain?"

An uncomfortable giggle rose from the audience.

Oh shit, Hennie thought. That fuckin' kid.

"People really like us," Bebe added quickly. "Honest. They really do."

The audience sighed at the boy's innocence, his moxie. They applauded as the Captain clapped Bebe on the back.

"All right then, boys. All right," he said. "Let's hear what you've got."

Terrasini played a couple of ringing chords. Bebe tapped his toes. One, two, a one, two, three, four…

"Cause my hair is curly," the trio sang in unison.

"He's got curly hair," Bebe added.

Glancing sideways at each other, the other two sang, "Just because my teeth are pearly."

"Look at those Chiclets shine," Bebe chimed, his smile wide and bright.

The crowd edged forward in their seats. They bobbed their heads in time to Terrasini's rhythm, smiling as they took in Bebe.

Hennie clapped her hands in delight, raining cigarette ash on the audience below.

"Like to dress up in the latest style."

"I'm hep!" Bebe mugged, tossing in a Durante ha-cha-cha.

The audience howled.

Before the Hudson Four reached the chorus, Hennie was heading backstage.

Show over, she cornered the Captain, who drew up as she approached. Stage mothers were boils on his ass, the worst part of a job he enjoyed and was finding increasingly profitable. The wise guy columnists mocked him for his drawl and low-key demeanor, but they knew he was a formidable businessman. A native of North Carolina, Bridges was a shareholder in Liggett & Myers, Lorillard, R.J. Reynolds and other tobacco companies. At 67 years old, he was a wealthy man.

"Ma'am, your son did a fine job," Bridges said as he tried to sidestep her. Her boy was the one who'd mentioned a product by its brand name. Tomorrow, the Captain's men would remind the American Chiclet Company that no one rides for free.

Hennie planted herself between the men's room and the stage door. Behind the Captain, a crew was breaking down the *Amateur Hour* set.

"A fine job indeed," he repeated. "Now, if you would kindly excuse me."

"Captain, I only wanted to thank you," Hennie said. "My son was nervous and I know you took the trouble to calm him down. That was very nice of you."

The Captain stopped. He looked at Hennie, a bulldog in fox and beaded lavender. She was a schemer, a bulldozer, but now she was doling out soft soap. He gave her credit for the shift in tactics. She'd read him right. "Why, you're welcome, ma'am."

"Mrs. Rosiglino," she said. "Billy's mother."

"Your son is a clever boy."

Nodding, she clutched her purse.

"Truth is, ma'am, I'm thinking we might find a place for his little group on the traveling show."

Captain Bridges' Traveling Vaudeville Show. He had one touring north of Boston, another south to D.C., a third in the upper Midwest, a fourth in California.

"That would be grand, Captain," Hennie replied, her excitement contained. "Billy would love that."

Bridges told her to come by the office in a day or so, well aware she'd be there tomorrow morning.

"One thing," he said as he maneuvered past her. "He has to change his name."

Hennie didn't hesitate. "Any suggestions?"

"Staying Italian is fine. There's more of you by the minute in the major markets. But make it simple and sweet. Something everybody can say."

A week before Bebe was set to head up to Monkton with the Traveling Vaudeville Show, Hennie returned to Bridges' office in midtown, taking the tubes under the Hudson to Herald Square. She brought her husband along, Vincenzo the Fireman, who was more hurt than angry as he trudged beagle-eyed through slush and snow. "Marsala," she told the Captain, "is the name. Every American can pronounce it."

The Captain approved. He came around the desk to shake the fireman's hand, acknowledging the man's sacrifice, the family name tossed aside. "If I were a betting man," Captain Bridges said, "I'd wager that soon a great many people across America will know your boy."

CHAPTER THREE

Mimmo decided Narrows Gate needed to make a big deal out of the Feast of San Gennaro, an event that took over Little Italy across the Hudson every year just as the kids were going back to school. Come September, using St. Francis Church as cover, Mimmo's crew got the shopkeepers to set up stalls along Polk Street. Vito and Gemma Benno agreed to fry up sausage rings and grill some peppers and onions. Dommie's would provide the bread for the sandwiches. This one would fry zeppole, that one would hand out torrone slices, Pooch the Grocer would sell watermelon. In a generous mood, Mimmo told them to keep the added profits minus the usual 10 percent cut.

At the north end of Polk, Mimmo had some guys build a wooden stage and parked next to it was a brand new 1936 Buick Coupe, a beauty Freddie Pop boosted off a lot in Hartford. Mimmo was raffling it 10 tickets for a dollar, pressing a booklet on everybody who came down the street; he even sent a couple of kids over to the Lackawanna Station to work over the commuters. (The winner was already chosen—the daughter of a general manager at a trucking firm, a guy Frankie Fortune wanted deeper in his pocket.) By the time the feast was ready to begin, Mimmo had enough money to buy 12 Buicks. Five hundred dollars would go to Father Gregory, the rest to Mimmo minus Fortune's take, which was considerable. Nothing bumped up to Corini and

Gigenti on this, an independent operation and Mickey Mouse by their standards. As for Farcolini, not even Fortune knew where he was: New York District Attorney Thomas Dewey was on Don Carlo's back with a phony prostitution charge, persecuting him in the papers and on the radio, driving him underground.

The point of the stage was to allow Bebe to sing. Hennie convinced Mimmo that he needed more than ponies for the kiddies—games where you can't knock down the lead-bottom milk containers or where the wheel is going to land on 00 whenever the board is covered—and that creaking carnival ride down by Observer Road that looks like it'll topple if somebody sneezes. Hennie agreed to lend Mimmo the public-address system and microphone she bought Bebe and the Hudson Four before they went on the road last year with the Captain's regional troupe. In turn, Mimmo had two of his boys bring the piano from St. Francis's basement up to the stage. Hennie made a couple of calls and booked a few acts for the festivals—comedians, singing sisters, a guy who juggled plates, all fresh from Italy, plus the church's marching band and Bonifacio, the violin player.

As for Mimmo, he had a little scheme of his own for *La Festività de Saint Januarius*. His niece, Rosa, he decided, was a perfect match for Bebe. She was sweet and pure with dark hair and dark eyes; at 17 already a woman, soon to be shapely rather than plump. The picture of a housewife and mother-to-be. Mimmo figured the time was ripe: Hennie had told him to be ready—something special was going to happen to her son at the feast.

"What?" Mimmo asked as he adjusted his sunglasses. "He's going to go back to his old name?"

"The new name is good. It's fine," Hennie said, annoyed. "We've beaten this to shit, no?"

They were standing on Polk Street, cleared of parked cars, watching carpenters hammer and saw the little booths at the curb. The feast was kicking off tonight. Bebe would entertain tomorrow at sundown. The press had been invited. On Sunday afternoon, the statue of the Virgin would be paraded, dollar bills pinned to her gown, the marching band wailing. Then the phony raffle.

"So. What's the announcement, Hennie?" Mimmo asked.

"You'll see," she said confidently, waiting for him to light her cigarette.

"He ain't getting married, is he?"

She leaned back. "Where did you hear that?"

"Ain't he knocked up that girl in Fairview?"

She blew a stream of smoke. "That's been taken care of."

"Again?"

"Mimmo…" She saw a reflection of herself in his sunglasses, a scowl on her face.

He held up his hands in mock surrender. "Maybe you tie a string on it for a while."

"Yeah," she said dryly, "I'll do that."

"Good. 'Cause I'm thinking it's time he settles down."

"You are, are you?"

Mimmo nodded definitively.

"Wow," Leo Bell said. "It's worse."

Benno put the piece of gauze back over his eye. A sty that had started out a couple of days ago like a tiny pimple on his upper lid was now chickpea-sized, red and aching. His aunt had dipped the gauze in olive oil, the all-purpose elixir, but this time it didn't do a damned bit of good.

"You need a doctor," Bell said.

"Where do I get a doctor in the middle of this?" Benno pointed toward the festivities. Polk Street was overrun with a couple hundred people, Italians coming down from all over the county, plus all the neighbors eating their way from one booth to the next, Gemma stuffing sizzling sausages into rolls, fried peppers going on top. Italian music blared from a Victrola on a fire escape, another one played in Antonio the Barber's shop. Benno saw Mimmo was onto something: The neighborhood was making a fortune and there was good cheer in the air. Already you could sense tonight was going to see a celebration like back when Prohibition ended.

Benno wore a colorful short-sleeved shirt; Bell, a suit jacket, a collared shirt, and prescription eyeglasses, which added to his air of maturity. They were both 13 years old and had pretty much cast off their childish ways—not that Bell ever had many. Now that the death of Benno's mother was no longer a shocking reminder of life's depravity, he had returned to his easy way with everybody, which made him a top-rank flirt and though he was still short for his age, he was no longer plump. All the hard work around the store had put him in tip-top shape. As for Bell, with girls he was often reduced to one-word answers, if not gulps and nods like he left his brain in his locker at the junior high school. A couple of times, Benno tried to nudge his pal into something like a double date—meaning two girls, the cover of night, and Elysian Fields—but inevitably Bell declined.

Even now, as they stood in front of the salumeria, an oily gauze pad over Benno's eye, a couple of ninth-grade girls out in the street gave them a little wave and stopped, waiting for an encouraging reply. They were pretty, both of them. Scatta was from Lazio on the mainland, Maria from Trabia in Sicily, yet they were friends.

"Let's get out of here," Benno said, thinking his sty had him looking like a gargoyle.

"A doctor," Bell repeated. "Let's go to St. Patrick's."

"I wanna ride the ride." Benno started south toward the creaking Ferris wheel.

"With the gauze pad over your eye?"

"What's the difference?"

Bell trotted to keep up. He preferred to amble on his long legs at a pace that gave him time to think. Benno, meanwhile, hurried everywhere, like wherever he was going might disappear before he arrived.

"Maybe we make a patch for your eye," Bell said. "To keep it clean. An eye patch."

"What? Like a fuckin' pirate?"

"Sally…"

Benno pulled up.

"Let me see again," Bell said.

Benno turned his back to the jostling crowd. He took down the gauze.

Bell grimaced. "I swear it's worse than a minute ago."

"It throbs," Benno admitted.

"Come on," Bell said, grabbing Benno's elbow. "We're going to the hospital."

Benno knew the emergency room at St. Patrick's kept the Italians at the bottom of the list next to the coloreds. He saw himself spending the entire festival waiting for some doctor to tell him whatever happened was his fault because he was born wrong.

But the sty hurt, the mass pressing against his eye, and he had a headache like a little drill was at work in there. Every now and then, it struck a nerve. His right cheek was numb, though he didn't mention it to Bell.

"We ride the ride first," Benno said.

"I swear to God, there's another Ferris wheel," Bell told him.

Benno hesitated. He looked toward Observer Road. "OK," he said finally.

They stepped into the crowd, letting it pull them uptown like an undertow, which neither of them had experienced, seeing as the Hudson River didn't make waves unless a ship hurried by, the garbage bobbing by the piers and those white birds soaring down for a feast of their own.

At dusk, the marching band played a fanfare. With Nino Terrasini waiting patiently at the piano and Bonifacio holding his violin at his side, Bebe came from Church Square Park looking like a million dollars. The blue-serge suit brought out the magic in his eyes, the bow tie did too, and the silk shirt took in the light and sent it back out like stardust. He was still as thin as vermicelli, but he seemed formidable, like he knew a secret.

The crowd on Polk Street stretched all the way back to First, people up on their toes to see. There were people on the rooftops looking down. Reporters were on hand—not just the *Observer*, but the *Mirror*, the *News* and *Il Progresso* from across the river, and the *Evening News* from Newark.

At the stairs to the stage, Bebe paused to kiss his mother's cheek, shake his father's hand and give a little nod to the army of aunts and uncles, also to the mayor and his wife and to Father Gregory in his brown robe and sandals.

"Bebe," said Hennie, who wore a royal blue gown and had her silver hair done up.

He was taking a last look at his shoes, which were shined to a gloss.

"Bebe, say hello to Mimmo."

He felt a spark of annoyance. He had gathered himself right, ready for the event, the walk across the park clearing his head. Now it was time to sing. But he knew the game. "Mimmo, hey," he said. "*Come va?*"

"Bebe," Mimmo said as they shook hands, "there's somebody I want you to meet."

Bebe saw the girl next to him.

"My niece, Rosa. Rosa, Bebe. Bill Rosiglino."

She was wide-eyed and bright, a pretty moonfaced Sicilian, and Bebe saw she was nervous. He cupped her hand the way he did whenever he met a pretty girl and held her gaze for an extra beat or two.

"Hello, Rosa."

Rosa Mistretta was thunderstruck. Years later, she would tell people that she fell in love with him as soon as he said her name, her hand in his.

"She's a big fan," Mimmo said.

"Why, that's nice to hear, Rosa." As he released her hand, he gave it a little squeeze. "I hope you can stick around for the show."

"Of course we're going stick around," Mimmo roared. "All this, Bebe, this is for you." He gestured to the stage, the bunting, the crowd, the fire trucks that blocked off the side streets.

Bebe had nothing lined up for tonight. He'd be free after he talked to the papers. Considering it was Mimmo's niece, he'd go slow. A meal first, maybe.

Hennie said, "You'd better get up there, Bebe."

Still looking at the girl, Bebe shrugged sheepishly. "I should listen to Mama," he whispered.

Now Rosa smiled too.

Hennie gave the Irish mayor a little whack on the arm. "Showtime," she told him. "Make it rich."

The mayor climbed the stage to welcome Bebe with an introduction Hennie had approved. His thudding footsteps echoed through the PA system along Polk Street.

"You people," said the emergency room doctor, shaking his head.

Benno was sitting on a gurney, his feet dangling, his head back under some kind of medical spotlight. Seven hours they'd waited. Seven. Might've been more if Bell hadn't approached the doctor as he tended to a woman who had sliced her thumb peeling apples for a pie. Her crying under control, she and the doctor shared a smoke and chatted like old friends.

Bell had seen enough. Defying all protocol, he stepped behind the curtain. "A word, Doctor," he said, adjusting his glasses. A young nurse hurried over to admonish him.

The toothy doctor looked astonished.

Bell remained calm. "My friend's eye is much worse than when we arrived."

The nurse put her hands on Bell's arms and tried to turn him away. He looked at her—she seemed younger than Bell—then held up a hand and smiled politely.

"Sir," she said. "Please. You have to step outside."

Bell mentioned the name William F. Flanagan, the hospital's chief administrator. He'd read it on the plaque in the lobby when he went out to get Benno a lemon ice. Benno had put the paper cup against his eye, but the cold didn't do a damned bit of good either.

"Mr. Flanagan," Bell repeated. "I'm going to his home now." He said it so evenly that the doctor believed him.

"I'll be with you in a moment," the doctor replied finally.

"In one moment," Bell said, "I'll be gone."

And so Dr. Horan had Benno brought from the now-empty waiting room to the bay next to the woman with the little cut on her thumb. Seated on the gurney, Benno fidgeted nervously, tinkering with the knees of his slacks and jiggling his cap.

Horan arrived in a huff, snapping up the chart. "Salvatore Benno," he muttered. "Inflammation of the eyelid."

Benno looked over to Bell, who smiled in an attempt to comfort.

"Let me see," the doctor said.

Benno pulled off the gauze. He'd been tempted to swipe a new one while they waited, but he believed in the olive-oil coating even if the eye, blood red and inflamed now by the pressure of the sty driving against it, had gotten much worse.

The doctor tossed the pad on the floor, then smelled his thumb and forefinger.

"You people," he said. He rolled the spotlight over and told Benno to look up.

"Hordeolum," he said. "A sty."

"It hurts like a son of a bitch," Benno said.

Like he wanted to show him real pain, the doctor pressed the swollen lump with a bare finger.

Benno howled.

Horan snapped off the light. "Put a warm cloth on it."

Bell said, "The eye's full of blood."

The doctor ignored him.

Benno wiped his face with the back of his wrist.

"Put a warm cloth on it," the doctor repeated. "It'll drain."

Shooting Bell a look, Dr. Horan threw back the curtain and disappeared.

Red-faced, Benno jumped off the gurney. "I'm going to kill that fuck," he said. "You seen that? He poked me on purpose." Suddenly Benno wobbled, his knees buckling. "My head. The damned thing wants to explode."

Bell said he'd take him to his father's house. He should've done it hours ago.

Bebe looked over the crowd, the young girls in front gazing upward, couples further back. Men who worked the shipyards and piers lined the sidewalks, their arms folded as they waited to be impressed. The old neighbors watched from their stoops.

Over by the big Buick, Mimmo was raffling away, that dunce Freddie Pop sitting behind the wheel like he wanted to drive off. Hennie paced nervously, her skin tingling, her chest tight, counting the ways it could wrong. Vincenzo the Fireman looked around, amazed that all this could be for Bebe. Maybe 500 people packed Polk Street. For Bebe. America. Some fuckin' place, huh?

Behind the stage, the Irish were strolling across Church Square Park; they'd boycotted the San Gennaro Festival but were intrigued by rumors of Bebe's announcement. They'd read about him in the *Observer*: Bebe Marsala is singing with the Hudson Four in Bangor, Schenectady, Providence, winning them over in Philly, Wilmington, Baltimore. In D.C., Captain Bridges posed with him, slinging his arm across Bebe's shoulders; that photo ended up in the *Daily News*. The Irish wouldn't go so far as to say they thought Bebe a young man to be proud of. But he had sloughed off some of his native grease.

Taking his time, Bebe studied the people on the fire escapes. He stared past the busy food stands a couple of blocks away and at the Ferris wheel on Observer Road.

At the piano, Terrasini waited.

Stoked by the mayor, the crowd expected Bebe to burst onto the stage and kick off with a frantic version of "Shine." But Bebe wasn't doing nothing but standing there. They began to murmur.

Mimmo turned to Hennie. He figured Bebe forgot the words to his opening number.

When he felt the tension in the crowd peak, Bebe turned to Terrasini.

The pianist started an up-tempo introduction that was nothing like the corny, hopped-up pace he'd whip up for "Shine." Quick and snappy, but it swung, too.

Bebe snapped his fingers and the audience followed, clapping their hands in rhythm. Looking into their eyes, seemingly one at a time, he helped them find the downbeat. When the crowd was locked in, he stepped up and began to sing. "Over somebody else's shoulder, I fell in love with you."

An Eddie Cantor tune Bebe and Nino rearranged, getting to the heart of the song about the singer stealing his pal's girl. They junked Cantor's gay approach and more or less stole a sound they heard from Bill Basie, the pianist in Benny Moten's band. To Bebe, it was like Basie took the frills off the music, like he made rhythm king, putting the listener's body in motion.

Swinging Cantor's tune, Bebe's voice floated along Polk Street, its timbre far richer than the high-pitched tone he used with the Hudson Four. His idea was golden. He'd out Crosby Crosby, using the mic for intimacy with his listeners, swinging like the Negro cats do. Crosby was 12 years older than Bebe—a great singer still but old news. Bebe could improve on his style—and in doing so, declare himself a man and no longer part of the boyish quartet.

Hennie thought her son was going to stand up and tell Polk Street and the press he was leaving the Hudson Four. Instead,

Bebe was announcing he'd come up with a new way to sell a song.

"Over Somebody Else's Shoulder" wrapped up with Bebe holding a note as Terrasini played a Basie-like outro. The duo ended in unison—hell, they'd been rehearsing the number for weeks—and the crowd burst into applause. If the new music confused them, Bebe's confidence won them over.

"All right, Bebe!" someone yelled.

"Hey, Bebe, way to go!"

"Thank you so much, ladies and gentlemen," Bebe said as the violinist, Bonifacio, stepped up. "Here's a little number I think you know." He pointed toward the crowd. "Hey, fellas, if your loved one's nearby, grab a hold of her right now."

As Terrasini held a G chord so Bonifacio could check his tuning, Bebe said, "For you old-timers out there..." Then he repeated his introduction in Sicilian. Big applause.

Mimmo said, "He's got your head on his shoulders, Hennie."

She was looking at Rosa, an idea brewing.

An arpeggio by Terrasini, and then the opening chords over which Bonifacio played the melody. Tall, thin, a pencil mustache, hair slicked, the violinist played the old way—soppy, overwrought, melodramatic, Sicilian—tugging at heartstrings as Terrasini kept the tempo for "I Surrender Dear" slow and steady for romance.

Bebe sang, "We've played the game of 'stay away.' But it costs more than I can pay."

Vincenzo put his hand on Hennie's shoulder. He whispered, "*Ciò è buona, no?*"

"Better than good," she replied. She'd begun to think her beautiful boy made a bargain with some devil who'd turned him into a man with a new set of brains.

Bebe continued, taking the second verse just like Crosby. In fact, he preferred Louis Armstrong's approach to the song, but he'd pushed his idea far enough. The bridge from where he'd been with the Hudson Four to where he was going needed to be built slow. A false move would bring the whole thing down.

After the third verse, Bebe stepped back and let Bonifacio solo. The violinist laid it on with a trowel, but it went over. As if inspired, Bebe repeated the third verse in Sicilian.

The old-timers sitting on the stoops and leaning on the window ledges smiled with pride. On Polk Street, couples danced in tender embrace.

At the side of the stage, Mimmo grabbed Hennie and gave her a spin.

Rosa looked at the girls in front of the stage. They were swooning, too.

CHAPTER FOUR

Benno's pain was desperate now, a jagged stone dragging across his eye every time he blinked, a worm made of steel drilling its way through his brain. Earlier, he vomited, and when he tried to stand, he fainted, Leo catching him and easing him to the floor. When Leo's father walked in, he drew up in shock. Behind the giant growth on the lid, the boy's eye looked like it had been turned inside out; the right side of his face was swollen like it had been beaten.

Benno tried to listen as Mr. Bell made a phone call, but he couldn't understand the language. After he hung up, Mr. Bell wriggled into his topcoat. "Not to alarm, Sal. But an expert is needed. Leo, call for us a taxi. To Manhattan—Sixteenth and First."

Bell turned toward the hall.

"Leo," his father shouted, "better to make it two. I want you should go to his family. Bring them."

Benno was too queasy to protest.

"Sal, I'm getting a blanket," Mr. Bell said, as he buttoned his vest under the jacket. When he returned, he found Benno had passed out again, his head pressed against the table, one arm dangling.

The taxi stopped at the entrance to the emergency room. Under a wash of stars, an orderly in white down to his socks and shoes was waiting with a wheelchair.

"Sal. Salvatore," Mr. Bell said. He held out his hand. "Let's go, son."

Benno groaned. In the backseat, his head cradled against the door, he'd fallen asleep. Now a wave of nausea rushed in.

"Where's Leo?" he managed.

"He's with your aunt and uncle," Mr. Bell said, stepping aside as the orderly positioned the wheelchair.

As he struggled into the seat, Benno saw, in the lights of the bay, Mr. Bell accept a muted greeting from a tall man in a long black coat. The man wore a black hat with a wide brim and had a dark beard and long curls that spun past his ears.

They brought me to a Jew hospital, Benno thought as the chair bounced on cobblestone. He tried to remember if this might be a good thing and he concluded it was better than St. Patrick's, where they made you sit around seven hours so they could poke you where you hurt, then walk away.

In Yiddish, the man in the long coat assured Mr. Bell that the best doctors would tend to the boy. An eye specialist, a superior surgical team if, and we should only hope it wouldn't be a necessity.

Mr. Bell said, "Eli, I can't begin—"

"Tend to the boy," said Mr. Kreiner, his boss and dearest friend.

At Albini the Tailor's, Bebe washed up good. He talked to the press boys, telling them of his plans to head out solo, saying good-bye to Captain Bridges as well as the Hudson Four. Then he walked Polk Street in a fresh suit and clean, crisp shirt. Starstruck high school girls were waiting—their older sisters, too, and a few young mothers, looking at Bebe with muted lust and unbridled admiration. As

Terrasini watched, his girl Ruthie on his arm, he thought, Which will you choose, Bebe? Nobody wants to see a man with a 15-year-old blonde at his side. But you fuck somebody's wife down here and you turn up under a bridge, body parts scattered.

A couple of men came over to shake Bebe's hand, guys who a year or so ago thought him an imbecile, an eel. Some guy called him "Bebe Hollywood." The crowd around him was closing in. He signed a few autographs. Then, with the flick of his head, he summoned Terrasini.

Bebe gave Ruthie a peck on the cheek. "We do OK, kid?" he asked as they moved on, the crowd following.

"You did fine, Bill." She was 25, a secretary at Western Union in Manhattan. A brawny Pole, she once told Marsala that if he grabbed her ass again she would crush his larynx. She believed the singer was keeping Terrasini from settling down.

When they reached Madison Street, Bebe looked over his shoulder. "Dinner on me tonight?" he said to Terrasini.

Before Ruthie could protest, Terrasini said, "What's the plan?"

"The Blue Onyx. Mimmo wants me to meet his niece."

"Mimmo?" Terrasini laughed. "I hope she don't look like him."

"Watch yourself," Marsala replied. "This is a lady we're talking about."

Leo, his father, Gemma and Vito had spent the night in the hospital waiting room, praying that the surgeon would do his best by Sal. Hours ago, an intern had mentioned the possibility of an intracranial tumor. "Whether there is permanent damage to the eye, we don't know. But," he added with a forced smile, "your son is in excellent hands."

Now pale morning light filled the long, narrow room. Still wearing his surgical scrubs, the doctor came in, his professional detachment strained by fatigue. "Dr. Finkelstein," he said, introducing himself. He withdrew a pack of Luckies from his pocket. As he lit a cigarette, he turned to Gemma and Vito, who sat on the sofa facing the Bells.

"Well, the boy is out of danger."

Leo Bell stood and walked gingerly toward the doctor.

"No sign of a tumor. This is very good news. It was my greatest concern, frankly."

Vito nodded as Gemma dabbed at her nose with her husband's handkerchief.

"However, the eye could not be saved."

Mr. Bell inched to the edge of the sofa.

Frowning, Vito said, "I don't understand."

Hearing the thick accent, Finkelstein turned to Leo. "Could you translate, please?"

"You took the eye?" Leo asked softly.

Finkelstein nodded.

Leo shuddered. "Aunt Gemma, Vito," he said. "*L'occhio. È andato. Sono spiacente.*"

Gemma gasped.

Later, there would be talk of irreparable damage to the cornea and sclera, *Staphylococcus aureus* and the risk of reinfection, and how very rare it is for a meibomian cyst to cause such damage. But now Finkelstein said carefully, "This is a healthy boy. The prognosis is very, very good. Perhaps we could think of ourselves as lucky."

Said Leo Bell, "*Salvatore vivrà—lungo e felice.*"

An ocularist would be recommended, they were told. The boy would be measured before he left the hospital and the fitting would take place after healing. He would stay at the hospital for at least one month.

Gemma took Leo Bell's hands onto her lap as he began to cry.

Freddie Pop couldn't help himself. First, Mimmo told him go boost a new car far, far out of town. So Pop went all the way to Hartford up in Connecticut, farther away from Narrows Gate than he's ever been, and walked around car dealerships until he saw that Buick Coupe, shining like a black diamond under the September sun, the machine calling to him, key in the ignition. And then he got it back home—the thing drove like the road was made of marshmallows—and Mimmo says sit on it, keep it clean and by the way, get some kids together and make them sell raffle books over at the train station.

To Freddie Pop, it was like being told to raffle off a chance to marry Lucy, his girlfriend. He knew the game going in but still felt betrayed. Mimmo should've known he'd have a good thing going with the Buick.

So the day after the feast, when Mimmo told him to deliver it to the daughter of that boss at Olson Transport, she lives in a nice house in Fort Lee, Pop thought maybe he should say something. Like why not give the girl some dough instead? She can buy any car she wants. This Buick, it's not for some girl, Mimmo.

But he said nothing. Only 17, Pop had no standing with the crew. They considered him a goopy kid; his only talent the ability to hotwire a car in seconds, then drive off like a choirboy.

"Don't fuck up the delivery," Mimmo advised, explaining Frankie Fortune was interested, but leaving the details out.

It was raining, the drops beading on the coat of wax Pop had applied with love. The ride up to Fort Lee was one sad journey, and he took the long way so he could have a few more minutes with the Buick, a beauty with dual side mounts, mohair interior, the whitewalls ringed in red. He was so blue the cherry lollipop tucked in his cheek brought him no joy.

The Fort Lee neighborhood was green and lined with big houses with driveways.

Ah, fuck it, he thought, and the next thing he knew, he was on the other side of the George Washington Bridge, going north.

And the sun came out.

The call to the candy store was for Frankie Fortune, but Mimmo took it.

"But he left here three hours ago," he tried to explain, but the boss at Olson Transport was shouting. Apparently, his wife and daughter had waited for a big surprise, standing outside their beautiful home, hope melting to disappointment when nothing happened.

Hanging up, Mimmo's first reaction was to bury the thing. Go boost another Buick, rush it up to Fort Lee, end of story. But there was tension in the crew. Don Carlo was on the run, nobody certain where, and it wasn't too clear who was in charge—Corini, Gigenti, Geller down in Florida. Maybe it makes sense to fix the problem before it goes to Frankie, given the state of affairs, but it could be he already knew about the missing Buick and he's sitting there thinking Mimmo kept the car to sell.

After calling three restaurants over in Manhattan, Mimmo found Fortune up at the Saint Tropez, which wasn't too far from Fort Lee.

Fortune listened.

"Send Boo," he said.

Mimmo couldn't tell what Fortune was thinking. When he was angry, he shut down like an icebox when the power dies.

"Tell Boo to bring him here."

Mimmo figured he'd better say he was sorry. But Fortune cut the line.

"Boo," Mimmo said to Chiasso, a big slab of muscle, his skull full of sharp edges. "Freddie Pop stole the Buick." They were behind the candy store in Mimmo's weedy backyard, the pisser boy statue dribbling. Suddenly, gray clouds threatened to burst again. "Find him and deliver him to Frankie."

Boo Chiasso nodded.

Mimmo peeled off $100. "Bring the Buick back, too."

It took Chiasso less than 10 hours to turn Pop over to Fortune.

First thing, he went uptown to Superior Baking Supplies, walked onto the noisy factory floor where they took the pits out of cherries, melted chocolate and shredded coconut, groaning conveyor belts moving product. Over the industrial din, he asked for Pop's girlfriend, Lucy, a kid from the neighborhood, too. The supervisor, this little fat Swede with a pencil behind his ear, told Boo he had no business in the building.

"Lucy," Chiasso repeated.

Furious, the Swede put his hand on Chiasso to turn him.

Chiasso, who had a foot in height on the guy, grabbed him and rushed him over to a mammoth machine where long blades chopped chunks of dried coconut into pieces to be shredded. One arm around the Swede's throat, Chiasso stretched the guy until his hand was heading toward the piston-pumping blades. The Swede struggled, but Chiasso had him good. He was born for tasks like this.

A girl's voice rose over the clatter. "Wait!"

Chiasso kept driving the Swede's hand toward the blades.

"She left," the girl shouted. "Freddie called her."

Chiasso threw the Swede down.

The girl, quivering and crying under a hair net, told Chiasso that Lucy had taken a bus to Connecticut.

As he left the building, Chiasso calculated and he figured it right.

Lucy went home to grab some clothes and write a note to her kid sister. Then she walked to Buchanan Avenue to take the bus over to the depot on 42nd Street for the Danbury Inter-Urban Line.

Chiasso was sitting six rows behind her as the bus to Connecticut wheezed and pulled out. Nervous, she kept twirling her auburn hair. Boo knew they were getting close when she pulled out her makeup and applied a fresh coat of lipstick.

Freddie Pop was waiting at the roadside stop in Milford, cherry Tootsie Roll Pop in his cheek. Connecticut to him was some kind of heaven, rivers and streams, trees, open spaces. Given he had a big, beautiful Buick, he and Lucy could get started good up here.

Lucy stepped out the front door, Chiasso the back.

Pop lifted Lucy up, kissed her face and spun her around. He couldn't wait to open the door to the Buick and let her slide inside.

He didn't see Chiasso coming.

Chiasso punched him once in the kidney. Pop dropped to his knees in pain. Lucy tumbled to the gravel, her cardboard suitcase flying open.

Frozen in horror, she watched as Chiasso shoved the barrel of his gun so far into Pop's mouth that he began to gag.

On the way back south, Pop sat subdued in the passenger's seat, his left eye bruised and swollen from the short right Chiasso hit him with when he protested outside Bridgeport, the Buick swerving with the blow.

A bus driver delivered Lucy into Massachusetts even though she was $1.40 short on the fare. He had a 14-year-old daughter at home and hated to see any kid frightened and defeated.

"Go ahead. Sit down," Fortune said.

They were in a storeroom at the Saint Tropez, a club up by the George Washington Bridge, cartons of liquor and cigarettes stacked to the ceiling. Fortune sat at an old wooden desk, a bottle of rye half empty. Two thirty in the morning, the room was lit by a dull bulb overhead in a tin shade. Fortune's handsome face glowed, his expression cold.

Freddie Pop sat. The side of his skull still ached from Chiasso's punch. Plus, he'd pissed blood near Greenwich.

Chiasso stood with his back against the door frame.

"What were you thinking?" Fortune asked.

Pop didn't know what he was supposed to say. "It don't make no sense now."

"You were making a move?"

Pop shook his head. "It was the car, Frankie. Just the car."

Fortune nodded. He pushed the bottle across the desk.

Pop declined. Liquor burned his throat down to the belly.

"Mimmo knew. Right?" Fortune asked.

"Nobody knew nothing. I was driving and all of a sudden I'm crossing the bridge."

Fortune nodded, the liquor failing to ease the strain. Freddie Pop was the least of his woes. With Farcolini still on the lam, nobody knew who was in charge or what was next. Corini and Gigenti needed a fuckin' referee between them. He said, "Nobody knew, but your girl is waiting for your call."

"No," the kid said.

"But she knows where you are."

Pop said, "She didn't know, Frankie." He looked over his shoulder at Chiasso. "There was no reason to leave her on the side of the road."

"So you're thinking we're even, seeing as Boo wasn't nice to your girl."

"I'm thinking at least the car is all right," Pop said. "I know I've got to settle up with you, but at least the car is all right."

Fortune sat back, Pop staring at him like maybe his expression would crack, maybe he would send a signal that said it could work out. It was so quiet in the room that Pop could've sworn heard crickets in the surrounding woods.

"You have one of those Tootsie Pops in your pocket?" Fortune asked.

Pop nodded, dug one out, held it high.

"Go ahead. Calm your nerves. We'll find a solution."

Pop took the wrapper off and shoved the lollipop in his mouth.

Fortune sprang across the desk. He grabbed Pop and, as they toppled to the floor, used his palm to cram the candy so deep into Freddie Pop's throat that the little white stick disappeared.

As Pop gagged, Fortune straddled his chest.

Pop tried to throw a punch. He pawed for Fortune's face but couldn't reach it.

Fortune kept pressing on Pop's mouth, one hand on top of the other, his arms trembling from the pressure. A thick vein pulsed in his neck.

Pop's eyes bulged. He banged his head against the floor, once, twice, several times. He was dying and he knew it, choking to death. He was thinking about the goddamned Buick shining in the sun, Lucy in the passenger's seat shining too, when he stopped struggling and collapsed, dead.

Fortune stood. He dusted dirt from the knees of his slacks. Fixed his tie.

Chiasso stepped in to remove the body.

CHAPTER FIVE

Rosa Mistretta: bright, quick-witted, attentive, warm, polite, confident among strangers. You could take her anywhere and she knew how to fit in. Didn't need the spotlight, stood comfortably in the shadows. Wasn't a gold digger. Didn't see Bebe as a stepping stone, didn't want to be a singer herself or an actress. Didn't want to meet Captain Bridges. Didn't ask him if he knew Crosby or Gable. She was solid. Whole.

Hennie approved. Vincenzo joked, nudging his son with his elbow. "Bebe, she's the one, huh?" Up in Bayonne, her family welcomed him when he called. Fearing a band of morons like Mimmo, he went in filled with dread, but no, they were fine. Told him he sang like an angel. Mentioned his clothes. No third degree. Nobody staring him up and down. He relaxed.

In Narrows Gate, Hennie made a big show of greeting Rosa in the street. "Rosa!" Hugs. "*Benvenuto, cara!*"

"She's proper," she told her son. "The kind of woman you marry, Bebe," she said, wagging a finger in warning.

All this after two weeks. Four dates, not including the double with Nino and Ruthie at the Blue Onyx. Cocktails at the Union Club. Dancing at Lubanski's Casino in Clifton. He asked her to come along when he dropped in on WHOM. The radio station sat above the Stanley Theater in Jersey City and broadcast throughout Manhattan, Brooklyn, and northern New Jersey, in Italian in the a.m., in English in the afternoon and at night. Their fourth date was at the Rosiglino home, Hennie at the head of the table, her sisters Rosalie and Dee running the kitchen like servants. "Rosa, dear, sit next to me," Hennie said, taking the girl by the hand.

While his mother chewed the girl's ear off, Bebe studied her. Maybe she loses the baby fat, cheekbones emerge, legs become long and firm. She fills out. Four dates and he hadn't touched her but to kiss her goodnight, with passion after the night at Lubanski's. The girl liked good music. To his surprise, she mentioned Ellington before he could. In reply, he said he'd take her to the Cotton Club in Harlem. "I'd like that, Bill." He told her his goal was to grab the singer's chair in a group led by a Dorsey, a Pollack, even a pompous bastard like Guy Simon. The exposure, sure, but what those cats can show a man about music. Better than a degree from Juilliard, baby.

Soon, he saw her four, five times a week when he was free, no matter his mood. Up, he showered her with flowers. Down, his neck stiff with anxiety, they shared a pot of coffee and she listened.

Hennie saw it was the right move. Bebe and Rosa: They looked like two sweet American kids. "Bebe, take her to meet the Ear," she told him.

He was in his boxer shorts, ironing a shirt. Nobody could iron a shirt like Bebe Marsala. "I don't think so, Ma."

The Ear—Eddie Moran—owned the Lakeside Inn, a half-hour's drive north from Narrows Gate. Moran was also a high-ranking official in the New Jersey chapter of the musicians' union, but as far as Hennie knew, he was connected to nobody, running his own action. A sly operator and a glad hand, he gave himself the nickname the Ear, which he threw at musicians who didn't bow to his taste, which, admittedly, was first rate. Hennie thought him smart for grabbing onto Bebe while he was still riding the high from the Captain Bridges road show.

"You bring her, Moran sees you're serious. You're ready."

"I bring her and she sees I'm a singing waiter," he said, his doe legs sticking out, his ribs like a xylophone against his undershirt.

"You tell her it's how everybody starts out." Hennie dropped her ass on his bed, the creak echoing. "It's how you earn your keep."

Bebe made a face.

"This girl, Bebe. I'm thinking maybe you don't know how to handle a girl like this."

"Ma, stop. OK?"

"You talk to her. You make it so she understands. People see you together and they know you're serious. You're a serious person."

"Yeah, all right, Ma."

"Besides, you planning on being a waiter for long?"

"It's out of my hands."

"Or you could go sing at the Saint Tropez."

A club owned by Farcolini; Anthony Corini was the front. They'd let Mimmo run it, and it's a miracle it survived. Fortune stepped in and turned it around, though the Lakeside was still number-one on the Jersey side of the George Washington Bridge.

She added, "I'm surprised you didn't go there in the first place."

"Good that you're surprised."

"I'm saying you date Mimmo's niece, but you don't want to sing at one of Farcolini's nightclubs."

"Ma, are you going to let me iron this shirt?"

"Bebe—"

"The *Saturday Dance Cavalcade* on WNEW. Where's it broad-cast from?"

That stopped her. "The Lakeside," she said finally.

"All right?" he said, staring.

"As long as you got a plan."

"I got a plan."

She pushed off the bed. "Still, you bring Rosa to meet the Ear. He sees you as something more than a singing waiter."

Bebe sprinkled some starch on the cuffs.

"And don't let me hear you're back with that *puttana* from Fairview—"

"Ma, for Christ's sake."

Sal Benno was sitting up in his hospital bed, a funny book on his lap. For the past few days, the nurses came in and showed him flash cards with letters so big maybe they fell off a movie mar-quee. Then colors. Shapes. Animal drawings next, cute ones for little kids. "Bunny," Benno said. "Correct," the nurse replied. Next one. "Bunny," he said again, though it was some sort of monkey, a gorilla or chimpanzee. "Bunny," he said a third time. The nurse, catching on, went back to the bunny. "Chimpanzee," said Benno. They took his eye, but not his spark.

"Would you like something to read, Sal?" said the nurse, also a Jew.

"Not if you gave me my eye back."

"Mr. Benno…"

"OK. The funnies," he said. She was only doing her job.

Every day Leo Bell came to visit. Between school and stop-ping by the store to help Vito and Gemma, he didn't have much free time, but he took the tubes to 14th Street and walked all the way across town, arriving just as the sun began to set, just as Benno was losing his will to pretend like he wasn't the only one-eyed 13-year-old in the world. They were going to stick a marble in his head and maybe if that son of a bitch over at St. Patrick's didn't make him wait seven hours and then throw him into the street…Ah, fuck it. What's the point? I ain't drawn a good hand yet, Benno thought. But there's Leo.

"Hey, Sal." Bell reached under his topcoat like he was going to pull a .45. Instead, he came up with a fat sandwich from the store, which he brought whenever he came. Tonight's dinner: *prosciuttini*, provolone, roasted red peppers, bread from Dommie's.

"The drawer," Benno said, nodding to the nightstand. He'd like to keep the thing a secret from Moskowitz, the only other guy in the six-bed ward, 58 years old with a hernia removed. He had a bloodhound nose—even if he was dead asleep he woke up when the food arrived. Thanks to Benno and Bell, he was going home from Beth Israel fatter than when he came in.

Cheeks red, the tip of his nose, too, Bell rubbed his hands together to shake off the cold. He took off his coat and draped it across the foot of the bed. "Mrs. O'Brien wants to bring the class over," he said as he pulled up a chair to Benno's good side. "A field trip."

"The zoo's closed?"

"How's the headaches?"

"Not worse. But I could die from boredom."

Bell said, "They gave you a new patch. It's better."

"A new patch. A funny book. A Spaldeen I can throw at Moskowitz when he snores. It's fuckin' Christmas."

"Not in here it ain't," said Bell.

Benno shifted, his pillow sliding. "Now that you brung it up…" The conversation was inevitable from the moment his father decided to seek help from his boss, Mr. Kreiner, who had influential friends.

Benno lowered his voice so Moskowitz over there didn't hear. "All the doctors that come in, the nurses, the guys they bring the food. They're all Jews, right?"

Bell nodded.

"They know your father from the shop?"

"They know his boss. Eli Kreiner."

"And what? Somebody owes them and I'm the chit? The nurse told me I'm getting some kind of super treatment over here."

"They go to the same temple in Brooklyn. Mr. Kreiner and some of the doctors and administrators," Bell said. "And my father. It's my father's temple, too."

Benno stayed silent.

Bell figured the information didn't hit. "My father's temple," he repeated.

Benno tilted his head. "Meaning?"

"Meaning he's a Jew," Bell replied, his stomach in his throat. "Me too."

Benno stared at him.

"You angry?"

"Wait. I seen you make confirmation," Benno said.

"I went along with it."

"Whoa. I don't think that squares with God."

"The point, Sal, is a secret's no good between friends. True friends."

"I wouldn't know. I ain't never kept a secret from you."

"Sal, how about you let me explain?"

"Do me a favor first. Go give Moskowitz half the sandwich. He's drooling."

Benno knew he was supposed to say, "You don't have to tell me nothing, Leo." The Bells saved his life, for Christ's sake, and it was more than that. Leo being like the other half of the coin, Benno and Bell, like they were one, not two. And as far as being a Jew goes, he'd met more Jews in the past week than he had his whole life and all he knew was they didn't bust his balls because his mother came from Sicily. Turns out all those stories he heard on Polk Street—Jews this and Jews that—were bullshit.

But the truth of it was, right now, here in this hospital bed, sitting with a new hole in his head and he don't know if he has a big scar or what, Benno was feeling a little stung by the idea that Bell could keep such a thing from him. He couldn't figure out how to feel, which was strange since he never had a doubt in his life. His opinions popped into his head already fully formed like boulders nobody could move.

Bell returned from across the room, the scent of peppered ham and red peppers in the air. As he sat, he said, "No way in hell my father thinks I'm going to find a friend like you. After he took the job at Kreiner's, he figured we'd move to Brooklyn. We'd go back to being, you know, ourselves."

"Which is?"

"My real name, it's Józef Herlitz. My father's is Abraham Herlitz."

"Herlitz."

"We're from Rabka. It's in Poland."

His father was a typewriter repairman who'd lost his young wife to the Spanish flu and a beloved brother to the Battle of Warsaw. They had no reason to stay in Rabka. Abraham Herlitz sold everything for forged documents, and soon he and his baby son had a new name, a new nationality, a new everything.

"So we went to Irpino and then Naples to sail to America—on a steamship named the *American*, believe it or not."

"You remember this?" Benno asked. All this information had his brain spinning. "You remember coming here?"

Bell shrugged. In the sanctity of their home, his father repeated the story so often that Bell no longer knew memory from legend. The Italian women on the *American* smothered him with affection. They helped his father improve his Italian enough so it would satisfy the officers at Ellis Island.

"That's some accent you got there, Mr. Campanello," said the uniform at Immigration.

"My wife was Polish. I think I spent too much time with her family," he replied. "So maybe you could put 'Bell' as our name. It's better for America, no?"

A few scratches with a pen, the thud of a rubber stamp and they were accepted.

"So that's how we got to Narrows Gate," Leo Bell said. "That's the story."

"Józef Herlitz," Benno said, trying the Polish pronunciation. "Herlitz. Explains everything. The name, it's serious like you. Bell, I don't know. It's light. Maybe you should've stayed Campanello, which is Italian for bell, by the way."

"I know."

"Herlitz," he said, still trying it out. "Herlitz."

"Forget the name, Sal. You call me Herlitz when you get out of here and I'm fucked. This secret has to hold."

"I can tell you this, Leo. If you want to keep getting away with being Italian, you shouldn't go around like you're the professor of Polk Street. I mean, you seen Mimmo carrying books?"

Bell said no.

"Maybe try to be like me. Except keep both eyes. Between us, we're going to need all we got. With Farcolini on the run, it could all go to hell."

"This matters?"

"You want Maguire and the other Irish cops back?"

"I'm asking if this is what you think about all day."

"I'm thinking if they leave us with Mimmo and his band of *idioti*, we might as well get back on the boat."

"Speaking of Mimmo," Bell said, relieved the subject had changed, "you heard about Bebe and his niece?"

"From who?"

"Bebe's in with Mimmo's niece."

"Fuckin' Bebe," Benno said, grimacing in distaste.

"What's the matter with Bebe?"

"Bebe Marsala. What kind of name is that? He's ashamed he's Sicilian. Pretty soon he'll be telling people he never heard of Narrows Gate. You watch. He'll put a thousand million miles between us and where he's going."

Bell had no feeling for Bebe, a stuck-up prig if there ever was one, but he was about to defend him. Leaving Narrows Gate seemed a sensible ambition. But he let it pass, considering. "Feel good to get mad at Bebe?" he asked.

Benno sat up. "You know what? It does." He balled his fists, bobbed his head. "Let's go a couple rounds, me and you."

Bell help up his hands. "Listen, are we all right on this thing?"

"What? The Jew thing? I forgot it already."

"Not possible."

Benno said, "No, no. Your father, he made the right move. A Jew gets no shot in Narrows Gate, believe me."

Cy Geller was reluctant to leave South Florida, where he was protected not only by his own security team but also by a succession of local cops and government officials. They were never the obvious choice—a captain, a mayor, a congressman—but people deep in the machine who made things go, people who were no more obvious than a coat tree in a corner or dust on Venetian blinds.

A pensive man of regal bearing in his late 50s, Geller conducted his business from an office behind his 9,000-square-foot plantation-style home in Coral Gables. Under a Mediterranean tiled roof, the office had only three walls surrounded by dense, shoulder-high bushes. At the front, behind a lounging area filled with wicker chairs and tile-topped tables, was a wide entrance that revealed Geller's desk, seats for visitors and an armoire. Inside the armoire was a safe that was bolted into the concrete floor. Most days, it held up to $1 million in cash.

Geller occasionally spent a few minutes under the palm trees in his yard, enjoying the hibiscus his wife had planted and watching tiny lizards dart across the grass. But then he would return to his desk. His guards knew if Mr. Geller was at work, a good reason was needed to disturb him.

Geller was Carlo Farcolini's most trusted advisor and ally and had been since the day they walked along Mulberry Street to announce their association while Gus Uccello's bullet-ridden body lay in a Coney Island morgue. He helped coordinate many of Don Carlo's strategies to synchronize the underworld throughout the country and the Caribbean. At present, Geller was developing a plan to improve the flow of heroin imported from Sicily through Havana into Miami and New Orleans. In addition, he was responsible for monitoring the infiltration of Los Angeles, an action coordinated by Ziggy Baum.

Now Geller was to be pulled away from these enterprises, at least temporarily. A message had arrived: Farcolini instructed Geller to go to New York and meet with Corini and Gigenti. Geller understood this meant Farcolini could no longer outrun Dewey and the feds. When he surrendered, the void in leadership would have to be filled until a deal could be struck.

Geller flew immediately to Newark Airport and a driver brought him into Lower Manhattan. He checked into the Grosvenor Hotel under an assumed name, showered, put on a wool suit he'd brought north in a carry-on and took a taxi to Pell Street. When Geller arrived at the Chinese restaurant, which was situated underground, Anthony Corini was already seated in a red vinyl booth, a pot of tea at his elbow. Short, broad at the shoulders, his nose once broken at the bridge and now hooked, Corini stood to greet Geller. They embraced.

Geller sat across from him, his back to the door.

"We wait for Bruno," Geller said.

Though he tried to conduct himself as a modern business-man, Corini bristled at any measure of disrespect, which is how he took his rival's decision to be tardy. "Maybe I send him a watch for Christmas."

Geller poured himself a cup of tea.

Gigenti arrived 20 minutes later with Eugenio Zamarella, a tall, thin man whose skin was scarred with deep pockmarks. He took Gigenti's hat and coat, folding the latter over his arm, and sat at a table on the other side of the small restaurant.

Rather than sit next to Geller or Corini, Gigenti dragged a chair from an adjoining table. A large, bearish man, he sat and crossed a thick leg. A cuff of his gray slacks seemed of more inter-est to him than the presence of Geller and Corini.

"Bruno," Geller said softly. "I have a message from Don Carlo."

"And you already told this one," he bellowed in Sicilian, nodding at Corini.

Geller sighed. Though the restaurant was nearly empty prior to the dinner rush, the idea was to be as inconspicuous as possible, but here Gigenti had brought along his button Zamarella, sat himself in the aisle and barked in Sicilian.

"Bruno, please," Geller said. "The situation is difficult enough."

Anthony Corini studied Gigenti. Under Farcolini, they had become rivals. Responsible for the traditional work including drugs, loan sharking, prostitution and the waterfront, Gigenti scorned the organization's legitimate businesses and its ambitions in politics and entertainment. He thought Corini's activities were costly and naive; investing in anything less lucrative than crime was stupid. But Corini could see the logic in Farcolini's plan to diversify. Were it further along, Don Carlo wouldn't be under threat of prison or deportation: He would own the man in Dewey's seat. If the troubles brewing in Europe cut off the supply of heroin from Sicily, a diverse portfolio of legitimate activities could fund operations until new sources for the drug were developed.

To Geller, the two rivals, men in their early 40s, represented different aspects of Carlo Farcolini's personality. Gigenti was the brute, the cold, conscienceless killer. Though he was in on the Uccello hit, Corini had come to believe finesse was almost always less costly than violence. Geller believed both men would profit from a thorough collaboration and ultimately both would fail if they undermined each other's efforts.

Corini leaned his elbows on the table. "Bruno, what's on your mind?" he said in Sicilian. "If we have a problem, we tell Cy and work it out."

He didn't disagree. Though he had joined him after the Patti hit in '29, Gigenti still felt he had no personal relationship with

Farcolini, who had met Corini in reform school when they were teens. Don Carlo and Corini spoke as friends. For all his efforts, Gigenti felt Farcolini held him at arm's length. With Geller, maybe he could be heard.

"The problem," he said to Corini, "is you take, but you don't bring. I told you this a hundred times."

"I don't dispute your facts, Bruno. But this is an investment and it needs time."

Gigenti waved his hand. He'd heard this before.

Corini said, "We shouldn't be at each other's throats. We're at a crossroads here, no?"

"The thing runs right," Gigenti insisted. "Where's the problem?"

Corini looked across the table.

Geller said, "Bruno, come here." He tapped the seat next to him. "Sit over here. Come on."

Gigenti hesitated, then moved into the red booth.

Zamarella watched from across the room.

"Here's the issue," Geller began. "Carlo can't continue to flee the feds. He will either end up in prison or in Sicily—whether he's deported or leaves on his own."

"So what Dewey says in the papers is true," Corini said. "There's no chance he beats the rap."

Geller nodded. "It's done. He takes the hit."

Corini shook his head in dismay. Three whores and a soldier up in the Bronx had testified to a grand jury about Farcolini's involvement in prostitution. Dewey couldn't make anything else stick, so he went with it.

"It's up to you two to keep everything moving," Geller said softly. "Don't see this as an opportunity."

Before either man could protest, Geller raised his hand. "It's not a matter of your loyalty. It's a matter of judgment. You both believe what you want to do is right. Fine. But we continue what Don Carlo planned, regardless."

"Of course," said Corini.

Gigenti grunted.

"We have a big challenge with the situation in Italy," Geller continued. "Mussolini will open the door to Hitler as soon as the Germans want to make a move. The Stresa Front is pointless."

This meant nothing to Gigenti. They should all kill each other over there.

"War in Europe is bad for us," Corini said, nodding. With less product to sell, expenses would be cut and plans to legitimize put on hold. This troubled him: Without that part of Farcolini's scheme in action, there was no place for him in the organization. He'd begun to appreciate the comfort of his new standard of living.

Geller said, "We have to prepare for all eventualities. Bruno, you must ensure our hold over the ports up and down the East Coast, including the airports. You make sure interstate trucking is content. You have full authority."

Gigenti nodded.

"Anthony, you continue your work with the politicians, the newspapers and the nightclubs," Geller continued. "Don't hesitate. Everyone has to understand we're in business."

"All right," Corini replied.

"Tonight, you come with me to Chicago," Geller said to Corini. "They have to know we'll uphold whatever their agreements are and they must honor ours."

Gigenti said, "Chicago? You give them the impression this one is sitting in for Don Carlo." He sat back in disgust.

Geller said, "The people who need to know understand you run the engine, Bruno."

Gigenti glared at the old Jew. Then he reached into the aisle and angrily snapped his finger. Zamarella got out of his chair and started across the restaurant. Gigenti edged out of the booth.

Corini drew the .38 from his ankle holster.

Zamarella held open his boss's coat, and Gigenti slipped his arms into the sleeves.

"Bruno, don't make a problem for us," Corini warned, the pistol on his thigh.

Gigenti spoke to Geller. "You gave this one too much."

"Myself," Geller replied, "I refuse to question Don Carlo."

Quicker than expected for a man of his heft, Gigenti snapped his hat from Zamarella's long fingers and stormed toward the door, scattering waiters and arriving customers.

CHAPTER SIX

Four Saturdays in a row, each chillier than the last as winter arrived, Bebe brought Rosa up to the Lakeside Inn. The first time, Eddie the Ear went so far as to pick up the tab for his mid-week singing waiter and his date while WNEW's *Saturday Dance Cavalcade* was broadcast right there from the dance floor. The program featured Lonnie Cornell, a dopey-looking, long-faced bastard from Oklahoma who Bebe figured couldn't touch him. The second week, Moran greeted Rosa warmly, asked her if she liked the inn's Western theme and its cowboy motif. He gave them a nice table, but no, he didn't pick up the tab. The third Saturday, he started with, "Rosa, hi, sweetheart, you look lovely as always," and she beamed sweetly, sincerely, unaware Bebe had a scheme going. They got a crap table near the kitchen; they practically had to stand to see Cornell. At week four, Stubby Wilson, a colored bouncer, took Bebe to a corner off the main bar.

Longhorns overhead, Wilson said, "Cornell drops dead tonight and Eddie puts me up there before you. And I sing like I gargle."

"I don't—"

"Stop begging and earn it."

"Earn it how, Stub?" Bebe said over the dance music. "I get three songs a night and when I go on there's not enough people to start a fight."

"And you don't think Eddie sees you think it's a bullshit gig?"

"It *is* a bullshit gig."

"Lonnie Cornell walked here from Oklahoma, Bebe. What did you do?"

Marsala was going to mention his success with Captain Bridges, but he'd learned from the Ear's other singing waiters that, given the number of touring vaudeville shows the Captain had crossing the country, a lot of guys on the come-up had that credit in their caps. Cornell was in his 30s and sang his way up to the New York–area nightclubs by playing cafés, county fairs, honky-tonks, juke joints, roadhouses, second-rate hotels and piss-scented dives for almost a decade. As Wilson liked to say, he bled for his shot.

"You got moxie, kid. I'll give you that," Wilson told Marsala. "But nobody's handing it to you."

"Eddie doesn't think I want it?"

"You want it, Bebe. Hell, everybody knows that." Wilson headed back to his post by the rear door.

As the band played the "Cavalcade" theme and the announcer took his post, Bebe collected Rosa, tossing a few bucks on the tablecloth. Ten minutes later, buffeted by a harsh December wind, they crossed the George Washington Bridge, 50 cents poorer for the toll. New York City stretched out before them. In midtown, the night had barely begun. No one knew what would happen next. The dice hadn't rolled.

"Bill," Rosa said, "maybe I can help?"

"Believe me, doll. You don't want to know." He stole a glance, the headlights from the oncoming traffic sweeping their faces. "What do you say we drive and let it die?" Marsala maneuvered the late-model Ford onto Riverside Drive for the trip south. The lights of the bridge quivered on the Hudson's black water. The curvy drive was quiet. An uneasy silence lay heavy in the car.

Soon, they drove past Grant's Tomb on its grassy isle and Rosa saw the gothic towers of Riverside Church high above barren trees.

"Bill, if you don't mind, pull over across from the church."

He turned like he was surprised she was there. But he eased the car into the right lane and parked. Across the drive, the limestone cathedral, scored with shadows, seemed timeless, as if it had been transported from centuries ago. Though they were raised just across the river, neither Bebe nor Rosa knew it had been completed within the decade. Just kids, 22 and 17, they had no idea how little they knew.

Bebe lit a Chesterfield.

"There's something bothering you, Bill."

He hung a wrist on the steering wheel. "The music business. It's a rough road. A long, rough road."

"You've got time." She turned to face him. "Haven't you?"

"Seems like I've been chasing the dream my whole life. You climb a mountain and you know what you find at the top? Another mountain."

"You'll climb that one too, Bill."

He forced a smile.

"No, I mean it, Bill. I can't say I know you for long, or very well, but I see you've got what it takes. Not just the voice. Not just the look." She stroked his cheek. "But you've got the will."

"Right now, I'd throw it all away for a chance to feel fine. Do you know what I mean? Not high, not low. Just fine." Marsala gave the steering wheel a light punch with the side of his fist. "I want it, Rosa," he said. "I want it so bad. I wish I could explain."

"Try. Please."

Marsala stared into the night mist. "All right," he said finally, crushing out the cigarette as he turned to face her. "Say you wake up one morning and you've found a new way to breathe. You feel lighter. Man, you can just float wherever you go. The blood rushing through you is filled with the good stuff—you glow. You've got it all. You're going, doll, you're going and you feel so damned good you know nothing can stop you."

He took her hands. "You go to bed at night and you can't wait for another day. Counting sheep? No need—you'll have the most peaceful sleep you've ever had in all your ever-loving life. Because you know tomorrow is going to swing even better than today.

"Then you wake up and, bam, it's gone. The magic, the excitement, the thrill, the possibilities—all gone. Everything is like it used to be. The air is dull—it's flat. The past is back. But since you remember how swell you felt yesterday, the old way is no good. You're not back to square one. You're busted back to zero, baby. You're weighed down. You're nothing."

"But, Bill—"

"You want to talk about desperation. That's the definition of desperation." Marsala pulled back his hands and retreated until his back was against the driver's side door. "You look in the mirror and what do you see? Nobody."

"You feel that way now, Bill?"

"You tell me. What have I done? I'm a singing waiter on slow nights in a club maybe ten miles from where I was born. I been nowhere and I haven't done a thing."

Rosa held out her arms in an open invitation.

He shook his head.

"Bill, I look at you—"

"Don't. I'm nobody, baby. Turn away."

"I look at you and I see somebody. A young man with dreams and talent. You're impatient. Impetuous, I'd say. What you want, you want now. I've a feeling you found out it's not going to come that easy. But you know what, Bill? You can do it. The voice, the look, the will—what else do you need?"

"I wish I knew."

"Come here, Bill."

Marsala dropped his head into her lap and curled up his legs until his knees met his chest.

She stroked his hair.

In the silence, they could hear the river run.

The world suddenly at bay, Bebe sighed.

"Love is what you need," Rosa whispered as she comforted him. "You need to know someone loves you."

"Do you, Rosa?" he asked, his voice soft and small.

"Of course I do, Bill. Of course I do."

"I long for it…"

They kissed.

Spindly trees at the roadside seemed to sway in the light. The river continued without pause, patient and assured.

Then Bebe got his shot.

January, February and into March, he waited tables at the Lakeside like a son of a bitch and when it was his turn to sing, he showed the kind of enthusiasm that would've impressed Jolson. "Hey, folks, join in on this one, will you?" he'd say. Or "Here's one I know you love. What do you say?" On the one ballad he was permitted per night, he'd bring the microphone toward tables where, moments earlier, he delivered steaks and chops. He sang to the women, the men amused by the kid's nerve. At the end, he'd throw it back to the band, thanking them for their support. Then he'd trot to the wings where he'd slip back into his waiter's jacket to retrieve the bones, empty glasses, the butter-smeared bread dishes.

Mid-March, Moran asked if he could fill in on a Friday night. Two sets. The bandleader Mel Keenan would pick the tunes. Forty minutes on, 20 off.

"I'll do sixty straight for you, Eddie," Bebe said.

"Forty is fine, Bill. Get together with Mel." There'd be no time for rehearsal.

Rosa came up with Hennie. The Ear understood their enthusiasm and moved to a table at the edge of the dance floor.

The band warmed up the audience with a couple of tunes, and then Bebe bounded from the wings to a nice round of applause, the Friday night crowd greased and gay. "Deed I Do" was the opener, followed by "That Old Feeling," Bebe straining, the arrangement in a key a bit higher than he preferred, but all right, all right, the crowd had spirit, they were on his side. The first ballad, Crosby's "Soon," went over, too. His feet under him now, Bebe talked to the audience, praising Moran and the room's cowboy theme. He turned to Keenan and talking into the mic, he said, "Mel, how's about we do one for Eddie?" The band played "Don't Fence Me In," Bebe pretending to ride a horse, the drummer making clip-clop sounds on the wood block. The audience howled. "Can you believe Cole Porter wrote that one?" Bebe said when it was done.

The second ballad, "I Surrender Dear," Bebe dedicated to "my two best girls, Mama and my special honey, Rosa. Stand up, ladies. Say hi to the folks."

A couple up-tempo numbers, and then it was over.

"Thank you, ladies and gentlemen. Don't forget to drink up! Oh, and tip your waiter. Big!"

As the audience laughed and applauded, Bebe hurried to the corridor, expecting Moran to shake his hand, tell him to go out and do one more, saying he was better than fine, quality all the way, a pro.

But no Moran.

Stubby Wilson, the bouncer, told him Moran was in his office. He hadn't seen the set.

Moran stayed in the office for the second set, too.

"Don't take it personal, Bill," Wilson told him as the band packed for the night. "Eddie runs a business, don't forget."

The bouncer was aware that Marsala could slide into a dark mood. "He'll hear from the regulars," Wilson said. "Hell, I'll tell him myself how you set 'em up and knocked 'em over."

The following week, Marsala was back on the midweek shift, where he stayed. Three songs, Tuesdays, Wednesdays, Thursdays. March, April. He simmered, tossed and turned. He was furious and inconsolable. Feeling foul, he picked up a ditz at a bus stop in Narrows Gate, fucked her standing up in a parking lot behind a diner, then dumped her back on the corner. Then he began to mope. He sat silent in Hennie's kitchen for hours, his aunts tending to him with homemade pasta and pastries.

Anger and arrogance returned in May. He decided to confront Moran. On a late Monday afternoon, the sun hovering above the Palisades, Terrasini, who was driving, tried to provide counsel. It wouldn't take.

Marsala said, "I give him the best Friday he's had in a year, two years, and what? No 'Thank you, Bill.' 'Nice work, Bill.' Nothing."

"All right. Nothing," Terrasini replied. "But the point is to find out where you stand, not to make the guy know you think he's shit. You say, 'Eddie, what did you hear about me? Did I give you what you wanted? How can I improve?'"

"I grovel, in other words."

"See, that's all in your head, Bebe."

Leaving River Road, they caught a red light on a hill, Terrasini struggling to keep his car from rolling back.

"Maybe you ask him, 'What did you hear?' and he says, 'I heard you were phenomenal.'"

"Phenomenal? Then why doesn't he tell me?"

"Bebe, you know these club owners," he said as they drove on, entering Fairview. "They think if they praise you, you're going to ask for a raise. Besides, you say you did fine. Why isn't that enough?"

"Because I'm still singing between delivering soup. Jesus, Nino, what's the matter with you? You take his side."

"I'm not taking nobody's side. I'm saying if you did fine, you did fine. Put in your time and if the guy don't come through, you move on."

"And what? Leave the *Saturday Dance Cavalcade* for some other singer? Fuck that. I earned it. It's mine."

Marsala rolled down the window and flicked out a half-spent cigarette.

"Bebe, I know you. Right now, if the world don't bend over for you, you think it's shit. Next week, you'll be happy as hell to have the steady gig. You'll regret—"

"No regrets, buster. Never a regret."

"Look, I'm telling you to play it smart, that's all. Play it smart."

"Moran's going to tell me where I stand," Marsala replied stubbornly.

"And if you don't like what you hear?"

"You let me worry about that."

Have it your way, Terrasini thought. They proceeded in silence and minutes later pulled into the Lakeside's gravel lot. Terrasini parked near a side entrance.

"Bebe—"

But Marsala hopped out and slammed the passenger-side door.

Moran was behind his desk, gooseneck lamp shining on a stack of bills of lading for liquor, cigarettes, gas and electric, maintenance, the band. He had an adding machine at his right hand and a pencil between his teeth.

Bebe stood in the doorway. When Moran failed to look up, he rapped the frame.

"Oh, hey, Bill," Moran said, emerging from a head full of numbers and calculations. "What are you doing here?"

"I've got something to say."

Moran waved to a soft, cracked leather chair in front of the desk.

"How come I never heard anything from you after I filled in back in January?" he said, still standing.

January? Moran thought. He'd met the payroll a dozen times since and hadn't shorted a vendor. The business was standing on steady ground, the *Saturday Dance Cavalcade* making the Lakeside Inn the number-one nightspot in North Jersey.

"What did you want me to say, Bill?"

"What could you say? You didn't bother to listen."

Moran raised a finger and pointed to a speaker on the wall. "I heard."

"Yeah? So?"

Moran sat back.

Marsala said, "You can't say the crowd didn't go for it."

"No, I won't say that."

"I think I earned another shot."

"We haven't needed a fill-in."

"Maybe you need to move things around. Keep things fresh."

"You telling me how to run the club, Bill?"

"I'm saying talent is hard to come by."

Moran reached into a drawer and pulled out a small stack of acetates, each with a song from an aspiring singer, and a pile of letters, maybe 50, held together with a rubber band. He put them both on his blotter. "These are from this month alone, Bill. Sixty, sixty-five, seventy singers a month." To make his point, Moran punched numbers into the adding machine and pulled the handle. "Seven hundred and twenty a year, minimum. Two a day."

"I mean talent like mine, Eddie. Talent like mine."

Moran stood and came around the desk. "Sit down, Bill."

Defiant still, Marsala didn't budge.

"Bill," Moran said gently. "Sit."

Annoyed, Marsala sat, the cushion wheezing. "I'm sitting. What's it mean?"

Moran perched on the edge of his desk. Big with too much weight in front, he had thick lips and the gray pallor of a man who worked long hours indoors. But his eyes conveyed a compassion necessary in a profession where fantasy and reality conflicted. Moran knew there was little glamour in show business, at least in proportion to the vast landscape littered with broken hearts and shattered dreams. If he had children, he'd advise them to do anything but try to succeed as an entertainer. The odds were astronomical, the pain very rarely worth the struggle or the goal.

"Bill, you've got something. You wouldn't be here if you didn't," Moran began.

Teeth clenched, Marsala stared up at the club owner.

"But you're not ready—"

"That Friday crowd didn't agree."

"Bill…"

"The midweek crowd goes for it, too."

"Bill, listen. You do fine. Is that what you want me to say? You do fine. The crowd, sure, they go for you."

Marsala nodded in satisfaction.

"You've improved. That's a fact."

"But I still sling hash. I still count tips."

"But you've got room to grow."

"You just said they go for it. If they go for it—"

"Bill, you're not listening. I'm here to tell you that you're not ready. I put you out there now and I'm hurting you."

"I'd say that's my call."

"No. It's mine. You fail and I'm the guy who sent out a kid before his time. My reputation gets clipped."

Marsala lifted from the chair and began to pace. "Tell me how I'm not ready. I know you're wrong, but go ahead. You tell me."

"It's a matter of seasoning, Bill. It comes from getting up there night after night, year after year."

"Eddie, you forget I was on the road with Captain Bridges. I've been playing bars since I was a kid."

"You're still a kid," Moran said, not unkindly. He'd been through scenes like this before. Sometimes his advice took, other times no. Usually, it was a matter of maturity, of understanding the nature of the job.

"Bill, your show is all energy. It's shtick. It plays in spurts. The ballads—that's something else. You've got a feel for them. But your voice isn't there."

Marsala stared at Moran, incredulous. "The voice isn't there?"

"It's pleasant enough, but it drifts between tenor and baritone. You can't control it at the bottom and it's ordinary in the upper register. When you sing a ballad, Bill, you want it to shake a woman down to her soul, like a tenor solo by Coleman Hawkins or that kid, Webster, with the Ellington band. You want to drive a man into a mood." Moran shook his head. "Your voice…Not yet."

Marsala was stunned. He searched for a way to deny what had been said, but he found no rebuttal.

Moran said, "A couple of years and that baritone will be burnished and you'll have a shot. You keep working, you learn your stagecraft, find the right material and you'll have a shot."

Marsala returned to the chair and sat on an arm.

"You're not there yet, kid," Moran added. "You try, but you're not there."

Bebe burst in, said nothing to nobody, raced upstairs, slammed the door to his room and threw himself on his bed. Drowsing on the sofa, Vincenzo spun upright, alarmed. Eyes glazed, he stared at his wife. Before he could speak, Hennie slid her glass next to her ashtray and wriggled out of the chair. "I'll take care of it," she muttered, housecoat stretched across her jiggling frame.

The stairs moaned under her weight.

"Bebe," she said, knocking on the door. "Bebe."

He was crying. "Go away, Ma."

"Bebe, don't make me get the key. Bebe."

When he didn't reply, she pounded the door with the side of her fist. "Bebe, open up, goddamn it!"

Bebe opened the door a crack.

Hennie saw his waiter's jacket on the floor behind him.

"What happened?" Her hands were on her hips, her voice graveled and phlegmy. "Look at me. What happened?"

"I'm out. I'm never getting Saturday night."

"The Ear said this?"

He nodded, his blue eyes ringed red. "He's not putting me on the radio."

"That son of a bitch. Who's he bringing in?"

"I don't know, Ma," Bebe replied mournfully.

"Who's he think he is, this stuck-up prick." Hennie calculated. Bebe had a mouth on him, but he wasn't so stupid to throw away a job that could've put him on a radio program popular all over Manhattan. "Sit down, Bebe," she said. "Tell me what happened."

He did, dropping Moran's kind words and fatherly tone.

Hennie calculated. Finally, she said, "That fat bastard slugged you, didn't he?"

Bebe shook his head.

"He say anything about us?" she asked. Up in Bergen County, far from the waterfront's grime, they looked down on Narrows Gate and the rest of Hudson County.

Bebe sat on the edge of his bed, staring at his shoes.

"Listen to me," she said angrily. "He gave you a whack and said the guineas from Narrows Gate are scum. Ain't I right, Bebe?"

"Ma…"

"You want to throw this away? Do you?"

He looked up. "Throw what away? It's over. I'm not putting in five more years as a waiter so I get a few songs a week."

"So you give up." She snorted derisively. "Ain't that you in nutshell?"

"I saw him. I confronted him. What more do you want me to do? You want I should show up on Friday and knock down the Okie?"

She leaned over him. "I want you to fight for yourself."

"How? How do you fight the guy at the top?"

"Moran hit you, didn't he?"

"Ma…"

"Say it."

"Ma, for Christ's sake."

"Bebe, goddamn it."

He stood. "All right. Moran hit me," Bebe repeated, touching the side of his head. "What good does that do?"

"He said the guineas from Narrows Gate are all scum."

"Sure. We're scum. So what?"

"He's going to put the Saint Tropez out of business. He said that, right?"

"All the time," Bebe lied.

"What did he say about Don Carlo?"

Bebe said, "Hey, you go too far, Ma."

She reconsidered. "Maybe he says Mimmo is an idiot. Yeah, he tells the vendors that Mimmo's an idiot."

"Make it the customers," Bebe said. "The vendors would say something to Frankie Fortune."

"You tell Rosa?"

"That Mimmo's an idiot?"

"No, what happened with Moran. I don't want her contradicting me."

"I didn't see Rosa."

Hennie stepped back. She smelled a woman on her son. "You went to Fairview, didn't you?" Hennie charged. "You went to that *puttana*." She reached up and smacked him on the side of the head.

He recoiled.

"What is wrong with you? What is wrong with you?"

"I needed a break—"

"Mimmo should break your fuckin' neck."

Bebe grimaced. The last thing he was thinking about when he was in Fairview was Mimmo. Or Rosa, for that matter. He was thinking of his career in ashes and seeing himself a nobody again. The girl in Fairview didn't know better. She thought he was all right.

"Stay here," Hennie said, lumbering away in disgust. She went for her shoes and coat.

One o'clock in the morning, and the candy store had that muscle-bound monster Boo Chiasso standing guard.

"I need Mimmo," Hennie wheezed.

Chiasso held up a finger and left her under the stars as she coughed violently, out of breath from the short march to the end of town.

He returned and waved her in.

Mimmo was sitting at a table near the pinball machine, the money tallied and tucked in a drawer. The lamp dangling above him, the only light on in the store, shone on his thinning hair, his odd-shaped head, his smoky sunglasses.

"We got a problem, you and me," she said. "Moran up at the Lakeside Inn, the Ear, he smacked Bebe around."

Frankie Fortune appeared from the back storeroom. "Maybe he had it coming," he said in Sicilian, leaning against the door frame.

She shivered. Fortune scared the shit out of her. Still the best-looking man she'd ever seen, he wrapped it in style, but there was nothing behind it, like they had shipped him from the factory before they put in a soul.

"Frankie," she said with a nod.

"Smacked him around," he repeated.

She calculated. "He said he didn't want nobody associated with Mimmo in his joint."

Mimmo turned and looked up at Fortune.

"Is that a fact?" Fortune asked.

"I know," she said quickly. "Bebe shouldn't have mentioned you guys, but you know Bebe."

"Yeah, we know Bebe," Mimmo said with a smile.

"Moran says he's putting the Saint Tropez out of business," she said.

She gestured at the rail-back chair across from Mimmo who, with a sweep of his hand, told her to sit.

"To tell you the truth," she said with a sigh, "Bebe wants to be on WNEW. You know, the Lakeside has that Saturday night thing they broadcast. Brings in a lot of money. A big bump, I heard."

Farcolini's crew operated the jukeboxes and cigarette machines in every joint in northern and central Jersey. Counting coins gave them an idea of how much the clubs pulled down in food and liquor. So Fortune knew she was right—the Lakeside was paying out; people were crossing the Hudson to hear good music away from the bustling city.

Her hand played, she reached for one of Mimmo's Camels. "In the end, Bebe's on the radio. OK?"

"If I could do something for Bebe and Rosa, I would," Mimmo said, flicking his lighter under her cigarette. "But you ain't going to get those WNEW sons of bitches to switch. You know how many times I told them—"

"OK," Fortune said, staring at Hennie. "But when we go, Bebe comes with us."

She sat back. "What for?"

"Bebe comes with us," Fortune repeated.

A curl of smoke drifted toward the tin ceiling. Jesus Christ, she thought, they want Bebe deep in their pocket. They think he's good. They think he can make it big.

"Sure, Frankie," she said. "I'm not going to question you."

CHAPTER SEVEN

It was about two in the morning, a few weeks later, when they pulled out of Narrows Gate, Boo Chiasso driving, Bebe next to him, Mimmo and Fortune in the backseat. As they passed the Esso station by the viaduct, Mimmo said he needed to hear Fortune go over it again. It didn't make no sense.

"Makes sense," Fortune said.

Pretty soon they were driving alongside the Hudson River, the piers quiet. Bebe's heart was pounding, his stomach bumping against his throat. "Go along," his mother had said, and she dressed him in dungarees, a turtleneck and a leather jacket, like one of the Dead End Kids.

"We had the Saint Tropez since when?" Mimmo said. "Since before Prohibition."

When Bebe turned, he saw Fortune staring at him.

Mimmo said, "I swear to Christ, we were raking it in. Hand over fist. Back then, the Saint Tropez was some shit hole named Joe's, Joey's, Johnny's, something…"

"Hey, Mimmo. Stifle, huh?" Fortune said. He wriggled down in the seat, slipping his fedora over his eyes. Mimmo owed him for the embarrassment with Freddie Pop and the Buick, he figured. The least he could do was shut the fuck up.

"But this…" Mimmo said. "This I don't get. Our own joint…"

Chiasso looked in the rearview.

"Burning down our own joint," Mimmo muttered.

A few minutes before three, Fortune told Bebe and Mimmo to stay in the car while Chiasso threw Molotov cocktails through the windows. The Saint Tropez was on fire, the flames visible in the Bronx. By the time the fire engines and the cops arrived, the four of them were gone, heading to the Lakeside.

Moran's big neon sign out front was shut down, its steady buzz silent.

"The bouncer's not here," Bebe said.

"You sure?" Fortune asked.

"His car's gone. Stub usually puts it under the sign."

Chiasso parked in the back under dense trees.

Mimmo and Bebe watched as Chiasso jumped out and hurried around to the trunk. A moment later, his arms full, he crouched behind the only other vehicle in the lot. With little effort, he popped its trunk and stashed a gas can, empty liquor bottles and oily rags inside.

Fortune leaned on the backseat. "Bebe, where's Moran?"

"In his office," he said. His throat was as dry as sand. "There's a safe in the floor."

Mimmo laughed. "Bebe wants we should rob the place."

"Go say hello."

Bebe protested.

"Go say hello," Fortune repeated.

Bebe eased out of the car and walked across the lot, limping a bit as he looked for the orange sky above the Saint Tropez. Chiasso had left the side door unlocked. Bebe entered the inn. The main room was empty, chairs upside down on tabletops, the dance floor swept clean. At the bar, the cash register drawer was open.

Bebe stopped and took a look at the bandstand, then went toward the long corridor that held the restrooms and, at the far end, Moran's office. Halfway down the hall, he tugged his sleeves until they covered his wrists, checked the cuffs on his dungarees, lifted his cap to smooth out his hair. He cleared his throat to greet his former boss, who, in Bebe's mind, hadn't given him solid advice but had only treated him like he pissed the rug.

Bebe pushed the door. "Hey, Eddie Moran—"

The Ear was tied to his desk, his arms and legs splayed, clothesline around his ankles and wrists, his stomach like a mountain. He had a big mouse above his left eye.

Bebe watched as Chiasso prepared a gag for Moran's mouth.

"Bill, what did I do to you?" the club owner said, turning his head. "Tell me."

"You should've let me sing on the radio."

"And this is what I deserve? He tried to take my head off."

Chiasso watched as Moran struggled.

"You're going to give yourself a heart attack," Bebe said. Hennie told him to put up a front. Nobody in the crew should see him scared.

"What's he gonna do, Bill? For God's sakes, Bill, don't let him—"

In went the gag. Chiasso tied it so tight Moran's lips tore at the corners.

Bebe felt a hand on his shoulder.

"Sit down," Fortune said. "Over there."

An old leather sofa rested against a wall lined with old photos of log cabins out West, a few coated in snow, scowling big-boned men and women posing in front of them. Bebe sat like he was told.

Then he saw Mimmo had carried in a brown paper sack. He wore workmen's gloves.

"Somebody burned down our club," Fortune said as he walked toward Moran. "Mimmo here thinks maybe it was you."

"You're some son of a bitch," Mimmo said, "burning down our club."

The Ear rattled in denial.

"So we're taking your club," Fortune said.

The gag muffled Moran's protest.

"Look," Mimmo said. "He thinks it's a good idea."

Moran continued to argue. But then he stopped and sagged.

"You keep the union job," Fortune said as he nodded to Mimmo.

Mimmo dug into the brown paper bag and pull out a can. "Paint Thinner," read the label. Next, he produced a funnel.

"Go ahead," Fortune said.

Moran's eyes opened wide, and he let loose a high-pitched scream, his back arching off the desktop.

Chiasso grabbed his head in two hands and snapped it to the side.

Without realizing he had, Bebe left the sofa and was standing next to Fortune. He was shaking. "Oh Jesus," he moaned as Mimmo shoved the funnel deep into Moran's ear.

With a swipe of his thumb, Mimmo spun the cap off the paint-thinner can.

"Acid," Fortune said, loud enough for Moran to hear.

As Chiasso pressed Moran's head against the desktop, Mimmo filled the funnel. It flowed down smooth, no problem, but, as it began to burn through tissue, it started to bubble. What came back up was laced with blood.

Moran continued screaming, his face turning purple, the veins in his temple pulsing, legs trembling.

Mimmo stopped the flow. He looked down, but the smell made him recoil.

Mouth open, jaw slack, Bebe stared in shock as the scent of searing flesh filled the office.

Fortune said, "Let's go, Bebe."

When he didn't move, Fortune grabbed his arm.

"Bebe, *andiamo.*"

Retreating, Bebe watched as Mimmo brought a towel from the sack. He placed it around the narrow end of the funnel as he wriggled it from Moran's ear, going careful like he didn't want to scar his face, too. As Chiasso undid the knots in the cord, Mimmo said, "Moran, you want to keep the other ear…"

Squirming in anguish, Moran tumbled off the desk, hitting the floor with a thud.

The burning sky behind them, they went back the way they came. Every now and then, Chiasso raised his right hand off the steering wheel, flexed it, and studied his bruised knuckles. Down below the Palisades, he pulled over to lose the brown sack and its contents, including the blood-tipped funnel.

"Why do that?"

Fortune sat up and stared at Bebe. "What?"

"He would've gave up the club," Bebe said, talking to the windshield, the dark winding road up ahead. "You had him beat."

"There's no rules, Bebe," Mimmo said, clapping the kid on the shoulder. "The fuck stood in the way."

"I didn't think…" he stammered. "I didn't know…"

"Yeah. Well," Fortune said. "Now you do."

They headed up the bumpy cobblestone road to the boulevard that led back to Narrows Gate.

Frankie Fortune didn't want anything to do with the Lakeside Inn, but he had to move in until things settled. After a few days behind Moran's desk, he called Anthony Corini and asked if he could recommend someone to run the joint. Corini owned a slice of a talent agency in midtown Manhattan—personal management, booking tours, contracts, accounting and the like.

"The sooner the better," Fortune told him. Then he took a shot and asked Corini if he'd heard from Don Carlo.

"When you call me, you're talking to Dewey," Corini replied. "The phones are tapped."

The next afternoon, a guy from the agency turned up. Not long ago, Rico Enna was midlevel at best. Now his former bosses were asking him if Corini would keep them on the job, seeing as how he handpicked Enna out of a back room. Enna was a dark-skinned Sicilian, tall with a long, thin nose, soft hands, finely tailored suits and a service mentality. After Enna looked at the books, Fortune saw he wasn't a total mope.

"You do nothing and you earn," Enna said, closing the ledger.

"We didn't move in to do nothing," Fortune replied. They were sitting at the bar, lights up, a guy washing glasses the only one within earshot. The rest of the employees went about their business, cleaning, stacking, checking electricity, not certain why the Ear was gone, but glad no one had put them back on the breadline. They were veterans of the nightclub business and had seen this act before; though Fortune didn't seem to notice, two guys in the kitchen had worked in a restaurant he'd taken over in Englewood Cliffs a decade ago in much the same way.

Enna nodded. "Mr. Corini says the radio."

"The radio," Fortune agreed.

"You can do better than Cornell," Enna said, mentioning the Okie singer.

"We've got a guy."

Enna nodded, though Corini hadn't mentioned anything. "He has representation?"

Fortune stepped from the stool. "That's your department." He looked around the room at the longhorns over the bar, the Indian blankets, framed photos of the Old West, outlaws with six-shooters.

"I don't get this cowboy shit," Fortune said.

"It's a log cabin," Enna replied. "Either you go with the Old West or you get the staff dressed up like Abe Lincoln."

"You want to be a cowboy, why the fuck you live in New Jersey?"

A couple of days later, on time to the minute, Bebe, Hennie, Terrasini and Mimmo entered the Lakeside. Fortune was seated at a table off to the side of the bandstand with Rico Enna and a doughy Jew Enna proposed as Bebe's manager.

"Frankie," Hennie bellowed gleefully. In a blue dress, her silver hair done up, handbag swinging, she held out her arms expecting Fortune to rise and kiss her, which he did not.

Looking through her as she stomped across the dance floor, Fortune said to Mimmo in Sicilian, "What are you doing here?"

Mimmo shrugged and made a slight gesture with his hand, indicating to Fortune that Hennie had asked him to come along, a bullshit excuse. Mimmo had it in his head that there was a chance Fortune would give him a shot at running the Lakeside, an idea too impossible even to be considered fantasy.

Midafternoon sunlight filled the ballroom, chairs atop most tables, the doors open to encourage a breeze. Fortune, Enna and the Jew were drinking ice water, the pitcher replenished by a redheaded waitress still in her saddle shoes and brown slacks.

With a wave of his fingers, Fortune called Bebe over to the table. He introduced Enna as the club's manager loud enough for Mimmo to hear.

Enna stood. He wore an impeccable, pale-olive, lightweight suit and a tie with an olive-and-red pattern and he looked almost as good as Fortune in his gray sharkskin. The other man, whose wrinkled blue suit shifted on his rounded shoulders, suffered double from the comparison. In his mid-50s, his remaining hair was in disarray. A tip on his shirt collar stuck out.

"Meet Phil Klein," Enna said. "He's someone you'll want to know."

Klein shuffled around the table to shake hands with Bebe, who, in khakis and a silk shirt that matched his eyes, greeted him with a smile.

"Good to know you, Phil."

"I've been hearing a lot about you," Klein said earnestly. He offered his seat to Hennie. She settled next to Fortune, who continued to ignore her.

From the moment he entered the room, Terrasini trained his eye on the man at the piano, Chu Kirby, who played in Mel Keenan's orchestra. He'd been with Pollard, too.

"Bebe, sit down," Fortune said.

Klein took note of the nickname as he poured Hennie a glass of ice water.

"You want your shot, you work with Rico," Fortune began.

"OK, Frankie. Whatever—"

Fortune held up a finger. "This isn't the Chatterbox with your cane, your lil' Crosby routine. This is the radio, this is New York City. *Ciò proviene da Don Carlo.* You understand me, Bebe?"

Bebe said he did.

Fortune said, "In the desk, there's a couple hundred singers—"

"I'm going to give you what you want, Frankie," Bebe replied. "We're putting this over the moon, my hand to God."

Hennie said, "Frankie's never steered you wrong, Bebe. Don't forget that."

Enna stood. "Come with me, Bill. Please." He put his hand on Bebe's back and guided him toward the piano. "Let's be clear, Bill. This isn't an audition. It's an opportunity for us—you, me, Phil, if that's fine with you—to find the best way to put you across."

Bebe nodded. He felt nice, mellow down to the marrow. All the shining light heaven could afford was about to find him.

Enna said, "What do you think you need to make it work?"

"Nino—Nino Terrasini—knows the arrangements."

"You're familiar with Chu?" Enna asked, nodding toward the pianist. "He put in a good word for you."

Bebe looked at Kirby, who smoked two at a time and hunched like he was trying to surround the keys. "I like working with Nino. But it's your call."

Enna snapped a finger. Kirby stood obediently.

Terrasini slid onto the piano bench.

"Let's use the mic, too. Chu can run the PA."

Over at the bar in his sunglasses and his best suit, Mimmo sagged. Fortune didn't even give him a shot to impress. He had ideas to dress up the log cabin, to bring back the original crowd from the Saint Tropez, maybe once a week there'd be music from the old country and always the right menu. He'd line up whores like the kind he ran out of the Blue Onyx: you'd think they were models. And discreet? Guys brought their wives to the joint and sat 20 feet from a broad who cleaned their pipes the night before and no one was the wiser.

Bebe settled by the piano. He tapped the mic with an index finger until he heard it was on. "Frankie, Rico, Phil, I think Chu over there will tell you the up-tempo numbers work fine. What I'd like to suggest is we add a few ballads to the program."

"Go on, Bill," Enna said with interest as he returned to his seat.

Elbows on the table, Hennie leaned toward her son as if in rapt attention. Sweat beaded under her girdle, a blue cloud of cigarette smoke over her head.

"On radio, you're not fighting the crowd noise," Bebe said, rubbing his hands together. "You can bring down the volume for the folks at home."

Cooperate, Bebe told himself. Be part of the team before you become its star. "Rico, I think you'll find you've got yourself a first-class orchestra here at the Lakeside. They can make it sound like it was sprinkled with stardust."

Enna leaned toward Klein. "Phil?" he whispered.

Klein nodded thoughtfully. "The ballads? It's an idea."

"The package," Enna pressed.

Klein saw that Marsala had a versatile style—you could play him a kid or a young man on the way up—and confidence. He wasn't a looker, but he had charm. And those eyes.

"Personality," Klein replied.

"You comfortable with the name?"

"You're asking if we can break big with an Italian crooner," Klein said. "Nobody's done it so far."

"So you be first," said Hennie, stubbing out a cigarette.

Klein nodded. "Someone will be first."

Enna turned. "All right, Bill. Whenever you're ready."

Bebe smiled. He was ready.

He looked around the room slowly, surveying the terrain. Mimmo over there, the redheaded waitress behind the bar. The house empty in back. At the table, Enna, Klein, his mother, Fortune. All attention aimed in his direction. He knew what they wanted. He was sure he would deliver. The warm glow of inner peace continued; he was ready to be judged.

Fortune shifted in his seat.

Bebe whispered off mic. "Nino…"

Terrasini played the intro to "She's Funny That Way." He and Bebe had studied Billie Holliday's version for hours. They took it slow, more lento than adagio, letting it swing with the bass tones.

"I'm not much to look at," Bebe sang, his voice a soft and steady baritone, "nothing to see…"

Klein listened intently.

"I got a woman crazy for me…"

Bebe felt it. Sixteen bars in and the room eased into the palm of his hand.

Even as he and Terrasini stepped up to the tricky bridge, no problem. "Though she'd love to work and slave for me…" Bebe sailed straight through.

Enna turned to Kirby, a curious expression on his face. The pianist told him Marsala was a mediocre vocalist who made it work with antics. Kirby shook his head, his jaw slack in disbelief. He wouldn't have bet the kid, or any singer, could improve so much in, what? Three weeks? The final verse was flawless.

The redhead behind the bar stared at the singer.

"Nino Terrasini," Bebe said, introducing his accompanist.

At the table, Enna started to stand, the deal done.

"Wait," Klein whispered. "Let's see what he picks next. Ask him to let it swing."

Terrasini played a walking bass line to kick off "All of Me," with Bebe snapping his fingers to the breezy tempo.

Three minutes later, Enna was even more convinced. But he asked Klein for an opinion.

"The voice is good enough," Klein said. "He knows how to present himself."

Hennie said, "He's smart. My son adapts."

"Frankie?" Enna said.

"Call me when he fucks up," Fortune replied as he stood.

From the piano bench, Terrasini watched, fearful Bebe had failed the audition as Fortune walked across the dance floor without looking at the singer. Enna and Klein were whispering, their hands covering their mouths, Hennie desperate to eavesdrop. Mimmo wore a big smile that told them nothing. That redhead glowed, but even on a bad night, Bebe could win a girl with a song.

"Bebe," Terrasini whispered.

"I'm in," Marsala replied.

Sal Benno pulled up on his bicycle, sweat dripping off the tip of his nose. The kerchief tied around his neck was as saturated as his white sleeveless undershirt. A few weeks ago, as he pedaled along Church Square Park, some Irish kid called the shirt a "guinea T," and now the dentist was making a cap for his front tooth. Benno always said a fistfight would be the last hurdle in his recovery from his surgery. Seeing as it lasted but one punch, it wasn't too much of a test.

As far as Polk Street was concerned, the glass eye looked so real nobody knew which was which, the doctors and nurses taking care of everything perfect.

Bell stood under a storefront awning. He liked the way Benno jumped off the bike while it was still moving, bringing over one stumpy leg while the other one stayed rigid on the pedal. You couldn't say Benno was graceful; puberty decided he'd be broad and stocky while she let Bell grow like a crane, but he came off the bike happy, a kid doing what he wants, roaming, hustling, even on a 102-degree Saturday in July.

"What's this?" Benno said as he approached.

Bell wore a dark blue blazer over a white shirt and one of his father's neckties. His shoes were buffed. "I'm going for a job."

"Where? The Rapanelli Brothers'?" It was the funeral parlor for the downtown Italians.

"The A&P."

"The A&P?" he said as he stepped up to Bell. "Why the fuckin' A&P?"

Bell grimaced. "Whoa, back up. No offense, Sally, but you stink like old sweat."

"Why the A&P?"

"They got jobs." He was growing moist under the damned jacket. The A&P was way up on 13th Street. By the time he arrived, he'd be as soaked as his friend.

"And there's no jobs down here?"

Bell shrugged.

"Did you ask?"

"Who? Mimmo? No thanks."

"Maybe you should go see if they got jobs in Ireland."

Bell began his retreat. "I'll come by later," he said. He was going to ask Vito to put in a good word for him if the A&P manager called, but he'd try after Sal cooled down.

CHAPTER EIGHT

Two things Bebe had to do to make the thing take off and both needed to be done at the same time. As they sat around the kitchen table, Hennie said, "I'll take care of it."

Still in an up mood, a kite flitting around the sky, Bebe said, "Hey, Ma, I hate to tell you, but the one—"

"Not that one. The other one," Hennie replied, laughing.

Vincenzo watched them, their conversation incomprehensible, like they were talking in code. These two, he thought, either they go skipping hand in hand through the daisies or they glare at each other, knives in their fists. Maybe he would like to interject a thought, but he never knew whether they'd throw him a death stare or reach out to stroke him like a pet.

Bebe clapped his hands. "Now's as good a time as any."

Hennie told her husband she'd be back in time for a double celebration at the Grotto.

I'm invited? Vincenzo thought as the two walked off on clouds.

Hennie Rosiglino took a bench by the gazebo in Church Square Park, the sun high above the Jersey City Heights, its rays careening off St. Matty's slate belfry. She shaded her eyes, looked around, checked her watch, lit another cigarette.

Finally, here comes Nino Terrasini, his hands deep in the pockets of his slacks.

"What'd you think?" she asked.

"Of what?"

"Today. The whole thing. Enna, Klein."

"Klein's a pro and he knows music," he replied. "He'll help Bebe."

"And what about Enna?" She had a pile of butts at her feet.

"He's Frankie's guy."

"He's not in the crew."

"I'm not saying he's in the crew. I'm saying he's running the Lakeside for Frankie."

Hennie said, "And what about this Chu Kirby? He plays good piano?"

Terrasini knew what was next.

"Mel Keenan thinks so." No point in making it easy for her. Or Bebe.

"What do you think?"

"I haven't heard an orchestra yet that needs two piano players."

"Bebe should put up a fight for you. Is that your thinking?"

Terrasini didn't reply.

The bells in the church tower began to peal. Hennie took out another cigarette. Maybe it would prevent the acid from rising any higher in her chest.

"You had a good run," she said as the last bell rang seven o'clock.

"You're firing me, Hennie?"

"Enna will fire you. Or Frankie Fortune will fire you. Me, I'm getting you a new job."

"What? Another night at the Blue Onyx?"

"Don't be wise, Nino. Bebe likes you so nobody's letting them put you on the street. From now on, you stick with Bebe. That's the job. Make sure he keeps his head out of his ass."

"You want me to be Bebe's babysitter?" he said, recoiling. "Why would I want to babysit Bebe?"

"I'll make sure you get a cut on his take. And maybe you work it so you can do some arranging. This Kirby and the bandleader Keenan can teach you a few things."

Terrasini sat next to her. "Go on."

"Plus you double up at the Blue Onyx when Bebe's not working. You could build up a nice nest egg for you and Miss Weehawken."

"Why you, Hennie? Why isn't Bebe telling me this?"

"For one, he can't know you're babysitting him. Two, he's up in Bayonne asking Rosa to marry him."

"Really?"

"If you're done pouting, go grab your girl and join us in the Grotto. But don't say nothing if Mimmo comes in. I want to tell Frankie myself that Bebe is making the thing run smooth."

Why not? Terrasini thought. Then he said, "Damn. I lent Bebe my car."

Hennie reached for her handbag to throw him a dollar for a cab. She held out the bill, then snatched it back. "You'll tell Bebe you're stepping aside?"

"You're buying me off for a dollar, Hennie?"

"Nino, everything goes the way it should and it'll be more than a dollar ends up in your pocket."

Bebe found a nice park overlooking the harbor, the Statue of Liberty glorious in the setting sun. Of course, everything was glorious today. Plump leaves, the sweet smell of grass neat and trim, geese floating by, their heads held high. It was a perfect evening, one for the books—the ideal ending to the best day ever.

Bebe and Rosa walked arm in arm, light as air, the happiest couple in the world. The world? The solar system, baby!

Easy and in love, they followed a curve in the path and found a bench surrounded by bushes. He told her every triumphant detail of his performance at the Lakeside.

She wore a yellow cotton dress, thin brown belt and brown loafers, her hair held back with a simple brown barrette. Even without makeup, her face shone with happiness for him. As they sat, she tucked her skirt and said, "Tell me more, Bill." She had a little white sweater on her shoulders.

"Oh, I've said enough. You get the picture."

"I wish I had been there."

"You were, doll. Those songs, I was singing to you."

"You don't have to say that."

"I was. Every word. You know I'm no good without you."

She smiled and looked out at the harbor and the towers of the New York skyline.

"You know it's true, baby. There's nobody for me but you." He jutted out a leg and dug into a pocket of his chinos, then went to one knee.

"Bill?"

"Let me sing those songs to you forever, Rosa." He opened his hand. There in his palm was a diamond ring. "I'm asking you to be my wife. You and me, always."

"Oh my goodness, Bill." She clasped her hands in front of her face.

"Baby?"

"Yes, Bill. Yes, of course."

He stood and dusted the grass from his knee. She leaped into his arms. They kissed long and happily. He spun her and they kissed again.

"Bill, I've never been so…God, I'm overjoyed."

"Me too, doll. This is the beginning of one fabulous, fabulous ride. Me and you like nobody's ever done it before."

She kissed him, running her hand along the back of his neck.

A hell of a topper to the day, he thought. Let's see somebody try to take this feeling away from me.

Benno pedaled all the way uptown to the A&P, which had more vegetables and fruit on display than Pooch the Grocer carried in a month, enough canned goods to line Polk Street, three cashiers, kids who bagged, and a butcher in the back. Even with his face against the window, he could see they had chickens and roasts all over the place. No sausages, though, which was some good news. And where was the cheese and the *ceci* and the *baccala* and the rest of the stuff that made the world go round?

He couldn't figure out why the supermarket was still open. It was after seven, everybody ate already, by now his Uncle Vito was stocking the icebox in the back—and then he remembered he didn't know nothing about what they did uptown. Maybe the Irish on the 4-to-12 shift at the shipyard and the piers had supper after midnight, the kids staying up, though if the men had a Gemma sandwich during their break, they wouldn't be hungry until tomorrow.

"What are you doing here?"

Benno turned, the voice coming from his blind side.

There was Leo wearing a red apron, a little A&P logo on the chest, and a white short-sleeved shirt.

"What do you think I'm doing here? I'm looking for you."

"Well, you found me." The little black bow tie bobbed when Bell spoke.

"They hired you already?"

"A guy in produce quit this morning."

Benno's eyes went wide. "Produce? Like you go to the Washington Market?"

Benno considered the daily pre-dawn trip through the Holland Tunnel to the market on the Lower West Side the job of a lifetime, the chance to elbow through the shouting buyers and vendors, sort through goods to come up with the best, the stars shining in the sky, freedom. Then over to the Fulton Fish Market, same thing only from the ocean instead of the ground and trees, Benno all excited as he told Bell how they throw the fish and another guy catches it in wax paper. In the morning, everybody wakes up and there's the food. A miracle. Christmas every Monday through Saturday. Now people drove to Benno's from Jersey City and Weehawken, maybe even a few people from north of Church Square Park, too. Quality draws the crowds.

"Right now I'm washing lettuce," Bell said. "They taught me how to stack the apples so the bruises don't show."

"The customers are too stupid to notice?"

"I don't know, Sally. I just got here."

"Listen, I got news for you."

Bell looked over his shoulder. "I ought to go back inside."

"Bebe's getting married. He got the radio job at the Lakeside. Terrasini's out."

"Hey," said Bell, "that's news, all right."

Benno went for his bike, lying on the ground by the cars parked nose in. "Meet me at the Grotto. They're having a party. I want to hear."

Bell had to walk all the way to the other end of town to get to the Grotto, but what the hell. He had something to celebrate, too. The little plan he'd devised during the dull moments at school was taking shape. A new job meant money in his pocket, which meant he was free to go. He loved walking New York City, but if he couldn't afford more than a subway token and a cup of coffee, it wasn't going to keep him engaged much longer. Maybe Narrows Gate would see him standing there waxing cucumbers at the A&P, but he knew he was entering a new world, one step at a time, and learning how to make a life of his choosing.

The Rosiglino party took over the Grotto's main room—red checkerboard tablecloths, candle wax dripping onto the straw-covered Chianti bottles, a full seafood menu. The booze was flowing; there was lots of shouting and good cheer. Hennie had Bebe on one side of her, Rosa on the other; and over there was Mimmo with his brother and sister-in-law plus Rosa's sisters chatting with Vincenzo, happy father of the groom; plus Bebe's aunts and uncles, Dee already tipsy. Hearing there were free drinks, the old downtown crowd, bronzed and grizzled, waddled over from Polk Street to congratulate Vincenzo, who looked a little dazed, to tell you the truth. And who should walk in but Phil Klein, Bebe's new manager, who kissed Hennie polite and shook Vincenzo's hand. Bebe made him kiss Rosa on the cheek. Klein was overwhelmed by Sicilians. "Hey, Phil," Hennie yelled, "the next round's on you!" Everybody howled when Klein turned his pockets inside out. Everybody but Mimmo.

Nursing a cup of free clam broth, Benno sat by himself, stared at Bebe and Rosa, and played out Mimmo's situation in his head. Mimmo was thinking he was Bebe's main guy, the marriage making him the real connection. Mimmo called Frankie Fortune and said, "Frankie, come to the Grotto and celebrate." Instead, Fortune worked it so Klein showed up and now Bebe's walking him around saying, "This is the man who's putting me on top." Little round Phil Klein, not Mimmo.

Weaving through the crowd, Leo Bell arrived, his red apron rolled up and tucked under his arm. "What did you find out?" he asked as he sat.

"The ring she's wearing," Benno said, pointing with his chin. "It belongs to Hennie."

"That's Rosa? She looks dazed," Bell observed.

"She won't get a chance to talk until 1940."

"And Terrasini? I thought he's dumped."

"Ah, Nino's a good guy," Benno said. "He won't ruin somebody's good time."

"And what's with Mimmo? He looks like his horse broke a leg."

Benno explained his theory, which included the phrase "a regular New York Jew" to describe Klein. The poor guy, he don't know what he's getting into.

Bell let it pass.

People were yelling at Bebe. "Sing, Bebe." "Hey, Bebe, give us a song." "Come on and sing one for the bride." Bebe shrugged like maybe he'd say no, make them beg a little harder and wait for the room to call out all at once. He had it in his mind to pay tribute to Nino when they made music together one last time.

"I guess everybody's invited to the Lakeside Inn," Bell said.

"Not the Ear."

Nor Freddie Pop, thought Bell, remembering the dreamer who never came back from stealing the Buick, and nobody knew what happened to his girl Lucy, that little thing with her stick legs and big eyes.

Old Man Sfuzzi backed up, and his fat ass made the table rock.

"Let's get out here before we get crushed," Benno said as he stood.

They swam against the crowd. Finally, out on First Street, the fresh air felt good. The night sky was dappled with magenta clouds.

Benno's bike was parked against the Grotto's bay window. The noise from the party crawled through the glass. Benno said, "Jesus, I hate that fuckin' Bebe. I'm telling you. I can't bear the guy."

"What's to hate?" Bell asked as they started toward Observer Road, the bicycle rolling on Benno's blind side. "He's the same snot nose he was when we were kids."

"I told you. He can't wait to tell people he never heard of Narrows Gate."

"So who gives a shit?"

"Me. I don't think nobody should be ashamed of where he's from."

"Sally, you can't begrudge the guy a shot to get out," Bell said.

"Who wants to get out?" Benno stopped. "That's the point. He makes it like what we got it's…it's a place you escape, for Christ's sake."

Bell shrugged. From the train yard came the sound of a hand-car rattling along the tracks.

"Plus this whole thing at the Lakeside," Benno continued. "The Ear, Corini's guy to run the place, this guy Klein becoming Bebe's manager—Farcolini's behind it."

"Farcolini gives a shit whether Bebe gets on the radio?"

Benno shook his head. "He wants somebody on the radio. Who else? Me? I'm telling you this is big. It says Farcolini goes along with Corini's plan to push the entertainment. If I'm Bruno Gigenti, I ain't too happy right now."

Though he heard of their exploits at least once a week, conveyed by Benno like he was repeating a gangster tale he saw in a serial at the Avalon, Bell could hardly tell one big shot in the crew from the next. He wouldn't recognize Gigenti the Killer—apparently the only time he'd seen him was when he was throwing Maguire off St. Matty's years ago. He hadn't seen Corini the Politician, the guy who talks to newspapers, either. Or the other guys Benno spoke of—Geller the Miami Jew and Ziggy Baum out in California, also a Jew, no doubt. Maybe they existed, maybe not. All of Benno's stories had the aura of legend.

To his great disappointment, Benno had never seen Carlo Farcolini, his hero like other kids admired Einstein or Edison. Downtown Narrows Gate was stuck with Frankie Fortune and Mimmo. Why Benno looked up to the people who would employ them was a mystery to Bell, who challenged his friend, the issue being you can't approve of people who torture and kill, who sell narcotics. Benno pointed out nobody was selling drugs on Polk Street and somebody deserves credit for getting rid of the dirty cop Maguire.

"They skim from your uncle," Bell argued.

"He raises the price to cover the hit," Benno replied, failing to see that the scam landed on working Italians. "All I can tell you," Benno once said, "is when I was a little kid I used to think that some wicked fuckin' giant, some McSomebody with a nightstick or a fire axe, was going to lift Polk Street and everybody who got off the boat would slide uptown and into New Jersey Bank and Trust we'd go, its gray columns the giant's monster teeth. But I don't think that no more."

"How about this?" Bell said now. "How about for tonight there's no more Bebe and Farcolini and Mimmo and King Kong and whoever the fuck else they bring in? How about we talk about, I don't know, the moon. See the moon, Sally?"

"Listen to me," Benno said. "Pretty soon Farcolini is finished with the killing and the drugs and the whores. Corini's setting him up nice for when he leaves Sing Sing. Bebe and the radio is the start. Mark my words."

At the corner of Cleveland, a woman in a navy suit stood under a streetlamp alongside an Oldsmobile, its front passenger-side whitewall flat as an anvil. To Bell, she looked desperate, like she no more knew how to change a tire than to lift the car over her head.

Passing the bike to his pal, Benno veered toward the worried woman.

She nodded gratefully as Benno retrieved the jack, telling Bell with a wink and a wave that it's no two-man job, making a thing right.

Later, as they sat on a stoop, Benno said, "Now maybe she goes and tells everybody we all ain't crooks."

Which confused Bell good and deep, even when he was learning how to slice watermelons so you could profit off the ones the ants had invaded. He also thought it was a pretty good trick Benno learned, how to wink over a blind eye.

PART TWO

PART TWO

CHAPTER NINE

Of course, on December 7, 1941, everybody's plans were blown to shit along with the *Arizona*, the *West Virginia*, the *Oklahoma*, the *Nevada* and our other battleships, light cruisers, destroyers, seaplane tenders and repair vessels at Pearl Harbor. Everybody's plans, that is, except Bebe's. He was enjoying the high life on the road and didn't give a good goddamn for nobody. That famous trumpet player came into the Lakeside Inn in '39 and seen the boy singer he needed. Bebe had answered his questions, saying that what the guy heard about Carlo Farcolini and Anthony Corini was bullshit: He knew them as a kid from the old neighborhood. This is something all Italians face and it's un-American. Meanwhile, Bebe met with Enna and told him he'd like to quit the Lakeside—in the long run it's better if Bill Marsala moved up: A dime on big is better than a dime on a little. Besides, Enna's man Klein would be along for the ride. Enna conferred with Fortune, who knew this day was coming the moment he realized Bebe never again mentioned the Ear, his conscience as cold as his mother's when she made up her mind somebody should go to hell. Fortune pushed the idea up to Corini, who approved. "Book them in our joints," Corini added, "and tell Enna to find another kid for the radio." A year later, Bebe ditched the trumpet player and joined a band with a bigger national reputation, the leader in a couple of movies. "Fuckin' Bebe," said Mimmo.

"You're surprised?" Fortune replied.

Then came the band's big hit, Bebe's singing about how he couldn't smile no more because his girl dumped him. He was on the radio everywhere in the country, a household name, and the bandleader better be alert because sooner than later, a shiv is going to land between his shoulder blades, courtesy of Bebe Marsala.

But none of this meant nothing to nobody on that Sunday in December. "We interrupt this program to bring you a special news bulletin. The Japanese attacked Pearl Harbor, Hawaii, by air, President Roosevelt has just announced," said John Daly on the radio. The church bells started ringing, their deep, solemn resonance shaking the sparrows from the trees, and people began to pour out onto Polk Street, a sense of foreboding moving like fog. "*Che cosa significa*? What does it mean?"

Somebody said there was going to be a lot of work at the shipyards because the Americans had to rebuild and these Japanese fucks were going to pay, and then everybody went away quiet, realizing that soon their sons and brothers were going to go off to die. And then Roosevelt got on the radio again and a few days later, that weak fascist bastard Mussolini, who already took it up the ass from Hitler, declared war on America, too. Which was a dumb play, because if he thought Polk Street was going to run and sign up to fight for Italy, he learned fast he was an idiot. The war effort went into high gear. American flags were everywhere and the Sons of Italy marching band changed its name and learned the right songs. Sal Benno, 18 years old, put himself and his glass eye to work to build the "Arsenal of Democracy" like FDR wanted, selling bonds and collecting scrap, using his uncle's truck, new scents competing with the aroma of cured meats, chunk cheese and fresh fish.

Leo Bell had spent most of December 7 in the back room at Benno's with an atlas and a globe showing everybody where was Pearl Harbor, where was Hawaii. As the radio flooded the room with news, he pointed to Malaya, Hong Kong, Guam, the Philippines, Wake Island and Midway and showed them how Hitler had swept across Europe and how Mussolini went into North Africa to control the Mediterranean. "And there's Sicily." Bell tapped it with the point of his pencil. Scratching his day-old growth, Pooch the Grocer was thinking everything is a long way from Narrows Gate, but who knows what kind of super airplanes and submarines the Japs and the Nazis got. Pretty soon we could be surrounded.

On December 8, Benno came back a few minutes late from the produce-and-fish run to Manhattan, slowed down by eaves-dropping on those guys at the markets shouting opinions, this frigid morning especially. Though it wasn't even sun up yet, Leo was waiting outside the store, wearing a suit and tie under his topcoat. On his way to enlist, he had brought with him a little duffel bag with his toothbrush and toothpaste, a comb, a rag to clean his glasses and a couple of books he grabbed off the nightstand.

Benno parked on Polk rather than backing the truck into the alley and even though the fresh fruit and vegetables were in the cab and the fish in the icebox, he jumped out and ran around the truck, the engine running. He stood right in front of Bell, both of them knowing maybe this could be the last time they'd be together. Jesus Christ, Sal Benno was thinking. Oh, Jesus Christ.

"I figured you'd do this," Benno said, his breath rising. Frost hung from the telephone wires.

"Sal…"

"But you'll outsmart those Japs." He noticed Leo was shivering a little bit.

Bell smiled. "In this corner, Imperial Japan. Over there, Leo Bell."

"And me. I'm with you. Ain't I with you?"

"Always, Sally. Always."

They took off their gloves and shook hands. And then they gave each other a big hug, right there on Polk Street.

About a month into his hitch, Bell was lying on his bunk, muscles aching, but feeling worse for the state of his unit. The Army had been engaged in a military-preparedness program since '39, but drills at Fort Dix were accompanied by the sounds of the Corps of Engineers hurrying to build barracks, an administration building, hospitals, storage warehouses, additional mess facilities and housing. New equipment was in short supply. Training with World War I weapons, Bell wore an oversized tin doughboy helmet, the chinstrap keeping it on his head. A few regular Army infantry divisions were close to combat-ready and the National Guard and Army Reserve had been called to active duty. Morale was high and no one doubted President Roosevelt, but it was hard for Bell to believe that the ragtag bunch he bunked with, men who could barely fall in without stumbling over each other, could go up against Hitler's war machine, the world's most powerful army. It would be damned funny if it weren't so damned sad.

He called his father whenever he had time. "Be resolute, Leo," his father said. "Look what they did to Poland. The Blitzkrieg was our Pearl Harbor."

He could see his father over on the Lower West Side, surrounded by typewriters at Kreiner's shop, tiny tools in his shirt pocket, ribbon ink smeared on his fingers. Bell said, "Maybe now is the time we come out from under our shell, Pop."

"Leo, I could not imagine a worse time for a man to admit he is a Jew." He reminded his son what they had seen in the newsreels at the Avalon and in *Life* magazine: Kristallnacht and the September Campaign, the Nazis marching along the Champs-Élysées, the Blitz in London and the Imperial Army's Rape of Nanking. There was no reason to think the Axis powers wouldn't hesitate to attack the U.S. mainland with the same savagery and lack of moral code.

Now, as he revisited the conversations, Bell lay with an arm across his eyes, his glasses on the cold floor. He was about to drift to sleep when he heard a man clear his throat.

"Private Bell."

He sprung out of bed, almost whacking his head on the top bunk.

"Come with me," the lieutenant said.

Bell groped for his glasses.

The scent of fresh-cut wood permeated Lt. Tyler's office, which had newspapers for shades and was as cold as the new barracks. The desk was uneven, as was the chair in which Tyler sat. Trying to give the place a sense of official decorum, Tyler had requisitioned a green blotter, a pen and pencil set and an in-and-out box. A U.S. flag, along with the company colors, was in a corner.

Keeping his trench coat on against the cold, Tyler took off his gloves and pulled a folder off the top of a pile. "Leonardo Bell," he said.

Bell stood at ease. "Yes, sir."

As he sat back, Tyler slid the folder against his stomach. He was blond, bland, tall, fit, maybe 30 years old. It was hard to tell. Bell had a sergeant who was rumored to be 50, another said to be 22. They looked the same to him: living blocks of gristle with flatheads and leather lungs. In comparison, Tyler looked like he spent much of his time behind a desk.

"They want you to go to Fort Benning for OCS, Private Bell."

"Sir?"

"Officer Candidate School. Or are you asking where Fort Benning is."

Bell knew it was in Georgia, but he said nothing.

"OCS," Tyler repeated. "But I said no."

"Yes, sir," Bell replied.

Tyler looked into the folder. "You speak Italian and Polish fluently. You speak German?"

"I studied German in high school, sir."

"Why?"

"Hitler, sir."

"Hitler?"

"I figured he'd be coming."

"You did?"

"Yes, sir."

"Too bad you didn't study Japanese."

"They didn't offer Japanese, sir."

Tyler flipped a sheet. "Says here you were first in your class."

"Yes, sir."

"A believer in independent study."

"Sir?"

"You spent hours in the school library," Tyler said. "Apparently the curriculum wasn't satisfying."

"Sir, I—"

"But you didn't apply to any colleges."

"No, sir."

"Why not?"

"I hadn't decided, sir. I was thinking of traveling. Or joining the Armed Forces."

"Tojo made the choice for you."

"I suppose you could say that, sir."

"Why Polish?"

"Sir?"

Tyler closed the folder and dropped it back into the pile. "Why do you speak Polish?"

"My mother's family was Polish. My father studied it and he taught me."

The lieutenant leaned his elbows on the desk, which rattled under the weight. "You love your father, don't you?"

"Yes, sir."

"You'd like to be the kind of man he is."

"What kind of man is that, sir?"

Staring up, Tyler said, "This isn't a conversation, Private."

"Yes, sir."

"You admire him."

"I admire my father, yes."

"Explain."

"Well, he does what he says he'll do. If you need a friend, he's…" Bell let the thought drift. It wasn't a conversation. Nor did Tyler want to know if Abramo Bell was forthright and reliable or had a wry sense of humor—though Bell wasn't sure what the lieutenant was looking for.

"He's what, Private?"

"He would boil Hitler in oil if he could," Bell replied.

"I see."

Bell remained silent as Tyler sat back again, the chair squeaking.

"Interested in typewriter repair, Private Bell?"

"No, sir."

"You see bigger things for yourself."

"I hope so, sir."

"I assume you intend to return to Poland one day."

"Italy, sir. Irpino."

Tyler glanced at the folder, but let it lie. "You intend to return to Italy, then."

"If I could put one in Mussolini's brain, yes, sir."

Tyler nodded. Then he stood. "All right. We're done."

Bell saluted, turned and left the office.

Nine weeks later, as the members of his unit were waiting to be reassigned, Bell was told to report to Tyler's office. A Corporal O'Neill intercepted him and said he was to be in Washington, D.C., tomorrow at 0800.

So began Leo Bell's recruitment into the Office of the Coordinator of Information, which was organized by Gen. William J. Donovan. Its mission: to collect and analyze information and data that might bear upon national security; to collate it and make it available to the president and government departments as the president may determine; and to carry out such activities that may facilitate the securing of information important for national security.

Bell had spent 13 weeks learning to kill. A good shot with an M1 despite his eyeglasses, he was looking forward to nesting in a tower in France or under brush in a Pacific jungle and cutting down the enemy. But the U.S. Army had decided Leo Bell was going to be a spy. In late 1942, after indoctrination and class work in Washington, he was assigned not to Berlin or London, not to Corregidor or elsewhere in the Pacific theater.

Bell was assigned to the New York Public Library, the 42nd Street main branch.

Cy Geller was sitting outside his office in Coral Gables as the palm trees' long shadows craned across the width of his swimming pool. For the moment, he was lost to the complexity of his calculations. The flow of heroin through Sicily to the United States would be interrupted when the Navy took control of shipping lanes in the Atlantic. The cache stored in Cuba would soon be depleted. Suppliers in Latin America had raised their prices to the level of extortion. From Los Angeles, Ziggy Baum reported that his Mexican sources were running dry. Shipments from Asia were impossible. No other segment of the business, no matter how prices or events were manipulated, could make up for the shortfall in income.

"Mr. Geller. Excuse me."

Geller shaded his eyes from the setting sun.

"There is a man to see you," said the jockey-sized Cuban who went by the name Felipe. Geller's wife thought of him as their houseboy, but he carried a pistol under his white jacket. "He says he is from the FBI."

Geller greeted his visitor and offered him a lawn chair. The agent, who said he preferred to stand, was middle-aged with gray hair, a pale complexion and a wool suit.

"We have a proposal for Mr. Farcolini," the agent said, peering over his shoulder at Felipe, who hovered nearby.

Geller didn't reply. To deny he knew Carlo Farcolini would be absurd. To admit that they could communicate would expose him to conspiracy charges.

"We're having problems with New York Harbor," the agent said. "The shipyards, the docks, the unions. We're at a standstill again. Nothing is moving."

"Why come to me?" Geller asked.

"We can't figure out if it's Corini or Gigenti we should talk to."

"Why not see Mr. Farcolini? I believe he's still in federal custody."

"Now he wants a free pass. That's impossible."

"You want to negotiate," Geller observed. "What would you propose?"

"Let's be frank," the agent replied. "All priorities have changed."

"Even for the newly elected governor of New York?"

"For everybody, Mr. Geller."

"Maybe you should approach Mr. Farcolini in a day or so. He may come up with an idea that would be acceptable to Governor Dewey and Mr. Hoover." Geller gestured for Felipe to lead the man to his car.

The gray man in the gray suit brightened a bit. Charged with the task of recruiting Farcolini's growing empire to back the war effort, he'd flown to Miami with two assumptions: that the Farcolinis, as ruthless as they were, would support the defeat of totalitarian regimes and that Cy Geller was a reasonable man. He'd return to New York with a sense of mission accomplished.

As for Geller, he was relieved the government had asked only for additional help with the waterfront. That left Don Carlo with a big chip to play. Roosevelt's generals understood the strategic significance of the island of Sicily. Its airfields, now in the hands of the Axis powers, were vital to all plans to invade Europe from the south and would give the Allies complete access to the Mediterranean. Carlo Farcolini knew this, too. Before surrendering to Dewey, he'd initiated a discussion with Maurizio Marra, the head of the Mafia in Sicily. Don Mauro agreed to contact his peers in Catania, Licata, Messina, Palermo, Sciacca and Siracusa and tell them the Allies would need their cooperation.

Geller went to his private phone, secure in the knowledge that business would soon improve.

CHAPTER TEN

Each time Bebe's return from the road was delayed, Rosa Rosiglino—her name on the marriage license, though everyone called her Mrs. Marsala—believed what he said: He had obligations. He was tied up. He said, "The music business is a competition, doll, a fight to the death. You've got to earn it wherever you can." How could she question him? What did she know about business? She was over the moon in love, a kid who had gone from a Roman Catholic high school for girls to the arms of Bill Marsala, singer for one of the most popular orchestras in the country. Her only experience with men and marriage came from her father, who was a good man. If her father said something, it was so.

Bill said he wanted nothing more than for them to be together. He told her he imagined she was always at his side. The time the band was held over for two additional weeks in Newport and she wasn't allowed to join him? The bandleader, not her Bill, said no. "I'm dying for you, baby," he said. That extra month out in Hollywood doing fundraisers for the USO? Of course he wanted her there, but was it fair to the boys heading overseas to have his angel by his side when they were going to do without theirs for years?

The time he was gone seemed endless. Rosa yearned for his caress, the words he whispered, the almost unbearable tenderness, the joy she felt as they walked through a park, went on a drive along the Hudson, held a conversation over candlelight and a cocktail. She ached for that feeling of contentment at hearing his voice as he sang while he shaved, brushed his suits in their bedroom, whisked eggs for their breakfast. In his absence, she listened to his records, dusted the frames around his photos and cooked his favorite meals as if he would be home by suppertime. She practiced doing his shirts the way he liked and pressed his slacks to a scalpel's edge. She kept busy, making the little apartment a home. "Are you lonely, Rosa?" asked her sister Bev.

She said no. "I know he wishes we were together." She pointed to the gifts he sent, the pins and pendants, a necklace for their second anniversary. The flowers always came with a note signed "Your Bill." She didn't mention the long, desperate calls when the bandleader was displeased or when the audience didn't respond; she couldn't tell anyone how much he needed her at those moments, how he longed to fold himself into her embrace and make the world go away. "You keep me safe, baby," he whispered. "You're my sanctuary." Nor did she mention how she had to calm him down when his temper detonated. "This son of a bitch acts like he doesn't know my name. Meanwhile, I'm carrying his crap orchestra on my back. You think they come out to listen to his syrup? Baby, they turn out to hear *me*. They want *me*."

Of course I'm lonely, she thought. The phone calls, cables, postcards, gifts and flowers weren't the same as if he were here. She'd spent many more days and nights in the apartment alone than together with him. But how could she complain? Her friends from school were alone, too, their boyfriends off to war. Their brothers and fathers. Bev's husband. Her Uncle Teddy. A girl who worked at the telephone company had lost her fiancé. A teacher at the Bayonne High School lost a nephew. The newspaper said three soldiers from Bayonne who survived the attack on Pearl Harbor were in a platoon trapped on the Bataan Peninsula.

Now the city in which she was born and raised was populated only by women and girls, old men and little boys. Flags in the parks and on public buildings flew at half-staff, sagging in autumn's dying light as if defeated. The radio reported the Allies had been overrun; London and Moscow were in ruins. Hitler could not be stopped and the savage Japs were choking off the Pacific. Innocent women and children were being slaughtered by the Axis troops.

Every day, she faced the endless and impossible news from overseas by herself. Finally, she was inspired to action. Everyone was needed, the president said. Her kid sister, Ida, planted a victory garden in the small strip of land behind their parents' brick house, and the neighbors followed suit; people who spent their entire lives in a cozy New Jersey city now believed they were farmers. "The Green Thumb Brigade," as the *Observer* called them, donated what they grew to the veterans' hospital.

Enough self-pity, she told herself. It'd be good to get out for more than grocery shopping and going to church. "Bill, I'd like to volunteer at the Red Cross."

"Go ahead, doll," he said. "It'll do you a world of good."

Excited, she took a bus to their offices in Jersey City the next morning. They were glad to have her. A girl who had been a grade behind her in grammar school was there to show her the ropes. They shared a sandwich like old friends. Bill called that night from a hotel in Los Angeles. She couldn't wait to tell him what happened, how proud she felt of herself. He said, "On second thought, baby, I'd like to know you'll be home if I need you. Isn't there something you can do around the house? Write letters to the boys overseas, maybe. Send them my picture."

She felt abandoned, though her family invited her over, setting an extra chair at the dining room table. When her mother visited—"our little coffee klatch," Alice Mistretta called it whenever she brought along a crumb cake or some *anginetti*—Rosa told her about Bill's latest phone call. She showed her a photo of him taken near Niagara Falls or on Bourbon Street in New Orleans, all the guys crowding around. "Look how happy he is, Mama," she'd say, grateful for her company. Later, when her mother tried to press a few dollars into her hand, she'd say, "No, I have more than enough. Bill provides. He's a good man. He's just…Oh, never mind. Mama, next week the lemon cookies are on me." Then she added, "When he calls tonight, I'll give him your love."

But later, when she realized he wasn't going to call, the night having gotten away from him as he stole a few hours' sleep on the bus, she'd nestle on his side of the bed and call up an image of her Bill singing to an adoring crowd, the spotlight in his blue eyes, his head tilted just so, his arms open wide when he held a note. But soon the vision haunted her. "Bill…" she moaned as she padded through the dark railroad flat wearing a nightgown he'd sent but had never seen her wear. Then she chided herself, repeating Hennie's words. "Rosa," she'd say aloud, "your husband has to build his career. It takes time." She repeated what he said when he finally called from Denver or Santa Fe: "The time we're away now, well, we'll double that—no, triple that—with the time we're together when I'm running my own shop. You watch."

More gold stars appeared in the neighborhood windows: a young man who had been the paperboy when she was a child was killed during a training exercise at Fort Bragg; two boys she knew who were going to attend the teachers' college were killed by a landmine in Libya; a nurse who had studied at St. Claire's was killed in New Guinea; a colored man who worked at the Flying A filling station lost two sons when a transport was torpedoed in the Atlantic.

How could she complain? Her Bill was coming home. She'd hold him, cuddle him, stroke him, tell him there was no other man in the world, and when they made love, he'd attend to her and then they'd make love again and she'd know she was the luckiest girl on the face of the earth to have a husband who wanted to build his world around her. Her dreams were their dreams; his dreams were hers. It was a beautiful life full of love, devotion and song.

Finally, the taxicab pulled in front of the house. From the second-story window, she saw him exit, waiting as the driver hurried to retrieve his bag. Tanned, a silk scarf around his throat, a suit she didn't recognize. Still skinny, those ears, those beautiful eyes: her Bill, glowing in the late-afternoon sun. With one last look around the bedroom, one last glance in the mirror at her dress and hair, she flew down the steps.

Bebe was sliding bills into his money clip when the building door opened. He turned as she ran to him. She was as lovely as he remembered. No, more so. A woman now. His wife. A rock at his side.

She jumped into his arms.

He couldn't wait to tell her.

They kissed with passion, forgetting they were on the street with its draped flags, its air of trepidation. In his arms, she felt secure. They were building a life together.

He stepped back and took her hands, his smile wide and shimmering with satisfaction.

On the front porches, neighbors smiled at the young lovers.

"Hi, Bill," she said, a tear streaking down her cheek. She loved him so much it hurt.

"Baby, great news," he said. "We're moving to California!"

Cpl. Leo Bell found Tyler waiting outside the closet-sized room he'd been given at the New York Public Library, home to the Office of Strategic Services' Psychoanalytic Field Unit.

"Where have you been?" the lieutenant said.

"The St. Regis Hotel, sir."

Tyler nodded for Bell to step into the space, which was on the first floor, off the newspaper room.

"Sit," said Tyler, who remained standing. He was in civilian clothes, a tweedy suit, the kind popular with the unit, almost all civilians, all graduates of Ivy League colleges. "Who's at the hotel?" Tyler asked.

"A former ambassador from Turkey," Bell replied. He was in his khaki uniform, which was better suited to the mid-May heat.

"And?"

"General Stansfield and Mr. Lowell."

"The cartographer," Tyler said.

Most of the men in the unit had doctorate degrees, including the CO, Major Landis, a Yale man. Tyler didn't and to compensate, he broadcast to Bell whatever fact he had on the subject at hand.

"I don't know, sir." When Bell arrived with the document, Lowell was showing his work to Stansfield, who reported to General Eisenhower, commander in chief of Allied Forces, North Africa. The Turk studied the large, detailed map that was unfurled across four card tables.

"What did you deliver?"

"Eyes only, sir."

The unit used Bell as a research assistant and courier. He combed the library shelves for books for them, dug out old journals and microphotographic copies of newspaper stories. He hurried to the United Nations, the British embassy, the Free France consulate, the New School in the Village or uptown to the New York Psychoanalytic Institute. Now and then, Bell took a train down to Washington or up to Harvard in Cambridge, always carrying a locked attaché case. In the 17 months since he enlisted, Bell translated a handful of intercepted documents in Polish and Italian, ranging from official Axis reports to personal letters. He had been pressed into service when the Ivy Leaguers who knew the languages were unavailable.

The Ivy Leaguers all smoked pipes and rarely remembered his name. Bell couldn't say they were rude, exactly; in fact, they were exceedingly polite. But they treated him as if he were a lesser species—like a chimp who could read.

"I'm incidental," he told Benno over lunch near Grand Central.

"Means what?" Benno replied, holding an oyster cracker up to the light.

"Never mind," Bell said with a shrug. "I was hoping to be useful."

"Hey," said Benno, "we don't win this thing unless everybody pitches in."

Bell still didn't know what he wanted to do when the war ended. But he was certain he'd prove to himself that he was as good as the guys with the PhDs up on the third floor. He already knew he had it over Tyler, except for figuring how he'd bluffed his way in.

Tyler held an envelope.

"Where do I take it?" Bell asked.

"No," Tyler said. "You read this."

"Polish or Italian?" Bell asked.

"Open it."

Bell used a knife to slit the seal. He withdrew a carbon copy of a report perhaps 300 pages thick and stamped "Confidential." The authors were Landis and the guys at Harvard, the New School, and the Psychoanalytic Institute. The title page read, "A Psychological Analysis of Adolf Hitler."

"They're dizzy up there from looking at it," Tyler said. "Proofread it hard and tight. It's going to Wild Bill on Sunday."

Wild Bill. Like they were pals.

Bell quickly scanned the first page. If he didn't put the fan on, he'd be asleep before he got to the second. "When do you need it by?" he asked.

"I'm locking you in until you're done," the lieutenant said, pulling the skeleton key from the door.

"Maybe I could grab some lunch?"

"No," Tyler replied.

Yanking the front door open, Bruno Gigenti barreled out of his social club onto Mulberry Street and pointed sharply at Fredo Pellizzari, his driver, who was dipping his thick fingers into a small brown bag of salted *ceci*. A dark, broad-shouldered Sicilian in his mid-40s, Pellizzari snapped alert, burying the bag in a pocket. Usually, Gigenti sent a boy out to tell him to start the car up, reducing the risk he'd be left standing in public should someone advance with a grievance. But Gigenti had been in a foul mood all week and now Pellizzari figured whatever had been gnawing at him had finally torn through. He held a rear door open for his boss and could feel the heat when Gigenti passed. Pellizzari knew someone was going to pay for sins, his own or otherwise.

They headed north along a street crowded with peddlers and their patrons. Gigenti never told any of his drivers where he was going until the car reached Canal, and then God help him if he tapped the blinker, pumped the brakes or made any kind of move Gigenti interpreted as a signal to a tail. If it was true that Gigenti trusted nobody, he especially didn't trust the people who were paid to keep him upright. As his drivers knew, he always wrapped his fist around a .38 Special throughout the trip.

"Make a right," Gigenti said in Sicilian.

At the Bowery, he said, "Go ahead." Meaning the Manhattan Bridge, which would deposit them across the river in Brooklyn.

No one in his crew knew, but Gigenti had been boxed out, again, by Geller and Corini. Neither man had revealed that they'd had to negotiate with the feds after Farcolini surrendered until the deal was done and all they needed was someone to enforce the plan. "Open up the piers," Geller had said. Gigenti replied, "My piers? Says who?" It was then that Geller said, "I had a visit from the FBI. Anthony Corini went up to Sing Sing and Don Carlo says open the piers." Then he added, "You're going to see a story in the newspapers. Don Carlo is being deported to Sicily. Don't interfere. This is what we want."

The call from Florida chafed Gigenti's ass. Corini had gone to see Farcolini and Gigenti knew nothing about it. If the matter was the waterfront, Gigenti should've been the contact. Plus the way the Jew said, "We." We, thought Gigenti. Who the fuck is "we"?

"Take Myrtle," Gigenti said, spitting the avenue's name at Pellizzari.

The Brooklyn Navy Yard, the driver thought. When he glanced quickly into the rearview mirror, he saw Gigenti was still seething.

Furious, bitter, insulted, Gigenti nevertheless did what he was told. The piers opened up overnight. Then he learned that Peter Verkerk, the head of a longshoremen's union, whose father had sway on the docks before the Sicilians moved in, had gone to the feds and told them the order on the slowdown came from Gigenti. This the FBI already knew, but then Verkerk proposed that the feds, who were still new to the waterfront, work through him instead of Farcolini's crowd. "Force them out," Verkerk said, "and I'll keep the waterfront running like you want."

The deal between Don Carlo and the feds fucked Verkerk good, but not long and hard enough to Gigenti's mind. Eugenio Zamarella, Gigenti's preferred button, proposed Verkerk would take off and volunteered to track him down. But Gigenti knew Verkerk would wait to see whatever shook from Don Carlo's departure. Maybe he recognized a void in the leadership; maybe he heard the feds went to see Geller, not Bruno Gigenti. Maybe he learned Corini, not Bruno Gigenti, took the train up to Sing Sing to meet with Don Carlo. Gigenti paced the social club, his home out in Queens, his mistress's apartment under the Williamsburg Bridge. Soon, all Gigenti's roiling anger at the insult from Geller and Corini centered on the head of Peter Verkerk, a degenerate whose idea of fun was to fuck a skank with another guy in on the action.

"Make a left," Gigenti said. He gave an address.

Pellizzari turned down a seedy side street about a mile walk from the Navy yard. He crossed an intersection and entered a grimy block rank with potholes and rotting garbage. Pellizzari grimaced at the foul scent that rose from the river.

In the backseat, Gigenti flexed his fingers on the barrel of his .38, adjusted his fedora and rolled his shoulders under his brown suit jacket.

Pellizzari pulled in front of a decaying two-story building with a wooden staircase in back. A flop upstairs, thought Pellizzari.

The second the car stopped, Gigenti reached for the door handle.

"I'm coming, Boss," the brawny driver said.

Ignoring him, Gigenti stepped out, crunching broken grass under foot.

Pellizzari checked the pistol in his shoulder holster and hurried from the car.

Gigenti crossed a patch of yellowing grass, moving quickly along the cracked driveway to the side of the paint-chipped house. With the driver trailing, he marched resolutely toward the stairs.

"Boss," whispered Pellizzari, thinking, Jesus Christ, what happens if Gigenti walks into an ambush? "Boss."

He stiffened as he anticipated the wood's revealing creak under Gigenti's weight, but the boss went up the stairs quietly and with surprising grace.

Pellizzari waited, unsure whether he should do the same.

Gigenti paused at the landing. He knew the dump's layout. On his way up in Patti's organization, Gigenti had whores working the neighborhood. As he considered the hideaway's door, he figured Verkerk would have the broad on the Murphy bed, either he or his crony pumping her or the other guy's gone and Verkerk sleeps. Or they're in the kitchen, coffee at the table, the *puttana* dismissed.

Pellizzari climbed the stairs on his toes, his hand clutching the shaky banister.

Gigenti then stepped back, drew up and slammed his foot against the door, exploding it off its hinges.

All three people on the bed jumped in fear. The bottle blonde was on all fours, sucking a guy while Verkerk rammed her from behind.

Gigenti's first shot took off Verkerk's jaw.

The broad screamed as the other man tried to wriggle free.

As Verkerk toppled over, his erection bobbing, Gigenti crossed the room, his gun held high. The second shot went into Verkerk's back. He landed on top of the screaming woman.

The other man, his face now coated in Verkerk's blood, leaped from the bed, grabbing in vain at a sheet. He looked at Gigenti, then at the doorway, now filled by Pellizzari.

Gigenti fired his third and fourth shots into Verkerk as he lay dead on the *puttana*. Both bullets penetrated his body and entered the slit's back.

The other guy ran to the window and dove out, head first.

Pellizzari lumbered down the stairs and found the man in the dirt and stone driveway of the decaying building next door. He'd hit the ground with his head, which bled in a stream. Pellizzari raised his gun, then flopped the man's body over with his foot. Dead and, look, he still had a hard-on.

Some *puttana*, Pellizzari thought as he holstered his pistol.

When he turned the corner, he saw Gigenti ambling down the stairs, calm, like he was going out for a loaf of bread. The fury that had gripped his face for a week was gone. He handed the .38 to his driver.

"We go," he said in Sicilian.

"Mulberry Street, Boss?"

"Sure," Gigenti replied. "Why not?"

Benno was sitting on the hydrant outside the salumeria, watching the guys coming off the 8-to-4 shift at the shipyards, lugging empty lunch pails, their faces and T-shirts coated in dirt from hard labor. "Hey, Sal," said this one. "Sally!" cheered that one, waving a knobby hand. Benno nodded like he always did, smiling as he spun his fedora on a finger, letting the sun over the Palisades warm his face. He had no plans for the evening unless he could find a girl in the neighborhood who wasn't off-limits, her boyfriend overseas. *Madonna mio*, he died when he saw Scatta strolling by, saying, "Sal..." wicked like she did, then laughing, her dress swaying this way and that. Her boyfriend was in France, they said, and she was true.

"Sal."

Benno turned. There was Mimmo, his suit jacket over his arm, one of his suspenders twisted.

"Making the rounds, Mimmo?" Benno asked as he stood.

"Too early."

Benno nodded. Every evening, Mimmo walked up and along the downtown streets like he was surveying his kingdom. The shopkeepers said hello and so did the women out on the stoops after the dishes were put away. By now, everybody knew Mimmo was in charge of nothing, so he couldn't be blamed for the weekly shakedown, his authority down to zero.

Three or four times a week, Mimmo moseyed over to Benno's, looking for somebody to bullshit with. Sal asked him how come he don't chat with Boo Chiasso or Fat Tutti or one of the other guys Fortune had on the payroll, but Mimmo said, "You never tell the help what you know or pretty soon their ass is in your chair," which made sense to Benno.

"You heard what happened?" Mimmo asked.

Benno said no. He'd heard lots of things that happened, but he didn't know which one Mimmo meant.

"With Bebe."

"He's going to California. Rosa don't want to go, but he says it's a good place for babies. Nino's going, too."

Mimmo leaned back offended, his rat eyes wide under his sunglasses. "I thought you ain't heard."

Benno said, "I don't know, maybe you wanted to talk about Don Carlo getting kicked over to Sicily."

"That's what you think happened? They kicked Don Carlo out? Jesus."

"That's what they put in the papers."

"The papers. Who gives a fuck for the papers? What's wrong with you?"

Benno found them entertaining, but he said nothing, seeing as Mimmo was winding up to tell him everything he shouldn't.

"You know why Don Carlo's going to Sicily? One," Mimmo said, counting on a finger, "he wants to be in Sicily. Two, we got business in Sicily. Three, the Army needs him in Sicily."

"The Army? The American Army?"

"No, the Martian Army."

Benno heard the government needed Farcolini, Gigenti, Corini and the rest to keep the waterfront in business—Mimmo told him—but he didn't know nothing about this move.

"Why do they need him?" Benno asked.

"Ah," Mimmo said triumphantly. "Maybe they don't put the right shit in your newspapers."

"I don't get you."

Mimmo held out his hands. "You're so smart, you figure it out."

"Whoa, Mimmo, you never heard me say I was smart."

"Well, think about it," he replied as he walked away, pausing for passing traffic on Polk Street.

Benno stuck his head into the store, the crowd thin so Vito was doing his numbers in the storeroom, the calculator churning.

"You need me?" Benno yelled. "I'm going to see Leo."

Gemma scurried around the counter, her slippers skidding on the sawdust. "Wait, I make a sandwich—"

He told her no, they were going out to eat. Then he went to wash up and throw on a fresh outfit. One thing he noticed about going to see Leo: A lot of good-looking broads liked to go to the library, wander around. They got a billion books over there, and then the women would sit on the steps with whatever they found, concentrating and looking happy to be in somebody else's story. Which made Benno have this little tweak of regret; he didn't give a shit for books. Soon he would turn 20 years old. It was too late to start in with them now.

CHAPTER ELEVEN

Leo Bell was lost to concentration, time flying as he reviewed his typed notes, comparing them to what he'd written on a legal pad the first three times he read Landis's report on Hitler. He was thirsty, hungry too, but he didn't mind. The work was good; he was moving in. Finally, he figured out what was wrong. All the facts he needed were in front of him—a puzzle put together wrong, but the pieces available. After a while, it was like they wanted to be set right.

Now, hours later, the 300-page report was edited down to 255 pages. With a glue pot, a brush and a ream of typing paper, Bell made the thing new, filling in the blanks by reworking flat language, trimming dubious conclusions and retyping new sections, bringing ideas into focus that had seemed vague. He liked what he was doing. He felt renewed, like he'd found a purpose. His father would say God had intervened, giving a frustrated messenger his chance to shine.

Just in case no one else liked his work, Bell kept careful notes that Tyler or any of the Ivy League boys could use to correct the typos and punctuation errors in the original document.

He looked at his watch. It read 8:45.

Tonight or tomorrow, he thought as he stood and stretched.

He took off his glasses and rubbed his eyes. Sitting on the corner of the desk, he dialed Tyler's number.

Major Landis answered.

Startled, Bell explained he was locked in his storeroom. A security measure, he said, while he proofread the report.

"Are you finished, Leo?" Landis took the fatherly approach.

"Yes, sir."

"Good. I'll send someone down."

Moments later, the dead bolt turned. An elderly Negro in a New York Public Library uniform opened the door.

Bell washed up quickly in the men's room. Then he took the marble stairs two at a time. His footsteps echoed in the vast stairwell, the building having been closed to the public for hours now.

Landis was in uniform, his hat tucked under his arm as he waited for Bell in the corridor outside Tyler's empty office. Landis greeted him with a warm, tired smile and returned his salute. "Did you find anything, Corporal?"

Landis was in his early 50s, his hair snow-white. His tone and the glint in his eye suggested he knew Bell wouldn't hesitate to seize the opportunity to express an opinion.

"My proofreading notes are in here, sir," Bell said, holding out the envelope, its flap taped shut. "I also made some recommendations."

"Find it enlightening?"

"Amazing is more like it," Bell replied as he took a breath. "It sounds like you've been following Hitler for years."

"In a sense, we have been."

Bell nodded. He really didn't understand how a psychological report could be prepared on someone none of the authors had met, but Hitler had been carrying on in public since 1920. According to Landis's report, his psychoses were obvious. Future actions could be predicted with relative reliability. For one, Landis concluded Hitler would commit suicide rather than be called to account for his actions.

"Well, good night, Leo," Landis said as he put on his hat. "Thank you for your perseverance."

"Good night, sir," he replied.

As the major reached the landing below, Bell sagged with disappointment. He'd hoped Landis would look at his work now, without Tyler standing between them. He believed Landis would appreciate the initiative he'd shown.

By the time Bell kicked down the library steps to Fifth Avenue, it was almost 10 o'clock. And there in the forecourt was Sal Benno, flipping his hat in the air and catching it, flipping it, catching it. Alone in the moon glow except for the pecking pigeons.

"They wouldn't let me in," Benno said.

"They told you I was in there?"

"No, but I went to the Y and you ain't there."

The Army had Bell bivouacked at a YMCA downtown.

"Maybe I'm out on a date, Sal."

"You?"

They stood between the stone lions, the lights of passing cars sweeping across Bell's face. "Is everything all right?"

"Except for we're fighting two wars, yeah."

"With Gemma and Vito."

"Yeah, sure. But you heard about Maria's boyfriend? He got it in on Guadalcanal."

"Jesus. Artie, right? From Second Street." Bell went down a step toward Fifth. Now he and Benno were the same height, looking eye to eye.

"Some Irish guy from Cleveland Street, too. In Tunisia," Benno added. "That makes twenty-one men we lost, and still I'm twisting arms to collect scrap iron."

Bell took note that Benno counted the uptown Irish in his tally, making Narrows Gate one town with one population, at least during wartime.

"You want to get something to eat?" Benno said. "I mean, I hate to tell you but you look like shit."

They went to a fish joint, the place long and narrow like a canoe. The jug-eared waiter wore a black vest and an apron that hung to his ankles. He stood silently as they looked at the menu.

"What's good?" Benno asked.

The guy shrugged.

"Keep it simple," Benno told him. "And bring lemons."

The place was almost empty, a couple over there polishing off a bottle of wine.

Bell tried to stifle a yawn and failed.

"Let me ask you something," Benno said. "The Axis got Sicily, right?"

Bell nodded.

"You think Farcolini could be working for them?"

Bell snapped alert. "What?"

"I mean, he wouldn't go against us, would he?"

"Jesus, Sal, that's a hell of a question," Bell replied as he took a breadstick from the glass.

"Look, they worked it so he gets deported, Corini, Frankie, the crew..."

"They worked it?"

"Sure. They opened up the waterfront if the feds let Farcolini out of Sing Sing."

Bell paused as he chewed. "OK. I'll buy that." He remembered Tyler's suggestion that organized crime was involved when a Nazi sub infiltrated Long Island Sound and torpedoed a tanker, then a freighter near a Coast Guard base in southern New Jersey.

"You think the feds are dumb enough to let Farcolini go help Mussolini?"

Bell said, "No. They'd keep him here if they're concerned."

"So Farcolini is over there helping us?"

"If he's helping anybody."

Benno sat back proud, a satisfied smile crossing his face.

The waiter returned. The flounder looked pretty good, fresh, ample. Benno would rather eat his socks than a boiled potato, but the broccoli was firm and bright green. He dug in. Bell, too.

"You got a pencil?" Benno asked, his cheek plump with dinner.

Bell nodded.

Benno took the cloth napkin off his lap and moved his plate aside. "Draw me a map. Show me why we need Farcolini to get Sicily back for us."

Soon, Bell had a crude drawing on the napkin, North Africa here, the southern tip of Italy over there, Sicily like a football at the boot's toe, little waves to show the Mediterranean and Tyrrhenian seas. For good measure he put an arrow showing the way through Austria to Germany and, what the hell, here's how you get into France.

Never for a moment did he stop thinking that right now Major Landis was looking at what he'd done to the report. As his fatigue grew, the warmth in his stomach lulling him toward sleep, Bell began to question whether he'd gone too far.

"You can't draw for shit," Benno observed as he dropped a finger on the map and slid it toward Tunisia and Algeria. "Boom," he went, lifting his hand like it exploded. Then he dragged it toward Calabria, then up through the tip. "Boom," he said again. For good measure, he blew up Germany, then made a left and tapped his finger on France.

"Boom?" asked Bell.

"No. Don Carlo won't blow up no good guys."

"You don't think so?"

"I'm telling you. Dewey, Roosevelt, they need us. Farcolini gets settled and pretty soon that fuckin' Mussolini, he's finished. Next, the goose-step fuck."

Bell held up his water glass. "Your lips, Sally, to God's ear."

Benno tapped the glass with his fork.

The detectives came straight to the club, badging the guy out front, and a minute or so later Pellizzari, leaning over there against the car, saw Bruno Gigenti come out handcuffed, his face a stone mask. Old man Questo, who poured the espresso, was trained to call the lawyer if anything happened. As the cops' car pulled away, Pellizzari walked inside. Questo was on the phone.

Maybe it was a half hour later when Eugenio Zamarella turned up on Mulberry Street, his fedora tipped down but his pockmarks visible. "Driver," he barked and waggled a crooked finger. Pellizzari followed him into the club.

Questo wore a brace and dragged his foot, and as he brought a cup of espresso to Zamarella, he quaked a little bit. The rumor was when Zamarella killed you—up close with a .38 or at a distance with a Carcano bolt-action rifle—you didn't know why you were dead until the Devil told you. Questo worked the club when it belonged to Gus the Boss, who Farcolini and his men ambushed out in Coney Island, a breach of protocol. Since then, Questo didn't trust nobody.

"What happened?" Zamarella said, not waiting for Pellizzari's ass to hit the chair.

"When?"

"By the Navy yard."

"Three down," Pellizzari replied.

Zamarella held up two fingers.

"Bullshit," the driver said. "I saw the guy on the sidewalk. Dead."

"The broad," Zamarella said as he dropped his palms on the table. He stood, putting on his hat as he made for the exit.

In his olive skivvies, Leo Bell took a call at the Y from one of the Ivy League guys, pleasant as usual, "Good morning, Leo, sleep well?" and all that. And then he was told to go to a brownstone on 44th Street between Eighth and Ninth where the Free French kept their operatives. A stylish woman met him in the vestibule and handed him an attaché case. To his surprise, they walked out together, arm in arm, toward Times Square. They spoke Polish. She was seeing her hairdresser, she said, before the concert tonight at Carnegie Hall, chiding him over whether he'd forgotten. When they folded into the crowd, she let go and disappeared down the steps of the IRT station. Bell continued along 42nd Street, refusing to look back to see if he had been followed. When he reached Sixth, he heard a voice call to him by rank.

It was Tyler, walking behind him, angry, his customary blandness vanquished.

"What in the name of God did you do?" he said as he approached.

Bell said, "Sir?"

"With the report. What did you do?"

Confused by the subterfuge with the Polish-speaking French woman, Bell had forgotten the report, at least for a moment.

"I proofread it, sir," Bell replied. "Then I tried my hand at editing it."

"Editing it?" Tyler was incredulous. "You ripped it apart."

"Sir, I—"

"You might as well have called Major Landis incompetent."

"I didn't intend—"

"He's furious, you know. Furious."

A light drizzle had begun to fall on Bryant Park.

"Permission to speak freely, sir," Bell said.

"Go ahead. I'd love to hear what excuse you have for your insubordination."

Bell took a few steps toward Tyler. "If you read it, you know it was bullshit until the conclusion. That tells you it was poorly organized and you know damned well the whole thing was puffed up with ten-dollar words."

Tyler shifted impatiently.

"We all know Hitler's a sick fuck," Bell continued. "From the first page, the report needs to tell everybody why—and what he's going to do next. Otherwise, all you got is this parade of rumors from Germans trying to save their own asses and some stuff from a thousand documents people up the chain already know. Did you read Hitler's quote I put up top? 'I carry out the commands that Providence has laid upon me.' Doesn't that tell you more about him than—"

"Hold on," Tyler said. "You're telling me you know better than Major Landis and the experts on the task force? You know more than the Ivy League boys?"

"This report isn't going to be read by experts or guys from the Ivy League, sir. It's going to be read by officers like yourself who aren't much interested in theory."

"Now you're going to tell me what I'm interested in. The gall of it…"

"When the war's over, Lieutenant, and those guys go back to the Ivy League, the OSS is going to need a Psych Field Unit. Our first hit better be a home run."

"So you want a part in this new unit."

"War isn't over yet, sir."

Tyler stared at him. Finally, he glanced at the attaché case.

"And what's with you and the Frenchie?"

"I never saw her in my life, sir."

"It seemed to me you were chatting her up pretty damned good, Bell."

"In Polish, not English."

"What did she tell you?"

Bell repeated the one-sided conversation.

"Hairdresser's. Carnegie Hall tonight," Tyler repeated.

"What's it mean, sir?"

Ignoring the question, Tyler gestured impatiently. "Give me the briefcase," he said.

Bell turned it over.

Tyler examined the combination lock. "You lay low, Corporal," he said finally. "Let's see if I can pull your ass out of the fire." He headed into the park and hurried toward a rear entrance to the library, passing a canopy set up for a Red Cross blood drive.

Hennie invited Rosa to lunch at the Union Club in Narrows Gate. Too late to do anything about anything, the moving van already packed and on its way to California, her son in a Beverly Hills hotel, recording sessions in Los Angeles already booked. But Bebe asked his mother to see Rosa. "Ma, she's not happy."

"Not happy? Here she has her family, Bebe. Who does she have in Hollywood?"

"Toluca Lake, Ma. In the San Fernando Valley. Beautiful. There's a lot of young couples."

"Oh, young couples. With husbands who come home at night."

"Showbiz people. The wives understand."

Now Hennie said, "He says it's the kind of place you raise kids." She was having bourbon, a double; Rosa nursed a ginger ale.

Rosa nodded. She dreaded meeting with her mother-in-law. Bill told her how she carried on, telling him he thinks his shit don't stink, walking away from the people who helped him, the town where he was born. Of course, it added up to Bill cutting the cord between mother and son. Rosa thought Hennie might ask her to talk him out of it.

"I've seen pictures," Rosa said, nodding. "It's lovely. The lake and the Santa Monica Mountains."

"The house is big, no?"

Rosa smiled. "Bigger than a one-bedroom flat in Bayonne."

"He can afford it?"

"I suppose so. He said I shouldn't worry."

Hennie reached for her hand. "What do you think, honey? A big adventure?"

"Bill wants it to be a fresh start," Rosa replied. "The new record deal, Phil says there's a chance he could be in movies…"

Hennie whispered, "I hope he's not trying to get away from Corini and the crew. They've been good to him."

Rosa shook her head. "Bill says everything is taken care of."

"He probably hooked up with Ziggy Baum." Hennie smiled bitterly. "The Jews. They're like a union." She heard Baum was weak for celebrities. Bill would have him nipping at birdseed. "Rosa, I got to tell you, I don't know what to think. I know my son's a married man and he could make a career out there. But, for Christ's sake, it's three thousand miles closer to the fuckin' Japs, ain't it?"

Rosa looked at her mother-in-law. She hadn't expected this. "He says it's where he needs to be," she replied. "He says if he stays in New York, the fans will always see him as a kid singer."

"What's wrong with that?" she snapped.

"Well, he's not always going to be a kid."

"He'll always be my kid."

"Oh, Hennie—"

"That fuckin' ingrate."

"Hennie?"

"Ingrate," she snapped. "Rose, I'm telling you, as soon as they don't need you anymore, boom. You are out the fuckin' door." Hennie snatched another cigarette, though she already had one lit in the ashtray. "You know how I found out he was going out on his own? Walter fuckin' Winchell—"

"Hennie…" Two men in suits at the next table were listening, their eyes cast sideways. Rosa nodded discreetly.

Hennie turned to them. "Mind your own fuckin' business," she bellowed.

The men cringed and hurriedly picked at their food.

"Rosa, you'd better keep him on a short leash," she said, smoke streams coming out of her nose. "I think he's up to something."

"Like what?"

"Like…" She wanted to say, "Like he's got a couple of broads stashed out there."

"Something, I don't know, thickheaded. You know how he gets."

"Well, he can be moody."

Moody? Hennie thought. This kid has no idea. Hennie gulped her drink, the cherry butting her lips. "But I don't know. I mean, that's it, right? Fuck. I don't know. I don't know what's going on."

Rosa signaled for the waiter. Despite the tight grip on gas-rationing coupons, she and Nino Terrasini were driving to California, Bill setting him up in an apartment close to the recording industry. The budget stretched, the old car would have to do. Since she didn't know how to drive, she wouldn't be much help. But she'd see America up close and feel the fighting spirit.

They ordered, Hennie demanding her Salisbury steak rare. Rosa took the turtle soup, one of Bill's favorites.

"What's your part of the deal?" Hennie asked.

"Deal?"

"He had to come across for you to agree, right?"

"Don't be silly," Rosa replied. "He's my husband."

"Jesus, you are a kid, aren't you?"

"Listen, Hennie—"

"No, no. I'm sorry, honey. I'm sorry. I'm a wreck. Look at me." She held out a hand and made it shake. "Twenty-eight years old. He don't need me to tuck him in."

Rosa stole a glance at her wristwatch.

"Listen, if he gives you any trouble, you let me know. He's not too big I can't box his ears."

But there are 3,000 miles between you and those ears, Rosa thought, as the food arrived.

Yeah, I'm fucked, thought Bell when his only afternoon assignment was a trip to a newsstand for week-old copies of *Le Soir*, the

Nazi-run French newspaper. Later, an OSS man he'd never seen before reviewed his conversation with the French woman. "Did you identify yourself?" the man asked.

"I was in uniform," Bell replied.

"You're sure this is everything she said?"

"Everything," Bell said.

The conversation took place in Tyler's office, the lieutenant sitting behind his desk, observing with his fingertips pressed against his lips. "That will be all, Corporal," Tyler said, dismissing Bell.

Now it was past 7 o'clock and Bell wondered if Tyler and the OSS would let him know what was going on. Maybe he could pitch in. It'd be a chance to make good, Bell thought as he grabbed his hat, locked his little room and went upstairs to see the lieutenant.

As he turned up to the third floor, Landis was standing in the hall in dinner dress, talking to someone who was blocked from view by a column.

"Leo," he said. "Hold on."

Stunned, Bell skidded to a stop.

Landis came down the steps. Bell froze in place, convinced he was about to be chewed to shreds. But Landis jutted out his right hand. "Leo, I'm glad I've run into you. I wanted to thank you personally for your work on the report."

"Sir?"

Landis beamed. "That is *exactly* what we need, boy. Exactly. Fresh thinking."

Confused, Bell said, "I was hoping I hadn't overstepped my bounds, sir."

"Glad you did." He clapped him on the shoulder. "Glad you did."

A week later, the beneficiary of an unexpected two-day pass, Bell, in uniform, was riding in Benno's truck, the scent of provolone lingering despite the Boraxo. Benno was dressed nice in a blue suit, his plan being to crash a dance up at St. Claire's Nursing School in Jersey City. Benno figured if he don't show, the girls would be stuck jitterbugging with each other, and he don't mind Leo tagging along, though he could see him standing shy over there by the punch bowl all night.

Bell told him why he was suddenly free, leaving out details of the report but boasting a bit on taking a shot at a step up.

"And then what happened?" Benno asked. He had to turn his head to see Bell, who was seated on his blind side.

"That's it. 'Glad you did, my boy.' Nothing else. I go back to work, Tyler more or less leaves me be, says hello in the cafeteria and then a two-day pass."

"What exactly is it you do again?"

"Again? I never told you what I do."

"You're in the Ivy League."

"What's the Ivy League, Sal?"

Benno swerved to dodge a pothole. "I could find out what you do."

"Like hell you can."

"I'll ask Mimmo."

Bell laughed.

"What? Mimmo's not good enough to talk to you no more?"

"I didn't say that. But Mimmo's not privy to everything. These guys are airtight."

Benno snorted as he slowed for a red light.

Bell said, "So now you're telling me Mimmo's smart?"

"I'm telling you this guy knows more than you think. You and the Ivy fuckin' League."

"I'm sure he does. But not about the Army."

"OK, smart guy, you think we're so fuckin' dumb—"

"'We're'? Who's 'we'? You and Mimmo?"

"You think Mimmo's so fuckin' dumb, ask your Ivy League pals about Operation Husky."

"Operation Husky."

Benno nodded. "Don't be surprised when they shit themselves."

"Operation Husky. I never heard of it."

"Ha," Benno said. "And you're in the Army."

CHAPTER TWELVE

Eugenio Zamarella had one mission in life: to kill at Bruno Gigenti's behest. When the matter was at hand, he could not be dissuaded.

But Pellizzari tried, seeing as he was in this thing up to his balls.

"Where are we going?"

"To get the whore."

"Yeah, I know," said Pellizzari, who was driving. "But where?"

"Jersey," he replied.

"Where in Jersey?"

"Not in Jersey," Zamarella said.

Gripping the wheel, the wipers flapping, Pellizzari tried his damnedest not to look over at Zamarella, whose steel-gray eyes and cold demeanor made him as scary as he was scarred. "Help me out here, huh? I've got to drive."

"She's in Staten Island."

Though one of the five boroughs, to drive to Staten Island you had to pass through the neighboring state. From Manhattan, the only way to get there was via the ferry, which wasn't too efficient, given the task at hand.

Pellizzari was thinking ahead. "How do you know she's there?"

"Watch where you're going," he replied as Pellizzari ran the yellow light at Sixth.

They rode into the Holland Tunnel in silence, Pellizzari deep in conjecture. A few minutes later, as they emerged into drizzle, he said, "Eugenio, how do you know? I'm just saying. How?"

Zamarella exhaled. "She goes by the name Angel, right?"

"I wouldn't know."

"You go on a hit and you don't know the mark's name?"

"I didn't know we were hitting nobody, my hand to God."

Zamarella pointed to a sign to Route 1. "Go south."

Pellizzari did like he was told.

"Find the Bayonne Bridge," Zamarella said after a few minutes passed.

The next time Zamarella spoke, they had crossed the span bridge, and he told Pellizzari to take Castleton Avenue. The wet asphalt was shining in the sun, and every now and then, when a little lagoon appeared on the strip, Pellizzari timed it so they'd pass through it before the rainwater receded behind the previous car. It gave him something to think about besides how he was sweating under his suit coat and how Zamarella was sitting there without an expression, breathing heavy, snoring almost.

"The hospital," Zamarella said, pointing. Zamarella reached into an inside pocket and pulled out a navy mask, but the opposite of what the bandits wore in the serials. To conceal his identifying pockmarks, the mask covered Zamarella's face from the nose down, with a little slit for his mouth. He pressed it against his cheeks without fixing it behind his ears, and then he put it back in his pocket.

"Park," he said. "Over there."

Pellizzari put the car in the middle of the small, crowded lot.

Zamarella gestured for the keys.

"What do you mean?"

Zamarella reached over, cut the ignition, took the keys. "She's on the third floor," he said. "Put her down."

Pellizzari recoiled.

"She seen you, too. Bruno she knew by name. You, no."

"You know this ain't my game, Eugenio. A hospital in broad day—"

"You shoulda took care of her before. Now go."

Zamarella leaned across and threw open the driver's-side door.

Pellizzari sighed. Killing didn't bother him as much as getting caught bumping off a two-dollar broad who already had a couple slugs inside her. Plus, the insinuation that this mess was his fault, like he should've taken her pulse before he ran down the stairs to see if the other guy escaped.

"What's the play?" he asked.

"Nobody cares. Make good."

"How do I know you'll be here when—"

"You don't."

Pellizzari hauled his heavy frame out into the sunlight. Like he had the other day, he checked his pistol in his shoulder holster, then he walked toward the hospital entrance, Zamarella's eyes burning a hole in his back.

Twenty-five minutes later, out of breath, Pellizzari arrived at the ferry terminal to head back to Manhattan, Zamarella and the car still waiting in the parking lot. Maybe he couldn't figure out how Zamarella knew the DA stashed the *puttana* in Staten Island, but he was smart enough to know that after she was killed, he was next, being the only remaining witness to Gigenti's rampage. All things being equal, he'd be dead and Zamarella would be driving his car home. Now that Zamarella had to put down the whore himself, Pellizzari figured he had maybe a half hour to disappear.

The cop outside her door was a 42-year-old rookie, the New York City police force decimated by its best young men volunteering to fight overseas. He was diligent, stopping doctors, nurses, orderlies and visitors, pacing like a tiger in a zoo. Pretty soon, the staff had enough and they called the captain, who told the cop to calm down. That was yesterday. Today his shift started at noon. By 1:35, he was on the floor unconscious, his dome cracked. Pacing despite the captain's advice, he hadn't heard the man in a mask come up behind him.

The whore's birth name was Ida Muttley. She was unconscious when Zamarella put a bullet in her cheek and up into her brain and a second in her heart, pressing the nozzle into her breast.

The next day, Bruno Gigenti and his lawyer, Nicolo Colla, met with an assistant district attorney. With the charge murder in the first degree, premeditated, and Gigenti denied bail, now was the time to deal.

"You have an eyewitness?" Colla asked as he shuffled his notes.

Gigenti sat back, his expression rich with disdain and defiance.

"We have an eyewitness, yes," said the ADA.

"Really?" Colla said, unconvinced.

"He's in protective custody."

Fredo Pellizzari, thought Gigenti, his jaw twitching.

Lieutenant Tyler asked Bell to lunch in Bryant Park. Of course, Bell said yes, though he'd intended to risk a call to a nurse-in-training he met at the dance at St. Claire's while Benno was out in the truck making time with an Italian knockout from Keansburg, a friend of one of the students.

Tyler handed Bell a paper sack. Ham sandwiches on white, yellow mustard, pickles. Nehi orange soda. Yeah, two-day pass or no, he hates me, Bell thought as he unpacked the sack.

They shared a bench near Sixth Avenue, the June sun bearing down.

"Major Landis is interested in you," Tyler began.

Bell nodded.

"Have you seen the final report?"

"Yes, sir."

"It's your report."

"No, sir."

"Why not?" Tyler asked, his mood as bright as the midday weather.

"You don't tell the cleaning lady it's her building, right?"

Tyler laughed. "No, I suppose not."

Bell looked with suspicion at the wafer-thin sandwich.

"I told the major of your interest in remaining with the unit," Tyler said. "He was delighted."

"Thank you, sir."

"But I wonder if you're not better suited to an assignment overseas. With your language skills and you have a certain demeanor, Bell. The way you carry yourself."

"Sir?"

"I assume you'd be amenable to representing the OSS overseas."

"I would, sir, yes. More than amenable."

Later, Bell would think it strange that a corporal had been asked to approve his assignment. But for now, whether it was the sense of pride he felt in knowing that Landis wanted to secure his services or that the U.S. Army considered him valuable or the rush of elation at the thought that his life might change, Bell was thrilled.

"I'll see what I can do," Tyler said as he slipped a straw into his bottle of orange soda. "For now, keep this between us. Frankly, I think we need to test your mettle."

"Sir?"

"Your commitment," Tyler said taking a sip of soda.

"I don't understand."

"You don't want this opportunity to slip away, Bell."

"No, sir."

Tyler watched the herky-jerky traffic on Sixth.

"Corporal, you tell me everything you hear, everything you know."

Bell said yes without reservation.

Tyler continued to stare toward the avenue. "Tell me something I don't know, Corporal."

The next moment would remain inked in the mind of Leo Bell, also known as Leonardo Campanello, also known as Józef Herlitz, for the rest of his life. And he never could decide whether his question had resulted in his biggest break or his greatest mistake.

"What's Operation Husky, sir?"

Gigenti made bail, posting a sizable bond and surrendering his passport. "Better stay away from Mulberry Street," the lawyer Colla warned him as they left the courthouse in Foley Square. "Don't fraternize."

Gigenti stepped into the street and flagged a taxi, leaving Colla at the curb.

When he arrived at his home, a squat, redbrick mother-daughter surrounded by a white fence that was identical to every other house along the one-way street, he found Frankie Fortune sitting in his living room. Gigenti's petite wife had served him coffee and figs, then retired to the kitchen. Fortune's good looks made her uncomfortable. She feared he'd recognize a long-dormant spark of lust in her hazel eyes.

Fortune stood. "Please excuse me for coming to your home, Bruno," he said in Sicilian.

Out of instinct, Gigenti reached into his pocket for his gun, but it was in the lawyer's briefcase, as it had been through the hearing. "What do you want?" he snapped.

He didn't wait for a reply. He tossed his suit jacket on the sofa and left the room. Soon Fortune heard running water. Gigenti retrieved a pistol he kept behind the silverware. Then he shut the tap and returned to the living room, a wash towel in his hands, pistol in his pocket.

He put on his jacket and, this time in English, said, "What do you want?"

"I have a message to you from Don Carlo."

"You. The Jersey boy."

Fortune nodded.

The two men stood on opposite sides of a coffee table, the figs and the espresso cup near Fortune's knees, his back to an open window, the curtains waving in a mild breeze.

"Why doesn't he call me?"

"Your phone is tapped. Here and the club." With a measure of discretion, he added, "All your phones."

Gigenti nodded dismissively.

"Also, the terms of his agreement prohibit—"

"What's the message?" Gigenti turned his body slightly and dipped his fingertips into his pocket.

Fortune had a stiletto in his shirtsleeve. Staring at Gigenti's right arm, he said, "You have to leave the country."

"I'm not leaving the country."

"Until we locate Fredo Pellizzari—"

"Simple enough."

"—and address the issue in the right way at the right time."

Gigenti was confused. "What's the right time? The right time is now. Today."

Fortune said, "Don Carlo believes Verkerk was a mistake, Bruno."

Gigenti sneered.

"We can't afford any problems now. Not with the feds."

We, Gigenti thought. Like Geller, when Fortune uses this word, it doesn't include me.

"Bruno, everything is falling into place."

Slowly, Fortune reached with his left hand to the front of his jacket. He opened it, revealing a thick envelope in his inner pocket.

"This is enough money to get you to where you are going. Also, there's a passport for you. If you want, we will arrange for your wife and daughters to join you."

Gigenti understood the decision had been made. To refuse would be to defy Farcolini.

"Bruno?"

"I haven't been to Sicily since I was a child," Gigenti said. Immediately, he recoiled at the display of sentiment.

"You can't go to Sicily," Fortune said as he removed the envelope from his pocket. "You're going to Argentina."

Gigenti stared at him.

Fortune slid the envelope next to the plate of figs. "Rosario, Argentina. It has a large Sicilian community. A port, railroads. You'll have a car, of course, and men at your disposal. They understand your authority."

Gigenti lifted the gun from his pocket but kept its muzzle pointed at the floor.

"I say no and what happens?"

"Bruno, please." Fortune was certain he could flip the blade into his throat before Gigenti could squeeze off a shot.

They looked at each other, their eyes shifting from the other's right hand to his face.

Gigenti calculated quickly. He could kill Fortune now, dump his body on Corini's doorstep, have Zamarella locate and kill Pellizzari, and then he would go to Florida to confront Geller. He could do this in two or three days. Then he would be on top of the world. Farcolini achieved his authority by killing his rivals. Gigenti could do the same. For the sake of the business, Farcolini would understand.

"Bruno…"

But if not, he would cut off the flow of heroin from Sicily into New York. Without the drug money to spread around, the waterfront would to fall into chaos. The take from gambling, prostitution, loan-sharking and the other old-time businesses was no longer enough to keep everybody in line. Gigenti would be hurt and Corini would prosper behind his so-called legitimate activities.

"What'll it be, Bruno?"

Gigenti put the gun on the coffee table. "When?"

"We have to move fast," Fortune said, concealing his relief. "Dewey is going to revoke your bail."

"I've got to talk to my wife."

"I'll be outside."

CHAPTER THIRTEEN

Bell was summoned to Tyler's office, the lieutenant back from a trip to Washington. Almost two weeks had passed since their conversation in Bryant Park, and Bell was still at his old routine, running uptown, downtown, crosstown with a diplomatic pouch or a box loaded with documents. He knew the bus drivers by name. The only change: Imogene, the girl he met at the dance at St. Claire's, joined him for coffee at the Automat. She put him at ease and the conversation flowed. She was even prettier than he remembered.

He trotted up the marble steps hoping the lieutenant would have news of a transfer, a new assignment within the OSS with training in Washington first, no doubt. But the moment he entered the gray room, he felt a tension so thick it seemed aggressive.

"Shut the door," Tyler said. "Take a seat."

Bell did as ordered.

"Tell me what you know about Operation Husky."

"I don't know anything, sir. Just the name."

"You're certain?"

"Yes, sir."

"Who told you?"

Bell hesitated.

"Corporal…"

"It's common knowledge in Narrows Gate."

Tyler groped for a cigarette. "Common knowledge?"

"Not common knowledge. Sorry, sir. People associated with Carlo Farcolini know."

"Do you know these people?" Tyler tossed his lighter on the blotter.

"I used to see them in the neighborhood."

"They know you?"

"As well as I know them, sir."

"I see."

Bell waited as Tyler brought a yellow pad out of his desk drawer.

"Names, please."

"Of Farcolini's crew?"

Tyler nodded, then blew a stream of smoke toward the ceiling fan.

"In Narrows Gate, you have Dominic Mistretta, who they call Mimmo. He reports to Frankie Fortune. Fortune reports to Farcolini, but now that he's left the country, he could wind up with Anthony Corini. Or maybe he gets Gigenti's seat until he returns."

Tyler wrote quickly, the tip of his ballpoint scratching the paper.

"Who else is there in Narrows Gate?"

Bell told him about Boo Chiasso, who ran the streets for Mimmo, and Fat Tutti, Chiasso's sidekick. "After that, sir, they've got guys on the piers, in shipping, gambling, prostitution and in City Hall, but they come and go. I don't know them very well."

"Nor do they know you," Tyler observed.

"I hope not," Bell replied.

Tyler looked at him. "Why is that, Corporal?"

"I've done everything I can to steer clear of all that, sir."

"Yet you know this," Tyler said, tapping his notes.

"There's a candy store where we used to hang out," Bell said. "Mimmo owns it. You couldn't help but know."

Tyler nodded thoughtfully. In the logic of the Army and the still-evolving OSS, he was somehow to blame for the leak of top-secret information to one of his men.

"Sir, may I ask a question?"

"Go ahead."

"Operation Husky. Is it real?"

"Oh yes, Corporal. Quite real."

"Is it the invasion of Sicily?"

Tyler didn't know how to reply. It was assumed, by anyone who had glanced at a globe and read newspaper reports of the hard-fought victory over Rommel in North Africa, that the Allies would invade Sicily. But British Intelligence had prepared a plan, carefully constructed and entirely false, of an invasion of Italy via Greece. They let the plan fall into the hands of the Axis.

"What do you think it is?" Tyler asked.

"The invasion of Sicily," Bell replied. He nodded toward the legal pad. "Otherwise, those guys wouldn't be interested."

Operation Husky was in fact the top-secret code name for the invasion of Sicily. But Tyler knew nothing more of the plan. To manage Bell as he intended, he would have to query him without revealing how little he'd been told.

"What makes you think it has anything to do with them?" he asked.

"Carlo Farcolini is in Sicily. He was let out of prison for a reason, no?"

Tyler underlined Farcolini's name on his notepad. "Go on."

"He can deliver his counterparts over there. You'd get their cooperation."

"Corporal, why would the Allies need the cooperation of criminals to invade Sicily?"

"Well, I suppose it would be like the waterfront, sir. Maybe you don't need it, but it's easier if you have it."

"Is that what they're saying in Narrows Gate?"

Bell shrugged.

"What do you mean by that?" Tyler said sharply.

"They like to make themselves sound like they run the world, sir. And we know they don't."

Tyler crushed his cigarette in the ashtray, picked up a pad and began pacing behind Bell.

"If this were true, Corporal, if Farcolini had involved himself in some secret plan to invade Sicily, how would the information come back to the U.S.?"

Bell wasn't sure whether he should turn to face the officer. Instead, he addressed the empty desk. "Two ways, sir. One is that Don Carlo could—"

"Don Carlo?"

"That's what they call the boss, sir."

"Continue."

"Maybe Farcolini told Corini, who told Fortune, who told Mimmo. Or, two, somebody's cousin is in the plan in Sicily and he told somebody over here."

"I don't understand. Somebody told somebody?"

"Sir, there are more Sicilians in this area than in any city in Sicily. I assume they talk to each other."

"Good grief." Tyler returned to his seat, the wheels squealing as he settled behind the desk. As Bell watched, he squared the legal pad in the center of the blotter, then placed the pen on the pad, lining it up parallel to the top line.

"Corporal, until further notice, you will be assigned to Fort Jay."

Bell was stunned. On Governors Island, Fort Jay was the site of an Army disciplinary barracks.

"Calm down, soldier. You're not going to DB. You'll help the First with administrative duties."

"Sir, what about our conversation? I thought I could be of assistance."

"You're not to communicate with anyone about your new assignment, Corporal, nor are you to discuss what you think you know about Operation Husky. Am I clear?"

"Yes, sir," Bell said softly.

Tyler lifted the receiver and dialed a phone number. "He's ready," he said.

"I'm going now, sir?"

"That's right, Corporal."

"Can I tell my father?"

"I'm afraid not."

Ninety minutes later, Leo Bell was on Governors Island. A corporal greeted him, took his papers and brought him to an office where his desk sat next to one that belonged to a supply sergeant, a wiseass who informed him that all he had to do was count, type and shut up.

So long Berlin, thought Bell with a sinking feeling. Good-bye Paris. So much for a triumphant return to Poland.

Operation Husky began on the night of July 9, 1943. Six weeks later, when it ended, the American, British and Canadian infantry and airborne troops had routed the Germans and Italians, seizing control of Sicily's airstrips, ports and highways as well as the shipping lanes in the Mediterranean and the Tyrrhenian. The triumph, which also resulted in the collapse of Mussolini's government in Rome, cleared the way for the Allied invasion of Italy in early September, another decisive victory that made possible the Normandy landings and the liberation of Paris less than a year later.

Via the Gulf of Gela, the U.S. Seventh Army's Third Infantry and Second Armored Division landed near Licata and pressed north and west, following paths cleared by paratroopers who had disrupted the counterattacks. Quickly, airfields at Ponte Olivo, Biscari and Comiso were captured and troops cut off the enemy as it withdrew from the Allied charge from the east. Other units from the Seventh moved north toward the island's center.

On the morning of July 14, a small American plane bearing a bright yellow flag circled Villalba, a small town near Caltanissetta, and dropped a package containing a similar flag, on the center of which was the letter F. The flag was delivered to Maurizio Marra, "Don Mauro," the head of the Mafia in Sicily. The next day, the event was repeated, a signal that the U.S. Army would be arriving in Caltanissetta within days. Don Mauro gathered his *sotto capi* from surrounding towns; in turn, they sent their men into the hills to negotiate with soldiers who were fighting under Mussolini's colors. In exchange for food, clothes and a promise of free transport back to their families, the men laid down their arms. American tanks arrived in Villalba flying a yellow flag with the letter F just beneath the Stars and Stripes. One tank rumbled to the Marra home. The American soldier driving it spoke Sicilian. After coffee and cakes, Don Mauro climbed in the tank to accompany the unit north to Cerda in the Palermo province. The tank flew the Farcolini flag.

Much like the so-called Battle of Caltanissetta, which ended without a shot fired, the engagements on the road to Cerda were civil discussions rather than bloody skirmishes. Don Mauro held a meeting with the local *capo*, informing him of the value of the Allies' inevitable victory. At each stop, Don Mauro asked the simple question Geller had suggested to Don Carlo: Has fascism been good for your business and your family?

On July 22, the Seventh Army, under the command of Gen. George S. Patton, entered Palermo, a critical port on Sicily's north coast. The citizens welcomed the Americans as liberators.

Under a raging midday sun, Bell, in uniform, passed Fat Tutti and entered the candy store. Mimmo was cheating at solitaire while a couple of high-school kids smacked the pinball machine. Another boy was reading a comic, also killing time until an assignment came along. On the comic's cover, Superman was banging Hitler and Hirohito's heads together. Behind the fountain, old man Russo had a cool rag tied around his neck.

"Ding," said Mimmo, without looking up from his array of cards, "kill any Nazis lately?"

The same number as you, Mimmo, Bell thought. But he did nothing but smile. Boo Chiasso was sitting over there, too, flexing a handgrip as if his steely wrists and arms could get any stronger.

"How've you been, Mimmo?" Bell said finally.

"War is hell," he replied, as he adjusted his sunglasses.

Bell ordered a lime rickey and sipped it through a straw. The thing was so sour it puckered his tonsils, but he couldn't think of another reason to come to the store by himself. As a kid, he'd order a lime rickey now and then. Maybe Mimmo remembered.

Bell ran through his mind the subjects for small talk, but nothing added up to a gateway to a conversation about Farcolini's activities. He could ask about Bebe and Rosa, maybe, though maybe not, given the nasty gossip in the newspapers. Corini's nightclubs—no, Mimmo might still be bitter over how he got knocked out of the entertainment business, forgetting he fucked up the Saint Tropez and now was running the Blue Onyx into the ground, paying his whores out of the till, the men gone so couples weren't dining and dancing, the old-timers uncomfortable with the young thugs who hung around.

Bell thought he'd ask Mimmo about that Chinese laundry opening on Second and Monroe. As he slid down from the stool, the front door swung back. "Hey," shouted Sal Benno, bursting in. "You come to see Mimmo before you come see me?"

The idea, Sally, Bell thought, was to keep you out of this. He held up the glass. "Lime rickey."

Benno made this face that told Bell he knew he was full of shit and, in an instant, that he figured out why.

"Mimmo," Benno said, "buy a GI another drink, huh?"

"No," Mimmo replied.

On a long walk up to Elysian Fields, taking Observer Road along the Lackawanna tracks, then to Adams Street, Benno told Bell the number of soldiers from Narrows Gate killed in action was up to 31. He noted that gaining the upper hand over the Japs and the Nazis meant the good guys got killed faster and more often. "The price is high, no?" he asked as they took the crest to the park.

They found a bench that overlooked the piers, busy with work, and the shipyard, where sparks flew and metallic clatter rose, the air smelling like old eggs. On the Hudson, ships moved slowly, angling for a berth or heading to sea, tugs scooting port and starboard.

Benno's hat was tilted on the back of his head, the sleeves of his pale blue shirt rolled above his biceps. Bell stretched out his legs and his Army-issued shoes reflected the sun. Benno dug into his pocket and produced a melting Turkish Taffy bar. He bent it, stretched it and passed half to his friend.

"I'm in possession of stolen goods," Bell noted.

"Mimmo should've blew you the rickey," Benno replied as he chewed. When he was finished, he tossed the wrapper toward a Public Works can. "Let me guess where you went."

"How do you know I went anywhere?"

"You didn't wish me happy birthday," Benno replied.

"Happy birthday." They shook hands.

"Your face is red, so you been in the sun."

"They've got sun in a lot of places," Bell said.

"I'm thinking the Army could've put you up by Santa for what you knew."

True. But they put me on an island in the East River.

"So nobody was too happy you asked about Operation Husky," Benno continued. "Maybe they can't throw you in jail, but they're not going to let you walk around in public until it's over. Right?"

"It's your nickel, Sal."

"Now they figure you could be useful, seeing how you know Farcolini and the crew."

"I don't know the crew. Or Farcolini."

"You tell them that?"

Bell hadn't had a chance to tell them anything. Tyler's instructions were as vague as they were firm: Go find out what Farcolini is planning next. Bell couldn't decide whether Tyler was dumping or testing him.

When Bell didn't reply, Benno said, "You tell them about me?"

Bell shook his head.

"Mimmo ain't going to tell you nothing. You know that."

"They don't," Bell replied.

Benno stood and scanned the park. When he was satisfied they were alone, he sat and, his voice low, said, "Listen, even if they don't know you're a Jew, the Army knows your mother wasn't Italian, right?"

"So?"

"Everybody knows you ain't getting in the crew if you're half Polish. Hell, you're lucky to get in if you're Italian."

"Nobody wants me to join the crew, Sal."

"Sure," Benno teased. "The American Army doesn't want someone who can find out when they're invading Sicily."

With thumb and forefinger, Bell rubbed sugar from the corners of his lips.

"I'm right," Benno said.

"Maybe. But I don't intend to spend the rest of the war in Narrows Gate."

"Why not?" Benno asked. "I'm gonna."

CHAPTER FOURTEEN

Everything was breaking Bebe's way. The musicians' strike against the recording industry meant a shortage of new music for the radio, so the trumpeter's label released an old song featuring Bill Marsala on vocals. To make it seem fresh, they issued it under his name and it hit big, the lyrical theme touching the folks at home who were waiting for their sons, brothers, fathers and neighbors to return.

Klein negotiated a deal with the label for Bebe as a solo act, then booked him on *Your Favorite Tunes,* where each week he charmed millions of listeners with his sweet small-town kid from Jersey routine, taking on any song the producers threw at him and singing the bejesus out of it, almost always better than the familiar version. Bebe mixed boyish dignity and desperation to develop an appealing on-air persona. Soon, everybody was rooting for Bill Marsala. Women lined up at the stage door.

Klein said, "You know, Bill, the appeal here is that you sound like a kid again."

"No shit, Phil." They were in the dressing room, Bebe changing into a fresh suit to rush off to another appearance. "I know what plays."

"Sure, Bill, but—"

"And whatever you do, don't ever tell me how to sing."

Klein saw his client as mercurial rather than difficult. Marsala felt pressure acutely and had to be handled. "My point is, you've got your own little corner of the popular music world."

"Little?" Using the mirror, he fixed his bow tie, one of the three dozen he owned.

"I'm suggesting you take care to protect your image, Bill," Klein said as he brushed his client's jacket. "Don't betray your fans."

"Don't worry about my fans, Phil. I know what they want."

The press loved him, this kid coming out of nowhere, always ready to give them something they could use, a new angle. He hosted a barbecue for them at his modest home in the Valley. He toured VA hospitals with Rosa, a down-to-earth sweetheart. He appeared in a newsreel encouraging people to buy war bonds. Hollywood took note: He looked good on the silver screen. Radio played one of his V-Disks and he had an unexpected hit, the union furious until Frankie Fortune sent Rico Enna to shut them up, Boo Chiasso standing nearby.

Then Bebe's label settled with the union in early '44 and he had two more hits, both tender ballads that stroked the yearning women felt for their loved ones overseas. For young girls, Bill Marsala was the sweet, caring boyfriend they hadn't yet found. They hung his picture on their bedroom wall and kissed it before they climbed in bed at night, their saddle shoes and bobby socks tucked away.

Enna and Klein put him on the road. He played small clubs to cause a furor among his fans who couldn't get in, especially kids who were too young for the rooms. Bebe apologized—"But I'll be back to see you. You bet"—and sure enough, next time around, he played a ballroom or theater, building to an engagement at the Paramount on 43rd Street in New York City, the kind you bragged to friends you saw, holding on to the ticket stub for the rest of your life. Times Square flooded with crazy humanity, the excitement electrifying, every seat sold in advance, klieg lights bouncing off the clouds, cops on horseback. "Look, isn't that sweet? There's his mother and father," the fans shouted, pointing at the dumpy Sicilians, Hennie in fur, Vincenzo in that same old suit. Inside the theater, girls with dimpled knees and fleshy thighs screamed and swooned. Women—with their hair done up, tight sweaters, skirts cinched at the waist, and high heels—felt an ache in the hearts, their men far away and maybe tonight Bill Marsala would give them an hour's worth of solace, his appearance a brief respite from the war. When the show ended, they demanded he return to the stage. He did, sheepishly. He blew kisses. You could see him blush from the mezzanine.

And so on, all across the country, from Maine to New Mexico, Oregon to Alabama. Each city alive, primed by stories in the local press, in the national magazines; Bebe on the radio, his new album a smash, five songs on the charts. Then the big night: The houselights dimmed, the orchestra began, a spotlight at stage left—Bill Marsala!

But a few reporters weren't charmed. Cynical by nature, they took a hard look and saw a façade, a rank opportunist. Men his age—at 28 years old, he wasn't a boy singer, no matter how young he appeared with those skinny arms and legs, jug-handle ears and bow ties—were dying in defense of liberty overseas. Other entertainers enlisted and served, ballplayers, too, sons of senators and congressmen. The draft board says Marsala has a bum leg? He's making a movie with Ray Bolger, a dancer. The studio says Marsala has it all: voice, charisma, a flair for comedy. "Wait 'til you see him," the MGM flack said, "in a sailor's suit." Like there was no such thing as irony.

And of course everybody knew he was running around with any broad in Hollywood who'd have him. You could measure his potential by the women who stitched themselves to his side, the quality improving with each hit record, each tour. He's at La Dolce Vita with this one, at the Mocambo with that one, at Lucy's on Melrose with yet another. The reporters remembered Rosa, the way she greeted them at the barbecue, serving Italian food, explaining the difference between manicotti and stuffed shells, telling them how Bill's Aunt Dottie made the best pastries on the East Coast, maybe in the whole country. They heard he stashed her out in the Valley and wouldn't let her drive. And now she's pregnant and Marsala stays at his bachelor pad in Beverly Hills, his bedroom wearing a revolving door.

Yeah, but what can you do? You write this and the studios cut you off, the label too, you're no good at the clubs, you can't get a reservation at a restaurant, your sources dry up and you're on the copydesk, the graveyard shift.

But the Hearst empire mocked him. They had the clout, and Marsala had thrown the first blow. Klein had warned him against backing FDR in public, saying USO shows for the troops was one thing, politics another when even in a landslide 40 percent is for the loser. But Marsala ignored him and on election night celebrated in Hearst's face, taunting him to rival reporters. Though Klein pleaded, three weeks of attacks in print followed, claiming that while Bill Marsala was catting around Hollywood, cozy with this one and that, his pregnant wife fled to New Jersey and our boys are dying overseas. Finally, Klein got the flow tapped and an uneasy peace ushered in '45. Then Marsala sent Hearst's columnist a telegram announcing the income line on his tax return was $1 million.

That broke it.

By heart, Klein could recite the column that followed: "Mothers of America, when you say your prayers tonight, put in a kind word for our hero Bill Marsala who, though he dances on the silver screen, is too infirmed to march with your sons in defense of our freedom. Mr. Marsala gleefully informs us from his new home outside sunny Los Angeles that he earned $1 million in the past year. Think of how many war bonds he'll buy for your boys with that."

Twenty minutes after he read it, Marsala found Klein on Hollywood Boulevard, having flannel cakes at Musso & Frank's. Before he could slide off the banquette, Marsala shoved the *Examiner* in his face, snapping his glasses and smearing his jowls with newsprint. Two days later, Klein watched as a baby blue Cadillac Sixty Special was delivered to the carport outside his bungalow office on Sunset, a gift from his lone client.

Bebe and Rosa named the boy Bill Jr. Rosa wanted her dad to be godfather, but Bebe thought Anthony Corini, who was running the crew in Farcolini's absence, was a better choice. He sent the request up the chain—Enna to Fortune, who stopped it cold. "He's busy. Ask Hearst," he replied by telegram, mocking the singer. To Fortune's mind, Bebe hadn't changed. He was still a punk. He hid behind his fame and talent like he used to hide behind Hennie when somebody threw a punch at him in the schoolyard. He couldn't wait for Bebe's star to flame out. He promised he'd put him down himself.

Bebe knew it was Fortune who cut him off. Corini liked him. Geller did, too. He earned like Man o' War—the sold-out dates at the clubs they owned, points on every contract he signed, jukeboxes paying off like a slot machine stuck on three bells. He knew Corini had plans for him; Ziggy Baum said so. The way Bebe saw it, he had immunity. Talent was the only coin that mattered. You make, you take. What else?

Just in case, Bebe sent a gold watch to Farcolini in Sicily.

Two more songs from Bebe's debut album made the charts. *Life* magazine ran a spread featuring Rosa and Bill Jr. In the photos, Rosa wore dresses made by Orry-Kelly. On the cover was a stark depiction of the invasion of Okinawa in which 12,000 American troops were killed.

A Hearst columnist called Marsala "the most hated man in America."

The movie musical was a hit, Bolger and Bebe dancing their way through a three-day pass in the South Pacific. Bebe sang two songs. In one, he stood on a pier, his hat over his heart, and sang a love song, all the while staring at the sun setting, an American flag flying in silhouette in the distance. "You mean everything to me," he sang, the lyric hitting home twice. It topped the charts for six weeks.

To stem the heat from Hearst, Klein suggested Marsala donate a portion of the profits to charities sponsored by the *Los Angeles Examiner* and the *New York Journal American*, both part of the newspaper magnate's chain. "How about he kisses my ass in Macy's window instead?" Bebe replied as he tried out his new golf clubs. He made his mind up: he was going to seduce Marion Davies, mistress to that fuckin' hypocrite Hearst.

Instead, he went to FDR's funeral at the White House. They treated him like a *nessuno*, a nobody. He had to beg his way in. He made a pass at a woman at the Hay-Adams Hotel and she slapped his face. He called Narrows Gate, but Hennie wasn't home.

He returned to California certain that Harry Truman didn't know who he was. Farcolini hadn't acknowledged his gift. His throat ached, but it was time to make another album. The charts the arranger sent over were shit—music for kids. The baby cried whenever he lifted him. He saw a photo of Mussolini and his mistress hanging upside down from scaffolding, their bodies riddled with bullets. Then came the news that Hitler killed himself. Everyone was looking at Europe, victory in sight. No one was looking at him.

Bebe couldn't breathe. His pulse raced. The walls were closing in. From behind a cloud somewhere, somebody was laughing. The higher you go, the farther you fall. Fearing bad news, he wouldn't come to the phone when Klein called.

One day Rosa looked out the window and saw him by the pool in his terry cloth robe, sobbing uncontrollably. She called Nino Terrasini.

The doctor was called in. "Nervous exhaustion," he reported as he tucked his stethoscope into his bag. "What can you expect, given his pace? I can recommend a spa in Palm Springs."

Nino put Bebe in the car. "He'll be fine," he said to Rosa. As he tickled Bill Jr. under the chin, he added, "I'll bring Daddy back in tip-top shape."

Hennie called, unaware Bebe was ill. "Your uncle has a message for him," she told Rosa. "'Grazzii dal vostro zio Carlo.' Why is Farcolini thanking Bebe, Rosa?"

Phil Klein drove to the Valley. Rosa explained Bill's sudden absence. "He needs a lift," she added, dabbing at her own tears. Why wasn't she enough? She'd given him her passion, loyalty, a son.

"Maybe I've got the tonic," Klein replied. Though Marsala had warned him against discussing business with her, he told her Louis B. Mayer was offering a three-picture deal. And the record label was willing to renegotiate the contract on Marsala's terms. "Let's call," he said.

"No phones at the spa," she replied. "But we can send a telegram."

The next afternoon, Bebe turned up in their driveway, the picture of health. "I'm back, kid," he said as he hugged and kissed her cheeks. "Top of the world."

She looked over his shoulder. Terrasini held up his hands and shrugged. It was V-E Day. The war in Europe was over. That was good news, too.

Now what? Little Boy and Fat Man leveled Hiroshima and Nagasaki, the Japs threw in the towel and the Psychoanalytic Field Unit at the New York Public Library was shut down even before they swept the confetti out of Times Square. Sure, Leo Bell celebrated like everybody else, getting a random kiss on Broadway that left him weak-kneed, but he couldn't help but think he'd missed an opportunity. He'd joined the Army, and they put him on 42nd Street. He made a mark at the OSS and they sent him to Narrows Gate. Most of the men he'd worked with were on their way back to Harvard, Yale, Princeton. Landis was down in D.C., Tyler, too. For two weeks, Bell sat at his desk, staring at the phone, reading a book a day the clerks pulled off the shelves for him, from Freud's *Civilization and Its Discontents* to *All Quiet on the Western Front.* Looking for information about the missing chain of command, he walked upstairs to the typists' pool, but they were gone, too, their men on the way home. He bought coffee for the Negro janitor. Turned out he had a grandson who had fought in France and decided to stay there. "Paris is better than Normandy," Bell said, mentioning the new American cemetery.

"Amen to that," the man replied as they toasted with cardboard containers.

"They give you something to do yet?" Benno asked. They were sitting on the library steps, the truck parked on Fifth Avenue. It was a chilly afternoon, though the late September sun was bright.

Bell turned and pointed toward the façade. "I'm in charge."

"Of who?"

"Yeah, well, that seems to be the question." Bell looked up at the sky, as if he'd see a sign of an Indian summer. Imogene was back in school, but he was still hoping for that trip to the beach.

Benno stifled a yawn. He was coming down off a two-week celebration. He had made up his mind to throw one last good time at every dame he met since the war began. Not that he was scared of competition, but he figured the hour was ripe with everybody in an ace mood. Except Scatta, who lost her boyfriend when his B-29 crashed as it returned from a bombing run over Dresden. Benno saw her crying in the gazebo in Church Square Park and he held her, rocking her gently. Then he walked her home; the whole time he didn't think of nothing but her broken heart, passing her off to her mother, who was crying, too, seeing as the war would never end for them. He told Gemma, who went to St. Francis to light another candle.

"Leo, I suppose it's OK I ask you now what the fuck you did in the library for four years."

"I was a messenger for a branch of the intelligence service," Bell replied.

"A messenger?"

"I'd prefer if you emphasized the 'intelligence service' part of the job."

"With who?"

"In your own head. Don't tell anybody, Sal."

"That's why they sent you to Mimmo?"

"I think that was an experiment."

"A dumb experiment," Benno said as he cleaned his glasses on his sleeve. "You ain't gonna find no intelligence there."

After his second trip over to Narrows Gate, Bell told Tyler a guy half as suspicious and twice as dim-witted as Mimmo would realize something was up, a man in uniform sitting at a soda fountain and asking questions. Better you should let me read the reports on Farcolini's crew you get from the Army and the cops and let me tell you what they mean. Tyler agreed and soon Bell learned the feds were tailing Corini and were still sitting on Gigenti's phones but as long as the New York crew stayed out of the war effort, they let them run free. Pretty soon, he was relegated to reviewing copies of booking sheets and interview logs pulled from precinct houses throughout Hudson County.

"They asked me why Bruno Gigenti fled to Argentina," Bell told Benno.

"You tell them there was a war going on in Europe?"

"I told them that since Gigenti came over from Nunzio Patti's crew a million years ago, he had no shot at taking over."

"You figured that out?" Impressed, Benno patted his pal on the thigh. "Good for you."

They sat in silence for a while, people going up the library steps empty-handed, coming down cradling books. Surveying Fifth, Bell wondered if GIs had already returned to their jobs in the office towers. As lunchtime came to an end, the streets seemed more crowded than they had in several years.

"So what's next?" Benno asked.

"I'm hoping they can use me overseas. You read about the Morgenthau Plan? They're going to need people in Germany and Poland."

"Messengers?"

"Don't be a wiseass, Sal."

Benno didn't respond. Already he knew Bell felt he didn't do nothing to help the war effort, which was bullshit and if it wasn't, it was somebody else's fault, not Leo's, who could've been killed just like Scat's boyfriend or every other dead GI who were real heroes in Benno's book.

"And if they don't need you?"

"I guess I go back to the A&P."

"You don't have to spy on Mimmo no more?"

"Unless he knows something about the Soviets, probably not."

"'Cause I got something interesting if you want it," Benno said. He leaned back, his elbows on the step behind him.

"Farcolini's got his eye on Stalingrad?"

"Not close, but you got the right guy. The feds ain't letting him back in the country. The deal's off."

"No kidding? There goes the waterfront."

"Nope," Benno said. "It's hands off. The crew don't do nothing and the feds owe."

"You think the feds will come through?"

"They got to. They're the feds."

Bell stood and dusted off the back of his uniform pants. "I ought to get back—"

"You ask me, I think you should tell your guys what I just told you," Benno said, looking up. "This way, they don't send you to Poland."

CHAPTER FIFTEEN

Frankie Fortune took the Canarsie Line to Brooklyn and walked south, the morning sun peeking over the Williamsburg Bridge and warming the October air. The plan was to meet Anthony Corini on the Queens-bound platform. No phone was safe, said Corini, who assumed his car radio was tapped, too. Now he had guys on the payroll who did nothing but clean listening devices out of his clubs. Couple of weeks ago, he had dinner with a city councilman and a Wall Street broker at a chop house in Greenwich Village. Three days later, he and his wife treated two executives from U.S. Steel and their wives to a Broadway show; afterward, they had dinner at Rosoff's—the same hovering waiter in both joints, fed haircut, fed shoes.

Fortune turned the corner and looked up at the El. Except for a trip or two to Luger's for the porterhouse, he hadn't been to Williamsburg in years and he couldn't remember the last time he took the subway. But what the hell. Maybe Corini knew best. As Fortune approached the steep stairs to the platform, a train rumbled into the station. He looked at his wristwatch. Not yet. He had five minutes until it was time to jump onboard, third car from the back end.

Two decades ago, Corini was a vain wiseass who couldn't string together a sentence without three fucks in it, a reliable button man who helped take down Gus the Boss. Farcolini thought he ought to apply the kind of polish he needed to cozy up to politicians and industry captains. As Fortune dressed this morning, he conceded that Don Carlo picked the right man to implement Cy Geller's plan, though he wondered if Corini's veneer would wear off under pressure, the old thug showing through.

"Hey."

Fortune turned.

Corini stepped from behind a pillar. He had his fedora pulled down, shading his hooked nose, and as a disguise, wore an old gray topcoat, baggy slacks and scuffed shoes.

Despite the cold snap, Fortune hadn't worn a coat. His blue silk suit, white shirt and cream tie were out of place in the working-class neighborhood.

"Walk with me," Corini said. "There's cops on the train."

They headed along busy Havemeyer Street.

"Carlo wants Bruno to come home," Corini said as they passed a shoe store with a display table on the sidewalk.

"Now? The DA's still hiding the driver," Fortune told him. "Pellizzari."

"That's not what I'm talking about."

At the curb, they watched a taxi turn the corner.

In Sicilian, Corini said. "Bruno comes back and it's bad." He faced Fortune. "He's trouble for us. You know this."

"How? Everything is moving. Don Carlo is pleased, no?"

"Whatever we do," Corini said bitterly, "we have to deal with Bruno before it goes. We waste time, we waste money."

The crosswalk clear, the men continued their stroll.

"What do you think?" Corini asked.

"I can't argue," Fortune replied carefully. "But we stand with Don Carlo, no?"

"Sure, sure. But maybe he doesn't see the big picture from where he is. Maybe the feds fucking him over has him confused. Nobody wants to make a move on Don Carlo. Clear. No one is saying he's not the boss. The feds, they can put him on the moon and he's still the boss."

"No question," Fortune said in English.

"But he has to see what we see. Bruno is what they call a demerit."

A detriment, Fortune thought.

"Don Carlo needs to see we don't need trouble on the other side of the house."

Fortune decided to take a chance. "Anthony, I'm not saying I disagree. But I take my orders from Don Carlo."

Corini stopped directly in front of a five-and-dime. "Listen to me. You know what fuckin' Bruno can do to what Don Carlo wants? I'm sitting in the mayor's office and he's shooting union guys and whores. What the fuck is that?"

Fortune suppressed a smile. Last year, Corini asked him to blow up a rival club in North Bergen.

"Now you know and I know, you had the go-ahead to take him down if he refused the order to leave the country. Am I right?"

Fortune shrugged.

"What does that tell you?" Corini asked.

A delivery truck pulled to the curb. A man in shirtsleeves came out of the five-and-dime to open the grate to the cellar. Corini gestured and the two Sicilians resumed their walk. For a moment, the conversation stalled.

Truth told, Fortune didn't give a damn for Bruno Gigenti. But Don Carlo went to the trouble of stashing him in Argentina rather than have him put down.

"The fuckin' idea, Frankie, is to make sure Don Carlo gets what he wants all the way around."

"Until Don Carlo says Bruno goes, Bruno stays. What else can we do?"

"Ah. So you're telling me you can't listen."

"I can listen."

"You like delivering messages and blowing up nightclubs?"

"Anthony…"

"You can't see how if we help Don Carlo, it's good for you? You know, owning a club is different than running a club, Frankie. It's what they call esteem."

Another curb and this time a Buick was waiting for a parking spot to open. Corini went one way around the idling car, Fortune the other.

When they came together, Fortune said, "I told you I can listen."

"I'm taking a chance on you," Corini said as he began to reveal his plan. He turned up his collar when they crossed into a stretch of shadows.

Soon, the two men were in agreement. The scheme would profit Don Carlo, as well as Anthony Corini and Frankie Fortune.

Phil Klein did what he could with the press, but the truth of Bill's breakdown was too big. Any reporter who didn't write about it was bound to come off an asshole, especially with the Hearst chain gloating. The war over, the men home and the show-business scenery had changed. No one needed a boy singer. Almost overnight, Bill Marsala's music seemed part of the past, a time best forgotten.

Yet Bebe was on a high. He said he saw a future with golden rays coming through the clouds to show the way. Something happened? When? Tides ebb and flow, the Rockies may crumble, Gibraltar may tumble, but I'm still standing, no? I'm still singing my tune. Box me in and this baby zooms.

"We need a plan, Bill," Klein said carefully. For weeks, he felt like he'd been talking to a kid on a pogo stick.

"What are you worried about? I told you. I've shown them before. I'll show them again."

Here we go, Terrasini thought.

They were in Bebe's bungalow on the MGM lot, Terrasini sitting over by the piano, Bebe with a script on his lap, shooting to start next week. Like he needed a script to know his role: a scrawny "dese, dem, and doser" from Brooklyn who, it turns out, can sing and dance, which allows him to blossom. No longer a sailor or a GI, this character is a stock boy trying to win a girl and please his boss who—what a surprise—is her father. Gene Kelly had all the big numbers. Bill Marsala sang a ballad to a cat.

"Here's how you boot their asses to hell," Bebe said, jumping off the sofa and clapping his hands together. He wore a white shirt open at the collar, boxers, black socks and shoes; his jacket and slacks were on the suit rack. "You book the Palladium. You book the Paramount in New York. You tell them I'm changing with the times. America's at a new stage and Bill is, too. I'm growing with my fans. You know how to play it, Philly boy. Whip up a frenzy."

Klein nodded. "Sure, Bill, but—"

"We bring in some new material. Nino?"

Terrasini was sipping an iced tea. "Maybe it's not the material. Maybe it's the arrangements."

"Needs balls, right?"

Terrasini nodded.

"Phil, talk to the label. Tell them I want to meet some new blood. Tell them Bill Marsala is ready to fly."

Klein decided he'd better write down his instructions. Marsala had a way of denying he'd given an order when it flopped.

"The press," Marsala continued, his energy mounting. "Bring in the friendlies."

Klein looked up from his notepad. "You sure you want to talk to the press?"

"Sure. Why not?"

"Make it the music press," Terrasini said. The regular columnists would ask about Rosa. Bebe's constant catting didn't do much to combat the rumors that their marriage was on the rocks.

"I don't care who," the singer said as he went for his suit. "Friendlies. Guys who can dig where I'm headed. Guys who know this train is an express to the land of milk and honey."

Terrasini stood.

Klein looked his watch. "Bill, don't forget your three o'clock with the second-unit director."

"Blow it off."

"Bill, you asked for the meeting."

"I'm gone, Philly. Gone."

He checked himself in the full-length mirror. The suit sat right. It'd better. Handmade. Eight hundred bills. "Never—never—count out this beautiful boy," he said as he stared into his own eyes.

"Bebe, you need a lift?" Terrasini asked.

He shook his head. "Flying solo."

Klein followed him toward the bungalow door. "Bill, where can I reach you?" he asked urgently.

"You can't."

A broad, Terrasini thought.

Klein and Terrasini could hear him whistling a happy tune as his Cadillac convertible turned over with a roar.

Snapping his notepad shut, Klein let out a long, tired breath.

"Yeah," said Terrasini. "Boing boing."

Leo Bell was lying on his back, hands behind his head, Imogene's naked thigh slung over him, wiry auburn hair between her legs tickling his hip, her head on his shoulder as she purred contently. He was staring at the ceiling, water stains, light bulb and string, when the telephone in the hall rang.

He wriggled free. Imogene stirred and pulled up the top sheet.

Bell slipped into his trench coat, his bare feet creaking the coarse floorboards. Only Benno had the number, but he thought the phone was in the Bells' brownstone, not in a one-room flop under the 14th Street viaduct that he rented from a liquor distributor he met at the A&P. The apartment wasn't much—bed, third-hand dresser, little row of books, some blinds and curtains Imogene contributed—but it allowed Bell and his girl to get away.

"I need a meet," Benno said. He was in a booth in the Lackawanna station, the morning rush gone. "Come for lunch."

Bell returned to his room, threw off his coat and tossed back the sheet, exposing the candy-cheeked girl.

"Leo," Imogene groaned, "please." She rolled onto her stomach.

Bell gave her a gentle slap on the rump, then leaned down and kissed her where the blow had struck.

She spun and sat up, raising her knees, her thighs pressing against her pink nipples and plump breasts.

"I've got to run," he said.

"Tyler?"

He groaned. "Don't remind me."

"Don't remind you that your former lieutenant says he sees big things for you?"

"Big things. Giant things. Sure." The war ended almost a year ago, but Bell believed if he hadn't decided to return to Fort Jay on Governors Island, he'd still be sitting in the library staring at the phone. At least they boosted him to sergeant before the Army sent him packing.

"Let's shower at your dad's house," she teased.

"No can do. They've got showers in the dorms, right?"

"Showers, soap even. But not my Leo." She bounced to the side of the bed and opened her arms. Bell stepped in and put his thigh against her cheek.

As she stood, she said, "Escort me to the bathroom?"

He helped her slip into his coat.

"That shin isn't getting better," she said, pointing with her brush to his purple egg. Offloading a truck behind the supermarket, he'd bashed it on a hand truck. "We ought to lance it."

"You're not a nurse yet," Bell replied as he opened the door.

"And you're not a college boy yet, either. But I think we're cute."

She scurried toward the rusty bathroom, Bell watching her freckled calves, the bottoms of her bare feet. She blew him a kiss before closing the door.

"What's this? Halloween?" Benno said.

Bell wore a gray V-neck sweater and white T-shirt, chinos with cuffs, argyle socks and penny loafers. He carried a book from the Narrows Gate library.

"What's up, Sal?" Bell replied wearily. On Benno's table was a braid of fresh mozzarella, some sliced *capicolla* and salami, a loaf of bread from Dommie's and *carciofi* in oil with *peperoncino*. As he sat, he rolled up a sliver of salami and took a bite.

"Maybe you want some mayonnaise?" Benno asked. He tilted his head to read the book's spine. "*Philosophy of the Common Task*. Means what?"

Bell pushed the book across the table, spreading the silverware.

Benno turned the chair, sat with his arms on its back rails. "Mimmo says Frankie has a task for me."

"A task? What's a task?"

Beyond the door, hunched widows in black navigated the aisles, Vito following with a wire basket to help while Sal was on his lunch break.

"He don't say. You think this is it?"

"All through the war they leave you alone and now..." Bell paused thoughtfully. "A guy like you—no jail time, comes and goes, eager, loyal."

"I'm useful. To do what?"

"Pick up and deliver," Bell said as he reached for the bread.

"You know, Mimmo said not to tell you." He popped a piece of cheese in his mouth and closed his eyes in bliss: It was like eating a milky cloud. "So walk out like I ain't said."

"I can finish the fuckin' sandwich, Sal?"

Benno wiped his fingers on his apron. "Put your nose in the book. Look like you don't know nothing worth nothing."

"Sure. But don't kill anybody until I come back," Bell said.

"Leo," Benno said seriously. "You think that?"

Bell shook his head. But he was thinking they were giving Benno a task Fortune couldn't assign to Boo Chiasso or Fat Tutti. Maybe that fuckin' primate Mimmo is serving up Sal.

They ate in silence. Benno's aunt waddled in with a cannellini salad, patted Bell's cheek and stood on her toes to kiss him on top of his head. "*Ti amo, Leo*," she said.

"Me too, Aunt Gemma," he replied.

CHAPTER SIXTEEN

The Paramount was elbow to elbow all the way to the upper mezzanine. Not a sellout, but damned close. With Broadway and the jazz haunts nearby, almost any other singer in the country would kill to draw 2,800 fans in New York on a Tuesday night.

He'd hit a home run at the Hollywood Palladium. "Marsala Magic," the West Coast press called it. The boy singer could make it work as a man after all. His music might trump the crude element in his personality. "I've made mistakes," Marsala admitted to a writer from *Metronome* magazine. "But true-blue fans who gave their hearts—and I'm lucky I've got them, believe me—they forgive."

For the New York engagement, Klein had worked the press twice as hard. "A mature Marsala," they wrote. "He's still the voice of our times." "Can Marsala, the big thing during the war years, be the next big thing, too?" they asked. By showtime, anticipation ruled Times Square. Women who'd once worn bobby socks while they slow-danced to his tunes arrived high-stylish and eager on the arms of their dates, men who had served overseas and come home triumphant. His new followers, kids who felt the promise of romance in his baritone, hurried giddy past the box office.

"A great love song is never dated," Marsala had said from the stage in Hollywood. When he began to sing, entering tenderly, his voice floating above the reeds and brass, Tinseltown sighed. They would tonight, too. The Paramount lights dimmed. A squeal. A few girls rushed the stage. Men laughed at the spectacle.

Playing soft and warm, the orchestra rose from the pit, the music drifting easy like a summer's breeze. Four bars into the second verse, a bright spot lit the wings. Marsala appeared, thin and fit in his tux, his blue eyes sparkling. As he glided toward the microphone at center stage, everybody in the Paramount rose from their seats. Cheering echoed throughout the cavernous theater.

As the orchestra let the wistful music unfold, the singer clasped the microphone stand. Radiating confidence and maturity, he gazed into the crowd, a modest smile on his lips. "Embrace me, my sweet embraceable you…"

Women nodded in reply and began to sway.

Deeper, sturdier than during the war, Marsala's baritone drifted above the silky orchestra. "Above all, I love all the many charms about you…"

Their eyes closed, the women leaned against their dates. They were gone, adrift in reverie. Someone was stroking them, running his thumb along the outer edge of their ears, breathing on their necks, inching closer, his hips touching theirs, heat on their thighs.

Marsala shifted his jaw ever so slightly as he held the note and swept his hand toward the audience. "Don't be a naughty baby…"

Seven, maybe eight rows from the stage, a gangly man in Navy blues climbed onto his seat, then planted a foot on each armrest.

"Come to Papa, come to Papa, do…"

"Coward!" Navy shouted, his coarse voice rising above the music. "Coward!"

He flung something at Bebe. An egg. It hit him in the chest.

Puzzled, Bebe looked at the front of his tuxedo.

The women snapped back as if stung. They stared up at their dates.

Another egg hit Bebe square on the head and splattered, shells clinging to his shoulder.

"Coward!"

Holding onto his dignity, Marsala backed away from the spotlight, palms open at his sides.

The music stumbled to dissonance and then trickled to stop. The audience murmured in confusion. As the cops rushed in from the wings, Nino Terrasini raced across the stage and pulled Marsala to safety.

Another egg landed harmlessly near the bandstand.

As women pointed, the cops yanked Navy down toward the stage, his heels dragging the carpet. Struggling, his arms locked behind him, he was rushed up a short flight of stairs to an exit. A couple of cops, nightsticks in their fists, guarded the door as a few angry men approached from the audience.

A few minutes later, a nervous announcer in an ill-fitting dinner jacket took the mic and said, "Mr. Marsala, you'll be delighted to note, ladies and gentlemen, was unharmed. A change of wardrobe and he'll return shortly. Mr. Marsala thanks you for your patience."

A fistfight in the balcony spilled into the upstairs vestibule. A woman screamed. At the stage, a cop raised his nightstick to ward off the advancing crowd, officers and grunts side by side, eager to rescue the Navy man.

The spell broken, the women debated whether to stay. The men were ready to leave. They'd seen a man in uniform taken down to protect a singer who'd remained at home.

Nino Terrasini found Navy behind the theater, tossed aside. He pressed his forearm across his throat and drove him between garbage bins until he hit brick. Then he let him go. The kid was drunk. His eyes rolled in his head.

"He's a coward," Navy gasped, "Four-F—for fuckin' coward." Then he dropped to his hands and knees.

Suddenly, Terrasini was thrown forward.

Boo Chiasso and Fat Tutti filled the alley. Chiasso's square jaw quivered as his teeth clenched. He turned to Terrasini. "Beat it," he said.

Terrasini retreated toward 43rd Street.

The two big men began to stomp Navy, mashing him into the murky concrete. Grunting, they pounded his spine and the back of his head. Blood spurted from a fractured nose. Tutti flopped to his knees, clamped Navy's wrist, and held his throwing arm hard against the ground. Chiasso drew up, inhaled and with a bestial grumble, stomped Navy's elbow. It snapped.

Navy howled. Then he fainted.

The two big men looked at each other. Clapping their hands like they were knocking off chalk dust, they headed west, lost in the crowd in Times Square.

Marsala came out casual as the band resettled, the house lights still up. The milling, murmuring audience grew quiet when they saw him.

Strolling to center stage with a fresh jacket draped on his arm, his collar undone, he took the microphone.

"What do you say, folks? How about we take it from the top?"

"We love you, Bill," shouted someone up in the mezzanine.

"That goes double for me, baby," he replied. The remaining crowd cheered.

Ten minutes later, the lights dimmed, he returned dressed in a fresh tux. As the strings ushered him to Gershwin again, he eased across the stage to the spotlight as if nothing had happened. "Embrace me..."

Marsala's voice retained its honey tone. But he'd lost his swagger. He hurried the set, and when he left the stage, he told Terrasini to get the car now, no encore, and he went back to the St. Regis Hotel without changing his clothes, pancake makeup on his cheeks, sweat dribbling down his back. He waved off Terrasini's suggestion of dinner at Leone's, though they loved him there, his picture hanging in the vestibule.

"I show my face after what they did to me?" Marsala barked.

"Bebe," Terrasini said. "One kid with a grudge."

Showered, Marsala paced the hotel suite in his slippers, his robe fluttering. He chain-smoked Chesterfields and threw back the Johnny Walker.

To distract him, Terrasini said, "Mimmo came through."

"Nobody dies of a broken elbow."

"I'm saying you got friends. Instead of boiling over, why not take it easy? Call Rosa." He looked at the clock on the mantle. "It's still early out in California."

"And tell her what? Tell her they pelted her husband with rotten eggs?" He stopped at the ashtray. "That gets me off her shit list?"

"How about we go over to see your mother?"

Marsala shot him a look.

Terrasini dropped on the sofa. "I'm fresh out, Bebe," he said. "Maybe you got an idea."

Marsala hurried to his bedroom and returned with his address book, quickly thumbing through pages.

Terrasini sagged. "Which, Bebe?"

Marsala threw out a name. An actress who played supporting roles in Hollywood but was big on Broadway. Tall and stately, she had 10 years on Marsala, maybe 15 for all they knew, but she was firm, quietly flirtatious and a demon in bed. Her husband, who was old enough to be her father, was overseas making a picture for RKO.

Marsala tossed the address book to Terrasini. "You call," he said. "Get her to come to the phone."

"Bebe, is this the way to go? Somebody sees you—"

"Nino, make the fuckin' call."

Marsala came back to the St. Regis around four in the morning, took a shower and threw himself into bed. When he was on the road, he needed a pill, sometimes two, to get in the required eight or nine hours. Waking up was an unpleasant chore, no longer the reward for a quality sleep sweetened by a few extra minutes shaking it off. No dreams either, at least none he could recall.

Midafternoon, he creaked out of bed, went to the dresser and avoiding the mirror, withdrew a fresh pair of boxer shorts. Knees and ankles cracked as he walked into the adjoining room. The curtains were drawn.

Nino Terrasini and Phil Klein stood as he entered. Klein's face was etched with trepidation, though he was relieved that his client hadn't brought the married actress back to the hotel after drinks in public at the Rainbow Grill.

Marsala ran his tongue over his teeth. A Chesterfield, and Klein offered a light. "So," he said, "how bad?"

"Nothing in the morning papers," Klein replied. He looked every minute of his 58 years on earth. "Afternoon papers…It could be tough. The *Journal American*."

"Fuck Hearst," Marsala said, as he picked a tiny tobacco leaf from his bottom lip. "Winchell?"

"He'll play ball." Klein brightened. "I told MGM the boy who threw the eggs had a screw loose. Shell-shocked from the war. It's a disgrace they let a kid like that in the Paramount."

Terrasini said, "We leave in ninety, Bebe. Three shows today."

On stage, 40 minutes of peace. Marsala walked away on stick legs.

"The photos, Bill," Klein said hurriedly. "Seven hundred to kill them. Nino burned the negatives."

Last thing Marsala needed were pictures of him in the press wearing egg yolk and shells.

"And Bill…"

Klein's mother hen routine annoyed the living shit out of him. Halfway across the suite, Marsala stopped and told Terrasini to order breakfast.

"Bill," Klein repeated.

Marsala stared at him.

"Rosa's here," Klein said.

Shit. "Where's here, Phil? New York? The hotel?"

"She's at your mother's."

Marsala exhaled wearily. "Oh that is just fuckin' fabulous." He hit each word with flawless diction, just like he did a Larry Hart lyric. Then he headed for the shower.

Benno arrived at the candy store at the appointed time, the sun way up in the sky. Boo Chiasso sent him through the back, past pisser boy and the stout brown birds dipping in the fountain. And there in Mimmo's kitchen was Frankie Fortune.

"Where's the food?" Fortune asked.

Confused, Benno said, "What food?"

Fortune nudged him back toward the door. "Mimmo didn't tell you?"

"I guess not, Frankie," Benno replied earnestly.

"Look," Fortune said, his voice low, "put together a bundle for three guys and take it up to the Palace Motor Lodge. You know it?"

He did. On Tonnelle Avenue in Jersey City, two stories, painted a beigy pink. Truckers spent the night. It had hourly rates, too.

"They usually get from Santucci's, but they're closed this week. It's a break for your family."

"Three guys…"

"Two cops. Don't let anybody see you're making a delivery."

"I can use my uncle's car."

"Make it good, Sal. Better than Santucci's."

"You got it, Frankie."

Fortune gave him a thin envelope, sealed. "For the third guy."

Benno put it in his jacket pocket.

"Ask for Corduroy," Fortune said, as he went to open the door.

Shortly after noon, Benno took his uncle's rasping Ford and rattled up the plank road into Jersey City. After going local streets, he started down to Tonnelle Avenue, a steep grade, but the brakes held pretty good. He had his elbow out the window, his jacket folded nice on the passenger seat. If he could get some business for his aunt and uncle, swell. He put together something different— a pound and a half of sliced prosciutto, a pound of provolone, some hot meatballs in aluminum foil in case they don't want a cold sandwich, and frying peppers stuffed with mushrooms in oil. Six loaves of fresh bread from Dommie's. He was going to throw in some Chianti for good will, but then he remembered cops.

To make a left across Tonnelle Avenue, Benno straightened his arm and when he caught a break in traffic, he bounced the Ford into the courtyard. A few cars were parked here and there, away from the trucks big enough for the long haul. Cutting the engine, he jumped out and slipped into his jacket; maybe this Santucci comes with gravy stains on his apron. Then he went to the manager's office, put the box on the counter and said, "I'm here for Corduroy."

The manager stunk like iodine. Looking over his magazine, he said, "Where's Vinnie?"

"Santucci? They're closed."

He rubbed his scruffy chin. "Who's got mine?"

"Vinnie," Benno replied. Fuckin' dope.

"Room 231," he told him. "Second floor. I'm supposed to call."

Benno trudged up the stairs. The room was all the way on the other side of the lodge, over by the soda machine. Halfway there, Benno saw the door open and a uniformed cop came out. Hand on his service revolver, he walked toward Benno.

"Who are you?"

"This is for you guys," he replied. "Santucci's is closed."

They drew closer. "Put it down," the Jersey City cop said.

Benno laid the box on the walkway. Then he put his hands up by his hat.

The cop patted him down.

"OK?" Benno asked.

"Let's go."

Lifting the box, Benno followed all the way to room 231. A detective was inside, and right away Benno saw they had room 229, too, and whoever was hiding in there had the radio on.

"Freddy," shouted the detective. "Lunch."

Fredo Pellizzari lumbered in, no shoes under his gray slacks, no shirt, curly hair sticking out of the top of his undershirt, his suspenders hanging down. He put on about 20 pounds since the feds stashed him after Gigenti's crew started the clean-up following the hit on the union head Verkerk.

"Hot and cold," the uniform added. He looked up satisfied. "Where did you say this is from?"

"From heaven," Benno replied. "*Mangia.*"

Pellizzari looked at the cops as they peeled wax paper.

Benno tapped Gigenti's driver on the ass with the envelope. Pellizzari pocketed it quickly as the detective pried open a loaf of bread with his thumbs.

"Fellas, make me a meatball while I wash up," Pellizzari said with a Sicilian accent. "If you don't mind…"

The way the cops were going at the food, Benno figured the Santuccis were for shit.

Pellizzari returned dressed, a tie even, though no jacket. He sat on the bed to eat. "Something to drink?" he asked. His meatball sandwich oozed gravy onto a napkin.

Over by the credenza, Uniform said, "Hold on, Freddie."

"I got it," Pellizzari waved. "Enjoy." He opened the door to retrieve the sodas.

And his brains blew out the back of his head, splashing Benno on his face.

Pellizzari collapsed like somebody cut through his knees.

Benno was standing in the doorway.

"You! Get the fuck down!" the detective yelled. He was already by the window, his pistol drawn.

Benno sprang and hid behind the open door.

Crouched on the other side of the bed, Uniform strained to peer through the portal. "I can't see where it's from."

The detective pushed back the curtains with the gun barrel. "Me neither."

Crawling, Uniform headed into 229.

"You hit?" the detective asked.

Benno said no.

"We got to get that body out of—"

Benno scrambled and pulled Pellizzari's arm until the body was in the room. The hole in his forehead was no bigger than a dime.

"The door," the detective added.

Benno slapped it shut.

"I don't see anybody," Uniform shouted from the next room.

"Check the roof," the detective said.

"No. Nobody."

Meanwhile, Benno retrieved the envelope from Pellizzari's slacks and crammed it back inside his jacket.

"The shooter's gone," Benno said, gasping for breath. "Or he would've killed me. I was standing right there. One shot only."

Uniform threw open the door to 229, expecting gunplay. But there was nothing but blue sky, the sound of the rigs on the highway and people gathering in the courtyard below.

"Get in the bathroom," the detective said. "Go."

Benno scrambled. Then, looking in the mirror, he toweled the blood and brains off his face.

A minute later, he shimmied out the little bathroom window backward, expecting to drop some 20 feet. But as he hung onto the ledge, he saw the raw earth below and landed almost soft, tumbling sideways. Back on his feet, he adjusted his glasses and scrambled toward Tonnelle Avenue, coming low around the back of the building, then scaling a side fence. When he reached the courtyard, he saw the crowd and the uniformed cop out on the second landing, squatting behind the rail, pistol drawn.

If there was anybody on the roof across the way, Benno couldn't see him. He decided to jump into the Ford, back the fuck out and get down to Narrows Gate before—

The Ford was gone.

CHAPTER SEVENTEEN

Benno was walking uphill toward Hudson Boulevard, the crest not yet in sight. He's sweating and Mimmo better make a guy boost his uncle a car and this was the closest he's ever been to getting killed, and holy Jesus. Maybe I'm in shock, my brain don't shut up.

He didn't hear the car pull next to him, blocking the narrow street.

"Get in."

Benno bent over to see Leo Bell behind the wheel of his uncle's Ford.

"Sal, get in. Come on."

Benno went for the driver's side, Bell sliding over.

The gear stripped when Benno threw it in first. As they went east, Benno said, "Why are you shaking?"

Bell noted that he was, hands and legs. He clasped his knees. "I thought they shot you."

"They could've. But they didn't."

"Drop me off on the boulevard," Bell said.

"Why?"

"I got to go back and get the truck."

"My uncle's truck?"

Bell parked it behind a diner maybe a quarter mile from the Palace.

"Let me bring you down to Tonnelle—"

"Sal, drop me off and get back to the store. Be there when the cops come."

"The cops ain't coming after me."

"When they round up all the one-eyed delivery boys…"

"*Minga.*"

"You knew nothing about this. Right? Sal?"

"Nothing. Except Frankie Fortune sent me."

At the red light, Bell jumped out, then leaned back in the car window. "You'd better figure out whether you want to tell them that."

Benno watched his friend tug his lapels, run his fingers through his hair and return his hat to his head. Then, like he didn't have a care in the goddamned world, he started walking down toward the sirens.

Boo Chiasso was leaning on the mailbox when Benno strolled onto Polk Street.

"So?" he said.

"Nobody paid me nothing," Benno replied.

Boo followed him along Polk, which was busy with kids out of school and widows shopping slow and sloped. Rolling back his awning, Pete the Butcher greeted Benno but looked warily at Chiasso.

"Slow down," Chiasso said.

"Somebody owes me at least ten bucks," said Benno, who kept walking.

Chiasso snatched Benno by the collar.

Benno spun and shook free. "Boo, I'll drop your ass right here you don't step back."

Looking down, Chiasso laughed. "There's blood on your shirt," he said.

"Yeah and in my mouth, too. Also brains, Boo. Understand?"

"But not yours. Right?"

"Luck," Benno said.

Chiasso shook his flat head. "Not luck."

Benno paused to wonder who could make a shot like that, but he was too rattled to reason.

"It was Santucci who asked you to cover for him. Right?" Chiasso said. "You got a telephone call…"

"Vinnie Santucci."

Chiasso nodded. "You give Pellizzari the note?"

He said he did.

"You read it?"

Benno was offended. "It was sealed, for Christ's sake."

With that, Chiasso went back toward the candy store.

Pride battered, searching for solace, Rosa Marsala left Narrows Gate and took the jitney up to Bayonne to see her parents, sisters and brothers-in-law, nieces and nephews; hugs, hugs, kisses. "No, no I'm fine," she told them. "Don't believe those rumors. Really. It's all part of the game. When you don't hear something is when you worry."

Soon they grew quiet, reflecting on her impossible situation: living 3,000 miles away in a house that was hardly a home; life in the spotlight—the glare, but not its warmth; and a husband whose career meant more to him than anything or anyone. Rosa's mother saw a grim reality. Out in Hollywood, they divorced and remarried, divorced and remarried, playing a sacrament like it was hopscotch. "What can we do, Rosa?" she asked.

Fighting tears, Rosa left the table. Her father patted his wife's hand. "A private matter," he reminded her. "Not our business."

Bill Jr. stayed with Hennie and Vincenzo: an evening with doting grandparents and neighbors eager to see Bill Marsala's son. But the kid was colicky and cried constantly; he didn't respond when Hennie put a little scotch on his lips. Agitated and needing to get out, she passed the baby off to her sisters. Though Klein had arranged tickets for her and Vincenzo, she chose the Chatterbox over the Paramount, thinking her absence would pressure Bebe to visit. In her mind, he'd notice her empty seat and would well with regret.

"Bebe's coming home," she announced as she burst into the Chatterbox. The crowd at the bar cheered, hailing the mother of the local boy who made good, a few flakes of stardust landing on their shoulders. As always, drinks on the arm and Marsala on the jukebox. "There will be other lips that I may kiss..." he sang, an accordion putting a satin pillow under his voice. One drink in, she looked at her son's picture over the bar and in an instant, she saw it like it already happened: teary-eyed Rosa on the front page, baby in her arms, abandoned by the draft-dodging wolf, the Sicilian with questionable friends, the perpetual child who rang the bell then flaunted his victory. Somebody wins, somebody loses. Guess who and guess who.

The vivid imagery drove Hennie to a booth in back where she sat alone with her elbow on the table, her head in her hand, an ache in her chest, acid in her throat. Klein told her he'd heard a rumor that wouldn't go away. Bill had fallen for someone, a Hollywood actress, divorced. A big name. The feeling was mutual, people said. He was skipping work to see her, keeping it a secret, even from Terrasini. It was more than recreation, more than a boost to sagging self-confidence. They hadn't been seen in public and their discretion gave the gossip its wings. It was only a matter of time until the story broke—and it would be big. Klein said his boss, Rico Enna, needed to be told, which meant Anthony Corini would know. For Bill, it could be serious trouble.

A song from '42 came on the jukebox and soon she was remembering how it used to be. Kids from all over the country would drive to the Marsala home, point, take pictures, mistaken in their belief that their Bill grew up in the Irish section rather than downtown. Here, they thought, is where he sang for pennies on the front steps, shoeshine box nearby, his newspapers delivered and duty as an altar boy done for the day—the story Klein spun. Every now and then Hennie came out dressed like Eleanor Roosevelt to offer milk and cookies and some words of comfort: "In America, you can be anything you want. Look at my beautiful boy…"

Lately, though, they didn't drop by like they used to. They weren't camping out, trying to steal the mortar between the bricks, rooting through garbage, putting pictures with telephone numbers into the statue of the Virgin Mary. The fan clubs liked to forward hundreds of letters from mothers seeking her advice, but now, few came.

Still, there was this engagement at the Paramount, following the triumph out in LA. Fuck the fickle ones, she thought suddenly, the newspapers, the magazines with their photographers from the sewers, turncoat fucks, green-eyed hypocrites. Who needs them? The *Jersey Observer* said the hometown boy was still bigger than Crosby ever was. A contract with the most important studio in Hollywood, his name above the title from his first picture. Bebe talked to presidents and millionaires, for Christ's sake. So who the hell are these nobodies with notebooks and pencils?

Wriggling out of the booth, Hennie hurried back to the crowd, elbowed her way to the bar, demanded another drink, a double. Soon, her throaty laugh rose above the music, troubles, if not forgotten, at least swept aside.

Rosa returned to Hennie and Vincenzo's at 11 o'clock, her body still on West Coast time. She felt a little better for the comfort of her family. But she was heartbroken. Confused. Humiliated. Lost. Sophie and Dee looked on as she went up to check Bill Jr. and change her dress, trying like hell to be more than a plump, pretty Italian housewife from Bayonne in case Bill came in. "Lovely," they told her while remembering the glossy magazine photos of Bebe with this gorgeous band singer, that knockout dancer, all over Hollywood, nightclubs, restaurants, the track.

Hennie led Vincenzo through the door a little before midnight. The lights still on, she thought a prayer had been answered. "Bebe," she shouted, arms extended.

"Ssh!" went Dee. Sophie jumped awake, her hair flattened by the sofa's bloated arm. "The baby."

"Hello," said Rosa, standing in the kitchen doorway, fist on her hip.

Vincenzo got the message. He kissed his daughter-in-law on the cheek, whispering, "*Buona notte, cara.*"

With a swipe of her finger, Hennie dispatched her sisters.

At the kitchen table, Rosa poured espresso. Hennie brought down the sambuca, but it remained untouched.

"Hennie, I'm leaving him," Rosa said as she sat. "He doesn't want me and I'm leaving him."

A rush of blood and who the fuck are you to leave my beautiful boy? But Hennie swallowed the thought. She knew it was coming.

Rosa's thick hands trembled on the table.

"Tell me why, honey," Hennie said, lowering her voice.

"It's no good. He's…he's different."

"Sure. He's Bill Marsala. But you're Mrs. Bill Marsala, no?"

"I'm Mrs. William Rosiglino, Hennie. We married at St. Matthew the Apostle, right here in Narrows Gate."

"What I mean is…" Hennie squirmed. "The women, sure. It's…it's embarrassing for everybody. A husband running around like that. But he comes home to you."

"It's more than that," Rosa said. "He's changed. And I don't mean he's, you know, a star now. That I can accept. When we saw him at the Lakeside Inn, we knew it could be big—"

"Not this big."

"No, but I knew I wasn't going to be like my sisters, my husband walking through the door every night at the same time."

"But you love him. So you compromise. You adapt."

Rosa tried to lift the tiny espresso cup, but her hand shook. She started twisting her rings, the thin gold band and the four-carat diamond Bill delivered two years ago as an act of contrition. She looked at her mother-in-law. "I think there's something wrong. If he's not sky high, he's wrestling with the blues. He fights with everybody, tells everybody to go to hell. He throws his weight around. It's dangerous."

Hennie dropped her meaty forearms on the table. "He didn't threaten you, did he?"

"No, no," she said. "I'm not—It's the pressure, I'm sure. But nobody's right but him. The people at the studio, the record company…He's making enemies."

"Like who?"

"Big shots," she replied.

"Oh, I don't think Bebe has to worry about big shots, Rosa. He's got plenty of friends, believe you me."

"I'm not talking about the Farcolinis. I'm talking about people who can take away his career. Don't you read the papers, Hennie?"

"Yeah. They say he's doing good."

"I'm not talking about the past couple of weeks. I mean the past couple of years. Where do you think those bums get that information?"

Hennie heard Bebe's voice when Rosa said "bums." Her own, too.

"And poor Klein—"

"You think it's Klein?" Hennie asked, drawing up.

"God no. Klein…Phil Klein is the only one who tells Bill the truth."

Hennie sat back, the truth seeping in. Rosa was pure. Not a schemer, no two-bit cheat. She loved Bebe when he was nobody. Rosa would've married Bebe if he'd jerked soda at a luncheonette and sang weekends at the Elks Club. The image Klein and the studio built for Bebe—the good child, the loyal friend, the helpful neighbor, the good Catholic, true-blue American, now the loving parent—that was Rosa.

And look at this. She comes up golden, the power in her lap. Rosa was simple but never stupid. Now she sips Champagne with those Hollywood wives and maybe they're giving her a tutorial on divorce, knocking Bebe to his knees, the whole thing blown.

The sambuca could wait no more. Hennie filled her empty espresso cup and drank it until it was gone, the scent of licorice lingering in the air. "You really want to leave him, Rose? With Bill Jr. and the new home? Is that what you really want—to give up without a fight?"

"I want a father for Bill Jr."

Hennie nodded. Sure.

"And I want Bill to be OK. You know, Hennie, OK. People out there know how to play the game. They know the score. But Bill, he's got to have it like he wants it and to the devil with the rest."

Hennie took another tug on the sambuca, its warmth spreading across her aching chest, as Rosa dabbed at her nose with a lace handkerchief, the letters *RM* embroidered in pink and green.

"I'll talk to him," Hennie said finally. "Maybe you're right, maybe he can't see clear. Maybe he needs a good whack." She stood, her chair squealing on linoleum. "Rosa, remember the time he brought the bandleader over and you made manicotti and we had the sausage from down Benno's and that trumpet bastard ate like there's no tomorrow?"

"You gave them meatballs for the bus." Rosa nodded with a thin smile.

"Maybe you should put up some gravy in case Bebe brings some of the guys home. Make him remember, right?"

Hennie saw it so clear she could smell it. Blue flames, garlic frying in oil at the bottom of a beat-up old pot. In go the peeled tomatoes and dried herbs. Rosa barefoot, her brown shoes set neat by the refrigerator, an apron wrapped around her new dress. Bebe comes up the steps, the guys behind him, laughter ringing as he pushes through the front door.

"Hennie, he's not coming," she said. "We both know that."

Yeah, Hennie thought. We do. Bebe had a stupid streak a mile wide. Thank God he could sing.

Bell decided they needed a drive. They went north in Benno's truck, the big moon following. When Narrows Gate was well behind them, they parked on a side street and finagled a couple of Yoo-hoos from the guy closing his roadside joint.

They took a bench outside Palisades Amusement Park, shuttered for the night. The Cyclone was quiet, but if you tried you could hear echoes of kids screaming in terror, the thing quaking under them like it could collapse.

The bulldog edition of the *News* told them the guy hit at the Palace was Fredo Pellizzari, a soldier from the old Broadway gang. He'd fingered Bruno Gigenti for the murder of some union leader. The district attorney's office had been moving him like checkers, keeping him breathing while trying to extradite Gigenti from Argentina.

Benno chided himself for not figuring out while he was still wearing Pellizzari's brains that Eugenio Zamarella made the shot. The crew had knife men and garrote men and concrete men and pistoleros. Zamarella was handy with a gun, but he liked the rifle too—capping some rat bastard from 50 yards out made it easier for him to return to invisible.

He told Bell, who'd never heard the hit man's name before tonight.

"Why aren't you dead?" Bell asked.

"Why should I be? I did what they said and I don't know nothing. In clean, out clean." He lifted his hips to dig into his pocket. "Frankie told me to give this to Pellizzari."

Bell reopened the blood-speckled envelope. "'AC is downstairs,'" he read aloud. "'Move.'" He looked at Benno. "What do you think it means?"

"It's amateur hour, that note. The cops could figure AC is Anthony Corini, but why would he want to spring a guy who could nail Gigenti?" he said. "Gigenti comes back from hiding and he's running the streets again. Now, you got Don Carlo in Sicily, Gigenti in Argentina and Corini don't have to listen to nobody but maybe Geller in Miami." Benno shook his head.

"Only some desperate cooped-up fuck like Pellizzari would buy that note."

"Which Fortune knows."

Benno nodded while he rattled the Yoo-hoo, the chocolate syrup stuck to the bottom.

"You know, Sal, the cops find this note on the body, and you'd be fucked worse than Corini."

"How so? I gave it to the guy sealed."

"You're part of a conspiracy."

"But I don't know what's in it, the cops ask. I brought food. For all I know, it's a bill."

Bell stood. On the sidewalk lay a discarded book of matches. Retrieving them, he set the note on fire, turning it as the flame rose. "Forget you read this and don't be cute," he said. "Let Boo and Tutti play with blood." The charred paper floated to the concrete.

They sat in silence, elbows on their thighs, Yoo-hoo bottles dangling. Benno stared at the ashes. "You think Frankie's double-crossing Corini?" he asked.

"Let it go, Sal, huh? Fuck them."

A couple buses passed and then a guy with a hose started spraying the amusement park's asphalt so it sparkled until it got dirty again.

As Benno looked up at the stars above the playland, Bell fell on the thought that had gnawed at him since he considered the possibility of being sent overseas: Mimmo and Frankie Fortune were going to drag Benno in deep and deeper. They'd already flipped him. Now Sal is the kid who was in on the Pellizzari hit. He's the kid they can trust. Which meant, sooner or later, they were going to use him until he bled. Bell had not an iota of doubt. He was certain if he left Narrows Gate now, one day in the bright distant future when he was sitting in a government office some-where, he was going to get a phone call from his father and it would begin, "Leo, I have some terrible news..."

By dint of his history, personality and ambition, Bell wasn't made to stack vegetables the rest of his life. He was better than those Ivy League boys, he was better than Charlie Tyler. He was eager to prove it.

But Sal Benno was going to spend his life on Polk Street and those Farcolini sons of bitches, who didn't give a shit for nobody, were going to take him down.

CHAPTER EIGHTEEN

Summer was going pretty good in Narrows Gate. Baseball on the radio filled the steamy air that capped Polk Street. Between jingles for razor blades, everybody heard about the DiMaggio brothers, Berra, Rizzuto, Crosetti, Furillo, Mickey Grasso from Newark, Lavagetto and Lombardi. The fruit peddler sold penny slices of watermelon. The stout Sicilian women tied kerchiefs around their necks and sat on their stoops, the floors mopped, the wash done. When their husbands came home from the piers, shipyards and factories, they were greeted with icy bottles they rolled across their foreheads before gulping down the beer. Trudging upstairs, the men washed like surgeons, put their heads under the faucet, took down a dish towel. Then they went over by St. Francis to watch kids smack a rubber ball with a broomstick, roly-poly Father Gregory sweating through his heavy brown robe. Soon dinner and then a walk along the river, maybe a cool breeze, a lemon ice. Plus the swish and sway of girls in their colorful dresses and, when the wife gave her guy a disapproving glare or a clap on the arm, he protested. "Hey, wasn't you young once?" Then he pinched her cheek and gave her a hug. "Give me a choice, I still want you any day of the week."

"Oh yeah. Sure," she replied, smiling sly, something fluttering deep inside.

One Saturday in early June, Mimmo told the Hook & Ladder to turn on the fire hydrants. "Go ahead, Sal," Leo Bell said, nodding toward the spray as they sat next to Benno's. "Dive in."

An Oldsmobile slowed down and took the cold water full blast, its wipers throwing off the cascade. Up the block, two sopping kids with a pail of soap, brushes and towels were poised to finish the job.

Benno and Bell took in the sun until Mimmo pointed and crooked a finger.

"Watch your ass," Bell whispered as Benno left the stoop and jumped the little river running along the curb.

"Mimmo," he said, fixing him with his good eye. "You did good over here." He threw a thumb toward the hydrant.

"You free Monday afternoon?" Mimmo asked, the glare reflecting off his sunglasses. "You got a delivery to make."

"No thanks."

"Not like that."

Benno shook his head.

"One, Bruno's back," Mimmo said. "Two, ain't nobody that needs…What's the word?"

"What word?"

"*Persuasione.*"

"Jesus, Mimmo. It's the same thing—persuasion."

"And three, I want you to do this. I been telling this guy about your aunt. The dish with the herring and the fennel, the rabbit with the pine nuts—"

"Yeah, but she makes that for you, Mimmo. Not some guy."

"I can't untell the guy, Sal. He likes it from the old country."

Benno felt special for a moment, Mimmo greasing him rather than having Boo Chiasso put a .38 to his temple to make him do the thing.

"I'll throw together a crate," Benno said. "My pleasure."

"Do it around three o'clock. I see you ain't too busy at three o'clock."

"Where to?"

"I'll tell you Monday." He pushed back his hat and mopped his brow. "Stop by the candy store."

"You got it."

Mimmo tapped him on the back of the head, a nice little smack. "Don't say nothing to Ding."

Nine seconds later, after jumping another stream from the hydrant, Benno said, "I'm up."

Bell stood. "For what?"

"*Bucatini.* Herring. I'm delivering."

"Who's getting capped this time?"

"Nobody," Benno said. "Mimmo gave his word."

"Well, then…"

"Oh, and I ain't told you."

Bell nodded.

"Want to come?"

"Not yet," Bell said.

Mimmo took a long time inspecting the goods, then Benno put the fish in the icebox and, whistling a tune, drove across 14th Street and into the Lincoln Tunnel, the address of his destination on the dash. Ten minutes later, he came around Columbus Circle and pushed past big apartment buildings like monuments to some kind of class, across the street Central Park, leafy branches hanging over the cobblestones, a woman out of a magazine on a bench fanning herself. Up ahead, museums and everything starched and folded.

Benno studied the address again—no name but an apartment number, 12C—then ducked to find a street sign. Guys dressed like ushers flagged cabs for serious men who didn't swagger and then held the door, a little bow at the end. Yeah, Mimmo was onto something. Nobody living here was queuing up at the Washington Market at four in the morning looking for escarole.

There it is, Benno thought. He let his eye run up the glazed brick, adjusting his glasses to see what kind of crown they put on top. Some building. He double-parked, popped out and with customary efficiency, repacked the crate and hoisted it onto his shoulder. To his surprise, the uniformed doorman greeted him and let him rest in the air-conditioning, the lobby the size of St. Francis Church, while he called upstairs.

"Use the service elevator," he was told.

"Will do," Benno replied, saluting from the brim of his cap. "Say, buddy, what's the guy's name, you don't mind? Polite helps the tip."

"Corini," the doorman said.

Benno retreated. "Anthony Corini?"

The doorman replied with a nod.

The produce unloaded, stacked and sprayed, Leo Bell went in back to help Vernon Buie, the only Negro employed by the A&P in Narrows Gate. Buie served in Cannon Company, 366th Infantry Regiment, 92nd Infantry Division and caught a round in the thigh in Sommocolonia, Italy, on Christmas Day, 1944. Now he hobbled down the viaduct from Jersey City to work under the butchers, which meant he swept, mopped and scooped out the chickens' insides before they went on display. Bell wasn't one of those phony pro-Negro liberals like Bebe, who demanded to be paid for his speeches on racial tolerance, but he figured no GI who took one ought to spend his days stained with chicken guts in order to have a job.

"Vernon," Bell said, as he opened the freezer.

Buie had a cigarette on his lip and an ice-cream scoop in one hand, a headless chicken in the other. He sat surrounded by crates of fresh kill. Dripping blood had frozen into grisly icicles.

"Still hot outside?" he asked.

"Like July. And I know," Bell said. "The faster we work, the sooner you're out sweating." Buie said the same thing whenever the temperature topped eighty.

As he went to retrieve the snow shovel, Bell heard the freezer door wheeze open.

"Sergeant Bell," the man said.

Buie eyed the visitor cautiously. The man was in uniform, a captain. Crisp, spit-shined, poster-perfect. Blond hair, Bell's height, maybe an inch or two taller.

Bell wiped his hands on his apron. "This is Corporal Buie," he told Captain Tyler.

Buie reached for his crutch, but Charlie Tyler waved for him to remain seated. Then he stepped outside. Bell followed.

There was the door, 12C, a gold knocker even, but knowing who was inside the apartment made him hesitate. Mimmo had cooked up something, sending him here, but Benno couldn't dope out the scheme. He cleared his throat. Before he could knock, a door opened behind him and there was Frankie Fortune. In gray sharkskin, he looked like two million bucks.

"In here," he said.

Benno would've shifted the crate to his left shoulder so he was ready to shake hands. But Fortune didn't offer.

Nice kitchen, airy, spick-and-span. Pots and frying pans hanging from the walls and ceiling like a restaurant. A butcher block.

"There," Fortune said with a nod.

Benno eased the crate onto the counter.

Fortune pulled out sacks of assorted greens, the paper-wrapped fish, a Ball jar of Aunt Gemma's gravy with hot peppers, a bunch of olives Sal packed himself, some fresh *campanata*. And a fat envelope Benno never saw before in his life.

Without checking it, Fortune nestled it in his jacket pocket.

Offered a Viceroy, Bell said no.

"Been thinking?" Tyler's lighter had an Army insignia.

Bell felt the sun on his neck. "Of course."

He waited. "So?"

"Tempting."

"Yes. A full scholarship to Yale goes well beyond the GI Bill. You'd agree, I assume."

Bell shrugged. "Yale isn't in Warsaw. Or Berlin. Or Paris."

"But you've already been accepted at City College."

"Yeah. I have." No longer was he impressed by how the intelligence community ferreted out information. "And New Jersey State Teachers College."

"Think the diploma will hold you in high regard among prospective employers, Sergeant? Unless you're following your father in the typewriter-repair business." Tyler lowered his voice in deference to a passing shopper, list in her hand. "Major Landis sends his regards."

Bell nodded. He respected Landis. Stored in the place he kept his hopes was the belief the old man would come through and secure an overseas assignment for him. "Tell him I said hello."

"Heck, get on the plane with me and tell him yourself," Tyler said.

"I've got to work." He tapped the breast of his red apron.

Tyler frowned. "Look, Sergeant—"

"Leo will do," he said. "The war's over."

"Over? You know better than that." Tyler snorted and tossed aside his cigarette.

"I'm thinking about the offer. I know what it could mean."

"Yes. Four years in New Haven, or six, and then you come to Washington and work with us. It's guaranteed."

"Doing what?" Bell asked. "After I graduate, when I owe you two, three thousand dollars…Then you'll tell me?"

"You work for us at State. There's a place for a man like you. With your specialized knowledge."

"My specialized knowledge. You never tell me what that's supposed to be."

"A measure of your experience."

"And what the fuck does that mean?"

Tyler laughed. "Exactly. Priceless. Oh, and thanks for the guesswork on Pellizzari. But Zamarella's got a witness who places him at Aqueduct."

Tyler reached into his jacket and gave Bell a thin envelope. With his thumb, Bell felt tickets inside.

"Open it later," Tyler said. "Also, I'd rather you not tell Miss O'Boyle where you got them. I like her, by the way. She's plucky. I'm sure she knows there are quite a few hospitals in Washington. Many opportunities for her, too."

Annoyed, Bell jammed the envelope under his apron. He'd never mentioned Imogene to Tyler or anyone else, not to Sal, not to his father.

"And Corporal Buie," Tyler said. "Good man?"

"Cleans a fuckin' chicken better than anybody I ever saw."

"You'd have the power to get him out of there, Leo. You could do a great many things. Well beyond your dreams."

With the tickets Tyler provided, Leo Bell invited Sal Benno to Yankee Stadium to see Joe Louis and Billy Conn fight for the heavyweight championship of the world. Before the war, Louis beat him, Conn choosing to slug after ducking and dodging for 11 rounds, ahead on points. Benno and Bell were kids back then, living in a simple world.

Now the truck rattled along the East River Drive toward the Bronx. Benno said, "I still can't figure what could be the fuckin' point of using me as the bagman."

"They need a straight guy in the crew," Bell replied.

"Though one delivery don't make me a bagman."

The cop at the gate told Benno to put the truck where it belonged. But Bell leaned across the steering wheel and handed over a pass. The cop looked at him and waved them on. Benno's truck snuggled next to two good-looking Packards, one of which had a bow-tied driver standing guard by the back bumper.

Bell came around and gave Benno his $50 ticket.

"A fifty-dollar blow?" Benno said. "From the A&P?"

An hour later, the preliminaries done, Benno and Bell went down to their seats, which put them behind the Yankees' dugout, maybe 20 rows of folding chairs between them and the ring. They were surrounded by men who didn't know Louis from Conn, a championship fight no more than some kind of midweek diversion. Eavesdropping, Bell realized Tyler had dropped them among staff from the United Nations.

Peanut shells mounted near Benno's shoes. Out in the bleachers, the crowd buzzed impatiently. To pass the time, Bell looked at the stadium's architecture, the copper frieze against the indigo sky—

Benno smacked Bell on the thigh and pointed toward the infield, the rows of seats blurring in the twilight.

Bell saw Joe DiMaggio and the brunette on his right, a little firecracker.

To Joe D.'s left was that actress—

"Eleanor Ree," Benno said.

And, next to her, on the aisle, Bebe.

"Fuckin' Bebe," Benno said. "A&P give him tickets, too?"

"What is wrong with that guy?" Bell replied in wonder.

Benno said, "Here comes Conn…"

Conn ran, Louis stalked, smoke gathered in the lights above the raised ring. The crowd booed.

"We should've sold the tickets," Benno said after the fourth round. "We could've watched it on television."

"You know somebody who has a television?" Bell asked.

After the fifth, Benno turned, excited. "Oh, get a load of this," he said, pointing.

Bell looked over to Marsala, who was leaning across Ree to confer with DiMaggio.

Mimmo was standing right behind the singer.

When Marsala felt a tap on his shoulder, he spun pissed and cocky, ready to tell the intrusive son of a bitch to grow up and let a man watch a prize fight, for Christ's sake. But he recovered quickly. "Mimmo," he said cheerfully as he stood, jutting out his hand. "*Come il suo va?*"

Mimmo shook it, his expression empty, his anger boiling deep inside.

"Mimmo, say hello to Eleanor Ree," Marsala continued. "Babe, this is my uncle and my childhood friend, Domenic Mistretta."

Ree gave him a firm handshake and a warm smile. With his sunglasses on, Mimmo showed Ree nothing.

"Bebe, you and me, we gotta talk," he said in Sicilian.

Surprised at the brush off, Ree shrugged and returned to her seat.

"Sure, but now? Here?"

"Bebe, don't give me none of your bullshit—"

"Easy, Mimmo, easy, easy," he replied, nodding toward DiMaggio, who was talking to his dame. The ballplayer understood Sicilian.

Marsala stepped into the aisle. "What's up?"

"Yankee fuckin' Stadium," Mimmo said as he turned. Maybe 40,000 people sat behind them. "You, a married man."

Marsala saw the veins on Mimmo's neck. "Rosa tossed me out. You know that."

"She should've cracked your skull with a rolling pin, Bebe." He threw a hand toward Ree. "What do you call this shit?"

"I'm watching a fight with—"

"With a broad who ain't Rosa. In front of everybody."

Marsala smiled. "Hey, I'm with Joe and friends. It's show business. It's good for the career."

"Running around on your wife is good for your career?"

"You don't know Hollywood—"

He jabbed the singer's lapel with a stiff finger. "I know you."

"Mimmo—"

"You keep it up and you're fucked. And me too."

Marsala tilted his head, a quizzical expression on his face. "This is from Don Carlo?"

"This is from common fuckin' sense. Ditch the broad and go home to your wife and baby." Lights flashed above the ring, indicating 10 seconds until Louis started chasing Conn again. Mimmo gave Marsala a cold, crooked smile. Then he clapped his nephew-in-law on the cheek.

As the bell rang, Marsala watched Mimmo fade into the crowd. The rest of the fight, he couldn't concentrate. DiMaggio spoke, but Marsala didn't hear. Ree hooked his arm, but he pulled away. When blood flowed from a cut above Conn's right eye, all of a sudden he remembered Eddie Moran, blood bubbling in his ear, Frankie Fortune and Mimmo putting him out of business and no one ever had to explain. "I love you more than life itself," he'd told Ree in bed at her house in Bel Air. Now he was thinking Mimmo dropped him on a spot where he might have to prove it.

CHAPTER NINETEEN

She was born Margery Mays Reardon, the third daughter of a South Carolina tobacco farmer. Entering junior high school, she declared an ambition to move to Johnson City and get a job as a receptionist. She wasn't yet the most startlingly beautiful woman most men, and a great many women, had ever seen.

When she was 16 years old, her photo appeared in her local newspaper after she'd won second prize in a baking contest. A professional photographer tracked her down, figuring he'd discovered a fresh modeling talent or a world-class piece of ass. Her mother allowed her to move north to model, sending her eldest sister as chaperone. They shared a one-bedroom apartment near New York City's Theater District until her sister met, and almost immediately married, a subway motorman 12 years her senior.

At age 18, Margery tested at MGM. The studio saw her sun-baked skin, sturdy nose, prominent cheekbones, and robust body as developing along classical lines. Assuming she might turn matronly in her thirties, they changed her name to Eleanor Ree, which suggested the cultured daughter of an aging business tycoon or the loyal wife of a conflicted attorney.

Though Metro had sanded her rough edges, by the time she reached 20, the earthy, sensual aspects of her femininity emerged, as if they had been hiding until she could unleash them under a veil of sophistication. On screen, there was boldness in even her simplest movement. She seemed to command the viewer to stare at her body and remarkable face. When executives gathered for the daily rushes, they looked at each other in amazement. They'd seen nothing like it before.

But she hadn't done a thing, at least not intentionally so. Hollywood was a lark, a castle in the sky. They paid her to take lessons in grooming, to have her dark hair styled, her makeup perfected. They taught her to walk, to sit, to speak without an accent, to improve her vocabulary. It took almost three weeks to fit her in a bra that would make it look like she wasn't wearing one. It was ridiculous and she didn't feel glamorous or any more special than a tobacco leaf would have on her father's farm. She felt insufficient, a fraud. Sooner or later, everyone would find out and she'd be sent back to Johnson City and she hadn't even learned to type.

Then she met the man who would become her first husband, an actor, famous since early childhood, fun, well-liked around town, his pictures still profitable. She was a virgin when they met and, after an intense courtship, a virgin when they married. Though they were the same age, he was an experienced lover and she learned fast. By day, he helped her with her lines and taught her how to play to the camera. He told her she was too beautiful for bit parts. Stardom was her only option in Hollywood.

In his memoirs, he wrote that the most achingly beautiful thing he'd ever seen was when she left their bed and walked away naked through moonlight. Until she returned, an uninhibited expression of desire in her emerald eyes, nothing could surpass the beauty in that. He claimed those two images were what every man who ever saw her yearned to witness for himself.

They separated four months later. He liked the sex but he'd enjoyed the conquest more. He found her dull and disconnected and she felt he needed applause and approval wherever he went. But they parted well. She'd take him in when he had no place else to go and he asked Louis B. Mayer to be good to her, unaware that the studio head had been against their marriage because he didn't want his perennial teenage star to be seen by the public as a married man and he didn't want Ree to be thought of as someone who could be satisfied by a boy.

A multimillionaire oil man—a renowned Romeo—was a better fit for her image. He gave her several thousand dollars in gifts, but he was a clumsy lover, had a peculiar odor, sent his spies to tail her. Out of raging frustration, he slapped her with the back of his hand. She hit him on the head with an inkwell, causing a gash that left a notable scar. As an apology, he bought her a house in Bel Air. "Hit me again," she said, "and a house won't keep me from shooting you."

Next came Guy Simon, the bandleader whose dreamy music she'd known since she was a teen. It was sophisticated and mature and so was he. He was full of himself but so were most men she'd met in Hollywood and he didn't seek her approval. He could talk a blue streak and she hardly knew what he was saying; it was like listening to someone read the encyclopedia. He volunteered for the service when the war began and led an Air Force band. He didn't think he was doing the war effort a damned bit of good and he had a nervous breakdown when he came home. He'd been married three times before he enlisted but hadn't touched a woman since he returned—until Ree, after she insisted. It worked. He called her "the pinnacle of his adult life." They were married and so full of modern ideas was he that one of his ex-wives was Ree's maid of honor. He said the two women were suited for each other, and they were—in ways he hadn't expected, though, knowing him, he might've calculated that, too. The ex said Ree's pussy tasted like honeysuckle.

Marriage put the bounce back in his step. He started a new band, maybe the best she'd ever heard with amazing musicians, including Roy Eldridge on trumpet. Anything Simon threw at them, they picked up instantly. They toured the California ballrooms. When the rhythm section stepped out to back him and Eldridge, it was magic. But the kids wanted the big band. They'd come to the ballroom to dance, not to listen. "Fuck it," he said and sent everybody home. He moved Ree into a house in Laurel Canyon he designed. Books arrived by the crateful and he insisted she read. She tried, but she preferred magazines and the movies. Thomas Mann made her nuts. She wanted a dog. He told her she was superficial, banal, a cipher. Though she told him to go straight to hell, she agreed. She knew she was a moron.

She left Simon and he hardly noticed. Then she got the part in a film adaptation of a Hemingway short story. She played the personification of sex as a weapon for power and gain. On screen, she walked into a nightclub and the audience gasped at her poise and beauty. Before the first reel ended, she was a star.

But by then, it didn't mean much. They've poured me some cocktail, she thought, equal parts fantasy, stardom and heartbreak. I'm an object. A punching bag. An imbecile. A goddess.

Bombay gin became her companion. When the picture's publicity tour ended, she checked into Good Samaritan and was diagnosed with ulcerative colitis caused by the stress of trying to match the expectations of others. Simon failed to visit her but her first husband did.

"I never felt adequate," she told him.

"*You?*" he replied with boyish amazement.

She decided she wouldn't give a shit. That's it. Life's a wild ride. Fuck it and just hang on.

For Rosa Marsala, peace settled over the 4,000-square-foot stone ranch in the Valley. Bill started coming home at night, and Rosa saw that his trip to New York somehow inspired a new passion for their marriage. He was working at MGM in Culver City, just 20 miles away. Her life found its rhythm within her new routine: mornings with Bill Jr. at Griffin Park or the lake where the air was crisp, the breathtaking Santa Monica Mountains all around. In town, she'd see Bob and Dolores Hope on the way to the club, Bill Holden filling up with Phillips 66. "Hey, Rosa," they'd say, waving.

In the afternoons, she shopped to make the house as beautiful as her Bill wanted, trying to adapt her tastes to the standards of the community. She loved to sit in the sun while the baby slept, an ear perked for his cry, and read long rambling letters from home. A social life emerged. Dixie Crosby invited her to lunch. She shared a doctor with Walt Disney's sister-in-law, who was home-spun, a real lady of the Midwest. As she waited for Bill to return for dinner, Rosa answered his fan mail, mimicking his signature on his latest publicity stills.

She told him she was thinking of taking painting lessons. "Go ahead," he said, fresh from a dip in their backyard pool. "It'll be good for you." When he said he'd be shooting late, he'd pop home in the afternoon to play with Bill Jr. He was always in a bright mood. He'd invite her into the music room when an arranger visited to work out songs for his next recording—a concert only for her. Phil Klein came by and gave her a paint set. It was wrapped just so with a card from her husband. "Baby, you're a master-piece," it read. "Love, Your Bill."

Maybe it was the flawless sky, the scent of the orange trees, his second top-10 hit of the year, a "swinging little affair," as he called it. It reached the charts despite an unexpected rasp in his voice and a touch of Narrows Gate in his diction. Whatever it was, Bill was happy; that it hadn't reached number one didn't seem to bother him. It seemed he'd settled into his new life in Southern California and he made ample room for her. Maybe his flings were over, out of his system for good. She lost seven pounds.

Turning 29 on Memorial Day, she awoke to a sense of contentment. She reached for her husband's pillow, pulled it to her side of the bed, consumed his scent. She'd begun to think they might try for a sister for Bill Jr. That night, over dinner at Ciro's, Bill promised to take time off, a trip to Tahoe. Later, he kissed her tenderly, met her in bed and in the afterglow, nestled in her arms. Twenty-nine pink roses arrived the following morning, after he'd gone to the studio.

Delighted, she returned with Bill Jr. from the lake and following his nap, decided to put on Bill's new hit. Spry music filled the house. Dancing on air, Rosa would've sworn the baby was smiling, squeezing his pudgy hands in rhythm. She didn't hear him come in.

"Shut that shit off," Marsala shouted. Seconds later, he smashed the record against the side of the cabinet. "Why do you torture him with that? Can't you hear? It's goddamned awful." Shards of black vinyl scattered across the rug. Bill Jr. wailed in fright.

By the time Nino Terrasini rushed in from the carport, Marsala had stormed into his office, slammed the door and locked it.

"What happened?" Rosa asked.

Terrasini shrugged. He didn't know—other than Bebe was furious. At a red light before the ramp to the 405, Bebe jumped out of the car and started marching along Sepulveda, horns honking. When Terrasini caught up, Bebe shouted that he was walking back to the studio to kick Louis B. Mayer's ass.

"I'll go see," Terrasini said, hurrying toward the office.

Crying baby in her arms, Rosa followed.

Behind the locked door, books flew. Marsala swore, his voice raw with rage. Then a startling crash. Glass shattered.

"Bebe," Terrasini shouted. He pounded the door. "Bebe!"

The door opened slowly. Marsala's ashen face was smeared with blood. He held up his hand. Already his shirtsleeve was soaked through. A gash crossed his wrist and it spurted with each beat of his heart.

Instinctively, Rosa put her hand across the baby's eyes.

Marsala stumbled toward Terrasini and fell into his arms.

"*Rosa*," Terrasini said, "*chiamata Phil Klein, por favore*."

Klein called the doctor.

Eleven stitches.

"Broken mirror," Klein told the press.

"Suicide attempt?" asked Louella Parsons in her column, alluding to rumors of Marsala's jump from a ledge when he was a boy. She included news of yet another Marsala temper tantrum on the Metro lot. Mayer had suspended Marsala, contract and the picture be damned, she reported. The not-so-young man from New Jersey was a menace, completely unprofessional.

Bill fired off a telegram. "Wrong. Wrong. Wrong," he wrote. "Get your nose out of the sewer, lady. Nobody in this whole wide world's got more to live for than me. As far as my temper goes, the next time I see you I'll show it to you—by punching you right in your nose."

The *Los Angeles Examiner* and Hearst papers across the United States printed it verbatim.

Rosa took the blame for his injury, saying she'd asked Bill to help rearrange the furniture in his office so they could move Bill Jr.'s playpen closer to his father's desk. When the mirror toppled, Bill grabbed for it and his hand smashed the glass. A jutting shard slashed him as the frame fell to the floor. "Bill Jr. is fine," Rosa said, reading from Klein's script. "A little frightened by all the noise. Bill would do anything for his beautiful boy."

Klein went hat in hand to MGM. Soon, *Variety* said, "Marsala Back on Board," reporting that he was returning to the picture. Two weeks of exteriors in New York City starting in a few days. The suspension was lifted—a misunderstanding, really—and the studio said it was glad the gifted singer-turned-actor had returned to the fold.

Rosa saw the magazine at the Piggly Wiggly and expected to be invited back East. She didn't know her husband was already over-the-moon crazy for Eleanor Ree. The actress kept a suite at the Hampshire House on Central Park South. On the drive to Union Station, Marsala told Terrasini to book him a room at the hotel and leave 50 $100 bills for Rosa. To annoy Mayer, he demanded a double on the Super Chief to Chicago and then on the Twentieth Century Limited, taking his time. Klein begged him to travel alone. For once, he listened and Ree flew ahead to LaGuardia Field.

Before they left, Marsala got into a shouting match with the tiny, hot-headed owner of Romanoff's in Beverly Hills, who, as usual, wouldn't bump a reservation to slip in celebrities, in this case Marsala and Ree. In the lounge, Deanna Durbin waited quietly, as did Van Johnson and his wife. They heard the row. So did everybody at the bar, including Ziggy Baum, who was hanging on as Farcolini's man on the West Coast.

The cops came and removed Marsala, struggling, sputtering, swearing. "You fuckin' Red!" he screamed. They escorted him to his apartment at the nearby Wilshire Towers, a bachelor pad Rosa knew nothing about.

Baum went to a phone booth and pumped nickels until he'd covered a person-to-person call to Anthony Corini, who was dining with a vice president of the American Stock Exchange.

The summer stretched into a lazy season, soggy asphalt, everybody angling for shade, kids jumping in the Hudson when the temperature topped 100. Benno delivered to Anthony Corini every other Monday, Central Park West no longer a big deal. A couple of weeks ago, he brought the food up and the fat envelope and Frankie Fortune hardly looked at him. Benno said, "Frankie, how about we ditch the routine with the food?"

Counting the cash, Fortune snapped, "Why don't we tell the feds you're the Jersey bagman?"

On the drive back, Benno could only see the "you dumb bastard" look Fortune gave him. That's it for me, he thought. Easy come, easy go and I ain't even met Corini. But Mimmo kept him on and palmed him $100, saying, "Anthony knows you work hard." Benno felt damned good about that and he sewed his mouth shut, saying nothing to Mimmo about what an asshole Bebe was in the newspapers, stiffing Rosa like that and embarrassing everybody in the neighborhood.

As he washed the store's windows, Benno was thinking about Bell, who he hadn't seen in days. Maybe he'd drive uptown to the A&P and just say, Leo, how come you don't drop in so much no more? You're too busy putting away fruit? You melted in the heat? Gemma and Vito ask after you. Or maybe you got a broad stashed and what, she's married? Maybe it ain't none of my business, but maybe it is and if you're keeping secrets, I'll ask you why. Have I ever blown a secret on you? I tell anybody you're a Jew, Leo, or the Army wanted you to sit on the candy store and hope Mimmo gives you the next Operation Husky, huh?"

For a minute there, Sal Benno was about to lose his temper, his ears turning red. But remembering it was Leo he was thinking about, he calmed down and admitted to himself he was feeling confused and, yeah, a little bit hurt. Deciding to bury his woes in work, he went hard at the glass, banishing streaks.

Then, reflected in the window, he saw Hennie Rosiglino hurrying along Polk Street. Her expression said she was chewing nails and swallowing castor oil at the same time. Without realizing it, Benno dropped his squeegee and followed her.

Boo Chiasso and Fat Tutti bit back a laugh when Hennie tried to stare them down. They unfolded their arms and parted like swinging doors. Hennie burst into the candy store.

To Benno, Chiasso said, "Store's closed, Sal."

Benno tried to look past him, instead of over, given the 12-inch difference in their height.

"Closed? There's, like, eighteen kids in there playing pinball."

"Well, you ain't a kid," Tutti said, Chiasso snorting a laugh.

Meanwhile, Hennie was across the weedy yard, already past the tinkling pisser-boy fount.

Mimmo summons *me*, she thought as she entered his house. Bill Marsala's mother. My Bill tipped more than Mimmo brought in, the fuckin' greenhorn. People came to the crew's crummy joints on the long shot Bill might walk in sentimental and if it was the luckiest day of their life, he sings a couple of tunes or signs their napkins.

Mimmo was seated on a sofa.

"Mimmo, what the fuck is so goddamned—"

With his finger, Mimmo told her to look that way.

Frankie Fortune was standing beside an empty armchair. He said, "Take a seat."

Hennie's outrage fled at the cold glare of Fortune's eyes.

"Take a seat," he repeated.

She obeyed.

The armchair wheezed.

Mimmo crossed his legs, his hands cupping his knee, sunglasses on though the shades were drawn. "Where's Bebe?" he asked.

"On location. The piers in Brooklyn, I guess. Maybe Rockefeller Center. Yeah, I think Rockefeller Center." She was sweating under her dress.

"He's at the Hampshire House," Mimmo said. "In his room. Or maybe now it's Eleanor Ree's room. He didn't go to work. Not yesterday. Not two days ago. Last week neither."

Seeing she had no play, Hennie said, "Is he OK?"

Fortune snorted. He couldn't believe they were going this route.

"This is no good," Mimmo said as he sat back. "This is an embarrassment."

"Maybe it's the director. The papers say he didn't want Bebe for the picture."

Mimmo said, "Rosa is his wife, the mother of his son—"

"Mimmo, I love Rosa. You know that. She's like my own daughter. But what are you going to do? People grow apart. They change. Am I right?"

"Hennie, you know and I know it's Bebe," Mimmo said. "Let's not kid ourselves. Yankee Stadium, the nightclubs, the restaurants. He throws it in her face."

Hennie nodded in agreement. "He's like me—you tell him not to do something and he does it. First thing."

"Look," Fortune said, coming around the armchair. "Let's keep this simple. He goes back to his wife. He stops acting like some *ciuccio* in the papers. He does his job like a professional."

Hennie waited for Fortune's expression to soften, but he remained ice and stone. "I'll tell him, Frankie," she said finally.

"He's got no right to blow up the career we gave him."

Which landed like a slap. Hennie shuddered.

Mimmo said, "And Rosa. She deserves better."

"Rosa." She nodded.

"Nobody wishes bad for Bebe," Mimmo said, softening. "Him in the Chatterbox, with his cane, singing..." He smiled. "Little Crosby. The sailor's cap. Then the Lakeside."

"It's true. We all go way back," Hennie said.

"So we can say it's Hollywood, the sun, the broads. He's on top of the world and maybe he forgets." Mimmo tapped his temple. "He forgets."

She sighed. "Mimmo, I—I'll tell him, my hand to God. But I don't know what he'll think about this."

Frankie Fortune said, "Nobody gives a shit what Bebe thinks. Tell him."

"I will, Frankie."

Fortune went toward the front door. He found his hat in the vestibule, looked in the mirror and tugged his suit jacket until it laid perfectly. Fuckin' Bebe. He couldn't wait for the day Don Carlo shrugged and said, We cut our losses, earn off his records and the jukeboxes and go find another singer.

Mimmo squirmed to the sofa's edge. A faint trace of a plea in his voice, he whispered, "Hennie..." His gesture told her it was out of his hands.

The door slammed as Fortune stepped into the sun thinking, Mimmo, he gets stupider every day. Bebe's gone, Mimmo. There's no more Bebe. He's Bill Marsala now and he thinks he can do what he wants.

"Hey, Frankie."

Fortune saw Benno at the bottom of the steps. "What are you doing here?"

"You got nobody out front," Benno replied.

Fortune drew up next to him. "So?"

"Hennie marching down Polk, Boo and Tutti with their arms folded. You should have a guy out front."

Fortune shot him a look as he went for his car. Benno watched as he drove off, pleased he came up with some bullshit to cover his curiosity.

A couple minutes later, the door opened again Hennie wobbled out, Mimmo slumped and trailing. He looked at Benno. "Walk her home," he said.

Hennie didn't realize she had an escort until they reached Third and McKinley. She was surprised to find that she'd been hanging onto a young man's arm.

"I know you," she said. "You're the one with the eye."

"Sal," he said. "I'm Vito and Gemma's nephew. The Bennos."

"Your mother...She died young, right? The trolley. It was raining."

"She slipped."

"But your father—"

"Nobody knows where that bastard went."

She put her hands high up on her bosom. "I think I'm having a heart attack."

"Nah," Benno said, though she did seem a little washed out. "You look like somebody who just got herself a second chance."

She stepped back. "You're a smart little son of a bitch, aren't you?"

He laughed. "Mrs. Rosiglino, I got to tell you that's a new one on me."

They continued, the steeple on St. Matthew's coming in and out of view to the west.

"You know my son? Bill Marsala?" Hennie asked. The color was returning to her face, a riot of gullies and fleshy knots.

"I seen him sing a couple of times. To tell you the truth, I seen him also at Yankee Stadium with that actress."

"What was in his head, that kid? Yankee goddamned Stadium." She bared her tombstone teeth, brown from cigarettes and booze.

"Well, Bebe wasn't too shy," Benno said. "I guess Bill Marsala ain't going to be too shy neither."

"They want me to straighten him out and how."

Even though Hennie was right up there with Bebe on his list of all-time shit heels, he said, "You ask my advice, Mrs. Rosiglino, I'd say you should tell him it's a matter of being useful."

Hennie stopped.

"There's no percentage in counting on friendship with them," he added, pointing to his glass eye like it was a gateway to wisdom.

The cute little bastard was right, she thought. It's as simple as that. Bill's got to stay on top.

"You never know," he said as he held out his arm. "Maybe they already got somebody who can sing a song."

"Not like my beautiful boy," she barked. "Never."

CHAPTER TWENTY

The next afternoon, Benno, fresh from a delivery to Jersey City Heights, was sitting on a crate under the store's awning, a dripping rag on his head. He'd sweated through his apron and clothes, and he didn't want to think what would happen when he took his shoes off. He grabbed the rag and, lifting his glasses, ran it around his face. When he opened his eyes, Hennie Rosiglino was standing over him. A good dress, handbag, shoes that matched, hose and she got her hair done. Still ashy gray, though, despite the rouge.

"Let's go, Sal," she wheezed.

"Go?"

"To see Bebe."

"I'm going to see Bebe," he said plainly. "When? Now?"

She nodded.

"Jesus, Hennie, I stink." Benno sniffed an armpit.

She leaned in. "Yeah, you stink. I'll give you ten minutes." She returned to the black limo at the curb.

The driver swung around Columbus Circle and continued along Central Park South. Hansom cabs and overheated horses waited across from a row of hotels, and Benno thought, We go this way and I see Bebe; we go that way and I see Anthony Corini. They

246

should meet in the middle, Corini gives him a good smack on his head and we all go home.

There was a limo right in front of the Hampshire House, so Hennie said something foul, the car stopped and the next thing Benno knew he was chasing her up a crowded Central Park South.

"Hennie…Hennie, hold up."

She'd built up a pretty good head of steam and barged to the front desk as Benno spun through revolving doors.

"Tell Nino Terrasini to come down," she demanded.

The guy at the desk frowned. "Who may I say—"

"Tell him Bebe's mother's here." Then she turned and stomped across the black-and-white lobby.

Chains rattled and then the elevator doors opened. Terrasini emerged still struggling into his jacket. "Hen—"

She put her hands on his chest. "Roundtrip," she told the operator as Terrasini retreated.

The door began to shut and Benno jumped in.

"Where's Bebe?" Hennie said. The cage lurched skyward.

The hotel was class, but Benno saw he could buy what he needed from the lift operator, the tiny pug listening so hard he tilted.

"I haven't seen him," Terrasini replied.

"Bullshit," Hennie said.

Terrasini recognized Benno from the old neighborhood. "Sal, what are you—"

Hennie said, "Nino, where's Bebe?"

"Hennie, come on. You know I can't say."

Benno watched the arrow dip to the right: 12, 13, 14.

"He didn't go to work today, did he?" she asked.

"I don't know." He shook his head. "I don't think so. No."

16, 17, 18.

With the back of her hand, Hennie rapped the operator on his epaulet. "Which room for Eleanor Ree?"

The pug looked up at Terrasini. "Ma'am, I'm not permitted—"

"Come on, pal," Benno said. "You don't want her banging doors."

Terrasini muttered the room number. The elevator settled on the 19th floor.

"Nino," said Benno, as Hennie burst into the hall, "throw the guy a fin, he didn't give you up."

Terrasini dug for his money clip, the one that said, "Nino, Forever, Bill Marsala."

They jumped at the sudden pounding. The door rattled.

"What in the hell?" a startled Ree shouted. She tugged her terry cloth robe to cover her breasts.

Marsala sagged. It was the same goddamned sound that had exploded his peace in his bedroom as a kid in Narrows Gate. For a second or two, he felt as queer and queasy as he did when he was a desperate child. He tied the belt on his robe as he looked for his slippers.

"Bebe!" That familiar grating screech.

"My mother," he told Ree.

"*Bebe!*"

Ree started toward the bedroom.

Marsala waved, saying, "No, doll, you stay."

"Fuck no," Ree said.

Recovering, he smiled mischievously as he went for the door. "Help me out, OK? Charm her. You're an actress."

Ree said, "All right. Fine."

"Who is it?" Marsala winked.

"Bebe, open this fuckin' door!"

"Mama!" He was laughing now.

She was in. Benno and Terrasini followed.

"Bebe," she panted, "answer the goddamned door when I'm calling—"

He hugged her and kissed her sweaty cheek. "For Christ's sake, Ma…"

"We've got to talk, Bebe. Now." Heaving bosom and then phlegmy coughs. "*Now.*"

Benno didn't know where to look. Ree was sitting on the arm of the chair, barefoot, her long brown leg exposed up to there and meanwhile, it was like a tornado landed off Central Park: bottles on the floor, silverware, cushions, clothes, newspapers, telegrams, too; a lampshade dented. *Minga*, he thought, that must have been some kind of fucking. He expected less from Hollywood.

"Ma, meet Eleanor."

Ree stood, but Hennie stayed. "I'm Rosa's mother-in-law."

"Ma, be nice, huh?"

Hennie started toward the bedroom. "Bebe, follow me."

"No, that's all right," Ree offered. "I'll—"

Hennie said, "Don't do me any favors, honey."

Marsala grabbed his forehead. In an instant, he had a headache and a knot in his stomach, too. He turned to Terrasini, over there helpless. "Bromo," he said.

Then he looked at Benno. "And who are you?"

Before Benno could reply, Hennie said, "He's with Frankie Fortune. You understand now, Bebe?"

Staring up at Marsala, Benno nodded cold but respectful, as he imagined Don Carlo might've done.

Marsala sidestepped the room-service trolley. "I'm sorry," he said to Ree as he passed, squeezing her shoulder, then running the back of his fingers along her cheek.

Now I know where he gets it, Ree thought as he disappeared, sealing the bedroom door.

As Terrasini grabbed up sofa cushions, slapping them back into place, Benno noticed a couple of crystal glasses, liquor and rocks, on the carpet.

"You need something?" Benno said to Ree as he sat, his tie hanging between his knees. "Coffee? Your cigarettes?" Not that he felt like serving Bebe's broad, but she was the most beautiful woman he'd ever seen in his life and right now he couldn't think who was number two. No makeup, her chestnut hair tangled— but the cheekbones, that dimple on her chin and those green eyes. She glowed like lightning.

I'm melting, he thought.

"So," Ree said as she groped for her glass, "who's Frankie Fortune?"

"Boy," said Benno, sitting back, clasping his hands behind his head. "There's lots of ways to answer that one…"

The bedroom was chaos, too, and Ree's perfume was overwhelmed by the scent of bodies and sweaty sex. Stepping over a pillow, Hennie scrunched her nose in distaste.

"Sit, Ma," Marsala said as he raised a window shade. "You're out of breath."

Ree's stockings lay across the back of the desk chair.

Marsala eased onto the foot of the disheveled bed. He tapped the spot at his side.

When she ignored him, he uttered, "Ma…"

She dropped her handbag on the chest of drawers. "You're stacking up enemies."

"Listen, I know what I'm doing."

"Really? You? Bebe Rosiglino."

"Don't be wise. They tried to make me out a *strunzo*, Mayer, the rest of them. Let them cool their heels. They can't make the picture without me."

"And this one?" She pointed toward the living room.

"She's a good kid."

"She's a *puttana*."

Marsala recoiled. "You're out of line, Ma. She's solid. All the way."

"Solid? Rosa's solid. You know, Bebe, I think they're right. I think you lost your mind."

Marsala dug out a pack of Chesterfields and offered one to his mother. She inhaled it down to her heels. "They sent for me, Bebe," she said, looking at the orange tip. "Mimmo, that creep. Frankie Fortune was there."

Marsala paced. "They had no right," he said finally.

"Oh, so you're going to punch Fortune in the nose. Like some restaurant owner."

"Ma—"

"Like Louella Parsons."

Marsala sagged.

"Frankie said you got no business fucking up your career. You know what he means?"

Marsala was at the window again, looking down at the green expanse of Central Park, the boats on the lake, serpentine pathways teeming with strangers. "They bet on me," he said.

"You paid off yet?"

He turned. "Las Vegas," he replied. "With Ziggy Baum. The casinos."

"But nobody's going to want you in Las Vegas—"

"They'll want me. Don't worry about that."

"—if first they bury you."

Hennie sat on the bed. She felt lightheaded, sour in her throat. She'd worked herself up good, calculating how to get him to understand what he'd done. She had to put her son in his place long enough for him to understand he had to get back on top. She had to remind him what she always said: Believe you're better than the rest and play the game. Simple.

In a way, she could see why he chose Ree, the hottest dame in Hollywood, the papers said, a magnet for famous men who'd had them all. But you make that move *after* you're out of reach, not when you're cashing in last year's chips, your movies for shit and new songs that sound like somebody wrote them over lunch.

"They swooned, why?" she asked, her gravelly voice low. "You were sweet and small-town, a skinny kid they could love while their boyfriends were overseas. Now, you pick fights, you're a big shot, you don't go to work, and you throw over Rosa—and my grandson.

"This is what the fans see, and they feel like goddamned fools. The GIs are still sore and they say, 'I told you he's no good.' Also there's this Mayer fuck in cahoots with the columnists. You gave them a loaded gun, then you put it against your own temple. Jesus. Maybe you are a *strunzo*."

Marsala stubbed his cigarette in the ashtray.

"I think maybe, Bebe, you should come home and shine a few shoes. Maybe work with your father at the Hook & Ladder. See where you'll be, you don't stop."

"I think I can do better than the Hook & Ladder, Ma."

The weight on her chest was sapping her energy. "Then go up to the Lakeside Inn and sing with an apron in your belt."

Sitting on the ledge, Marsala stared at his thin feet. Leave it to Mama to lay it out straight. There was nobody better at finding the sore spot and digging it until it bled. He could try to explain, but with her, he wouldn't find words she'd listen to.

"All right," he said, as he left the ledge. "I'll go see Corini."

"Put the *cumare* on the next train." Hennie hoisted off the bed. "Send a telegram to Mayer. Apologize. Then you call Rosa, then Klein, have him put you two together with that Louella Parsons. *Then* you go see Corini."

She let the cold ashes she'd collected in her hand drop to the floor. "This way," she said, "he knows you can do right and Frankie Fortune don't matter if Anthony Corini is on your side."

There was knock on the bedroom door. On command, Terrasini entered with a hissing glass of Bromo-Seltzer.

"Give me that," Hennie insisted.

"So there's this guy," Benno told Eleanor Ree, "his name is Fortunato Spaletti. He was born in Sicily, but he comes over here and pretty soon he meets up with Carlo Farcolini, who I'm sure you know from the papers, considering that son of a bitch Dewey. Naturally, if your name is Fortunato, they're going to call you Fortune, so he's Frankie Fortune."

"I see," Ree said, her green eyes fixed on the lively young man.

"When Mr. Farcolini makes his move back in the late twenties, Frankie gets New Jersey, which is everything coming in and out of the piers, and every joint Bebe worked on his way up plus a taste of this and that."

Elbow on the chair's plump arm, she'd cupped her chin in her palm. Hearing the punch line, she knit her brow.

"And I'm telling you, to this day, when he could be sitting pretty, Frankie goes at it. Which is good because with Anthony Corini making moves like he's a gentleman and Bruno Gigenti just getting back his routine, you need somebody who knows the game. See, there's muscle, but brains is the thing."

Ree unfolded her legs and leaned forward. She saw Benno steal a glance at her cleavage. A little smile formed on her lips.

"Me, I wouldn't be surprised if some day Frankie ran the whole thing." Suddenly, he snapped his fingers. "Oh, and I forgot to mention Mimmo, who you met at the Louis–Conn fight. He's in Frankie's crew, but he's also Rosa's uncle. So he's Bebe's uncle-in-law."

"Bill's wife is…" She sat back, amazed. "She's…"

Madonna mio, ain't she the most perfect thing? "By blood. Oh yeah."

Ree shook her head in dismay.

"See," Benno said, "I told you there were lots of ways to answer that question."

When she stood, Benno traced her from the ground up.

"Excuse me," she said.

"Sal," he said. "I'm Sal."

She nodded and went to the credenza for the phone. Benno watched as she told the hotel to book her onto the Pennsylvania Railroad's Broadway Limited bound for Chicago.

CHAPTER TWENTY-ONE

Returning from putting his mother and the glass-eyed kid in a car to Jersey, Marsala found Ree slipping a light coat over her emerald dress. "I've got to get back," she said. "You understand."

"Listen, baby, let me explain." He dropped his hands on her arms.

"Let's leave it at I've got to get back." She lifted herself up on her toes and kissed his forehead.

"Baby..."

"Could Nino manage my luggage?"

Scarf knotted under her chin, sunglasses hiding much of her face, she went directly to the private lounge at the station, sending Terrasini for magazines. Then, replaying Benno's soliloquy, she smoked one cigarette after another, swallowed down a gin and tonic, gin and tonic, then a double. She bit the lime and ran her sour tongue across her bottom lip.

"Ready?" Terrasini said, holding out his hand like she needed help out of the chair.

Her ankle buckled when she stood.

There was a walkway that permitted Broadway Limited passengers to go directly to the train without crossing under the stark light of the station's glass roof. The shadowy path had a red carpet and in her hazy state, Ree saw that the blood from the bullets Frankie Fortune's men would fire into her would seep into the rug and disappear. She jumped when the conductor shouted, "All 'board!"

"You OK?" Terrasini asked as they emerged near the waiting train.

"Swell," she replied.

Not so. She was terrified. She'd heard the rumors—her ex-husband Simon insisted on telling her. But when Marsala said they were bullshit, a slur against all Italians, she believed him.

"All 'board!" yelled the conductor again.

"Nino," Ree said, "walk me to my compartment."

Terrasini looked at his watch. He didn't like to leave his boss alone when he was blue. "Sure," he said. He couldn't figure why she was scared. Bebe was crazy for her.

Ree planned on sending a telegram when the train left the station. Maybe her oilman could send a plane to meet her, bring her back home. Maybe he'd fly it himself.

Benno told the limo driver to leave him by the A&P. "See you later, Hennie," he said cheerfully.

Hennie sat in the back, burping and stewing. "Yeah," she replied, staring out the other side.

No Leo at the A&P. His day off. Eight-to-five he ain't home, Benno thought, but he walked to his father's house anyway, his suit jacket on his arm, sleeves up, his tie hanging low.

At his desk, Bell heard pebbles hit a front window. As if caught peering at French postcards, he shoved the Yale brochures in a drawer, a wave of guilt rising in his head. Sliding into chinos and loafers, he met Benno on the brownstone steps, shady now with the sun setting behind the Heights.

"Eighteen years and still you don't knock?" Bell said as he ran his fingers through his hair.

"Hello. I'm Sal Benno." He stuck out his hand.

"What's on your mind?"

"You buy me dinner and I'll tell you a story. That is, if you can spare the time."

Bell said, "Let's go."

Imogene wasn't due back at St. Claire's until Friday, so she was enjoying the end of her summer vacation with her family down the Jersey Shore. Bell visited her whenever he had time off, abusing the cooling system in a car Charlie Tyler sold him for $400. "You give us Yale and sign on long-term," Tyler proposed, "and I'll sell you an eight-hundred-dollar car for half price."

"I'll give you Yale," Bell countered, "if you guarantee me equal time in Europe."

Tyler said, "I don't think Miss O'Boyle will approve for you leaving her behind for twenty-four months, Leo. I see what I see, and you two are getting serious."

"True," Bell admitted. She occupied his thoughts and made his heart skip a beat. When they spoke on the phone, his skin tingled. He was in love and she was too, and if he couldn't hold her in his arms, he thought he'd burst into flames.

Everything had fallen into place so easily. The first thing Bell did with the car was drive down the shore and introduce himself to Imogene's father, who shook his hand, threw him a Rheingold and pointed him toward his daughter, who was on the beach with her kid sister. Later, they went out to tap the sand for clams; Imogene carried the bucket and held his hand. Mr. O'Boyle told stories while little Ruthie O'Boyle collected shells tumbling in the foam.

Bell brought her to Narrows Gate to meet his father, the old man treating her like a china doll, Imogene insisting he sit down, she'll take care of everything.

"A winner," Mr. Bell declared later. "This one you hold onto."

He was waiting for the right moment to show her off to Sal.

"When am I going to meet him?" she asked. "You talk about him all the time."

He made excuses. "Sal's a busy guy. Up before dawn, rushing around, his aunt and uncle are getting old and he's all they've got."

"Leo, we've been going steady for almost five months."

"I know. I want it to be just right. You've got to love him the way I do."

"I'm sure I will."

It wasn't Sal and it wasn't Imogene. They'd get along fine. Hell, they'd be best friends, beaming smiles, the two of them flitting like fireflies on a summer night. But Sal would see what it meant. The conversation would turn. She'd say, "Don't you think Yale is a great opportunity for Leo, Sal? Tell him."

Now, as he walked toward downtown with Benno, Bell said, "You were going to tell me a story."

"Mimmo sent me with Hennie to see Bebe. And I met Eleanor Ree. In a bathrobe."

"Jesus."

"You ain't kidding. They left me alone with her. Me and her, a movie star. And the bathrobe, it ain't tied too tight."

"What color bathrobe? I'm trying to picture it."

"She's got an all-over tan," Benno replied.

Bell laughed. "I bet you wish you were Bebe."

"No, I wouldn't go that far. But I wouldn't mind being that robe."

Soon, they stopped at the Mirco Brothers' and settled on a table out on Pierce Street.

"So. Where you been?" Benno said as he sat.

Bell looked at him, detecting a trace of a grin at the corners of his mouth.

Benno said, "All of a sudden, you disappear like the fuckin' Shadow."

Clams on the half shell arrived, a dash of vinegar with *diavoletto*, and two ice-cold beers—the usual—delivered by a girl the guys called Knotty. One evening late in the war, Benno kissed her under her stairs until his balls turned blue. Next day he learned she was 15. He went straight to confession, but at the Irish church so Father Gregory don't find out.

"It's true. I've been busy," Bell tried.

"Cut the shit. You got a broad, right?"

"Not a broad, Sal. A girlfriend."

Benno slurped a Little Neck, cold, chewy and sweet. "I know her?"

Squeezing a lemon, Bell circled his fist over the cherrystones. "No."

"Why not?"

"The time's not right."

"What the fuck does that mean?"

Bell sat back, the little fork empty. "I guess it's part of a package, Sal. I've got a decision to make."

"She's pregnant?"

"I hope to hell not. Listen, I didn't mean to keep her away from you."

"Maybe when you first started dating you thought, she meets Sal and I'm done."

Bell smiled. "That's it."

Benno reached over and tapped his hand. "Only kidding. I know you're shy around girls."

They ate in silence save for Benno's slurping and cars passing on the side streets.

"There's something else," Bell said finally. He leaned in. "The Army wants me to go to college."

"That's good, no?"

"They want to pull strings and get me into Yale."

"What's Yale?"

"A college in New Haven."

"New Haven?"

"Connecticut, Sal."

"That's where they play the Ivy League?"

Bell nodded as he sipped the cold beer.

"Your girl, she's all right with this?"

He nodded.

"So you're asking me if I'm OK with it?"

Bell hesitated. "It's more…Yeah, sure. What do you think? I mean, I could go around here. City College, maybe. It's a damned good school."

"I thought you said the Ivy League is for the best."

Bell continued to dodge his own thoughts. "Maybe we don't see each other for a while."

"Well, I figure if the Army sends you to Poland, I ain't going with you, Leo."

"They have some kind of orientation program on campus next week. I'm thinking I should go."

Benno cleaned his glasses on the napkin.

"Sal, I'm saying that—I'm saying you've got to watch your ass with Mimmo and those fucks."

"I do. They ain't outsmarting me."

"It's not a matter of who's smarter." Bell leaned across the table and lowered his voice to a whisper. "Of course you're smarter. You're also honest and forthright. Those are—"

"What's forthright?"

"Straightforward. Direct. Trusting," he said, emphasizing the last word.

"That's good, no?"

"Not with these fucks. They already trapped you with Pellizzari. They turned you into their bagman. I'm worried they'll make you the next Freddie Pop, for Christ's sakes."

Benno frowned. "I ain't no Freddie Pop."

"No. Of course not. I'm saying you run your ideas by me and they become clearer in your own mind."

Benno reached for his beer glass, which was empty. He turned to Knotty and threw two fingers in the air.

Bell pushed his half-filled glass toward his friend.

"Well, I ain't coming to Yale Haven every time Mimmo wants something," Benno said finally.

"They got phones, Sal."

"I'll reverse the charges."

Bell took in the scent of the clams and the lemon juice. It reminded him of dinner at the O'Boyles' down the shore, Mr. O'Boyle shucking clams as they sat around a table on the screened-in porch, Mrs. O'Boyle chiding her husband to save some for her chowder, little Ruthie reminding her mother the ocean might have a few more to spare.

"Where's your girl live?"

Bell told him. Kearny, which was maybe a half-hour drive from Narrows Gate.

"They got Sicilians there, too?"

"She's Irish, Sal."

Benno snapped back. "Are you nuts?"

"You meet her and tell me what she's not."

"Holy Christ. I think somebody hit you on the head at the A&P."

Benno quickly finished off Bell's beer, then took the two fresh glasses from Knotty, who gave him a playful elbow to the ear as she turned to leave.

"Your girl—"

"Imogene. Imogene O'Boyle."

"*Minga.* You don't go halfway, do you?" Benno said as he lifted a clamshell. "She know your real name and Rabka, Poland? All that?"

"Nobody knows that," Bell said. "My father and you. Period."

"Not the Army? The Ivy League?"

"Period," Bell repeated. "Look, the point is, you've got to promise me you don't let yourself get trapped by these guys."

Benno thought for a moment. Then he said, "How do I know I'm trapped until I'm trapped?"

Hennie couldn't sleep—the weight on her chest, indigestion, frustration and thinking Frankie Fortune is out in the hall, can of paint thinner in one hand, a stiletto blade in the other. A tension headache, pain in her shoulder. Gas. Her husband Vincenzo out cold, purring, the guy at peace with himself. I wonder what the fuck that's like.

Hot night, the fan a worthless piece of shit from the five-and-dime. She looked at the clock. A little after one in the morning. Shit. Groping for her cigarettes, she tugged the doily, the lamp wobbled, and there goes the ashtray onto the carpet. She brought her bare feet down carefully, a miracle she don't step into a pile of cold butts.

Robe off the hook on the back of the door. A quick piss and she stayed on the bowl to smoke, leaning back to drop the half-gone cigarette between her chafed thighs. Stairs creaked under her weight on the trip down. She entered the darkened living room on her way to the kitchen. Maybe I'll sit outside in the back-yard, she thought. A cool breeze, maybe. Look at the moon.

Bebe sang in her mind. "It's not the pale moon that excites me..."

She smiled. Taking up with Eleanor Ree. The one they all want.

And he tells King Mayer to go fuck himself.

My son.

My beautiful boy.

Don't let nobody push you around, Bebe. You work Corini, too. Get what you want, what you deserve. He don't come through and you go see Don Carlo. He believes in you.

The sambuca was in the cabinet above the sink.

A plastic Virgin Mary glowed in the dark.

A plate and a fork: Vincenzo had stolen a piece of Dee's *torta di ricotta*.

Bottle and glass in hand, Hennie went for the key to the back door.

Suddenly a twinge in her chest, followed by a sharp, crunching pain.

Moaning, she struggled to Vincenzo's chair, glass smashing near her feet.

The moment she sat, it felt like something exploded behind her breasts, then some sort of electrical charge ran throughout her body. Then unbearable pain in her head.

She snapped upright and the chair tumbled back. She crashed on the floor, her skull slamming the linoleum.

She moaned again and then a sad little cry escaped as she thought, I showed those fucks.

And then, just like that, she died.

"Long day," Bebe said.

"Long day," Terrasini agreed.

"I'm turning in."

"Anything you need?" Coming off the Hampshire House elevator, after a late dinner at Billy the Oysterman on 47th, just the two of them, drinks until the joint closed, Terrasini alert to signs of his boss's changing moods.

"I'm good," Marsala replied.

Though their adjoining rooms shared a living area and kitchenette, they entered by different doors.

Marsala waited. When he didn't hear Terrasini at the radio, he turned gingerly and went back out to the corridor. He sealed the door and headed to the stairs, kicking down to the ground floor. Short of breath, he flagged a cab on Central Park South. "Harlem," he told the driver. "The Hotel Cecil."

"Mind I take the park?" the driver asked.

"Kid," Marsala replied, "I don't care if you fly."

The cab entered Central Park at the Grand Army Plaza and stayed on the east side, racing behind the zoo and along the reservoir up to Harlem Meer. Leaving the park, they continued north on Lenox Avenue and turned on 118th. There was the Cecil, home to Minton's Playhouse.

Minton's was on the hotel's first floor. The jazz club was closed for the night, but as Marsala approached, he heard music. While Terrasini was at the train station with Eleanor, Marsala made some calls. "The best tonight," he said. They responded. "But go in quiet," he was told. "No columnists, no reporters, no starlets, Bill. This one's for us."

Marsala rapped the code and the husky doorman let him in, nodding in acknowledgment but saying nothing. Though it was after hours, the tables were packed, Negroes outnumbering whites maybe 10 to 1. Everyone faced the stage and stared at the singer, who swayed with her eyes closed, her face a mask of serenity. Nobody gave a shit he was there. Marsala went to the bar.

On the bandstand, the musicians laid a deep groove under an up-tempo number. The bass player pumped four to the bar, matching the drummer's high hat. The piano player had a great left hand.

Marsala whispered for a scotch and got his drink before the trumpeter—it was Roy Eldridge—turned over the melody to the singer.

"All of me," Billie Holiday sang with Eldridge blowing low behind her, "why not take all of me? Can't you see I'm no good without you…"

Scotch in hand, Marsala smiled. Lady Day sang dangerously off the beat, like a tightrope walker threatening to fall. But she never wavered and swung easily into a reprise of the second verse.

Marsala's big band version of the tune was influenced by Holiday's. His was fine, hers perfection. He loved everything about the way she sang: her style; how she toyed with a lyric and riffed on a melody; her sense of rhythm. The columnists, wrong again, compared him to Crosby. But as a vocalist, Holiday was his model. They were the same age—he teased her that she was three months older—but she was his musical big sister, a success on her own when he was fighting to launch a solo career. When he took off, he praised her whenever he could. In turn, she introduced him to Lester Young and all the jazz cats. They were the greatest and they knew it.

The song ended and the pianist began a new number, a ballad this time, the drummer entering on the third block chord. Marsala recognized it before the first bar ended: "Solitude," the Ellington composition. Now Marsala closed his eyes.

She sang, "In my solitude, you haunt me…"

The beauty of Duke's impeccable melody and Billie's voice: Oh sweet Jesus, Marsala thought. This is it, isn't it? The whole ball of wax. That moment when song and singer become inseparable—buddy, that's what you call heaven on earth.

He leaned an elbow on the bar, his eyes still closed, his head perched on his fist. A sense of well-being engulfed him. He floated to his place inside the music where nothing mattered but the beauty that surrounded him. No pain, no aggravation, no confusion, no ups, no downs, no mood swings—now it was just him and the music. Sanctuary. He was somewhere between downy clouds and a tranquil blue sea.

After midnight, all calls for Mr. Marsala went to Terrasini's line. House rule.

Terrasini sat up at the first ring. Maybe it was Metro. Or Klein, forgetting the three-hour difference.

"Yeah," Terrasini said, as he cleared his throat.

Mimmo gave it to him straight.

"Oh, good God," Terrasini replied. "Yeah. I'll tell him. I'll tell him now."

Terrasini threw on the robe he kept at the foot of the bed. He hurried across the living area and knocked on the door to Marsala's room.

"Bebe," he said.

He knocked again.

"Bebe." He had a sudden thought he'd taken his sleeping pills.

He opened the door. The room was empty, the bed made. The bathroom door was open, the light off.

His mind raced.

Somebody had already called Bebe, he thought. They sent the call up and he knows his mother's dead. Jesus Christ.

Terrasini raced out of the room and down the hall. The window to the air shaft was open.

"Bebe, damn you..."

He reached the open window and stuck his head out, expecting to see Marsala in a crumble down in the courtyard below.

But only a few pigeons nesting on the ledges.

He rang the switchboard, identified himself and asked for a list of the telephone numbers Marsala called. Maybe he was with one of the broads he had stashed in town, maybe that Broadway actress again.

Then he asked for a long-distance operator. Certain Mimmo had contacted his niece, he requested person-to-person to Phil Klein. Knowing Klein, he told the operator to try his office first.

"Phil. Nino."

Klein stood. Hearing those two words, he could tell Terrasini was forcing himself to stay calm. "What is it?"

"Hennie's dead."

Klein slipped a pen out of the desk set and scribbled while Terrasini told him what he knew.

"Can I speak to Bill?" he asked.

Terrasini told him Marsala was out. He had to locate him before the papers and the radio heard the news.

Klein thought quickly. He'd have to release a statement on Marsala's behalf, expressing his gratitude for his fans' prayers and sympathy. In the morning, he'd contact Louella Parsons. She knew Marsala had been close to his mother. The entire country deserved to be reminded. He'd propose that she speak to him, an exclusive. She could convey his enormous sense of loss and devastation. People would see Bill Marsala for the sensitive man he was under the swagger and bravado, stardom's ebb and flow.

"I don't envy you, Nino."

Terrasini nodded. He'd already put away the sleeping pills and stashed the straight razor. "Do me a favor," he said. "Call Rosa and tell her I'll be with Bill. I'll be in touch as soon as I can."

"Of course," Klein said as he completed his notes. "I'll drive out. She shouldn't be alone."

A bellman rapped on the door and Terrasini crossed the suite, the long telephone wire snaking behind him.

He took the slip of paper. Two phone numbers, the second one Minton's. Terrasini could see it: He's surrounded by musicians, nobody gives a shit he's Bill Marsala, something sweet's playing and he's bought himself a few minutes of peace. I tell him one sentence and everything blows to bits. It's a toss-up whether he runs headlong into traffic or collapses into a catatonic state.

"He's up in Harlem," he said to Klein.

"I'll have a doctor waiting for you when you return to the hotel."

As he put down the phone, Terrasini tried to anticipate Bebe's reaction: Is he lost or is he free? With most people, it's a little of both. With Bebe, it's either one or the other.

All or nothing at all.

CHAPTER TWENTY-TWO

Mimmo waited at the TWA gate, his mind drifting. Then, through his sunglasses, he saw Rosa coming down the rolling steps of the silver bird holding Bill Jr.

Trailing with his briefcase and the baby's diaper bag, Phil Klein strained for the right tone meeting Mimmo, then offered to retrieve the luggage. The baby went to Grandma, who loved her daughter more than she despised her son-in-law.

"How's the trip?" Mimmo asked as they walked toward the terminal.

"Bill Jr. slept maybe five hours. He's an angel."

Rosa's mother looked at the baby. He resembled his father.

"Is Bill here?" Rosa asked.

"Bebe's at Kalm's," he replied, mentioning the funeral home. "With Vincenzo, the poor bastard."

Late-afternoon humidity followed them inside the building and Rosa walked next to her uncle in silence. By the time she saw Klein, who paced as the bags were stacked, she could wait no longer.

"Mimmo," she said, reaching for his arm. Her mother and Bill Jr. went ahead. "Did she really have a heart attack?"

"Sure," he said, staring into her eyes. "Why not?"

"But is Bill in trouble?"

Mimmo couldn't figure what she wanted to hear. "Not yet," he said.

"Is he drinking?"

Mimmo said no. "You forgive him, don't you?" he asked. "You're taking him back." They continued toward the baggage claim. "Rosa, you got to remember this is hard for him, not being nobody's beautiful boy no more." Then Mimmo quoted Anthony Corini. "Maybe he stops showing off and goes back to work. Buckles down."

"Maybe," she said. On the flight, she'd spent a lot of time thinking her husband was finally going to have to grow up.

Benno knew Catholics don't have funerals on Sunday and they didn't like to have them on Saturdays neither, that being the day for weddings and the last thing the bride wants is the smell of incense as she's coming down the aisle. So Hennie stayed in cold storage at the funeral home until Monday. Like a festival for some saint, the wake was going to last the entire weekend.

For the first afternoon, the old-timers on Polk Street, mostly women in black who knew Hennie and Vincenzo as kids, paraded uptown to Kalm's like they were on a pilgrimage. St. Francis sent the eighth grade in their uniforms, ashes to ashes even if your son is world famous. Flower trucks pulled up nonstop. Opening night, the men home from work and their wives got dressed and a line formed. Benno stood across the street, flat of his shoe against a brownstone wall, and he saw coming out a congressman he didn't see go in and then Joey Aaron, that wacky Jew comedian, and it dawned on him that they were using the back entrance and maybe Frankie, Mimmo and the crew were already in there, listening to bullshit.

Then Bebe and Rosa came out and walked the line, shaking hands, accepting hugs and Mass cards from people who hated

Bebe's bony ass when he was a spoiled-rotten kid and he hadn't given a thought since. A photographer appeared and Bebe and Rosa posed appropriately miserable and married.

The next day it was worse because Hollywood and Broadway arrived. Boo Chiasso and Fat Tutti were working the line with the Narrows Gate cops, and some guys from the county squad kept the kids across the street. Benno saw that Alan Ladd was four feet tall and not one doll who entered could touch Eleanor Ree, who had the good sense to stay away. Teen girls who never met Bebe were crying as they held up his picture and grown-up dames came to show support. Even a bunch of GIs dropped by, saying they seen him with the USO. Klein behind him, Bebe nodded humbly and shook their hands. He introduced them to Rosa.

"Fuck this," Benno said finally. He went around to Fillmore, intent on walking in where the big shots go. He figured Terrasini would be at the door or some Hollywood mook and he wondered if Leo was going to show, if they got the news in Yale Haven, down the shore or over in Kearny.

Bill Marsala made the cover of the *News* and the *Mirror*. "I've lost my biggest fan," he said. Shell-shocked Vincenzo was pictured in his fireman's outfit, flanked by his son and daughter-in-law.

"Hey, Nino," Benno said. "OK I come in?"

"Sal, where the fuck you been?" he replied. "We could use you here."

Terrasini was at the brink of disorientation. Besides keeping an eye on Bebe, he had to worry about the crew. Low-level guys were everywhere, rubbing shoulders with plainclothes cops. A florist brought in a wreath signed Carlo Farcolini. Cy Geller, that Jew who ran Miami, came in without ceremony. Terrasini told Benno he just got done passing off Milton Berle to Klein, plus the songwriters from the Wilshire Towers arrived thinking Kalm's a good place to meet broads in distress.

"What do you need, Nino?"

"Ask Mimmo if he can lend me Boo or Tutti. I'm going nuts over here."

"OK, sure. But first, seeing as I was the last one to talk to Hennie—"

A voice from down the hall said, "Let him in."

By the water cooler, looking splendid in black silk, a white shirt and a cobalt blue tie, stood Frankie Fortune. To Benno's surprise, Fortune shook his hand, clapped him on the back and led him to some kind of office, its accordion door pulled shut. Yanking it back, he let Benno enter.

And there on the sofa was Anthony Corini. He looked up, his expression calm and to Benno, even vigilant and wise. He stared right at Benno, his sleepy eyes wide. Mimmo was in the room, too, and the wise old man Geller, sitting. But Benno didn't see them. Corini seemed more formidable than he did in the newspapers, out with this candidate or some guy who runs a big company.

"This is Salvatore Benno," Fortune said in Sicilian. "The one who brings the food."

Benno watched astonished as Corini stood to shake his hand.

"My pleasure, Mr. Corini," Benno said in Sicilian.

"No. The pleasure is mine. The food is superb."

"You eat it? Really?" Benno said.

Corini laughed and everyone else did, too. "What do you think I do with it? Food like that..."

"My Aunt Gemma," Benno said, his stomach fluttering. "I'll tell her."

"Good," Corini said as he returned to the sofa.

Fortune took a seat behind a desk that belonged to the funeral home's owner, a picture of a saint on the wall behind him. Benno didn't know the Irish saints or the Germans neither, but the guy's head glowed right.

"Sal, tell Mr. Corini about you and Mrs. Rosiglino," Fortune said.

Benno explained. "She asked me to take her to Bebe, that you wanted him straightened out. Maybe not you, but Frankie. So I went with her to the Hampshire House."

The Jersey crew was listening for him to say the right thing. Benno could feel Geller studying every word.

"I didn't hear what she said too good," he continued. "I was entertaining Eleanor Ree when Bebe closed the door."

"Eleanor Ree," Fortune said with disapproval, glancing at Mimmo.

"But when Bebe came out, you could see he'd got his ears pinned."

"So he understands." Fortune led.

"She said so. Hennie."

Mimmo looked at Corini. "He's making good with Rosa and this Klein says he's set with the moving pictures."

Corini knew that already. He'd spoken to Rico Enna, who continued to funnel the agency's talent to Corini's clubs at a square price.

"What else did she say?" he asked.

"Not too much, Mr. Corini, to tell you the truth. She looked pretty bad. Gasping. But she did say he should stop with the pictures and go back to singing."

Corini nodded. He'd had the same idea. Shorten the leash.

"All right, Sal," Fortune said as he went for the door.

"Nice to meet you, Mr. Corini," Benno said. But the dark-skinned man, his silver hair shining under fluorescent lighting, had turned to Geller.

As he headed for the back door, Benno saw that Terrasini had gotten his relief. A cop in uniform was on guard and Fat Tutti was blocking the moonlight. Terrasini was leaning against a banister, blowing smoke, exhausted, thinking, all I wanted to do was play the piano. He said, "You pay your respects to Bebe, Sal?"

"Nah," he told him. There's no point when Frankie Fortune brought you into a special private room and you got a glad hand from Anthony Corini.

Bebe looked at his father, who sat on his side of the couch, staring nowhere, sorrow etched in every line of his face. He knew he should go over, hang an arm across his shoulder, kiss his cheek and say, "Pop, what are you thinking? Pop?" But his father wouldn't have replied. Never once in his life had he heard his father say what he felt.

"Be careful," he'd say to his son, who chose to take it as, "I love you."

"Pop, what are we going to do?"

Vincenzo sighed and tried a smile. "They broke the mold, huh?" In Sicilian, the old man said, "I can't do nothing without her."

"I know, Pop. I know." Tears welling in his eyes, he turned as Rosa entered the living room, carrying a tiny cup of espresso. The phone was off the hook. Sophie and Dee were in the kitchen putting away the dishes, their husbands gone for the night. The house was grim and unfamiliar without Hennie's spark. For a fleeting moment, Marsala wished they were back on Polk Street, crammed in a three-room railroad flat, everything fucked up but all right.

"Here you go, Papa," Rosa said.

Vincenzo looked up with empty eyes, accepted the cup with a nod and placed it carefully on the end table. Earlier, when it was time to leave the cemetery, he had looked around for his wife, ready to offer her an elbow to hold. He listened for her booming voice, knowing full well he would never hear it again. Now somebody else had made the coffee and they put it in the wrong cup.

Marsala slipped his arm around his wife's waist. The Irish have their wisdom, he thought. They drink at the wake, before the funeral, at the cemetery and late into the night to stave off the emptiness. Not us. We dive right into misery. We can't wait to feel our hearts break.

"You had a wonderful life together," Rosa said to her father-in-law.

Forlorn in his uniform slacks, starched white shirt, blue clip-on tie, the old man said, "We did, yes."

Later, he shaved with his straight edge, put on a fresh under-shirt and went off to sleep in the single bed in the room Hennie kept up for her son.

Now in the quiet of his parents' bedroom, as moonlight peeked past the blinds, Marsala said, "I can't do it. I can't sleep in here."

Earlier, Rosa had thrown open the windows, cleaned the carpet and changed the bedding, but Hennie remained, as if she was just over at the Chatterbox, maybe, or uptown at the Elks Club, regaling the crowd with the latest stories about her beautiful boy.

Even when she and Bill were 3,000 miles away in Southern California, Rosa could feel Hennie nearby, entering rooms where she'd never been, advising her on subjects she knew nothing about. As she signed her petition of separation, Rosa thought, What's Hennie going to say? Sooner or later, Hennie's opinion would be Bill's too, even if he claimed she no longer had much sway in his life. Rosa knew Bill was still fighting his mother's war against anyone who expressed a low opinion of him. She could feel it in almost everything he did, especially his childish behavior after the public's blind idolatry faded. Bebe Rosiglino's house was built on a cracked foundation. Bill Marsala knew it and could never forget.

"No, I can't sleep here either," Rosa said. "It's like she's still in this bedroom."

That's true, Marsala thought. But he needed to be with his wife and mend their relationship. It was his mother's last request.

"Baby, what do you say we get out of here?" Bill Jr. was in Bayonne and Marsala could get an uncle to take the couch in case his father woke up confused. A patrol car sat at the hydrant outside the door. "We'll just go."

Where? Rosa thought. The Hampshire House? "I don't know…"

"We'll drive. Up the Palisades or down the shore. Like we used to."

"It's late—"

"Not in LA."

He stepped in and kissed her, a peck on her bottom lip. The second time, he kissed her passionately and she returned it, relenting as he held her tight.

"Let me make things right, Rosa," he whispered. "Let me show you I'm not some Hollywood phony."

"Bill…"

"I made mistakes, sure." He ran his fingertips along her spine. She shivered. "But I learn, kid. I learn."

They kissed again. He probed long and slow. Gently, he nudged her toward the bed.

"Hold me," he whispered.

He fell asleep in her arms.

Bell walked the Yale campus, looking up at ivy-coated stone towers, green grass underfoot. All around him, walking the paths or crossing at a distance, were people with drive, determination and purpose. He was impressed, though the thought of guys in beanies humming some heartfelt anthem made his skin crawl. Also, he had to go two miles to get a decent loaf of crusty bread and some prosciutto. He fell asleep with a used copy of Kant's first critique on his chest, his question marks and exclamation points littering the book's margins.

He still couldn't tell if he belonged—not enough students around in the summer and the ones he saw were kids. Yale didn't scare him away, which was too bad. If it had, he would've dug in to stay. But he couldn't make up his mind. Maybe it was time to stop pussying around with reconnaissance and go talk to a counselor, the Army liaison. Maybe it was time to return Charlie Tyler's calls.

He was thinking about an early dinner and then back to the boardinghouse. Though dreading a cucumber sandwich on white, he started toward the Commons.

At the sound of scuffling shoes, he turned to see Tyler, in uniform, trotting toward him.

"Bell," Tyler said. He stopped and took a deep breath for composure. As they shook hands, he said, "I can't say I'd considered that you might be rude."

"I've got to make up my own mind, Captain."

"Why don't you tell us which way you're leaning?"

"Who's us?"

"Have you dinner plans?"

"Yeah, I'm—"

"This will be better," Tyler said. "I assure you."

Bell followed him to a black car parked near the cemetery, beyond the campus grounds, its engine running.

Five minutes later, they entered the Union League Club. At the top of the marble steps, Tyler was acknowledged, Bell's hat checked and they swept through a dining room of middle-aged men who were sharing canapés and cocktails. Out the corner of his eye, Bell took in the dark wood paneling and stained glass in arched windows, the carpet that had been worn to antique perfection.

At the end of a narrow corridor lined with framed prints of old New Haven, Tyler ushered Bell into a small room filled with plump leather sofas, armchairs and crowded bookcases as high as the ceiling.

Major Landis, who had been gazing out the windows on Chapel Street, turned to greet them. "Leo," he said. "Welcome."

Gray-haired and burly, clear-eyed and persuasive, Landis seemed no less impressive in tweed than he'd been in uniform.

"Good to see you, lad," he said. "Charlie here says you're considering our offer."

"Yes, sir."

"Well, perhaps I can answer any questions you may have," Landis added. "You'll join us for dinner?"

They moved to a corner of the main dining room. Landis acknowledged discreet greetings with a nod of his head. When a man arrived to pull out his chair, Landis waved him off. At the major's gentle insistence, Bell sat to his left, the room now spread before him.

Three drinks appeared. "Manhattans," Tyler explained softly.

"What's on your mind, Leo?" Landis said, lifting a pipe from a side pocket. "There shouldn't be any confusion."

"I guess I don't understand what you want me to do, sir."

Landis explained thoroughly, his voice barely rising above a whisper. President Truman was convinced of the need for a permanent intelligence agency with broad authority in domestic and international matters. Landis had been instructed to propose how his team's expertise could serve the new organization.

When Landis paused to spark his pipe, Tyler leaned in and said, "You keep this on the QT, Bell."

"Oh, Leo knows that, Charlie," Landis said, as smoke escaped his lips. "The data you saw...Am I right, Leo?"

"Yes, sir."

"We did a fine job. Did we not?"

"Yes, sir."

Tyler carefully sipped his Manhattan and returned the glass to table. "Leo, we've learned an awful lot about you."

"No secrets among us, Leo," Landis said softly, a paternal smile lighting his face.

"Your name isn't really Leo Bell," Tyler said. "It's Leonardo Campanello."

"We changed our name, sure," Bell said. "A lot of us did."

"Of course, Leo," Landis said. "It isn't an issue. Not at all."

Tyler said, "You came with your father on the steamship *American* out of Naples. You were born in Irpino. That must have been quite the journey for your father. A baby less than two years old."

Bell shrugged.

"The information is from our friends in the Bureau of Immigration," Landis said. "No need to be concerned."

"Leo, the point is, were we to consider you part of our team, you'd be the only native-born Italian among us," Tyler said.

"With a gift for analysis, I might add," Landis added.

Bell said, "But I still don't know what you'd expect me to do. I've already said I'd like to be considered for a post overseas."

"Leo," Tyler said, "it's not just the Reds."

Landis shifted in his chair. "Leo, our nation is under threat from many sources. Agitators of all stripes want to tear us down. One of our enemies is the criminal element. One aspect that is particularly troubling is Farcolini's ever-expanding syndicate. They are well organized and, as much as I'm loathe to admit it, quite savvy. Their infiltration of the political sphere in New York and Chicago is thorough and their increasing influence in the entertainment industry is equally troubling."

Landis laid his pipe on a bread dish.

"If our new intelligence agency is to be at all effective, we need to anticipate what they'll do," he said. "Reacting, as law enforcement prefers, is…Well, it's—"

"Shutting the barn after the horse is gone," said Tyler.

Landis said, "We have to gather intelligence about these men. Their personal histories, how they've come to their way of thinking, their pathologies. When we know them well—better than they know themselves—we'll know what they intend to do."

"Do you understand?" Tyler asked.

"Leo," said Landis, "your country needs you to infiltrate their organization."

"From New Haven?" Bell replied.

Tyler looked at Landis.

"Leo, we think we'd all be better served if you were to remain in Narrows Gate," Landis said. "As far as Yale is concerned, we know you can compete. Heck, you're about the brightest boy I've had the pleasure of working with."

"Stop," Tyler joked. "You'll give him a swell head."

"No, I'm quite serious. Leo, we are prepared to propose that you attend college in New York or New Jersey while you work with Charlie. Afterwards, should you still want to be posted overseas, you would be more than qualified."

Bell considered the cocktail at his elbow.

Tyler said, "What do you think, Leo?"

Calculating, Bell brought a long finger across his lips. Then, sitting back, he said, "Let me see if I've got this. I go on the payroll of this new intelligence agency. I infiltrate the Farcolini organization. I report what I see and hear. You cover my tuition and board. When I graduate, you'll give me my choice of assignments overseas."

Landis said, "That's a rather broad interpretation—"

Tyler interrupted. "No, I'd say that about sums it up."

CHAPTER TWENTY-THREE

Settling back in Southern California, Bebe Marsala returned to work. Metro's Brooklyn film was readied for Grauman's and his scenes in another feathery musical, shot on a nearby soundstage, were in post-production. Klein found a sponsor for a 15-minute midafternoon radio show and Bill Marsala was back in homes across America. "Bag the announcer," he suggested to Klein. "Let me spend a few extra minutes with my fans. They'll appreciate it." Marsala read the promos and needled the sponsor, a soap company with products in kitchen cabinets everywhere. But he always reminded the listeners that Rosa used the same detergents and floor wax as they did. "Gives one heckuva shine, doesn't it?" he'd say before launching into another song.

Inspired by Lady Day, his next project was close to his heart: into the recording studio with a selection of standards he'd sung for years that were now rearranged for a small combo—a vibraphone added to the rhythm section, only a single tenor sax and Sweets Edison, on loan from the Basie band, on trumpet. Marsala dubbed it "Music for People Who Get Laid." The boy singer would be buried for good.

He surprised Rosa with a new home, Spanish-style, five-bedrooms, secluded yet within walking distance of the lake. "Invite your family," Bill insisted. "Let's show them the good life." Dodging photographers, he took her to dinner at out-of-the-way places with good food in the Valley; they walked the beach in Malibu, escaped to Catalina. Some of Bill's celebrity friends came over, husbands and wives, Rosa cooking specialties she learned from her mother and grandmother. Oliver Hardy asked for her recipes; so did Lucille Ball, who cradled Bill Jr. in her lap.

For the first time in months, years maybe, Rosa heard Bill singing around the house, scatting the horn solos, tapping out the rhythm. Whenever she crossed the living room, he'd dart over and sweep her into his arms. They'd dance as he hummed into her ear.

"This mother's gonna swing," he told Terrasini as they worked on Bill's new music room. He decided he'd rehearse at home, putting the band at ease. Rosa and Sweets chatted while Bill grilled steaks and Nino tossed a salad.

He felt good. His mother was right: Fuck the pictures and let's get with the music. That was the pulse, the stuff of life. The music, baby. Pictures were publicity to sell records and to pack the ballrooms and nightclubs. Bill Marsala came alive on vinyl.

The snappy tap-tap on the high hat, the brush on the snare, the double bass chugging its rhythm and then a touch of piano echoed by warm vibes. And Bill Marsala singing just for you.

"What do you think, baby?" he asked when a song ended, the guys settling back.

Perched on a love seat's arm, Rosa smiled. It was good, better than good. Bill was enjoying music again and life was bliss. At night, when he complained of a tired throat—he'd spent hours singing without a microphone—she brewed tea with honey and massaged his neck and chest with VapoRub.

Best of all, Bill was happy. Every little thing seemed to buck him up. One late-autumn afternoon, Sweets drove up with Lester Young. "Pres," Bill cheered, going out to hug the great saxophonist. "Fine Wine," the beagle-eyed Young said in reply, hanging

Marsala with a nickname he cherished. Young had heard Marsala was growing into jazz. "Be sure you take care of those pipes," he advised, wagging a lean finger.

Downtown in the studio, Marsala worked three hours a night, starting at midnight, five times a week. To take advantage of the new, long-playing recording format, he wanted a couple dozen killer cuts in the can before he made his next move. Terrasini thought he was running low, riding the last of his burst of energy after Hennie's funeral. But there he was, on the other side of the glass, Johnny Walker on the music stand, his jacket folded with care on the back of the chair. When the sextet kicked it, Marsala seemed a picture of vitality, a man in charge.

"'Sweet Lorraine,'" he said now. "In the key of F."

…two, three…

"I just found joy. I'm as happy as a baby boy…"

He felt like he could just soar, man, then hover above the studio's parquet floor, floating like a feather in a breeze. He'd already given the LP a title—"Just for You"—and he told Klein he wanted the buzz to begin now: Bill's back and better than ever. "Bring the columnists to the studio," he said. "I'll sit with them on break and they'll see. Bring Parsons. Hell, bring Hearst."

Even they couldn't crash his plane. Back from the funeral, he called Parsons and asked if he could join her for lunch at the Brown Derby. He showed early. "Can I tell you something just between us?" A wary Parsons agreed. Marsala said, "I wasn't ready for it. Success. It caught me dreaming and I lost my head. I know it now. I understand. You know what I mean, Louella? Life has a way of telling you what's important."

She was impressed. Marsala wasn't so far down that he had to bend a knee.

"And Eleanor Ree?" Parsons asked.

"A great kid. First-rate. Mark my words, she'll be a major star."

"*Bill*," she said, eyebrow arched.

"Like I said, Louella, life tells you what you need to do." He waited for her next question. When there was none, he said, "Can you give me a fresh start? I'm not asking you to go to bat for me with Mr. Hearst. But the column…Can we—"

There was Rosa, approaching the table. Right on cue.

Marsala stood and kissed her cheek. "Louella, may I introduce you to my wife? Rosa, this is Louella Parsons." Behind Rosa were her two sisters in from Bayonne, their husbands playing golf at a country club in the Valley on Marsala's tab.

All right, Ma? he thought as Parsons met the in-laws. OK, Mimmo?

Parsons hadn't swatted him since and Klein made sure Marsala talked to everybody he could win over. Columnists and magazine editors were invited to the new house. Rosa served hors d'oeuvres. A few punks turned down the call and kept swiping at him, but the public caught on to their game, the piling on, the cheap shots. The loyal fans forgave. They'd been right about their Bill. He was true.

"Thanks, ladies and gentlemen. Thanks a million," he said after a tune on his radio show, the applause still ringing. "Listen, I've been meaning to say something and I'm going to say it right here, right now. You picked me up when I was down and, well, as my friends in the old neighborhood will tell you, I don't forget. You're swell, each and every one of you!"

He was elated. Free. Life seemed so uncomplicated. A new year, a new lease on life, everything glowing under the California sun. When the sessions were done and the first sides ready for release, he intended to get back on the road with his new combo. Rico Enna had approached him with a plan. He'd play the

Cocoanut Grove at the Ambassador, the Chez Paree in Chicago, the Palm Tree in Miami. Then he'd head back north to that new joint in Philly and the 500 Club in Atlantic City. Then three weeks solid at the Caribbean, where he'd show Anthony Corini how getting in line had put him on a shooting star. He was certain the pictures would pack them in, the radio show, too. There was money to be made. Bill Marsala couldn't be stopped.

The producer spoke over the intercom. "Bill, I'd like to take it again from bar forty—"

Marsala turned to the booth. "Hell, let's take it from the top," he replied. Snapping his fingers, he said, "I could swing with this lady all night."

The producer nodded to the drummer when the tape was rolling.

Marsala entered on the fifth bar. "I just found joy…"

The combo purred and Marsala closed his eyes and let the melody ride the rhythm.

"…why I love my Sweet Lorraine."

Sweets tossed off a little fill that ushered the singer to the B flat bridge.

Marsala threw open his arms as he prepared to move up in register. "When it's raining, I—"

His voice cracked.

The band stopped.

"Who the hell let in the frog?" Marsala joked. He took out a handkerchief, coughed a few times and wiped his lips.

The musicians laughed.

Shaking his head, Marsala put his fingers to his throat. "Baby, don't you fail me now," he warbled.

The producer said, "Bill, you want to take five?"

"I'd like to take five hours after that one."

As the musicians chatted, Marsala lit up a Chesterfield and gestured for Terrasini to come out from the booth.

"How bad was it?" he whispered. He'd started making his necktie.

"The clam?" Terrasini asked. "What the hell? You missed a note. You're tired…"

"That take seven any good?"

Terrasini shrugged. At bar 40, the tenor sax stepped on Sweets, marring the whole thing.

"I'm blowing the joint," the singer said. "Tell the boys I'll see them tomorrow."

Terrasini met his boss at the car, Marsala already in the backseat. The dome light went on when he inched behind the wheel. "Where to?" he asked.

"The Wilshire Towers," Marsala said. "And tell Klein to get a doctor."

He held up his handkerchief. Using the rearview, Terrasini saw it was blotted with blood.

Marsala watched as the doctor packed away his instruments. In his blue silk pajamas, pillows stacked behind his head, he was trying for an air of nonchalance but came up short.

"You have a hemorrhagic vocal cord nodule," the doctor said. "A capillary ruptured. It's not serious."

"For you, maybe," Marsala said.

Klein paced, hands clasped behind his back.

"In fact, you have two nodules. One popped. The other might. We call them singer's nodules. They're benign." He wiped his hands with his handkerchief. "They look like clits, if you must know."

"What does it mean, Doctor?" Klein asked.

"Mr. Marsala needs to rest. Nothing more." He returned to the singer. "At some point, you might consider having the nodules removed, but for now, rest."

"How long?" Marsala asked.

"Ten days to two weeks."

"Bullshit."

"They won't kill you, Mr. Marsala. But they'll make you hoarse and in time, they may affect your vocal cords."

Klein stepped in. "Thank you, Doctor," he said as he took him by the arm.

Terrasini inched aside to let them pass.

Agitated, Marsala lit a cigarette. "My vocal cord ruptured, but it's not serious."

"There's enough songs in the can, Bebe," Terrasini said. "Phil can get the agency to push the tour back a few weeks. You've been driving yourself awfully hard."

Klein returned, the doctor's bill in his jacket pocket. "What do you think, Bill?"

Marsala said, "Where'd you come up with this clown? Clits? And then he says the other one might pop, too?"

"Not if you rest, Bill," Klein said hurriedly.

"It's not serious, but I ought to get them removed." Marsala crushed out the cigarette, threw back the bedding and stood. "Fuck him."

"Bill…" Klein sank in dismay. "It's your call, of course. But how can rest hurt you, Bill?"

Marsala slipped into his silk robe and began to pace.

"Nino, get Eleanor on the phone."

Klein stammered. "Bill, she's on location."

"Nobody's talking to you, pal," Marsala snapped as he walked toward the bath. "Get her, Nino. Track her down."

Klein waited for Marsala to run the shower. Then he said to Terrasini, "It's almost one o'clock in western Europe."

"So she's on the set," Terrasini said. "Somewhere."

Klein slumped. "This is a nightmare."

Klein confirmed that Ree was in Madrid. TWA would get Bebe to New York, then onto Spain. Stunned but not surprised, Terrasini packed Marsala's bags. He watched as Marsala dressed, slamming drawers and closet doors, his eyes narrow, jaw clenched.

"Bebe—"

Marsala held up a hand and stuffed his passport in his jacket pocket.

Klein rode to the airport in back next to Marsala. He knew what to say but not how to say it so he kept quiet until Terrasini pulled up outside the terminal.

"Bill, hold on a second," he began.

Marsala sighed.

Terrasini was on his way around to the trunk.

"Bill—"

"Save it, Phil," Marsala said as he slipped on his sunglasses.

Klein could feel his heart pumping. "I'm sorry, but this is a mistake, Bill. You've got everything going your way now. Can't you give it two weeks?"

Marsala stared ahead. "No."

"The press is going to be there. They'll jump on you."

"That's your problem."

"They'll say everything we did—bringing them out to your home, introducing Louella to Rosa, talking about your family—Bill, they'll say it was a game. A sham."

Marsala turned to him. "It was."

"No, Bill. No. It was the right thing to do. It's right for you and right for your career."

"Hey, Phil, didn't you hear? There's no career. No voice, baby, no career."

"Bill, the doctor didn't—"

"Let Eleanor know I'm coming. I don't care what you tell the press."

"Bill, please. Don't throw it all away."

"Phil, do what I told you. Handle it."

"I can't, Bill. It won't wash."

"You can't or you won't?"

"Both," he said, his voice soft and desperate. "Bill, it won't play. I'm sorry."

"OK," Marsala said. "You're fired."

"Bill—"

"Get fucked, Phil. You and everybody else."

He pushed open the door and told Terrasini to bring the bags into the terminal.

CHAPTER TWENTY-FOUR

Daydreaming the truck could make the run by itself, Benno turned left off Central Park West and settled near the familiar fire hydrant, yanking the hand brake. He hopped in back, moving something like graceful, something like a busy chimp in a zoo. The *baccala* went into the crate next to the fennel, the *arancini di riso* with the chicken livers and the envelope, as fat as ever.

He was hoping Corini greeted him. Frankie Fortune blew cold and frigid, despite making a big deal out of introducing Benno around at Hennie's funeral. Since then, he treated Benno like a stain. Old Cy Geller, up from Miami, saw Benno entering the apartment with a crate and said, "Good afternoon."

"*Salvatore…*" Corini would say, stretching the four syllables.

Should Bruno Gigenti, for whatever far-fuckin'-fetched reason, find himself in his rival's apartment, maybe even he'd act like Benno wasn't just some fly buzzing the room. But not Frankie, who dug in the crates for the envelope, then walked away.

To hell with him, Benno thought as he crossed the street, a nip in the November air. Out of habit, he threw the crate up on his shoulder, blocking his good eye's side view so he could leave his right hand free to shake with the doorman, who also said hello better than Frankie.

Then Benno felt something heavy crack him hard above the right ear, and his hat flew off. The pain shook him down to his soles and back again. Maybe his head would burst. He landed on the sidewalk next to the crate, food rolling toward the curb.

Before the lights went out, he saw the bottom of the guy's shoes as he ran toward Columbus Avenue. Wiry little mother-fucker, wiry, but no kid. Holding his hat with one hand, the envelope with the other.

Leo Bell left City College's gothic campus for Amsterdam Avenue on his way to the IRT, humping a leather satchel heavy with texts and research, a sleeveless sweater over a white Oxford. The nuns at St. Claire's had given Imogene a breather, so they decided to visit the Metropolitan Museum of Art before dinner and a picture in Times Square.

Bell had introduced her to Benno and they got along like he knew they would, teasing, laughing, Imogene insisting she'd find him a steady girl, Sal telling her he didn't need no help. It was easy with her family, too. Ruthie was a pisser, his surrogate kid sister. Mr. O'Boyle insisted Bell call him Mike. Mrs. O'Boyle invited Bell to join the family at Sunday Mass. He declined politely, saying he was busy elsewhere. "But do you go to Mass, Leo?" she asked, her brogue thick with sincerity.

"I do, Mrs. O'Boyle," he replied. At the Church of the Central Intelligence Agency, Charlie Tyler presiding.

Bell met Tyler in New York City, the location chosen at the last minute. "So?" Tyler would begin. Bell told him Boo's crew hijacked a truckload of radios off the Pulaski Skyline; Fat Tutti bent back Albini the Tailor's knees over a cash dispute; the vig on street money is up to 12 percent: day-to-day stuff Tyler could've overheard walking Narrows Gate from the Lackawanna Station to St. Matty's.

Tyler wanted more.

"Let me get a semester under my belt," Bell replied. "Then I can spend time in town, talk to people, go to the clubs."

Though he dropped in on the candy store maybe a half-dozen times since he enrolled in City College, Bell hadn't gotten a single tip on his own. Everything he'd ever learn that would be worthwhile to the CIA would come through Benno, who'd get it from Mimmo. Stinking of discontent, Mimmo moaned to Benno about Ziggy Baum spending three or four times the budget Corini and Geller had approved to build the Sandpiper Hotel and Casino in Las Vegas. Mimmo bitched about how Gigenti wanted points on the heroin going into the projects in Jersey, too. Mimmo had turned into a spout. "Now he comes to my uncle's store, sits on the *ceci* and starts yakking," Benno complained. "I think there's a worm loose in his head."

Though everything Benno reported added up to tension between Corini and Gigenti, Bell repeated none of it, at least not yet. He wouldn't put Benno in a position of having to confirm speculation.

Now, strolling away from the City College campus, his topcoat open, Bell reached Broadway, crossing a strip of shade.

And there, near the subway station, was Benno, sitting on his truck's running board. Forlorn, he was as pale as his brown skin would allow, holding a gauze pad against the side of his head. Blood had dried on his collar and apron strap.

"I was hoping you didn't drive to school," he said as he struggled to stand.

Bell grabbed his elbow. "What the fuck happened to you?"

"They robbed me. They took the money."

"Let me see," Bell said, nudging the thick pad away from his friend's ear.

The skin was split open good and the gash hadn't stopped bleeding.

"The doorman took care of me. I didn't tell Corini or Frankie or nobody."

"Your melon...*Minga*."

Bell reached into his friend's slacks and withdrew the truck keys. "I'll drive." He helped Benno around the front of the truck. On the passenger's seat was a fold of wax paper, the dried tail of a salted cod peeking out.

"Lost the money," Benno said, as he climbed up. "But I saved the *baccala*."

They picked up Imogene by the Port Authority and she tended to Benno in the truck's cab, Bell driving through the Lincoln Tunnel back to Narrows Gate. "You might need stitches, Sal," she said, her professional demeanor shining through.

On the Jersey side, they stopped at a pharmacy and then went to Bell's secret place under the 14th Street viaduct.

They must've knocked my brain loose, Benno thought as he trudged up the stairs. Leo Bell has a love nest?

Taking off Benno's apron and his bloodstained shirt, they helped him down the hall to the rusted sink where Imogene poured peroxide on the wound. Benno yelped.

Imogene turned on the water. "Rinse it good," she instructed.

"You going to stitch me?" he asked as water ran along his ears and cheeks.

"Let's get the bleeding to stop and we'll see. I don't suppose you want the side of your head shaved."

"No, but I'll take a couple of aspirins. An ice pack, too."

They put Benno on the bed, an old towel covering the wound. Thinking concussion, Imogene insisted he rest.

Out in the hall, Bell said, "I'd better go see what's what."

"Are you going to tell me what this is about?" she asked.

"I don't think you want to know," Bell said as he inched toward the newel post.

"I do, Leo." She liked Benno. She thought he was cute, a big little boy.

"They robbed him," he replied. That was as thin as he could slice it. "They took the money."

"Oh."

"I'm not lying."

"But you're not truthing, either."

He decided he'd go down to the store to let Vito and Gemma know Sal was all right. When he arrived, Mimmo was sitting on a stack of canned tomatoes, his hat on a barrel of rice.

"Ding," he said. He gestured to the back room.

Bell held up his finger as he waited for Gemma to come around the counter. "He's fine," he said to her in Italian. "Maybe a stitch or two. But he's fine." He leaned down and let her kiss his cheek. He gave her a hug and as he held her, nodded at Vito, who was stiff with dread.

Bell followed Mimmo to a table in back.

"So?"

"They liked to take off the side of his head," Bell replied, staring into Mimmo's sunglasses.

"What about the money?"

He repeated what Benno told him.

"They took his wallet?" Mimmo asked.

Bell said no.

"He tell you what he was doing? The deliveries?"

"I figured," Bell said.

"Sally talked."

"About what?"

"About the bag. The take."

"To who?"

"Somebody."

Bell shook his head. "You know better than that."

Mimmo made a little shrug.

"How much was in the envelope?"

"Twenty-nine Gs and change."

And you don't provide protection, you stupid son of a bitch? "Maybe it's about Pellizzari and the hit at the motel."

"You heard about that?"

"Everybody heard about it," Bell said. "You like it when people know. This thing, though…"

Mimmo hoisted away from the table. "Maybe they'll ask where you were, College Boy."

"You think I took you for thirty large and sapped Sally? Come on, Mimmo. Be yourself."

Mimmo started toward the door.

Eleanor Ree had developed an appreciation for the tradition of siesta—especially after she'd been up until dawn in the bars on the Gran Via where she dazzled patrons. Throwing her dark mane back, she danced, hips swaying under her free-flowing peasant skirts, her boisterous laugh rippling above the guitars and rhythmic handclaps. They called her *gitana de ojos verdes*—the green-eyed gypsy. The Spaniards loved her as she strolled the Plaza Mayor, shopped in El Rastro, dined in the restaurants of El

Escorial, acknowledging their compliments in the few words of
Castilian Spanish she learned.

The cast and crew loved her, too: She was thoroughly professional, despite the aches and minor injuries she suffered in her
scenes in the rugged Sierra de Guadarrama. But alone she was
miserable. The entire picture was a difficult shoot with multiple
locations and a script that was an insult to Hemingway's source
material. The summer sun was brutal, at noon a heat lamp on
high. After lunch, she slept, grinding her teeth, tossing merci-
lessly until the wake-up call beckoned. Her thoughts taunted her,
her mind on a pendulum that swung between reflex and hammering doubt. She needed a lover to fight off the devils lurking
in her solitude, someone who could fill the inescapable hole in
her soul.

Now she awoke from a fitful sleep. A ceiling fan wobbled
above her.

He was in the shower. Antonio was a proud and fastidious
man. His sinewy brown body glistened.

She thought of joining him, coming up from behind, wrap-
ping her arms around his narrow waist, the cool water trickling
down her breasts. He'd turn elegantly and stare at her, his head
cocked, conquest in his eyes, as if he had an *estoque* in one hand,
a red *muleta* in the other and she were a seething beast about to
be taken.

She reached to the nightstand and rinsed her mouth with gin.
As she left the bed, she heard a timid knock on the hotel room's door.
Slipping into her robe, she said, "*Sí?*" though no one on the Palace
staff would dare interrupt Antonio Miguel de Zuera during siesta.

"Eleanor, it's Johnny Cornax."

A unit publicist for the picture. "Come back in an hour, John,"
she said.

"It can't wait, El. Sorry."

Ree wiped the sleep from her eyes and poked her head into the hallway. "Hi, Johnny," she said with a shy smile.

Cornax coated bad news for a living, but there was no way to sugar this. "Bill Marsala just landed at Barajas."

Behind her, the shower stopped with a prophetic groan.

"A reporter from United Press saw him. Marsala told him he's here to be with you. To see the sights."

"I know nothing about it, Johnny. Honest."

"He asked that you two be given some privacy, but…"

"Yeah, I know," Ree said.

"I can let you know when he arrives. I can move you to another hotel if you want."

"No, no," she said. "I'll—I'll—" What the fuck was Bill doing in Spain? Why would he tell reporters we're together again?

Because he's certifiable. A four-star filbert.

"I'll call up," Cornax said.

Ree shut the door. When she turned, there was de Zuera, towel around his waist, body glistening, black hair slicked back and off his lean, flawless face, his feet set firmly in place.

Bell brought Imogene back to school. When he returned to 14th Street, he found Benno waiting outside the decaying building, the now bloody towel pressed against the side of his head. The sun was gone and the streetlamps on the viaduct cast eerie shadows. They got into the truck, Bell behind the wheel. Benno said, "She asks a lot of questions."

She'd asked Bell, too, and he answered, walking a tightrope. "He knew some bad guys growing up" and "He can't say no" and "Maybe this will wake him up" was the best he could do.

She said, "What about you, Leo? You knew the same people."

"I caught some breaks. My father, the Army, Landis, college." He took her hand. "You."

The truck smacked a pothole. "What did you tell her?"

"I didn't tell her nothing," Benno replied. "I don't know what she knows."

"About the crew? She knows only what she reads in the papers. She sees the words Narrows Gate and she asks me if I know the guy or the place they found his body. I say no."

They turned onto Fillmore. Bell looked in the rearview for company. "Mimmo thinks you told somebody," he said.

"No, I ain't talked. I would've told you if I did."

"Then it was an inside job," Bell said. "Unless you stole the money yourself."

"After I hit myself on the fuckin' noodle?"

"You took a smack for thirty Gs."

"They said there was thirty Gs?" Benno grimaced in disgust. "Means fifteen. Or less."

When they reached Third Street, Benno told Bell to pull over and get out. "Bring your car behind the store," he said as he climbed over the stick.

Ten minutes later, Benno came out of the alley wearing his leather jacket and gloves. "The Holland Tunnel," he said, jumping in, pointing past the train yards. "I got an idea."

As instructed, Bell headed toward Observer Road.

Benno sat with his eyes closed. Bell saw a calm before a storm.

"Who could it be?" Benno asked.

"Corini, Fortune and Mimmo. They know. Boo and Fat Tutti, too."

"Give me odds."

"Mimmo doesn't play smart," he said, "and he can't make a move on his own, especially with Bebe on probation."

"So it's Corini or Fortune."

The tunnel was clear. Bell paid the toll and they cruised toward bright tile under the river. Soon they came out into the starry night. The Lower West Side was minutes away.

Benno said, "Go left, make a left, make a left." They headed east and Bell saw they were going to Little Italy, to the members-only social club used as a base by Bruno Gigenti, Corini's murderous rival.

"Hear me out," Benno said. "This is one of two things. This is Corini setting up Gigenti. Or it's Gigenti—he wants to show he can go after Corini's guy and he don't give a shit what's next. Either way, Frankie's in the middle of it. He's the go-between."

Bell looked at him. "This is the right move, Sal?"

Benno rolled down the window and tossed the bloody towel onto Leonard Street. Bell shivered at the rush of cold air.

Gigenti's club sat on the other side of a park on Mulberry Street. As stout, olive-skinned men in coats and baggy slacks played bocce under lamplight, shuffling to stay warm, Bell settled the car alongside a high, cast-iron fence.

A couple of big guys, Gigenti's version of Boo and Tutti, flanked the club's door, the Italian flag draped over its header. An empty chair faced the park and soon a young man filled it, an espresso cup in his hand, collar turned up.

"Him?" Bell asked.

"Not him. But the guy's in there," Benno said. "If he's not, he's coming. And if he ain't coming, somebody knows where he is."

CHAPTER TWENTY-FIVE

One of the big guys left, the little guy, too, and the other big guy went inside, pulling the door shut behind him. The park was abandoned now, Mulberry Street empty. Bell was drowsy, but Benno remained as vigilant as a cat. Suddenly he said, "I'm going in."

"Sally—"

"Gigenti's not in there. Not until two in the morning."

"You don't know that."

"Doing what? Playing *scopa* with the help? The guards are pulled, right?" Benno reached inside his jacket and eased out a dull, long-barrel pistol. He hefted it, hand on the wooden grip.

"Holy Christ, Sal." Bell hadn't seen the gun since they were kids and Benno showed him how he intended to shoot Maguire, the crooked cop Gigenti hung from St. Matty's.

"The big fat fuck who went in is still in there with I don't know what, a fuckin' cannon maybe. But the little shit, too. I hope."

Bell stared at him in astonishment.

"See, Leo, being smart with the books, it don't mean shit right now."

Bell reached for his arm. "You walk into Gigenti's club fixed and it's a new ballgame, Sal. You know that."

Benno tugged free. "Fuckin' right it is." He stepped onto Baxter Street.

Bell followed as they cut through the vacant park. Spindly branches bobbed in a breeze.

Benno said, "You in?"

"You ought to calm the fuck down, Sal."

Breathing heavy, his face red, Benno repeated, "You in?"

Bell nodded.

"Throw the chair through the front window."

"Sal—"

Seething, Benno said, "Straight through."

They crossed Mulberry. The storefront windows were painted navy blue to chest level. On the glass, in front of dusty sun-stained curtains, gold-leaf block lettering said "Mulberry Street Community Center" and "Members Only." Peering between the curtains, Bell saw the back of old wooden shutters and hanging plants.

Benno stood bold by the door.

Bell picked up the chair and charged. Giant shards of window glass crashed into the shutters, blowing them open.

"Stand back," Benno said. Head bowed, his arm stiff, he held the gun high and tight.

A second or two later, the big fat guy opened the door. And Benno reached up and shoved the nozzle between his eyes.

"The motherfucker who robbed me," Benno said, backing him up.

Bell rushed in. The club appeared empty, but he ran behind the musty bar to check. Nobody.

"The motherfucker who robbed me," Benno repeated, pushing the big guy back.

"I don't—"

Benno brought the barrel down hard on his nose and blood shot from the wound and his nostrils at the same time. "*Il suo nome, il suo indirizzo or morite. Semplice.*"

Blood oozed through his bloated fingers. "Who?" he managed. "I don't..."

Benno described him.

"He lives over on Pike," the guy said. "We call him Little Buff."

"Let's go," Benno said. He turned the big fat guy around and put the nozzle against his spine. "You got money?" he said to Bell.

He did. Enough for dinner and a picture show with Imogene.

"Throw it on the bar. For the window." Then he said, "Come on, fat man. We're going to kill somebody."

They crossed under the Manhattan Bridge, Bell hurrying to keep up. Half the time he scurried backward, expecting to see Gigenti, the killer Zamarella and the 200 soldiers in his crew storming through Little Italy.

The moon hidden by the overpass, Pike Street was coated in shadows. They came to the stoop of a ratty, redbrick tenement. "The next two minutes are the most important you lived," Benno said to the fat man. "You ring the buzzer, you tell him Bruno wants him."

"What if he ain't—"

"Then you're dead. Now ring the buzzer."

He did and they went in, all three of them, over cracked tile, steam heat sputtering.

The big fat guy grabbed the banister and looked up, waiting for Little Buff to show. He waited, then looked at Benno.

"Somebody's paying," Benno said, his voice as calm as warm milk. Veins pulsed at his temples.

"*Che c'è ora?*" came a voice from high up.

The guy wiped his bloody face with the back of his wrist. "Danny," he shouted. "Now."

"Don't look at me," Benno whispered.

"Now?" Little Buff shouted.

"Hurry the fuck down here," the big fat guy said.

When the door upstairs slammed shut, Benno bolted, leaping two steps at a time.

The guy turned to Bell.

"I sit if I'm you," Bell said. "Otherwise..."

Benno ran up four flights and arrived just as the little thief motherfucker reopened the door, stupid bastard struggling into his coat at the same time.

Benno broke his front teeth with the gun butt. Little Buff collapsed to his knees. "The money," Benno said, gasping. "Every fuckin' cent."

Little Buff looked up in terror.

Benno thought, What the fuck. I might as well... He aimed at Little Buff's forehead.

Little Buff knew he was dead.

At that moment, a bony, dark-haired woman with raccoon eyes appeared at the door. She wore a tattered nightgown, her breasts hanging. She said, "*Abbiamo un bambino.*"

"No, you don't," Benno said.

"No, we do. We do," Little Buff said, his voice jagged with panic.

Benno kept the gun poised. "Why don't he cry?"

"He cries," the guy said. "But not now. Not now, *Madonna mio!* I swear to God—"

"I bring him," the woman said. She trembled.

"What's his name?"

"Bruno." They said it at the same time, more or less.

Benno sagged. "You're fuckin' kidding me." Then to the woman he said, "Get the money. Get it now."

She ran off.

"She comes back with a gun and you got an orphan in there," Benno said.

The envelope came around the door. Benno snatched it. It was torn open, but it held its weight. "Who sent you?" he said to Little Buff, who now sat in the doorway, blood pouring down his chin.

"Please—"

"I said—"

"Some guy from Jersey." In Sicilian, he added, "Please don't tell Bruno. For God's sake, please don't tell him. My God!"

Benno stepped back. Then he swung and slammed Little Buff across the face with the gun, knocking him out.

As he dashed down the stairs, he buried the envelope inside his jacket. The gun hung at his side.

The big fat guy was sitting on the landing, Bell leaned against the lukewarm radiator.

"Let's go," Benno said.

Before he left, he turned. "Fat man, you'd better pray Gigenti don't think you stole from me, too."

The guy held up his blood-streaked hands in surrender.

"Good," Benno said.

Side by side, Benno and Bell ran back to the car.

The gun quaked in Benno's hand as Bell pulled the car out of parking spot.

Benno took a deep breath. "OK," he said, "that's the first part."

Bell drove too fast but he was mindful of the cops. The last thing he needed was to get pulled over with a bloodstained envelope full of cash. He made the squealing turn onto Watt Street, his heart pounding.

"No, no. Don't go for the tunnel," Benno said. "Get on the West Side Highway."

"What—"

"The second part, Central Park West. And slow the fuck down. We look like a couple of armed robbers here." He stashed the gun in the glove compartment.

Marsala slouched across the opulent hotel lobby in Madrid, unaware that Eleanor Ree was waiting on a banquette under the hotel's glass dome. When she saw him, she jumped up, brushed by potted plants and caught him at reception before he could ask for her room.

Marsala heard his name whispered softly, as if from a distance. "Bill."

He was flagged with fatigue, but his suit was immaculate, as if it had been pressed on the airplane. He was clean-shaven.

"Baby," he said. He hugged her desperately and snuggled into the warmth of her embrace.

"Oh, Bill."

"Let's get out of here." He looked over her shoulder for photographers.

"Bill, we're shooting tonight."

"Blow it off."

"Bill." She pretended to pout.

He stepped back and put a tired smile on his face.

Ree wore a green silk blouse and pale slacks. Her hair was tucked behind her ears.

"You look terrific," he said. "Spain's done wonders for you." He held his arms open wide. "Come here, doll."

Oh God, she thought as she leaned against him.

"I'm going to ravish you," he whispered. "You're going to know how much your Bill missed you."

She moaned as he kissed her neck and nipped at her ear.

"Upstairs," he said, "before I take you right here."

"Darling, I wasn't expecting you."

He let go. "So?" Then his face fell.

"Bill, I can explain."

Marsala charged toward a concierge and elbowed to the head of the line.

"Bill, please."

Startled, the concierge blurted the room number.

Marsala raced for the sweeping stairs. Ree's flats clacked on marble as she followed.

He stormed along the corridor, checking door numbers to the left and right.

"Bill," she said as she caught him. "Bill. Goddamn it, Bill. Would you wait a minute?"

He found the double doors to de Zuera's suite and pounded at them with the sides of his fists.

"Bill."

The bullfighter appeared.

"The gig's over, shorty," Marsala said, flicking his thumb. "Pack your bags."

Ree said wearily, "Bill, it's his room."

"Then let's throw this bum out."

In his black suit, his shirt open at the collar, de Zuera stood rail-stiff. He seemed thoroughly disinterested in Marsala.

Panting from the rush up the stairs, Ree said, "They'd empty the hotel before they move him."

"Oh, he's a big shot?" Marsala returned to de Zuera. "Are you a big shot, shorty?"

"I am Antonio Miguel de Zuera," the legendary bullfighter replied. "And you are?"

"I'm her guy," Marsala said. "Now move along."

De Zuera stood firmly in place.

Inching in, Marsala said, "How'd you like to wind up on your ass?"

De Zuera smiled. He didn't understand half of what Marsala was saying, but he could feel the challenge. "As you prefer."

Marsala threw a punch. De Zuera dodged it without moving his feet.

The next one missed, too.

Then de Zuera stepped deftly aside. He grabbed Marsala by the back of his slacks and tossed him deep into the suite's living room.

"What do you wish me to do, *camaleón?*" De Zuera called Ree chameleon: one moment, she was the epitome of sexuality, the next a freckle-faced innocent. Bold, then suddenly adrift with insecurity.

"We'll go," she said. "I'm so sorry, Antonio."

"No, my dear. Please take the room. It is my gift to you."

"Fuck off, shorty," Marsala said as he gathered himself. "Nobody here needs charity."

De Zuera looked at him. "I was not speaking to you."

"Well, I'm speaking to you," Marsala replied. He stepped up again. "You know, shorty, where I come from, we know how to take care of a punk like you."

De Zuera swept his hand behind his back and withdrew a small pistol, a .22. He tossed it to Marsala. "Use it as you wish."

"Don't think I won't."

De Zuera snorted in disgust.

Ree grabbed the Spaniard by the arm and tried to yank him outside the suite. But he wouldn't move.

Marsala waved the gun. "Go on, shit heel," he said. "Get lost."

"Antonio, please. For me, Antonio."

De Zuera yielded. "*Para ti*," he said softly. He gestured for Ree to pass into the corridor.

"You're going with him?" Marsala said.

"For Christ's sake, Bill, would you just shut up for a minute."

Marsala dropped onto a settee as de Zuera followed Ree into the hall. She shut the door. "I'm so sorry," she said. "I should have explained." She took his arm again and walked with him along the corridor.

"There is no need," de Zuera replied. He looked at her, a glint in his eye. "Nothing will change how I feel about our time—"

A gunshot echoed.

Ree and de Zuera stared at each other.

Ree bolted back to the suite.

The bullfighter waited. Then he turned and left. He spoke to the concierge in their native language, his speech so exceedingly calm and measured that it was clear de Zuera had been offended.

"There is a desperate man in my room. He has pretended to shoot himself and perhaps he has—a minor wound requiring sympathy, but nothing so serious. When the charade has ended, please find Miss Ree new accommodations, perhaps at the Ritz or the Canarias, if you don't mind. The desperate man will insist that he pay, but I ask that you send the bill to me."

"As you say, *señor*," the man replied.

"I thank you."

"*Señor*, do you know who this man is?"

"No. Nor do I care."

"He is Bill Marsala. The famous American singer. There are reporters who want to talk to him." The concierge nodded toward the bar.

"The Americans can have him," de Zuera replied. He left the hotel and as he walked toward the splashing fountains at the Canovas del Castillo Square, he wondered what a woman like Eleanor Ree could see in a man like that. By the time he reached the Paseo del Prado, he understood that she was more damaged, and more fragile, than he feared.

"No, he don't expect me," Benno said, answering the night doorman's question. "But he wants to see me. You bet."

The bewildered doorman scratched the back of his neck.

"Go ahead," Benno insisted. "Tell him Salvatore." He pronounced it in Sicilian, operatic and fluttery. "Say it like that. Salvatore from Narrows Gate."

He turned to Bell. "I seen Hennie Rosiglino do this. These guys, they're in charge of nothing."

And then they were on the elevator, going up.

Anthony Corini was at the door facing the lift. Over blue silk pajamas, he wore an embroidered robe with matching slippers. Bell thought the boss wasn't terribly surprised to see them.

"How can I help you?" Corini said. His hands sat in his robe's side pockets, his thumbs out.

"I got the money back, Mr. Corini." With a nod, Benno asked for permission to reach inside his coat. He handed over the bloody envelope.

"I don't know how much it is," Benno added, as Corini eased back the flap. "But it's all there."

Corini said, "Come in." He stepped aside to let Benno and Bell pass.

"The kitchen," Benno whispered.

"Really?" Bell said.

Corini closed the door and moved to the sink, putting a butcher-block table and a hanging garden of pots and pans between him and his guests. The window offered a glimpse of other castle towers.

"Tell me," Corini said.

"I found him near Gigenti's joint on Mulberry Street," Benno said, spinning his hat in his hands.

Corini nodded slowly.

"But the guy says Gigenti don't know."

"The guy?"

"Who robbed me. He has a new baby," Benno said. "But new teeth, too, when the swelling goes down. He wasn't lying."

Corini put the envelope on the counter, not far from the sink.

Somewhere deep in the apartment, a door closed. Benno lowered his voice, thinking he woke up Corini's wife, too. "Mr. Corini, I don't know what's going on," he said, "but I don't want you to think I could fail you. This bothered the hell out of me."

"No, you did good, Sal," Corini replied. Then he looked at Bell. "And you?"

Benno answered. "He's my friend. He goes to college." When Corini frowned in confusion, he added, "He drives."

"They cracked his head," Bell said as he tamped down his sweater.

Benno turned and pointed to the gash, which was now hidden under curls.

"Mr. Corini, I'm out of line, I'll just shut up, but I'm in the middle of something and I don't want to be in the middle of nothing."

Corini let a smile cross his lips. "What's on your mind?"

"I was there when Pellizzari took one and now this and I ain't said nothing to nobody. My hand to God."

Corini came around the table. "Everything is good," he said in Sicilian. "There's nothing for you to worry about."

Benno sighed. Then he said, gesturing toward Bell, "He speaks Italian, by the way, though he don't look it."

Bell smiled as if embarrassed.

"Sal, you don't say anything to anyone about this. You understand me?"

"No, Mr. Corini. I won't."

"And you—"

Bell jutted out his right hand. "Leonardo Bell, sir," he said.

"Keep this to yourselves."

"You got it, Mr. Corini," Benno replied, speaking for both.

Rosa thought he'd decided to have a few drinks with the band. A bottle or two in the studio, ice in Dixie cups, blue smoke clinging to the ceiling, cables underfoot. Or maybe he'd gone for breakfast with Nino, bacon and eggs on a roll, out on a pier, fresh-brewed coffee in a thermos, and maybe they'd kick off their shoes and walk the cold sand. A chance to relax while feeling fine about what he'd done and where he was going. A life back on track, music once again at the heart of things. Then he'd sleep until late afternoon and start all over again, Bill's career in flight.

But there was no mistaking the expression on Terrasini's face as he stepped through the morning haze, slouching toward Rosa in the doorway, Bill Jr. in her arms. Until seconds ago, having heard the car pull up, she was thinking her husband had come home.

"Go ahead, Nino. Just say it."

"He went to Spain," he told her as he hitched up his slacks. "She's there." Terrasini shook his head in frustration and disgust. "His voice gave out and he panicked. We got a doctor and the guy said it was nothing but rest. But Bill panicked."

She stared at him. "What else?"

"He fired Phil."

She slumped. "I don't believe this."

He followed Rosa into the house and watched as she paced. Look at her, he thought. Dressed nice and fresh for Bill—her hair pulled back sweet, lipstick, sky blue blouse, khakis, brown flats. When she turned, he studied her face. Her eyes darted as she calculated, her jaw clenched.

"That son of a bitch," she said finally. "He had this planned."

"No, no," Terrasini replied as he took the baby, cradling him against his hip. "We had to track her down—Phil tried to talk him out of it." He stopped. "Jesus, it's a mess."

"He's an idiot. An idiot."

Worse, Terrasini thought. Not an idiot. He knows what he's throwing away and he don't care. Not when he feels the world's got him cornered. Then it's to hell with everybody, which includes his wife and son.

"*Questa è la goccia che fa traboccare il vaso*," Terrasini said. "Right?"

"For me, yes," she said. "The last straw. *Finito*."

Terrasini had known women like Rosa his whole life. Anybody waiting for her to burst into tears this time was going to be hanging around forever. *Siciliana* like Rosa don't stand around waiting to get worked over twice. Odds are she already has her strategy in place.

But, oh, the way she'd loved him. Oh, Jesus. The way she'd stare at him, sitting at a front table in some joint, nursing a ginger ale; Bebe's singing for everybody but also just for her. He's a kid in a floppy bow tie, she's a budding young girl with a blush on her cheek and they don't know where this thing is going, but it promised a wonderful ride.

Which is now over.

Hennie in the grave and now this door is sealed shut.

Fuckin' Bebe.

"Rosa, could I ask you maybe we could see what happens when his voice comes back?" Up went Bill Jr. onto his shoulder and the baby pawed at the side of his head, tugging at his ear.

"His voice goes," she said. "I understand. But why isn't he here, Nino? Tell me."

"Sure, that's the sensible thing to do, to come to his family," he said. "But he's not sensible. We know that. He panics."

The phone rang and Rosa went for the kitchen.

Terrasini looked for a place to rest the squirming kid.

"Oh, yes, Louella," Rosa said. She gestured for Terrasini to join her. "Phil Klein—" She opened her eyes wide. "Phil Klein had a stroke."

"Oh shit," Terrasini uttered.

"No, Louella. Bill's not here. He can't comment. He's in Spain. With Eleanor Ree. That's right. He's left me and Bill Jr. He fired Phil, and he's left us. Of course, you can print it. Who can stop you? It's true."

Terrasini sank.

"A statement?" She paused in thought, all the while staring into Terrasini's eyes. "Phil Klein is in my prayers. He was a dear,

dear friend to Bill since the earliest days of his career. I'm sure the shock—Well, no, I can't say that. I'm sure I'll be down to see Phil this afternoon. He's a lovely man. But you know that."

They waited as Parsons asked a question.

"Heartsick? Do I sound heartsick? Well, then, I suppose I am. Foolish? No, not foolish. I do wish Bill had said good-bye to his son."

Before hanging up, she said, "Anytime, Louella. Yes, I appreciate that. Thank you."

Terrasini said, "Maybe that was too much, Rosa."

"Hey, Nino, that's how you do it in Narrows Gate, right?" She held out her arms and took the baby. "There's a bottle in the fridge. Maybe you could heat it, if you don't mind?"

Terrasini nodded. From behind the refrigerator door, he said, "Maybe I should call Ziggy Baum in Vegas and let him know about Bill leaving. He can pass it up the chain."

But Rosa was already dialing the candy store in Narrows Gate. If her uncle wasn't there, they'd find him. Mimmo would set it in motion.

Bottle in his hand, Terrasini said softly, "Rosa, *por favore*."

Her face steely with determination, she said no. "*Non questo volta*, Nino. Not this time."

PART THREE

PART THREE

CHAPTER TWENTY-SIX

With the bullfighter's gun, Marsala had put a hole in a lamp on the Baroque credenza and the silk-papered wall behind it.

When Eleanor Ree sat where he'd been on the settee, she noticed the trajectory was about even with her eye level, as if he might've shot the bullet with the gun near his head. A while ago, her oilman reported a rumor: Bill tried to kill himself as a kid, jumping off a ledge into traffic. She didn't believe it. And yet…

"You make me crazy, baby," he said when she returned, rushing in, terror and desperation on her flawless face.

She slapped him and he liked it fine. It meant she cared. She still burned for him.

He stopped the next blow by grabbing her wrist. Then he kissed her hard on the mouth. "I won't let you walk out on me," he said between long, swirling kisses.

She moaned and they fell into bed.

He was dead asleep when she went to the settee, naked except for the pillow she held against her breasts.

No, the fool didn't try to blow his brains out, did he? Maybe he thought about it, but then he jerked the gun away from his skull and shot it in anger at the lamp. That's it, isn't it? She looked at him, all peaceful and warm in the bed. She shook her head.

Racing across the ocean, taking on de Zuera like that. Taking me like no other man ever could. Asking nothing and making sure I get all I need. When it's over, when other men turned and slipped away, he holds me, stroking my hair and staying at my side, skin to skin.

Unpredictable bastard. Lightning on a beautiful summer's day. A man who didn't give a shit but cared more than anything. Exactly what I need, and to hell with anyone who can't understand.

Leo Bell watched as Tyler dropped off Vernon Buie at the top of the viaduct. Buie struggled out of the car, chicken gizzards in a bag. Tucking his crutch under his arm, he headed into the late-afternoon shadows on the steep concrete steps up alongside the soap factory. From a distance, he gave Bell a clipped nod in gratitude.

After an illegal U-turn, Tyler pulled in front of the supermarket. "You have something for me?" he said, talking across the front seat.

Bell stifled a yawn. His long face sagged; he had bags under his eyes. "Let's hump." He thought walking with Tyler wasn't much of a risk. In his raincoat and suit, he looked like a fed, but to passersby maybe he'd seem a salesman from United Fruit.

They went south, St. Matty's spire up ahead. "This thing with Corini and Gigenti could escalate," Bell told him.

"How so? You have something more on the Pellizzari killing?"

"I'm just saying," Bell replied. "Keep an eye on them. Could be one of Farcolini's lieutenants is making a move."

"Mistretta?"

"Mimmo? No. You couldn't give Mimmo away."

"Because of Marsala?"

"Because, in general, he's a nitwit," Bell said. "But, yeah, Marsala, too."

"Who is it?"

"Take a look at Frankie Fortune."

"Frankie Fortune," Tyler repeated. "Is that why you went to Anthony Corini's home last night?"

Bell stopped. Tyler did, too.

"You were at Corini's. We know this."

Astonished, Bell raised a finger to make a point, but he let it go.

"Who was the other guy? He looked damned angry in the photos."

Bell said, "He's just a kid I knew growing up."

"He's in the crew?"

"We don't talk about him, Charlie. He's just a kid."

"Visiting Corini in the middle of the night—with you, Leo— is quite a bit different than his Monday afternoon deliveries."

"He works in his uncle's grocery store," Bell said, as they continued along the street. "Mimmo recommended the food. Believe me, there's nothing there."

"He keeps turning up in surveillance photos and that might be difficult to prove."

"I don't care how difficult it is. He's off the books. No matter what."

They walked in silence past a row of brownstones, hopscotch board in chalk on the sidewalk and an errant rubber heel. Boys maybe 10 years old played on the other side of the street, pushing and shoving, punching and laughing.

"What's Corini like?" Tyler asked finally.

"It's hard to say," Bell said. "He keeps it close to the vest." Bell knew Corini was playing Benno. He'd chosen the fatherly approach, like he knew Benno's old man had run out.

"Think he knows anything about you?"

"Like what? I go to college?"

"He'd like that," Tyler said. "Maybe he'd groom someone to represent him with Tammany's lawyers, the unions—"

"Charlie," Bell said wearily, "I know where you're taking this. I told you I'll listen, I'll look around, I'll let you know what's what. But I'm not joining the crew."

"Your friend must've made an impression on them."

Bell stopped again. "Ah, Jesus, Charlie," he said. "Nobody makes an impression. Don't you get it? If they can use him, they'll use him. But they'd butcher their own children if it could make them an extra dime."

Tyler pointed to Church Square Park. There were kids everywhere, a football game, teen girls in the gazebo deep in a gab-and-giggle fest. Bell followed him to a bench facing St. Matty's, the noise behind them.

"Landis is in trouble," Tyler said as he rubbed the cold off his hands. "The report on Hitler. It remains classified, but people who've read it are challenging it. 'Unscientific,' they say. 'Armchair psychoanalysis. Anecdotal gibberish.'"

Bell bristled. "He nailed the suicide, didn't he?"

"He's marginalized, Leo, so he's not going to be studying Stalin or Chiang Kai-shek or anybody else. He's going back to New Haven. These days, desk jockeys don't count for much. They want people on the ground." Tyler stood, crunching brittle brown leaves. "I'm going over to the Department of Justice. I'm bringing our deal with me."

"Why? The CIA's no good?"

"It's the right move—for both of us."

"Does Justice want people on the ground, too?"

"One step at a time, Leo. Do this well and you'll have options."

Bell stood, too, and buried his cold hands in his topcoat pockets. "So now you work with the FBI."

"That's right."

Bell smiled. "I thought Hoover said there's no organized crime."

"It might be interesting to prove to him that there is," Tyler replied. "That's a fine ambition, isn't it?"

"For you, sure."

"We'll see," Tyler said. He tapped Bell on the shoulder. "By the way, you should know that Frankie Fortune was in Corini's apartment last night when you got there and he left twenty minutes after you did. If he's selling out Corini, he's playing it very, very cool."

Securing a sitter for the baby, Rosa Mistretta Rosiglino rode with Terrasini to Cedars of Lebanon Hospital. The whole trip along the 101 and then waiting in traffic on Sunset, they stayed silent. They were visiting Klein and then she was seeing a divorce lawyer, a Beverly Hills shark. Terrasini agreed to drive her to his office so he could take one last shot it at. Like maybe she could see there was still something in Bebe worthwhile. That he wasn't in his right mind when he took off. Yeah, he's a selfish jerk when he gets like that, but maybe we should see it as a weakness, Rosa, no? Besides, how could he know about Phil?

Terrasini parked in the shade. "You look nice," he said as he opened her door and held out his hand.

"Really? I don't feel too great." Her stomach had turned sour. She knew there was no turning back.

"*Sì. Bellezza.* Really."

She smiled weakly, closing her handbag.

"Rosa—"

"You know, Nino, he left you, too. You know that, right?"

She wanted to enter alone, so she went in through the front doors on Fountain, while Terrasini parked in the emergency bay and waited in the hallway outside Klein's room, oxygen canisters banning a smoke. Klein had yet to be moved upstairs and an intern suggested he might not be. "Mr. Klein," the young guy said, "is dying. A stroke is to the brain what a heart attack is to the heart. Since everything's connected, sometimes the heart goes, too."

Rosa came up a few minutes later. "How is he?" she asked.

"They don't think he's going to make it."

She titled her head. "It's that bad? My God."

Thin blue curtains around the bed blocked their view. From the hallway, all they could see were the shapes of machines and a body in the bed.

"Maybe you don't want to see him, Rosa."

"I have to," she said.

"He's unconscious, though."

"No, I have to."

She drew up and Terrasini saw her back in Narrows Gate, this beaming kid struggling to stand her ground with Bebe and the swarming girls, the next one more beautiful than the last. She always had character. Now she's fighting for her place—not with Bebe. That's done. She's fighting for her place in the world.

Terrasini nodded. "*Andiamo.*"

Klein was on the edge of death. Pale, with one side of his face slack, the other twisted, he had one tube in his nose, more in his arms. He seemed so small and helpless. He rattled when he breathed.

"Oh no," Rosa sighed.

Terrasini put an arm around her.

"Oh this poor, poor man," she said.

They stared for a moment, unsure what to do.

Rosa went to the side of the bed. Leaning over the protective rail, she kissed Klein's forehead.

"Maybe we wait for his son," Terrasini said. Klein was a widower. The talent agency had notified the young man, an accountant happily married down in Escondido.

Suddenly, Rosa started to sob. "What did he ever do but be kind? Nino…"

Terrasini pulled a handkerchief from his back pocket.

As she dabbed at her eyes, Terrasini looked at Klein, then at Rosa, and thought, Bebe, you are some lowdown motherfucker. You know that?

Now it was December and still nobody told Benno he was off the Monday run to the city, but he was. And nobody mentioned nothing about his visit to Corini and so he had all this time to do nothing but tell his uncle to nap while he ran the store in his place. He met this usherette at the Avalon, Italian, she lived in Union City and her father, a widower, worked nights so she had Benno over two, three times a week. What the hell, he tried to push it to a new level like Bell had with Imogene the Irish nurse, but it wouldn't take. The only thing she liked about him was the evening's worth of hammering he threw her now and again. He tried a book, but fuck that, too.

One evening, while the usherette worked at the movies, Benno sent his aunt and uncle upstairs and cleaned up, sweeping the sidewalk and laying down rock salt. Then he sat in the store, nibbling on a crust of bread and staring out the bay window. Night had fallen with a fuckin' thud and soon everyone was off the streets. Alone and, tell you the truth, wishing Leo would stop by, Benno put on his coat and hat and walked over to the pizza parlor, Nunzie's. Nunzie Jr. was in a T-shirt, the wood burning in the brick oven throwing off a hellish heat. Benno ordered a slice. A few minutes later, he said, "Nunz, what the fuck is this? You call this shit pizza? Where's the dough?"

"The Irish, they go for it like that. Flat," Nunzie said, flour in his hair, rushing, sweating. "My brother wants we should open a joint uptown."

And then 11 o'clock, half-past, midnight. Benno was back at his perch, a little frost gathering on the storefront glass, container of Coca-Cola in his fist. For no reason, Benno turned and there was Mimmo on the other side of the dull Fords and Nashes, surveying his turf, peering through shop windows like a beat cop. Every once in a while, he bent down to pick up a wrapper, a cigarette butt, maybe somebody broke a bottle.

Benno saw him disappear. What? A tissue, an empty book of matches?

The windshield in the car behind where Mimmo had been standing suddenly exploded into a thousand pieces. Mimmo rose and then, shot, he flew backward like he'd been yanked. Slammed to the sidewalk, he let out a guttural groan and rolled under a car.

Dropping the soda, Benno bolted into the cold, his jacket left behind.

"Sally," Mimmo shouted. "Where's it coming from?"

Benno had ducked behind the stoop, looking toward the Lackawanna yards for the gunman. "I can't see nobody. You hit?"

"I'm hit."

"Hold on." Benno stuck his head out and when a car approached, he dashed in front of it like he was trying to get run over. The guy slammed the brakes, providing a shield. Benno dove onto the cold cobblestone.

Mimmo's arm hung sideways, dead, and Benno saw by the blood on his back that he'd been shot through the collarbone, the thing probably split in two. Meanwhile, the shooting had stopped.

"You're bleeding like a son of a bitch," Benno said. "Hold on."

He crawled backward, came out from under the car's trunk and on his knees, ripped off his shirt. Under again and he told Mimmo to wad it up and press it against the wound. "Mimmo, you need a hospital."

"No," he said, the side of his face on stone, his sunglasses cracked. "The candy store."

The candy store, Benno thought, is over in the direction where the bullets came from.

They waited and heard cars pass. Neighbors appeared, winter jackets over pajamas and housecoats, women with their hair in curlers, everybody buzzing. Then everyone went silent when they heard a stampede rumble and soon a giant fat hand reached down. When Benno came out first, he saw Fat Tutti gasping and sweating and Boo Chiasso trotting.

"In the shoulder," Benno said, adjusting his glasses as Chiasso went to his knees. "He's bleeding pretty good."

Mimmo appeared and they got him to his feet. His face was ghostly and he wobbled so bad they had to lift him, making their arms into a chair.

Benno was looking for the bullet in the car with the smashed windshield.

"Sal, get out of here," Boo Chiasso shouted. "Go now."

As he opened the side door, Benno thought, Yeah. OK. Give me a minute.

"Sally, go!"

There was a hole in the upholstery and Benno stuck in his fingers. Sure enough, he found something besides springs. The seat already ruined, Benno tore it and dug out a little slab of metal that still looked enough like a bullet and why not—it didn't hit nothing but glass and padding.

Shoving the slug in his pocket, Benno started walking uptown. On Polk Street in an undershirt and slacks soiled with blood, he didn't even know he was freezing until he reached the Bells' brownstone.

He threw stones at the window until Bell answered.

"What the hell happened?"

"It ain't mine," Benno whispered, pointing to the blood. First words he said since he left Mimmo with his absent bodyguards.

Bell ran out barefoot, in his boxers.

"They shot Mimmo," Benno explained. He started to shiver.

"Dead?"

"No. Or maybe. They're fixing him at the candy store."

"You saw it?"

"From A to the end."

"Who?" Bell asked.

Benno slipped a hand inside his pocket and produced the spent bullet. "What are the odds it's from the same rifle that took care of Pellizzari?"

"Better than even," Bell replied.

"It's war. Gigenti against Corini. Like Farcolini versus Gus the Boss all over again."

Bell hefted the slug. "Could be."

"Maybe I should go tell Corini what happened."

"Maybe you should come in and not get shot."

"Yeah, I wouldn't mind a hot bath," said Benno, his lips blue.

Since the government had reneged on its deal with Carlo Farcolini, citing as its reasons his continued involvement in the trafficking of narcotics, particularly heroin, Cy Geller increased the number of armed guards he employed to six, each of whom worked four-hour shifts at his house in Coral Gables and another four hours at a marina in nearby Miami, though they were often at sea beyond the Florida Straits. Three of these men were Sicilian, the other three Cuban. They knew Geller had the support and protection of Don Carlo as well as the governor of Florida and had seen Gen. Fulgencio Balboa in his home, both when he was the president of Cuba and now that he resided in Daytona Beach. Well paid, they had killed for Geller and each assumed the other guards would kill any among them who betrayed their boss. Which was true, though it hadn't happened since '39 when a guard who had stolen antique silverware from Mrs. Geller's collection was fed to the sharks as chum.

When one of his inside guards approached, Geller was in his wicker chair reading an article about Bill Marsala in the entertainment section of the *Miami Herald*. He'd been dropped by his record label, the company claiming it was a matter of artistic differences, but the columnist said it was the bad publicity Marsala had brought on himself—leaving his wife and child, taking up again with Eleanor Ree, first in Madrid and now back in New York City, and his reply to a telegram from Louella Parsons, in which she asked for a comment about the death of Phil Klein. "Phil who?" Marsala cabled, causing Hollywood to turn its back, too.

Geller sighed. Marsala's declining popularity would put at risk any possibility of salvaging the mess Ziggy Baum had made of the Sandpiper in Las Vegas. Also, the strategy to build a series of nightclubs across the country based on the Palm Tree model depended on high-end talent willing to perform at less than their customary rates. Marsala was to lead the way and invite his show business friends to follow.

"Mr. Geller, *excúse me.*" The guard had a telephone in his hand and he asked permission to plug it into an outlet in Geller's office. It was Anthony Corini, he said.

Geller took the call, asking the guard to wait.

"Someone took a shot at one of my guys," Corini reported from a pay phone in the cafeteria at the Museum of Natural History. The victim was the uncle to Marsala's wife, who tallied the take in Hudson County. Corini speculated that Bruno Gigenti had sanctioned the hit. Geller knew this was a possibility: Gigenti resented the power Corini had accrued while he avoided a murder prosecution in Argentina.

Corini explained that one of Gigenti's men robbed the Hudson County bagman, who busted up Gigenti's social club in return. And there was the matter of the Pellizzari hit and the note found on his body.

"A note?" Geller asked. "I don't understand."

"The note, it said, 'AC is downstairs. Move.' Like I wanted him put down."

Geller had seen the police report on the murder of Fredo Pellizzari. There was no mention of a note.

Corini asked for advice.

Geller said he would reply in due time. "Stand your ground," he added.

When he got off the phone, Geller reached into his desk, pulled out his stationery and wrote a brief message. It read, "El Malecón. January 15. Three items."

Ten days later, the same guard returned with a reply. The message had come from Vallelunga, Sicily, via Havana. Geller recognized Farcolini's handwriting and saw he had understood the brief notation. "*Sí, tre. New York soltanto e la musica.*" Meaning there would be three items on the agenda. Corini, Gigenti and their deputies would attend, and Marsala. But Ziggy Baum would remain in Vegas.

Geller dispatched an aide to call Rico Enna at the talent agency and instruct him to arrange the event at the Hotel El Malecón.

CHAPTER TWENTY-SEVEN

Back at the Hampshire House in the suite Ree's flying billionaire boyfriend had bought her, Marsala settled in and ordered up a new wardrobe, the handmade suits and topcoats in deep blues and charcoal gray reflecting his desire to stay in New York. Rosa had filed for divorce. "My husband has no interest in upholding our sacred vows." Jesus, *queste donne Siciliane*, Marsala told himself. They go for the jugular. A judge threw her $3,000 a month in temporary support, even though the prick knew nothing was coming in. Meaning I've got to sing, to hell with the clits on my pipes. To hell with the label, too; do you know how many record companies would love to have Bill Marsala on their roster?

But without advisors, he soon walked into quicksand. Only the sound of Ree's voice purring his name or the glimmer in her emerald eyes took his mind off his tumble toward desperation. When he ran his hand along the firm curve of her calf, kissed the inside of her thigh, he could tell himself everything was just about all right again, at least for a little while. He wondered when his spine would return.

Ree had a piano brought into the suite and Marsala sat slumped on the bench, trying to sing along to lazy scales he tapped out with an index finger. His voice sounded like Bill Marsala's might've after he hadn't slept for a week. She listened as he played a chord and tried to dooby-dooby scat as it rang, but he couldn't center a tone. This went on for days.

She waited for the angry Bill Marsala to flash, the feisty Bill, defiant Bill, Bill the cock of the roost. In the meantime, she loved him as best she could and took no joy in seeing him weak, losing weight, worried. For advice, she called his father in Narrows Gate. "Tell him to be safe," the old man said.

Ree came up from behind, dropped her chin on Marsala's shoulder and nipped at his ear. "I've got an idea. It's a kind guaranteed to send you right into outer space." She zoomed her hand toward the ceiling.

He managed a laugh. "I could use a boost, baby."

She told him her arrogant ex, Guy Simon, was staying in the hotel. "I haven't said a thing," she added quickly.

Marsala stood. His shirt matched his eyes. An ascot was tucked to his chin. He knew Simon before Ree did. He'd had Negroes in his band in the late '30s, a pretty ballsy move. "So?"

"I think he can help you with your voice."

"No, thanks."

"Bill, hear me out."

She'd been walking on eggshells, lazing in the tub, combing through scripts, avoiding newspapers while sipping gin and tonics, as if to hurry the summer. She'd been taking a beating in the press, her lone statement throwing kerosene on a raging fire: "The marriage was over long before I came along. Bill deserves happiness and that's what I intend to give him." Home-wrecker was the nicest thing they wrote about her. Behind the scenes, the studio whispered naughty to the columns, seeing how it would help her picture in the can now that the bullfighter stories had died. Even if the picture flopped, which seemed likely, she was going to be a major star. So they arranged a photo of Ree and Marsala shopping at Harry Winston and she gazed in a mirror as she held a snowflake cluster of diamonds to her ear. Forty thousand dollars, it was reported, which was a fifth of what Marsala had to his name if they included the equity in the new house. When the photographer left, the earrings went back into the case. But the day after the photo appeared, Rosa's lawyer called Louella Parsons and said Marsala had been slow to pay for Bill Jr.'s booster shots.

"You know how he thinks he knows everything?" Ree said now to Marsala, referring to Simon, the self-styled genius.

He'd started to pace the suite, his cigarette smoke trailing him.

"Sometimes he's right," she added. "Bill, you have to admit he knows music. He's employed singers for a good long while."

"Baby, he takes one look at you—"

"Don't be ridiculous. The whole world knows I'm hooked on you."

He liked that. It was true. She's mine. "Get him up here," Marsala said.

Within the hour, Marsala was eating horseradish with a teaspoon. He felt like his nose was on fire. He had tears in his eyes.

"Breath deep, Bill," Simon instructed. "Open the nasal passages."

"You're giving me nothing but *agita*."

"This is all quite delicate, Bill," the bandleader continued. "You don't want to callous the vocal cords and yet we can't risk another hemorrhage." Simon couldn't resist a chance to show how superior he was. But Ree was impressed. For a minute or two, she didn't think of him as a bigheaded toad.

"The challenge is to keep the instrument in proper physical condition without stressing it," the bandleader said, beckoning Marsala to follow him to the living room.

As the singer passed, Ree latched onto his arm.

Tweedy jacket, billowy beige slacks, Simon went to the piano bench, ran a finger along his mustache in thought and played ornate scales worthy of Horowitz. He waited for flattery.

"Super," Marsala said without enthusiasm. To his surprise, his head had cleared. He breathed easily.

"You're a baritone so let's stay in the lower register. E flat, Bill. And keep it legato. Ready?"

Marsala sang along with the scale.

"Again and gently. Slur the tones."

The same result, maybe a little better, so the bandleader ran the scale up and down, up and down, and Marsala sang more fluidly with each attempt.

"Not too much, Bill. Not yet. Now, one note at a time."

Again. Beautiful, almost.

"And B flat..."

Marsala shifted effortlessly.

Delighted, Ree kissed his cheek. Marsala smiled. Simon had lifted a bank vault loaded with gold bars off his shoulders.

"F and we'll drop back down to E flat. Legato."

Marsala sounded like Bill Marsala, if only for a few measures.

"That's enough for today," Simon said, sealing the piano lid for emphasis. He stood, put his arm around Marsala. They were the same height, but with the singer sick with worry, the bandleader was more robust, his skin golden with that California glow.

Ree watched her ex begin to work his inevitable scheme.

"Excellent," he said. "Now chew some ice. Repeat once an hour. Avoid hot beverages. I'll check in before supper but we won't vocalize until the morrow."

"Thanks," Marsala said.

"So they dropped you. Morons."

Ree padded close to Marsala. "Complete morons," she said.

"I hear you've made some recordings," Simon said. "Jazz, I'm told. Have them sent to me. I want to hear what they missed."

"Call the label," Marsala told him. He didn't much like the snob fuck and now that their work was done, he wanted him out.

Simon reached for Ree's hand and kissed it gallantly. He said, "Bill, you made her happy, I can see. Good for you. Good for both of you."

When she closed the door behind him, she said, "What does he want?"

"You," Marsala said as he lit a cigarette and passed it to her.

"No. Really."

"He wants to impress you," Marsala repeated.

"With horseradish? Bill, he wants in. He knows your voice will be back. He'll listen to the recordings and he'll tell you he can make them better."

Marsala shrugged. Jesus, his throat felt great.

Benno was in the store's back room, eating a mammoth capicolla and provolone sandwich Gemma had put together, the bread loaf bloated to football shape. She's so happy he wasn't shot like Mimmo, who now made his rounds with Fat Tutti in front, Boo Chiasso in back.

Benno took a long hot pepper off the plate and holding his head back, let it slide down his throat like some college *strunzo* swallowing a goldfish. When he dropped his chin, there was Frankie Fortune, gorgeous in a steel-gray topcoat.

"You got a passport?" Fortune asked.

"What's a passport?"

"It's a document the government gives you. It says you're allowed to go into other countries."

"The American government?"

Fortune nodded wearily.

"Why does the government give a fuck what I do?"

"Sal, huh? Go to the post office and get a passport."

"It costs?"

Fortune dug into his slacks, peeled off a fifty and threw it on the table.

The second week of Guy Simon's lessons and Marsala was sing-ing fine. Better than fine: With a ruptured hemorrhagic vocal cord nodule on the mend, Marsala once again sounded like dark honey pouring from the clouds, like sex on a platter, like the score to a magical stroll with your best girl at your side under the most beautiful night sky of your ever-loving life. And he knew it.

"My God," Ree said, eyes wide in wonder. "Bill…"

He winked at her.

She thought, he sings and my skin tightens and tingles. No wonder they loved him. They'll love him again.

Simon had brought in a pianist. A fourth for the asylum, Ree thought when the bearish man lumbered in. But he was nimble on the keys.

"Let's confront the number that revealed the injury," Simon said from an armchair, pipe clenched in his teeth. "'Sweet Lorraine.'"

Marsala knew Simon had heard the cuts over at the label's West Side studios. To bust Marsala's balls, they played Simon the take where his voice broke. The bandleader called it "a cheap shot, Bill, after what you've done for them. Unacceptable." But he'd lis-tened and laughed.

"OK, baby?" Marsala asked. "'Sweet Lorraine.'"

Bare feet on the coffee table, a script perched on a thigh, Ree smiled, her Bill in an up mood.

Simon turned to the piano player. "Go ahead," he instructed.

"Hey," Marsala said. "The singer calls the tune, buster." He turned to the pianist. "Give me the chorus as an intro, kid. Let it swing."

Ree sat up, closed the script and feeling Simon's gaze, casually slipped her feet into her flats.

Halfway through the breezy introduction, there was a knock at the hotel room door.

Marsala said, "I thought you put a Do Not Disturb—"

"I did," said Ree, as she left the sofa. "Damn it."

Still playing, the pianist looked to Marsala, who raked a finger across his throat. The music stopped as Ree pulled the knob.

Standing there in sunglasses, fedora and a topcoat was Mimmo, his arm in a sling.

"You remember me?" he said to Ree.

She felt a chill. "Yankee Stadium."

"I need only Bebe."

Marsala joined Ree at the threshold. "Mimmo, *ciao.*" He greeted him with a kiss on both cold cheeks. "*Come il suo va?*"

Mimmo stepped into the room, oblivious to the bandleader and the piano player.

Marsala threw a thumb toward the door. "Boys…" he said.

The pianist left immediately, dragging his coat by the collar. But Simon insisted on sticking his hand out and introducing himself.

"Good for you," Mimmo replied.

Simon went quietly.

Ree said, "Bill, I've got some things…" Scooping up her script, she retreated toward the bedroom.

"Thanks, sweetheart," Marsala said.

Mimmo sat where Simon had been. When the bedroom door shut, he pointed toward the piano bench and gestured for

Marsala to tug it toward him. Then he told him to sit. Their knees were inches apart.

Marsala said, "I heard what happened. It's awful."

Mimmo tossed his hat aside. "No, we're going to talk about you, Bebe," he began in Sicilian. "I'm disappointed what you done to Rosa and little Bill."

"I know you are," Marsala said. "But it's over, Mimmo. We've got to face it."

"You embarrassed her. You embarrassed *us*."

"I didn't mean to. But I had to go."

"Carlo is unhappy."

Marsala dropped his arms on his thighs and leaned in. "I don't want that, Mimmo," he said in English. "Never would I want that."

"You know why I'm here? I'm here because Bruno Gigenti ain't. You understand?"

"I'm not sure—"

Mimmo reached, put his index and middle fingers against Marsala's temple and said, "Bruno comes and it's boom, Bebe. Boom."

Marsala shuddered. He tried to find Mimmo's eyes behind the smoky lenses, but only saw his own reflection.

"Carlo wants to see you," Mistretta said, returning to Sicilian.

Marsala was confused. Farcolini was in Sicily.

"He talks to you, you listen. And it ain't going to be advice, Bebe. The movie studio drops you, the record company. The tour you cancel. You walk out on the radio program and you run off to Spain for this one." Mimmo raised his hands. "What is this?"

Marsala knew a bullshit excuse wouldn't play. "I can fix it," he said.

"Maybe. But don't do nothing until Carlo talks to you."

Marsala paused. "I put you in a spot, didn't I?" he asked.

Mimmo tugged on his sling. "Carlo's going to talk to me, too."

"I'm sorry."

"You fucked up, Bebe." He shoved off the sofa. "You fucked up good."

As Marsala followed him to the door, Mimmo nestled his hat on his head. "Be ready and don't tell nobody."

"Sure, Mimmo—"

"Nobody," he said firmly, jabbing a finger toward the bedroom.

"Havana?" Bell said. "What the fuck are you going to do in Havana?"

They were at the crook in the crowded bar at the Grotto, leaning on their elbows as they shared a pot of thick *zuppa di vongole*, dipping in bread, a couple of beers nearby, sawdust underfoot.

"Sssh. For Christ's sake, Leo."

"I'm surprised, is all." He lowered his voice. "Havana."

Benno looked at the noisy four-to-midnight crew on lunch from the piers. Frozen to the bone, the men huddled by the Franklin stove and threw down whiskey like it was liquid heat. "Where's Havana?"

"Cuba."

"Which is?"

"Off the coast of Florida."

"I can drive?"

"A boat or a plane. They speak Spanish, you know."

"Not the guys I'm going with."

"Who else?" Bell asked.

Benno had a dab of the tangy tomato gravy under his bottom lip. "Frankie, maybe Mimmo. Corini."

"What? No Tutti, no Boo?"

"I'm thinking maybe a plane can't take off you put two giants like Boo and Fat Tutti in it."

Bell speared an errant clam with his fork. "When?"

"Frankie won't say. He goes, 'Be ready.'"

Benno drank half the beer and now he had a foamy mustache. Bell passed him a napkin.

"That fuckin' Frankie, though," Benno said. "He still don't like me."

"You jumped his head by going straight to Corini. You threatened the order of things."

"I'm not looking to make an enemy. I figure Corini had to say OK if I'm invited."

"Well," Bell said as he put a heel on the foot rail, "you get a trip out of it."

"You mean there's no chance I could say no."

They ate in silence, their hands taking turns dipping into the tattered pot. After a while, Benno called the bartender, Volpe, over, saying, "More *zuppa* and this time don't stint on the fuckin' clams."

Volpe groaned as he shuffled off.

"I hate that cheap fuck," Benno whispered.

"Like he don't know."

"We been in here maybe once a month since the war ended. You'd think he'd buy a round."

Bell said, "He holds a grudge."

"Since Little League?"

"You chased him across the outfield, Sal." Bell saw 7-year-old Volpe screaming in terror, the umpires trailing Benno and parents laughing in the stands, opening-day pennants and bunting on the fence.

Benno recalled how Volpe smirked when he threw strike three past him. "I should go over and knock that grudge out his ass."

Bell found a garlic clove in the sauce and offered it to him. "Imogene's got somebody for you," he said. "A nice girl. A nursing student. She transferred."

"What am I going to do with a nursing student?"

"Her name is Esposito."

Benno turned. "No kidding. We're in the nursing schools now, too?"

"I guess."

"Put her on ice until I get back."

Bell caught Volpe's eye. He pointed to the empty breadbasket, knowing it's even money the fuck delivers stale.

Ree took the hint and decided to fly back to Hollywood. A script interested her. Incredibly, they wanted her to play a goddess come to earth. A trip to Greece, she told Marsala. "You'll join me, won't you?" she asked.

Simon dropped in unannounced as she was packing.

"You waited until Bill was out, I see," she said. She rushed to the bedroom to complete the task. The plane was scheduled to take off in an hour.

Simon followed and stood in the doorway. "Is he too busy for you?"

"We're both busy people." Retrieving a few toiletries from her dressing table, she gave a quick glance to the mirror and saw only her flaws. "We have careers."

"His voice is back so you're disposable."

"Oh, why don't you just go to hell," she said.

Simon grabbed her arm. "Eleanor—"

Spinning, she kicked him hard in the shin.

Hissing in pain, he hopped red-faced and leaned against a chest of drawers.

"You wanted to move in on him," she said, continuing to pack. "He's down and you'd revive his career. Then you'll take the credit and you'll have something to do with your life."

"That's rid—"

"Bill Marsala's musical director."

"Well, he needs someone."

She said, "He doesn't need you."

"Perhaps he won't need you, either."

"Good." She snapped the luggage clasps. "He'll be with me because he wants to be."

He followed her back into the living room. "But why run off?" he said. "I'm here, you are too…"

She slipped into her coat and pulled a sheer scarf from its pocket. "You're kidding, right?"

"Eleanor, you have to admit it was always wonderful between the sheets with us," he said.

"No it wasn't, Guy." She tied the scarf under her chin. "It's wonderful with him. Better than you'll ever know." Sliding on her sunglasses, she picked up her bag and headed to the elevator. A car waited for her on Central Park West.

In its backseat were two-dozen red roses. The card read, "Come home soon, baby. Forever, Your Bill." Ree suddenly felt giddy.

Across the avenue, Marsala shivered as he watched from behind an ancient oak tree in the park. He loved her. He did. He was right about her: She was solid. A good kid who was there when he was down. Mimmo, Fortune, Corini, Gigenti, Don Carlo—they'd have to understand.

Forty minutes later in the suite, the telephone rang. Marsala was changing his outfit and he trotted across the room in his boxers and undershirt. Maybe it's her calling from the airport, he thought. Maybe one last sweet good-bye.

"Bebe. You ready?"

"Now, Mimmo?"

"Right now."

"Where are you?"

Mimmo spoke in Sicilian. "I'm in Miami, Florida. Be ready, Bebe, and do this thing right. Don't fuck this up."

There was a knock on the hotel door so loud that Mimmo heard it. "Go," he said. "Do what he tells you."

"All right," Marsala said. The new silk robe Ree had bought him hung behind the bedroom door.

"And don't fuck this up." Then Mimmo cut the line.

Marsala hurried to the bedroom. "Just a minute," he shouted. He wriggled into the robe and opened the door.

"Let's go, Bebe," Sal Benno said as he lifted the black suitcase at his side.

Despite the caramel suit and the spit shine on his brown shoes, Marsala thought the one-eyed kid had the look of somebody who'd have to climb to be second rate.

"Would you mind if I dressed?" Marsala said.

Benno stepped in, bumping him with his shoulder. "Me, I don't give a fuck what you do. But Anthony Corini says you carry this bag all the way to Havana. You start now."

"What?"

"Plus it's locked, meaning I don't know what's in it."

As Marsala watched, Benno sat on the sofa. "You got fourteen minutes," he said. "And don't worry about no topcoat. They got sun in Cuba."

CHAPTER TWENTY-EIGHT

Rico Enna met them at the airport in Havana, the air moist and warm. When he reached for the black suitcase Marsala carried, Benno said no and pushed his way between the two men.

"Rick, it's all right," Marsala said as he slipped on his sunglasses. He'd come to some sort of terms with this bulldog Benno who, over the Atlantic, walked through the curtain into first class and sat next to him.

"How can you read a magazine when you got those clouds?" Benno asked, pointing to a window. And then he said, "Bebe, the ocean is pretty big, no?" Then the stewardess shooed him back to coach. Benno, who'd never had a glass of Champagne in his life, lifted Marsala's flute and took it with him to 11C, where he resumed his study of sea and sky. "It looks like it don't end," he said in wonder.

In the silvery evening light outside the terminal, Enna suggested Benno sit in front with the driver, but he went in back with Marsala, the suitcase between them, an armrest for the singer. Soon they were driving along El Malecón, the waves slamming the seawall alongside the wide boulevard with its grand buildings with arches and ornate balconies. In the quiet time before supper, couples in white, the men in straw fedoras, strolled leisurely. Benno was taking it in, the swagger and brown skin, palm trees and a lighthouse. If he had turned around, he might've noticed

Charlie Tyler of the U.S. Department of Justice riding in the taxi behind them.

Marsala had taken off his jacket and folded it neatly on his lap.

Enna passed him an envelope. "It's the agenda for the meeting and your itinerary."

Benno craned to see. Luckily, Marsala was on the side of his good eye.

"Tonight?" Marsala said, raising the sheet.

"For Carlo." Enna nodded. "To set the tone."

Benno saw that Marsala was to perform at the welcome banquet.

"The band's ready. We've got all the charts. Real professional, these guys."

"Rick, I'm out of shape."

"Five or six tunes, Bill. You pick them."

"You should've let me know." Marsala struggled to stay calm. He wasn't sure he was up to a performance. "When I'm working, Rick, there's a way to do things. You know that."

"It's been hurry up and wait for everybody, Bill. Hurry up and wait."

"Carlo knows I'm on tonight?"

"This comes from Cy Geller. So I'd say, yeah, Carlo knows."

Benno heard the silence and knew it was written in stone. Bebe on stage, Don Carlo Farcolini front and center.

"We've got a nice suite for you. One of the best," Enna said. "Two stories in the tower. First class."

"What about me?" Benno asked.

"Yeah, you're all set, too," Enna replied.

"I'm with him, though." Fortune told him plain: Don't let Bebe walk away from the suitcase.

Enna looked back at Marsala, who replied with a shrug.

As he sat in his dressing room, fretting over his throat and whether the band would cloak his weak points, Bebe Marsala suddenly realized this was the first gig he'd done without Nino Terrasini taking charge. Terrasini would review the charts, verify Marsala's selections and stand by as his pianist, Ronnie Oliver, ran through a couple of numbers with the band, encouraging the woodwinds, muting the brass. He'd return to their suite to wake Marsala, pour scotch over ice and help him dress, maybe call out for a meal. When they arrived at the venue, Terrasini would ward off the well-wishers. When Marsala wore a tux, Terrasini would slip in his black onyx cufflinks. "*Buona fortuna,* Bebe," he'd say as he adjusted his bow tie and Marsala would reply, "*Non è fortuna,* Nino." Then Terrasini would escort him to the side of the stage and cue the lights, his hand on the singer's shoulder until it was time for Bebe to go to work.

Now a wave of panic rushed over Marsala. He needed somebody to tell him it was going to be fine, that his voice wouldn't go, that the band wouldn't expose him, that Don Carlo wouldn't be displeased.

He glanced at Benno.

"Bebe, I got to say, you look great and like shit at the same time."

Marsala looked at himself in the mirror. His eyes were pinwheels. The veins in his temples pulsed. Whatever good the time in Madrid and New York with Eleanor had done for him seemed gone and he was as frightened as he was when he fled Los Angeles. "Yeah, it's the jitters, kid. We all get them." He dabbed a bit of pancake makeup on the slope of his nose.

"You sung for some of these guys at the Chatterbox when you were thirteen years old. What's the big deal?"

Marsala looked at Benno through the mirror. "I'm like everybody else, kid. I want to be at my best."

"Why? They know the difference?"

Marsala smiled.

"Why don't you figure out what they want and do that?"

For some reason, this Benno kid put him at ease. "You're pretty smart, aren't you?"

Twirling his hat in his hand, Benno said, "You know, your mother told me the same thing. Maybe I got something that fools you guys."

He rose to answer a knock on the door. "I told Hennie it's a matter of being useful—"

Benno opened the door and was struck numb.

"Kid?" Bebe said.

Standing in the hall next to Frankie Fortune was Carlo Farcolini.

Unable to speak, Benno pointed to the black suitcase.

Farcolini waited impassively, his scarred eyelid drooping, his jaw chiseled stone. Silvery gray had crept into his hair at his temples, but he was tan and fit under a baggy brown suit. Fifty years old, he looked like he could snap a head off at the neck. He smelled of bay rum and talc.

Remembering how Bell did it with Corini, Benno said, "Salvatore Benno, Mr. Farcolini."

Farcolini shook his hand.

Benno noted that Farcolini had some serious air around him, a kind of electrical charge.

"You're the one with Mimmo?" Farcolini asked. "The gunplay."

"Under the car? That's me."

"*Siete Siciliani?*"

"*Sì,*" Benno replied. "*Sono Siciliano.*"

Farcolini nodded, then entered the dressing room, leaving Benno alone among the bare light bulbs and fire axes in the narrow corridor below the El Malecón stage.

Fortune sealed the door. The singer rushed to Farcolini, kissing both cheeks.

"I'm so happy to see you looking well," Marsala said in Sicilian as Farcolini sat on a folding chair.

"You've brought something for Carlo," Fortune led.

When Marsala hesitated, Fortune nodded toward the black suitcase.

Marsala retrieved the bag.

"Bebe wanted you to have this," Fortune said. "A sign of his gratitude."

Farcolini looked at the suitcase as Fortune produced a key.

It was loaded with stacks of one hundred dollar bills, one hundred to a bundle wrapped in rubber bands. Marsala calculated quickly. Six rows across, maybe eight rows deep. Almost a half-million dollars.

"He knows how important the Sandpiper operation is to you," Fortune said.

Marsala said, "I want you to understand how much I appreciate what you've done for me, Carlo. Since I was a child."

"And the future," Fortune added.

"That's right. Yes." Marsala waited for another cue, but Fortune wouldn't look at him.

Farcolini said, "We have to talk, Bebe."

"I know, *padrone*. I need your guidance."

"You see me tomorrow," Farcolini said as he stood.

Fortune opened the door and there was Benno, waiting. "Sal, you stay with Bebe."

Benno noticed Fortune had the suitcase now.

Farcolini left the dressing room and without acknowledging Benno, walked the corridor, Fortune behind him, the suitcase swaying at his side.

Benno came in and shut the door. "How much?" he asked.

Shaking, Marsala sat. "Five hundred Gs."

Benno whistled. "A tribute from who?"

"From me."

"Hey. Nice going, Bebe. Corini just fronted you five hundred large, which means you get to live to earn it back."

Marsala struggled to light a cigarette.

"How long does it take to make five hundred Gs?" Benno asked.

In '43 or now? the singer thought.

Rico Enna knocked on the door. "Ten minutes, Bill," he said.

Cy Geller hadn't slept well. Propriety had required that he sit through Marsala's performance and the celebration that followed, so he was late to bed. At dawn, he took a light breakfast in his room before joining his son and the talent agent Enna to inspect the third-floor boardroom. As he walked around the table, he adjusted the bottles of Sicilian wine imported by Farcolini that stood alongside pitchers of ice water. The centerpiece, an oversized display of tropical fruit, was thoroughly unnecessary, but it would be an insult to hotel management to have it removed.

Geller walked to the window and looked beyond the white water at the shoreline to the Florida Straits. A misty fog had settled over the northern edge of the city; otherwise, Geller believed he could see the outline of the Florida Keys, the gateway to America. He'd insisted the meeting be held in this boardroom so he and Don Carlo could point to the Atlantic Ocean, the Gulf of Mexico and the United States to reinforce the notion that their international enterprise was too vast to tolerate a petty turf battle in New York City. Frankly, with Farcolini in Sicily overseeing the flow of heroin from Central Asia and Northern Africa and Geller managing distribution throughout the United States and Canada from outside Miami, New York was no longer an indispensable base. If the Gigenti–Corini grudge grew into a war, affecting shipping into and transportation by truck out of the Brooklyn, Manhattan and Jersey piers, several other ports might serve to replace them: Baltimore or New Orleans, for example. But it would take years to transplant the operation. Peace was the most practical solution.

"The room is fine," Cy Geller said.

"We'll sweep it one more time," replied Saul Geller, who learned the value of caution from his father.

The meeting began on time. Farcolini sat at the head of the oblong table, facing the door, his back to the wall. Geller was to his right with his son, Saul, seated behind him. To Farcolini's left was Anthony Corini, with Frankie Fortune nearby. A representative from Farcolini's Cuban operation, Jorge Ortega, was to Corini's left. Directly across from Ortega sat Bruno Gigenti. All were dressed in business suits of light grays and browns. Since Farcolini had approved the seating arrangement, the third agenda item had already been addressed to a degree: Corini was at Farcolini's side, with Fortune, who was supposed to be a neutral party, at his back; Gigenti, who had his scar-faced rifleman Zamarella behind him, was positioned as equal to a Cuban thug who had no vote. His ink-black eyes mere slits, Gigenti breathed heavily, like a beast preparing to charge, raising the level of tension that already gripped the room.

Gigenti stared at Corini, who seemed oblivious to his implied threat. Fortune was not; his eyes shifted from Gigenti to Zamarella, who studied his long, tapered fingers as they rested on his thighs.

With the slightest gesture, Farcolini told Geller to proceed.

"Gentlemen, we have three items to address. I think it's best to begin immediately. The first is the matter of our Las Vegas investment and our expansion into the entertainment field. For the benefit of Señor Ortega and to refresh our memories, my son, Saul, will review the numbers. Saul…"

With a master accountant's precision, Saul Geller systematically detailed how the organization's initial investment of $700,000 in the building of the Sandpiper Hotel and Casino had grown by a factor of 10, with little prospect of recouping the $7 million if mismanagement under Ziggy Baum continued.

Cy Geller said, "We recommend replacing Mr. Baum."

"With who?" Gigenti asked.

"I think we can open it to discussion, Bruno," Geller said calmly. "Do you have someone in mind?"

"I have a dozen men who can run a casino."

"True, I'm sure. Perhaps you can suggest one or two who can correct the situation at the Sandpiper and move us deeper into the entertainment industry."

"I don't see how one has to do with the other," Gigenti said. "We're out seven million in Vegas. We need to earn and we need to earn now."

"Bruno's right," Corini said. "The loss at the Sandpiper is a big hit. Until we straighten out that mess, how do we know we can do these other things we've discussed?"

"Bruno?" Geller said.

Gigenti tried to calculate. His objective was to show the Sandpiper was no more than a glitzy version of the gambling operations he commanded up and down the East Coast for the past decades. Corini's entertainment angle was bullshit. People gambled. You throw up a game where there's people and you earn. Baum's idea to put a casino in the middle of the desert was stupid. "Bulldoze it," he said. "It was a mistake." He dusted his hands together. "*Finito.*"

Farcolini said, "I'm not sure it was a mistake. The mistake was in who we trusted with the job and this was my decision."

Corini said, "It's true that we have a major investment in the city."

"This is the issue, I think," Cy Geller said. "We wanted to do more than build a casino. We wanted an industry in a city we owned. We shouldn't lose sight of this."

Farcolini nodded knowingly.

"I'd like to make a recommendation," Geller continued. "My son, Saul, has done a very good job of managing the Palm Tree in Miami Beach. Very competent. I suggest we allow him to oversee the completion of the renovation at the Sandpiper and to run the property for a period of one year. Bruno, your men who know gambling might serve on the board and run the floor. Anthony, you could continue to develop the entertainment angle to bring in customers, so you would be represented on the board, as well. Perhaps you can suggest people in local and state government we can turn to."

Corini nodded.

"This is the proper way to proceed," Farcolini said. "Bruno?"

"He's got one year to get us out of the hole? That's seven million above the ten percent off the top we discussed when we agreed to the Vegas move. Am I right?"

Farcolini nodded.

"And that's all off the casino floor. Not prostitution or narcotics."

Corini said, "The casino floor *and* entertainment."

Gigenti snorted as he sat back. "Good luck, Geller."

It was decided that Zamarella would remove Baum from his post. Gigenti would be compensated for the assignment.

"Next item is Marsala," said Cy Geller.

Frankie Fortune walked to the door to retrieve Mimmo.

Marsala relaxed at the pool for a while, then snuck back into the cabana to use the phone. Last night's performance had him "higher than the moon," as he put it, and he was eager to talk about it. He figured Ree would still be on New York time and up early in Bel Air, which was right—but she was already out, her houseboy said. Breakfast with her agent, then she was going to the studio. He tried Terrasini at the Wilshire Towers, but there was no answer. Phil Klein came to mind and then he remembered—dead. Maybe I ought to do something for Klein's family. A college fund for his grandchildren. I'll tell Nino to find out.

He stepped back into the sun where Benno sat, a lobster's empty shell at his elbow. Earlier, Marsala told him to buy himself swim trunks, a terry top and lounging shoes.

"What's on your mind, kid?" he said.

"Bebe, you could fire a bullet in my ear, and it comes out the other side clean," he replied. He had his fedora on the back of his head and his hands folded on his stomach. "You?"

"I'm thinking it was pretty swell last night."

"They went nuts," Benno agreed. "Nuts."

The orchestra was grand and when "She's Funny That Way" ended, Marsala turned to them and said, "Gorgeous, fellas. *Muchas gracias*." The audience, which, according to Benno's count, was 500 Cubans, a couple tables full of Sicilians and the Gellers, applauded the song and the gesture. Spirits were high and by the time he finished with "All of Me," the crowd was overjoyed and Marsala was, too. "That all right for you, kid?" he said as he came off stage.

"You got something, Bebe," Benno said as the singer wiped his face with a towel Enna provided.

"You bet your ass I do," Marsala replied before he took one last bow.

"That's the sugar, kid," he said now with a nod. "Right there."

Benno was staring at the Cuban dames by the pool, the sunlight dancing on the turquoise water. They reminded him of the kind of Italian girls he liked—cool and hot at the same time, flowing dark hair, chin held high, a nice rack and they knew it. But these broads had a caboose a mile wide. *Madonna mio*, he thought. What do you do with that thing?

"Stop drooling," Marsala said as he stood behind him, sharing the view. "Make your move."

"They got their ways, Bebe?"

"Sure, but who cares? Go make your own. What are they going to say?"

Benno didn't reply.

"Am I right? You make your...Kid?"

Benno pointed. "Look."

There was Mimmo, luggage on his good side as he walked from the tower toward the parking lot beyond a flower-coated trestle.

"They kicked him out," Benno said. "Jesus."

"Go see," Marsala said, tapping him on the shoulder. He was concerned. Maybe $500,000 wasn't enough to make things right.

Benno stood. "Bebe, don't disappear." He held up a finger in warning.

"I'll be right here. Scout's honor."

"Ah, you ain't no Boy Scout."

He caught up to Mimmo in the lot, steam rising from the asphalt. Several limos waited, but Mimmo couldn't determine which were assigned to Farcolini and the crew. Mimmo looked deflated, slouched in his wrinkled suit, his straw hat, sunglasses, and that arm in a sling.

"Mimmo," said Benno as he skidded to a stop.

In a daze, he turned to see a young guy in a brown fedora, terry top and bathing suit. "Sal…"

"Can I help you with something, Mimmo?" Benno said.

"Which car?"

Hand over his brow, Benno searched. "Where are you going? Maybe that means something."

"The airport."

"Oh, Jesus, Mimmo. They told you to go home?"

"Yeah. Fuckin' Bebe. Somebody had to pay."

Benno grabbed Mimmo's luggage and headed toward the first car in the queue. "The airport," he told the driver. "This is a very important man you got here. You do what he says."

The little Cuban nodded.

Benno eased the bag into the trunk as Mimmo slumped into the backseat.

CHAPTER TWENTY-NINE

A commotion outside in the hallway. Alarmed, Saul Geller sprung from an armchair but with a casual wave, Farcolini said no, sit. He'd recognized one man's voice—Cy Geller had, too—and crossed the hotel suite to answer the door himself.

In the corridor, Farcolini's guard, a Cuban military man, was wrestling with Bruno Gigenti who, though maybe 20 years his senior, had the man gripped in a headlock. Gigenti threw a right uppercut that caught the center of his face.

"What is this?" Farcolini said in Sicilian. "What do you call this?"

Gigenti released the man, shoving him back toward a small table. A vase and flowers crashed to the carpeted floor.

"We're not finished," he said to Farcolini, spittle flying. "Me and you."

"We're not?"

"What you did. That wasn't right. You threw me over."

Farcolini stared at him.

"You think I set up Corini for that skunk Pellizzari and I robbed his Jersey bagman."

Farcolini didn't reply.

"But I told you I didn't do nothing to Corini, that fuckin' politician."

"So you said, yes."

Gigenti rolled his shoulders. "Now I'm here to tell you what's right. You're gonna know what's going on."

"Ah." Farcolini stepped back and opened the door wide. "Come then."

Gigenti stormed inside but stopped when he saw the Gellers. "This is none of your business," he told them.

Saul Geller was still standing, but his father remained on the sofa, surrounded by long sheets of accounting paper.

Cy Geller looked at Farcolini over by the door. "Carlo?"

"You stay. Saul also."

Staring at the Gellers, Gigenti said in Sicilian, "Carlo, this is another mistake—you following these Jews. You know who makes the most from these plans? Jews."

Farcolini walked slowly across the room. When he was an arm's length from Gigenti, he dropped his shoulder and drove his fist hard and deep into Gigenti's lower back, slamming his kidney. Howling like a wounded animal, Gigenti collapsed to his knees.

With terrifying speed, Farcolini grabbed the chair where young Geller had been seated, snapped off its arm and began beating Gigenti, rising off his feet and grunting as he struck each savage blow. When Gigenti toppled on his side, Farcolini kicked him in the stomach and chest three, four, five times.

He threw down the weapon. Looking at Gigenti, Farcolini drew a breath and said, "When you betray any one of us, you betray me. Do you understand this? Do you understand this?"

Gigenti felt as if his insides would explode. "I understand," he groaned, holding up a quaking hand.

Cy Geller looked up at his son. Fear had drained the young man's long, tan face. "Saul," he said, "Saul. Saul, get a washcloth and a towel."

When Farcolini turned toward him, the elder Geller said, "It's fine, Carlo. It's done."

"I apologize for this man," he said in English.

"No need."

Gigenti coughed and blood spewed across his lips.

Stepping back, running his hand through his close-cropped hair, Farcolini stared down at Gigenti. "Anthony Corini represents me. Cy Geller represents me. Understand this or you're through. Period."

Young Geller approached and looked to Farcolini for permission to treat Gigenti. Farcolini nodded.

As Geller put the wet cloth to his face, Gigenti shuddered and passed out.

Bell was playing penny-a-point gin with Imogene's kid sister, Ruthie, while Mrs. O'Boyle cooked dinner in time for her husband's return from work. He'd spent the day with Imogene in New York City, talking for hours over espresso, sitting by a glowing stove, in a tiny storefront in Greenwich Village and what's better than that? You do something that simple and you feel good, you know you're in the right company.

Ruthie was conniving something as she rearranged her hand, the freckle-faced kid chewing her tongue, the preamble to a triumphant shout, "Gin!"—which was followed always by "Ha!" Then "Ha, ha, ha!" as she started counting her points. Bell was down 65 cents. He promised himself he'd stop feeding her cards when the tally hit a buck.

"Leo," Imogene shouted from the kitchen. "Telephone."

"Don't cheat," he said as he stood.

"Don't have to," she sang, her head bobbing.

Imogene handed him the handset and waited.

"Leo. Charlie Tyler."

Bell made a silent plea for privacy. Imogene faked a huff before she fled.

"How'd you get this number?" Bell asked.

"Leo, you've got to find out what's going on down here."

"Down where—Wait, you're in Havana?"

"They just brought Bruno Gigenti out on a stretcher."

"Dead?"

"They're taking him to the hospital. They also sent Mistretta back home."

"What about Sal?" Bell asked, alarmed. "Have you seen him? Is he all right?"

"He's at the pool with Marsala. At least he was. They're probably up in the room now. Benno is sharing Marsala's suite."

"See if he's OK."

"I don't think I can do that, Leo. But you can."

"I'm not supposed to know he's in Cuba. No one is. I can't call Bebe's room and I can't page him."

"What do you think is going on?"

"The rest of them. Are they still at the hotel?" Bell asked.

"As far as I know, Farcolini, Corini and Geller are still here. So's Fortune. Eugenio Zamarella got into the ambulance with Gigenti," he replied. "Speculate, Leo. What does it mean?"

Calculating, Bell said, "Corini's in good shape. Farcolini wants him to keep up with the politicians and Marsala."

Tyler was using a pay phone on El Malecón. A young couple lingered by the booth, kissing and giggling as they waited.

Bell said, "Let me talk to Sal when he gets back home. But keep an eye on him while you're there, Charlie."

"Leo…"

"I don't want him to be the next guy who goes to the hospital."

Well after midnight, Corini and Fortune shared a corner at the bar in one of El Malecón's small, dimly lit lounges. Farcolini had retired to the villa he maintained in the hills west of Matanzas, its perimeter patrolled by guards provided by Senator Balboa. The Gellers had gone off to review information Farcolini had provided from Don Mauro and his other counterparts in Sicily. Across the lounge, under a cloud of violet smoke, were a handful of American businessmen who were oblivious to all but their own discussion.

Over cigars and dark rum, Corini told Fortune what he had proposed to Farcolini regarding Marsala.

Fortune was stunned.

Corini explained that Don Carlo wanted Fortune to stick to Bebe. "I should've known," he said. "Once again, you can't see the benefits."

"We never said a thing about this," Fortune replied bitterly. "Not word one."

"You're angry because I went to Don Carlo before I spoke to you."

"Because you knew I wouldn't agree."

"Because you don't know what's in your best interests."

"Babysitting Bebe is in my interest?"

"This opens up the West Coast for you. You sit on Bebe for a couple months, then you put somebody in your place. By then, he's on track or he's through. In the meantime, you're already tapping the racing wires, the numbers, the unions and whatever the fuck else Baum is up to. It's good."

"And when do I come back to New York?"

"You want to know when you're taking over for Bruno."

Fortune snuck a glance at the Americans in the corner. "Wasn't that the plan? Wasn't that the agreement we made in Brooklyn?" He lowered his voice and in Sicilian said, "Wasn't that why I'm teeing up Bruno for you?"

With a note of triumph in his voice, Corini said, "I remind you that Bruno's in the hospital, my friend."

Fortune snorted. "If you think a beating is going to change his ways, you'd better think again."

"Of course not. The man's an animal. But if Carlo gives you Baum's seat right away, Bruno puts two and two together. Then he's got no choice but to blow everything up. So instead of Mimmo, it's you or me at the end of the rifle shot." Corini clapped a hand on Fortune's arm. "Irregardless, we need a man out in California we can trust. You go with Bebe, and it develops slow and natural. It's logical. You in for Ziggy. Then you're the king of Las Vegas."

Fortune said, "Anthony, tell me. Does this bullshit work when you talk to your politicians?"

Corini smiled. "Sure. Why not?"

"Well, I ought to tell you I know when I'm getting fucked."

"Listen, this thing is going our way nice," Corini said. "I told Geller about the note the cops found on Pellizzari which put it on me. Then you caught a big break when your bagman went after Bruno's guy. Instead of me pinning the whole thing on it looking like Bruno stole from us, I get to tell Carlo the fuckin' truth: He tried to take out Mimmo. Over a fuckin' plate-glass window. Typical."

The plan was for it to look like Gigenti had one of his crew swipe the Jersey take from Corini as a sign of his frustration with the continuing investment in politics and entertainment. Fortune sent Chiasso to approach the kid they called Little Buff and tell him the robbery was a test of Benno's mettle. Chiasso said he could keep the money if he rode away clean. Fortune figured in a day or two he'd send Fat Tutti to retrieve the cash, but Benno moved too fast, smashing his way into the Mulberry Street club, embarrassing Gigenti in front of the neighborhood and his crew. Of course, Gigenti would want revenge, no matter that an attack on Mimmo looked to Farcolini and Geller like Gigenti was eager to bust up the organization over a minor grievance.

Corini examined his thick cigar, a serpentine plume of smoke rising. "That Benno kid did good," he said. "What are you going to do for him? Can he sit in Mimmo's chair?"

Fortune shook his head.

"Then?"

"I got an idea," Fortune said. "Could work out for everybody."

Nino Terrasini found a little bungalow in West Hollywood that would suit him just fine. He salvaged some crates off the loading dock at Ralph's, crammed them into the trunk and with Rosa in the passenger's seat, drove to the Wilshire Towers to move his stuff out.

"So this is it," she said as she removed her scarf. "His bachelor pad."

"This is it." Terrasini went to his bedroom. He'd made a silent pledge to leave behind everything he hadn't earned. He started tossing shirts, slacks and jackets toward the open luggage on the bed.

"No, Nino. Don't," Rosa said. "Let me do that."

She folded a pair of slacks over her arm and placed it gently in the suitcase. Next she started folding Terrasini's suit jackets.

"The furniture stays," he said.

"Too bad. I wanted to see you fit that chiffonier into a tomato crate."

Terrasini smiled. This was a damned difficult task, closing the casket on a long friendship and she was trying to make it easy for him. No way she had to be here, but that was Rosa. She knew the right thing.

"The clock?"

"A gift," he replied.

"Ashtray?"

"Ditto."

He had a few books, some magazines, toiletries. A photo of him and Bebe snapped outside the Paramount in '42 stood on the dresser.

"Take it," Rosa said, looking at the picture. "One day, when you're not mad at him, you'll wish you did."

He nodded and it went on top of pillows he'd bought for his cranky neck. "That's about it. Ten years on the road and it fits in one suitcase and a couple of tomato crates."

She said, "If you were married to him, half of everything would belong to you."

Terrasini closed one eye and gestured like he was chopping the bed in half, the chest of drawers, too.

"Show me his bedroom," Rosa said.

"Come on, Rose—"

"I want to see the notches on the bedpost."

"What did you tell me? '*Quando è tempo di andare, è tempo di andare.*'" When it's time to go, it's time to go.

"You're going, I'm gone," she said as she retrieved her hand-bag. "But I want to see."

Terrasini waited behind her as she stood in the doorway and surveyed the crisp, orderly room.

"Not a single photo of Bill Jr."

"It wouldn't serve the mood."

"I wonder if he would've brought me here. You know, if we weren't married."

"You?" Terrasini laughed darkly. "This is no place for a woman like you, Rosa."

She turned, went up on her toes and kissed his cheek. Then she said, "Come on, let's get out of here."

As he followed her across the living room, Terrasini dug into his pocket and withdrew the gold money clip Bebe had given him. He tossed it on the sofa and watched it bounce and tumble to the floor.

Fortune opened the door to Farcolini's suite. He waved Marsala in and told Benno to wait.

"Sure, Frankie," Benno said as he retreated. He didn't know what his role could've been in the meeting, other than to tap Marsala on the face after he fainted from fright. All night the guy had paced and whined, Benno reminding him it was a pretty good bet they wouldn't throw Mimmo out of the plane into the ocean and besides, there was the matter of $500Gs he had to earn, which he couldn't do if, say, Zamarella put one between his blue eyes.

To Bebe, a sit with Farcolini was the same as seeing St. Peter at the pearly gates. He took a deep breath and put on his best smile.

Farcolini and Corini sat at opposite ends of the sofa and neither stood as Marsala approached.

He dropped the smile and adopted an expression as somber as his black suit.

Farcolini pointed toward a chair. Marsala sat. Fortune did, too. They were both facing the boss.

To protect Marsala, whom Enna had described as fragile as a fresh egg, Corini had tried to explain to Don Carlo that celebrity corrupted even the most reasonable man. Farcolini didn't buy it. He felt the pursuit of fame was a sign of weakness and having known Hennie Rosiglino, Farcolini now understood he should've expected nothing more from Marsala than what they got: a needy, unreliable child who sought approval from strangers because he didn't approve of himself. A man of such low self-regard could never respect others, particularly those who professed to love him. Mimmo, who had become more ineffectual as the years wore on, tried to treat Marsala like a nephew, failing to see that family meant nothing to the singer, who humiliated his own wife and child. Farcolini wouldn't make the same mistake again.

"William Rosiglino," Farcolini said.

Marsala swallowed hard.

"What will you do to make things right?"

"I—What do you suggest, Don Carlo?" Marsala said.

Corini replied. "Did you have some problem with the plan, Bebe?"

"No. But I—"

"Then why did you try to destroy it?" Corini asked.

"It wasn't my intent—"

"The plan Rico brought to you," Corini said. "Didn't you agree?"

Marsala wasn't sure how to answer. "I agreed," he said finally.

"Then you follow it to the letter."

"Yes, Anthony. Sure."

"Rico Enna will manage you personally. He's going to find you a new record company and put you back on the radio."

In fact, Enna already had completed both tasks.

"You will begin your tour as soon as we can arrange it. In between, you will contact your friends in the music industry and introduce them to Saul Geller."

"Saul Geller? I don't—"

Corini said, "Geller will manage the Sandpiper for us."

Marsala knew better than to ask where Ziggy Baum was going.

"You agree to this, Mr. Rosiglino?" Farcolini asked.

"I do. Yes."

Corini pointed toward Fortune. "Frankie is going to take a personal interest in you on our behalf."

Marsala looked at Fortune. "Anything I can do to make it easier for you, Frankie?"

Fortune didn't respond. The assignment still made him sick to his stomach.

Farcolini said, "This situation with your wife…It's a disgrace."

"I handled it poorly, I admit. But the marriage is beyond repair."

"From now on, keep it quiet," Corini said. "We'll send you the right lawyer."

"Thank you." He turned to Fortune. "Do you mind if Terrasini stays?"

"Terrasini's moved out. You broke it. He's through with you."

"You're in a fix, Bebe," Corini said. "By our accounts, when the divorce comes in, you'll have less than one hundred thousand dollars to your name—and you have to pay off the mortgage on your wife's home."

Marsala laughed nervously. "I guess I'll be working awfully hard."

Fortune rose from the chair.

Farcolini said, "You'll be doing what a man in your position is supposed to. You'll take care of your career and the people who are supporting you."

"Yes, Don Carlo."

"What you did to your wife and said about Phil Klein, this offends any man."

Marsala slumped.

Fortune said, "Bebe, look at these two men," gesturing to Farcolini and Corini. "They stood by you. What you've done, it won't happen again. Hear what I say, Bebe. It won't happen again."

Marsala turned to Farcolini.

Corini dismissed Marsala with the back of his hand. "Go on. We're finished."

Farcolini said nothing.

Fortune led Marsala to the door and told Benno to keep him in his suite.

"Sure thing, Frankie," Benno said, but he was pretty sure Bebe would pass out before they made the elevator.

CHAPTER THIRTY

The weekend came and went, then Monday, then Tuesday and no Benno. Dropping by the store, Bell said, "Gemma, do you need a hand?"

No, Benno's aunt said, her other nephew was filling in. "He's a good boy," she added sadly and Bell figured the putz took a wrong turn with the truck and wound up in Pennsylvania.

On Thursday, Benno returned. "Hey, fella," he said as he entered the A&P's produce aisle.

Bell was stacking the last of the pumpkins, hiding their dents and scars.

Benno opened his new black topcoat to display an ocean blue sharkskin suit, a slim blue tie and a crisp white shirt.

"Bebe gave it to me. New." Benno pirouetted. "You dig?"

"Do I dig?" Bell asked incredulously. "With a fuckin' shovel I dig. What are you supposed to be?"

"Oh, you can dress up like Joe College, but I make a move and it bothers you."

Bell tried to follow the analogy. "What? You're Frankie Fortune Jr. now?"

"No. But he loves me, too."

"Ah. I guess I don't have to ask how Cuba went."

Benno looked around. An old humpy guy was feeling up the bananas, but Benno guessed he couldn't hear if they shouted in his ear. "Frankie's in charge of Bebe," he said, stepping closer to his friend. "Mimmo's out."

"Out out?"

"No, like, 'go sit in the candy store and shut up' out. Also, Carlo Farcolini kicked the shit out of Gigenti. Broke his ribs."

"You saw this?"

"Mimmo, yes. Gigenti, no."

"So no one said anything about you, the money, Gigenti's window?"

"Nope. And I ate a coconut."

"I'll order you a crate."

"Nah. I brung one back for Gemma, which is enough, seeing as nobody I know owns a machete. I got some perfume for Imogene, too. Bebe says it's the best."

"Speaking of which, Sal, you either declare on her friend Nina Esposito or she's looking elsewhere."

"I don't know," Benno said thoughtfully. "You swim with Bebe and a different school of girls come—"

"Saturday night. They get off the hospital at six. Dinner at eight."

"I pick the joint?"

"The joint? Sure. Pick."

"You drive."

Bell nodded. "Don't make me compete with that suit."

They knew Ziggy Baum had built an escape route into his suite at the Sandpiper, a tunnel facing the truckers' highway. It was originally designed to help him flee the feds, but it would also help Baum dodge someone like Eugenio Zamarella, who this morning was dressed like a member of the construction crew that paraded through pounding noise and clouds of dust in the hotel's otherwise-empty halls and casinos.

Baum, who took to the sunny lifestyle the moment he was assigned to LA almost 20 years ago, came out of his room wearing a canary-yellow sweater over a lime-green shirt and green slacks. He'd had plastic surgery that gave his skin an eerie sheen that was even more ghostly as he walked under the bare light bulbs that lined the ceiling. Right now, he was thinking maybe he should go down to the garage, jump in the big Buick and head south through Arizona and over the Mexican border, $375,000 hidden in the side panels, another $800,000 split between Banco de Mexico and the Cayman National Trust Company. The only thing holding him back was his unwavering belief that the Sandpiper—and the scheme Geller and Corini conceived—would pay off bigger than big. In his dreams, he saw machines that printed money, $100 denominations and up, the key in his pocket.

Since Geller and Corini were refusing his calls, last week Baum reached out to Frankie Fortune back in Jersey. The guy who answered the phone at Fortunato's said he wouldn't be back for days. He was out of the country.

Buy me six more months, he was going to tell Fortune. Talk to Carlo. I'm telling you, Frankie, if that son of a bitch Bebe comes through—if Bebe brings in Crosby, the Andrews Sisters, Peggy Lee, the movie stars and you see them at the tables. Glamour and gambling and it's a hideaway, Frankie. Who's to tell people they shouldn't do what they want?

Like Fortune didn't know Baum had turned the Sandpiper into a money pit he scooped from for his own pleasure. Baum was a button, not a businessman. To put him in charge of constructing a storage shed would've been stupid, never mind a hotel and casino 80 miles from nowhere.

Wearing his mask to cover his pockmarks, Zamarella walked up behind Baum as he approached the elevators. Within 20 yards of where they stood, maybe a dozen workers, their sweaty arms coated in asbestos and grime, shouted and sledgehammered through walls. As Gigenti had instructed, Zamarella jammed a .38 against the back of Baum's head below his right ear.

Baum felt the bump.

Then his head exploded and his brains splattered against the top of the elevator door. The shot's echo was lost in the din of construction.

Zamarella spun to leave. The workers continued their noisy demolition. Baum's body was discovered maybe 10 minutes after his killer had driven the dead man's car onto Route 91, heading toward Long Beach, the gun going into the desert. The cash was going to be shipped to Gigenti, who was recovering back in New York.

Rico Enna set up a luncheon at the Polo Lounge, a table in the sun for three. As he and Fortune were killing time, he looked up and there was Bebe and on his arm was Eleanor Ree. Under the dappled sunlight, she was stunning, an ivory dress off her tanned shoulders and a satin sinamay hat as cute as hell.

"Look at this," Fortune groused. He wasn't talking about Ree's beauty, though every head in the restaurant had turned, the sun following her like a spotlight of spun gold. He meant that clown fuck Bebe. The *ciuccio* was starting off the new life exactly like the old one.

The men stood.

"Frankie, Rico, say hello to Eleanor."

Ree jutted out a hand. As the maître d' slid in a fourth chair, she said, "Mr. Fortune, I've heard a lot about you." Smoke in her voice, a twinkle in her emerald eyes, she couldn't help but notice Fortune was the best-looking man in the place. "Can it all be true?"

She's halfway to drunk, Fortune thought, his mood souring even more.

A story she heard on the morning's news had sent her to breakfast gin. "Reputed mobster Sigmund Baumstein, aka Ziggy Baum, was found murdered at the Sandpiper Hotel and Casino in Las Vegas, Nevada. Workers at the hotel discovered the body of Baum, an associate of underworld crime boss Carlo Farcolini…" Coming out of the shower, Marsala listened as he toweled his hair. Naked, Ree sat up in his bed. "Bill—"

"Hey, it happens, kid."

As she tried to corral her thoughts, a mundane question popped out of her mouth. "What about your engagement at—"

"Don't fret, babe," Marsala replied. "It's all taken care of."

"I hope you won't be bored by the conversation, Eleanor," Enna said now as they sat. He moved the leather folder on the table to his lap.

"I've met with agents before," she said with an ironic smile. "It's not too terribly bad."

His spirits soaring, Marsala beamed. "What are you guys having?" He offered Ree a smoke and lit one for himself.

Ree ordered a gin gimlet while Marsala told the waiter he'd take a rum cooler.

"Bebe," Fortune said, leaning in. "It's time to go to work."

"Did you listen to the music I sent you?" He wore a baby blue jacket over a dark blue shirt and baggy khakis. He fit in with all the other *finochios* in the place.

Fortune nodded curtly. "Rico says nobody wants jazz but you."

Ree looked sideways at Marsala.

"One or two numbers in the act," Enna offered.

"Fair enough. Can you get me Sweets?" The trumpeter.

"I can get you Basie for the Sandpiper," Enna replied.

"The entire orchestra? Now that's a swell idea."

"Bebe." Fortune spoke in Sicilian. "Since when do you bring your mistress to a sit?" he said, using crude slang to describe Ree.

"*Non è il mio cumare.*" In English, Marsala added, "We're in this together."

Fortune turned to Ree. "Excuse me, but I need to be precise with Bebe."

She reached for her drink.

In Sicilian, Fortune said, "You ought to know better than to think this is a game with me, Bebe. I'm not Mimmo and I don't give a fuck. You understand? You're going to do what you're told."

"I understand, Frankie, sure—"

"I don't care if you fuck goats. Keep it quiet and do what Rico tells you. You don't change one fuckin' thing."

Ree was fascinated. The gorgeous man seethed and smiled at the same time.

"Gentlemen," she said, "before you begin your meeting, let me apologize. I asked Bill to introduce me to Mr. Enna. Not that I'm unhappy with my representation." She got up to leave, her fingers groping for her clutch. "Mr. Fortune, forgive me for intruding."

Enna stood, his chair scraping the brick. Marsala did, too. But Fortune barely stirred.

"Bill, I'll be in the café."

"Thanks, sweetheart."

As she crossed the pavilion, heads turned again.

Marsala sat. Frowning, he said, "Frankie, Jesus. She doesn't know how we operate."

"Go ahead, Rico," Fortune said.

Enna had the contracts in the folder. "I understand you've been informed of the terms of the agreements." The agency would now take 15 percent of everything—recordings, radio, live performances and endorsements. With Klein, it was seven.

Marsala nodded as he fished in his jacket pocket for a pen. "I won't question Don Carlo." He thumbed through the contract, searching for the dotted line.

"The Basie offer. Bill, it's legit," Enna said.

"You'll get what you need," Fortune added. "We don't want any excuses."

"No excuses," Marsala echoed as he signed his name.

Enna said, "I'm thinking Joey Aaron to open." A wacky Jew comedian from back in Jersey.

"Great, Rick," Marsala mumbled as he kept writing his name. When he finished, he passed the papers to the agent.

"We start a week from Friday," Enna said. "Kansas City, then Saturday and Sunday in Chicago." He dug into his folder again, bringing sheet music to the table. "When you get back, we can talk about songs for your next session. I think we have a couple of hits there."

"Are these hits, Frankie?" Marsala asked as he pushed the sheets across the table.

"They'd better be," Fortune replied.

Benno came out spiffy in a double-breasted camel suit and his familiar brown fedora, matching shoes, tie with little red streaks. Then he stopped dead. Imogene was in his seat—front passenger's side. And then he stopped dead again. This Nina Esposito was a knockout. Thick black hair cascading down to her shoulders, gorgeous black eyes, a perfectly prominent southern Italian nose, healthy olive skin. Plump lips. Long legs crossed at the ankles. Her violet dress fit her like paint.

"Nina, this is Sal Benno," Imogene said as she let him wriggle into the backseat.

Esposito nodded hello, both confident and shy.

Imogene put a finger against her neck right under those earrings Bell gave her last Christmas. "Sal. Here."

Benno came in and took a whiff. "Mmm. Nice, right?"

"I told Nina you bought it in Cuba." Imogene looked good in blue. Smart and happy, like always when Bell was nearby.

"Do you travel often, Sal?" Nina asked.

"Sure. Cuba. All over. Champagne, first class, free magazines. Me and Bebe."

They proceeded through the Lincoln Tunnel, the heat in Tyler's old car working good, the girls yapping nursing school, Benno watching the city say hello. Soon they took their seats at Porter's Chophouse off Fifth Avenue, a short stroll from the Hampshire House. The maître d' said, "Good evening, Mr. Benno. It's good to see you again."

Benno said, "Ernie, let me introduce you to my friends. This is Leo Bell and his girl, Imogene. And this is Nina Esposito."

Ernie nodded gracefully and after directing them to the coatcheck room, he led Benno and his guests through the crowded clubby restaurant with its leather banquettes and round tables with little lamps in the center. The place was alive with chatter, a bustling staff and a roving violinist. Clouds of cigarette smoke hung near the ceiling.

The waiter appeared. "Mr. Benno."

"Hay." Then he said, "Four rum coolers, OK, pal?"

Bell said, "Rum cooler?"

"We drink them in Havana. Me and Bebe."

"Sal knows Bill Marsala," Imogene said dryly, an eyebrow arched.

"He's from Narrows Gate, eh?" Nina asked.

"Yeah, but I know him better from Havana and also here in the city. He brought me here twice. Yeah, we get along pretty good."

Some other guy showed up with the menu. Of course, the ones he gave the girls didn't have prices on them, but Bell's did and his dimple liked to leap off his chin, the Famous Porterhouse going for more than he earned in a week at the A&P.

Imogene leaned over and looked at Bell's menu like they were already married. She whistled.

"This is on me," Benno said. "Bebe—"

"OK, that's enough with Bebe." Bell turned to Nina. "He used to hate the guy. Now they're *amici*."

"Is that true?"

"What? That I used to hate him?"

"No, that you're friends."

"Well…" He glowed with false modesty.

"Listen, Rockefeller, you're not picking up the check," Bell said.

"With Bebe, there is no check."

Imogene said, "Sal, don't be a jerk. Nina, he's usually not like this."

"Like what?" Benno said, his humor still in place. "I had a good week, babe. I like to share good times with good friends."

"Babe?"

"Let him be," Bell said, tapping Imogene's arm. "They sprinkled him with stardust."

"Bebe wants me to come to Hollywood with him."

Bell put down the menu. "What?"

"Hollywood, California. For which you don't need a pass-port."

The rum coolers arrived. As Benno and Bell parried, Imogene and Nina took sips. Immediately, they wanted six more. The thing was magic, like soda that dizzied your head and made your belly warm.

"When were you going to tell me this?" Bell asked.

"Bebe said don't say."

"So who gives a damn what Bebe says?"

"It's not a done deal. There's steps, Leo. First good-bye Ziggy, which you know, and then Frankie moves in, and then Bebe gets on the road and then he settles in at the Sandpiper and Frankie gets bored and Corini needs somebody he can trust so…" Benno snapped his thumbs toward his lapels.

Bell looked at the adjoining tables. No one seemed to be eavesdropping, though the way Tyler told it, maybe there was a microphone in the salt shaker.

"Plus Eleanor Ree approves." He turned to the dark-haired beauty at his side. Leaning in, he whispered, "Believe me, honey, she's got nothing on you."

"You'd better think about this," Bell warned.

He laughed. "Like I'm going to start doing that now."

Imogene said, "Leo, if you're not going to drink that…"

"This is delicious, Sal," Nina said, hinting for more of Benno's attention. He was a boy, showing off and all, but he was awfully cute with those glasses and the way his face shined when he smiled. The Espositos were big believers in potential.

"The drink. It's not too sweet?" Benno asked.

She said, "How can something be too sweet?"

"What are you going to have, Leo?" Imogene asked.

"I'm thinking a bowl of air."

"Don't be stingy," Benno said. "Nina?"

"You order for me, Sal."

Benno thought he detected an odd accent when she spoke. Not that he was an expert, seeing as how everybody he knew talked like him. Except Bebe, who took lessons, but there's no sense in bringing that up, Leo brooding over there.

"Nina, I heard you knew *amici* was friends. *Parla Italiano*?"

"*Sì*," she replied, drink poised beneath her lips. "*Parlo Italiano*."

"What are you, Sicilian or Italian?"

Imogene said, "Sal, how can that matter?"

"It matters, hon. Believe me."

Imogene looked at Leo. "There's a difference?"

"Ooh. Don't get him started. He was going human there for a minute."

"No, really," Benno said. "Italian or Sicilian?"

"Which do you prefer?" Nina Esposito asked.

"Hey, doll, I like you either way. I'm asking—Italian or Sicilian?"

"I'm Canadian," she said.

Benno blinked in confusion. "What does that mean?"

"That I'm from Canada."

"No, no. I—I mean, what about Italian or Sicilian?"

"Gosh, I don't know. I was born in Toronto."

"Toronto. Sounds Sicilian and Italian." He turned to Bell. "We're everywhere, see?"

CHAPTER THIRTY-ONE

The Beverly Hills Hotel was rich with memories for Ree: While they were dating, her first husband gave an impromptu performance here, dancing on the soda fountain counter as he belted out a song. Her billionaire boyfriend kept a bungalow on call where he insisted she let him bathe her in buttermilk at a time when she was impressionable enough to believe it meant he thought her special. As her second marriage dribbled to its end, she met Simon's ex three times a week in a bungalow Marlene Dietrich had refitted for the type of affair they enjoyed.

But from now on, the hotel would have a different connotation: It would be the place where she learned Bill Marsala was owned by gangsters. The rumors he said were rubbish and nasty anti-Italian slurs were true. The investors he spoke of were the likes of Frankie Fortune, who told Marsala, not long ago the biggest star in the country, to go fuck himself and like it. She was frightened. She loved Marsala but there was no way to win. She had to get out and had no idea how.

"Sorry," Marsala said when he joined her at the hotel's café. "That was rough."

"Are you all right?" she asked. She could see he was shaken.

"They oversold it, didn't they?"

No, she thought. It seemed right. He'd walked out on them. He abandoned his wife, the tour, the radio program and its sponsors. He was risking the open-ended engagement in Las Vegas. Fortune was furious and since he represented the people who owned Bill, he had a right to be.

"They want what's best for me," he explained as he lit another cigarette. "But subtle they are not."

"Oh, Bill," she said tenderly, touching his cheek.

He kissed her and didn't care who saw. "Let's drive," he said. "Fuck it all."

They stopped at her place in Bel Air for a sobering dip in the pool, a session on a lounge chair, Ree straddling him slow and easy as he lay on his back, and then a second round in the living room, Marsala entering her from behind. A shower, a friendly dispute over what to wear and they threw a suitcase in the trunk. By late afternoon, they were headed east, picking up Route 60, the San Gabriel Mountains to the north. They felt damned good, the desert ahead but the sun behind them. The pint of scotch was going down like nectar. Marsala sang tunes he said he'd fight to work into the new show. "This one's from Lady Day," he told her. "You know this number from Nat Cole." His baritone flowed smooth and gentle. Notes floated tenderly. It was wonderful.

Everything she loved about him was here now—"fuck it all," memories of starbursts as he slid inside her and they worked their hips in unison, laughing when it was over, the love still there. Just two damaged souls, puzzle pieces made to fit together, the world far away. And now the road, dusk, his voice. They were alone, nothing mattered and life was as uncluttered as the empty horizon.

She nestled next to him, and she thought, OK. Maybe it'll be all right. Maybe if he gives them what they want and just sings. He could buy us both a little time…

She took off her sunglasses, put her head on his thigh, kicked off her shoes and fell asleep.

She woke to the sound of gunfire.

It was nighttime in a small town. Sitting up in the car, she saw a café, a general store and on the other side of the street, a post office. They were all closed. Neon sizzled in the window of a bar slung out of adobe. Houses were behind them in the distance, but nothing lay ahead.

Standing in the high beams' glare, Marsala was shooting at the town's lone streetlight.

A few men in work shirts and denim dribbled out of the bar. Country and western music followed.

Marsala shot at the light again and missed. "*Va fungule,*" he spit.

Ree struggled into her shoes and skittered toward him.

"Want a shot?" he said. He pressed the gun into her hand. "Go ahead, El. You'll feel great."

She looked up. Stars were scattered overhead.

"Don't worry," he insisted. "You miss, you'll hit the moon."

Still groggy from her boozy nap, she closed an eye, lifted the barrel and to make him happy, squeezed off a round.

"Damn close, doll," Marsala said. "Damn close."

The gruff men outside the bar, who looked at the couple with bemused disregard, parted to let the sheriff through. He wore a beige cowboy hat, beige shirt with a gold star, beige slacks with a prominent buckle and pointy boots. He had his hand on the butt of his pistol.

Marsala shot. He missed the light but hit the lamppost.

"Say, buddy," the sheriff said. "What did that light up there ever do to you?"

"You say something to me, Hopalong?"

"Said you might want to think about putting down that weapon you got there, Mr. Marsala."

"And suppose I don't."

"Bill…" She couldn't figure him. He was sober but he wobbled, playing drunk.

The sheriff flexed his fingers slowly. "Then this will get ugly real quick."

"Give me the gun, Bill," Ree whispered.

"Think he can outdraw me?"

She looked at the sheriff, who stood with his legs wide, his hand coiled and ready. "Bill, he's not fucking around."

"She's right, Mr. Marsala. Be a damned fool way to die. For either of us."

Marsala eyed the sheriff. "Fair enough," he said as he let the gun fall to the dust.

Ree kicked it toward the law.

Shaking their heads, the crowd dispersed.

Rico Enna arrived four hours later by crop duster and the lone taxi out of Cabazon. The sheriff got $2,000 and Ree's pistol: The drunk and disorderly charge disappeared.

"Any reporters in the bar?" Enna asked.

"There's no call for that kind of talk, Mister," the sheriff replied. He said his town was the first piss stop before the next service station on Route 60, meaning Marsala wasn't the only Hollywood star to drop by and make an ass of himself.

The door to the jail's lone cell was open. Marsala sat on the cold floor while Ree rested on the seedy mattress. "You're free to go," the sheriff said.

Ree stood and tamped her slacks. "Are there photographers?"

"No, ma'am," the sheriff told her. He had seen Ree's debut in that hard-boiled Hemingway picture and thought she was hotter than July. He would've spent time pondering what she was doing with a dipshit swizzle stick like Marsala, but he learned long ago that opposites did not attract. "Mr. Enna will fill you in."

Enna was behind the wheel. Ree climbed in back, kissing her fingertips and tapping the agent's cheek. Marsala got in back, too. "*Grazie tanto*, Enrico," he said. He pointed to the bottle in the glove compartment. The desert air had dried out his throat.

"What were you thinking, Bill?" Enna said finally as they headed west.

"Don't put me in a box," he replied. "I'll sing for you but don't put me in a box."

Ree held the bottle now, debating whether to finish it or save Bill a final pull.

"You put me in a box and I fly. Baby, I fly."

"Let me ask you something." Enna looked into the rearview. "What do you think Frankie will say if he hears about this?"

"Is he going to hear about it?"

Enna didn't reply.

Marsala smiled triumphantly as he drew Ree to his side.

There wasn't a chance in hell Mimmo could drive through the maze of downtown New York City, the random intersections, narrow lanes, shadows even at noon. You make a wrong turn and you're over by City Hall and the courthouses when all you wanted to do was find Mulberry Street. Once he could've freed up a driver but not now. His boys knew he'd been slapped down. Everybody knew.

So he took the tubes, got off at the wrong stop and wound up by Macy's. He humped up the stairs, his hands in his pocket, the sling off, his shoulder tender. He told a taxi driver to bring him where he wanted to go but drop him off on the other side of the snow-coated bocce courts.

"Stay away from Bebe," Corini had told him, Don Carlo sitting right there, not a drop of compassion in his eyes. No link to Bebe, that brat fuck, meant he'd never have a say in the plan to move the crew over to entertainment. Never. And maybe Corini didn't remember and maybe Frankie Fortune forgot on purpose, but the Blue Onyx was the first club they owned that pulled in a couple large every week even though it was in downtown Narrows Gate, not up on the Palisades or in Newark where Jersey people usually went for a good time. Also, he had the Saint Tropez until Fortune burned it down, he still didn't know why—just to put Bebe on the radio?

Surely, Don Carlo would remember his contribution and one day Cy Geller would come to him and say, in his phony, hoi polloi, Miami Beach Jew way, "Domenico, would you be interested in moving to Las Vegas and show us how to run the operation proper?" Mimmo understood why Farcolini wanted Baum out West first: Ziggy had the kind of bullshit style that the slats out there could swallow. Mimmo figured Corini and Fortune kept him back in the candy store like he was warming up in the bullpen. As soon as the walls were in place in Vegas, the lights turned on and the slots plugged in, he'd get his due. Bebe in a tux, spotlight around him, announcing, "I'd like to dedicate this next number to my uncle. Folks, he's been like a father to me and well, you know him as the man who gets things done out here in Las Vegas.

Ladies, gents, how about a big hand for Mr. Domenico Mistretta. Come on, Mimmo! Take a bow!"

Fuckin' Bebe.

Mulberry Street was swarming with families coming from Mass at the Transfiguration, the kids bundled and wearing galoshes, old gray couples trailing their sons and daughters who were dressed up good. For a moment, looking at them nice and content, Mimmo forgot the rage that boiled his brain, but it came back like a fuckin' volcano blowing.

Gigenti had muscle men at the door who looked like they were carved from steel. They studied Mimmo and he could tell by their eyes they didn't make him a threat, just a guy in sunglasses past his prime, the clock winding down.

Mimmo kept coming, even as the kids ran around him like he wasn't there and their parents parading their youth, smiling and talking sweet, everybody fresh from Communion, the winter air putting color on their cheeks.

"Tell Bruno that Mimmo wants to see him," he said.

Green-eyed Superman in the brown suit said, "Keep moving, old-timer."

And then Superman found a gun pressed against his stomach.

"Tell your friend he moves, I make you dead."

"Tommy..." the guy said.

Tommy showed his palms.

"Hands in your pants pockets deep. Both of you," Mimmo instructed.

They did like they were told.

"I know Bruno since he was younger than you and he knows me, too." To Tommy, he said, "Go tell him the guy who put two in the Franklin stove is here."

For a moment, Mimmo forgot Gigenti wasn't in on the Uccello hit.

Tommy looked to his associate. "Do it," he said.

When Tommy shuffled toward the door, Mimmo stepped back and returned the gun to his jacket. As the happy parade passed, he said to Superman, "Was a day I shoot you first and then we talk."

The guy produced a handkerchief and mopped his brow. "You got style, old man. I'll say that."

"I used to," Mimmo replied as he adjusted his sunglasses.

Bruno Gigenti was at a round table across from the bar, pale and in pain and angry like a beat-down boxer who had some fight left in him and was biding his time. He had a cup of espresso in hand and a bottle of sambuca stood nearby, but neither dulled the throbbing from his broken ribs. Every breath reminded him he wanted Corini dead, like it was Corini who took an arm from a chair to him, driving him to his knees in front of the Gellers. He wore a sweater vest to hide the bandages under his shirt, but it only served to add to the bulk. They had given him a cane, but it made him look weak, so he bit his tongue, took the pain and concentrated on his revenge.

"I got to talk to you," Mimmo said as he approached. The price of admission was turning over the gun, which was all right, seeing as he had a boning knife inside his sock.

In the back of the musty clubhouse, four old-timers playing *scopa* didn't bother to look up. But at least the guy behind the bar brought over an espresso. He waited until Gigenti pointed Mimmo to a seat, then put it down.

"Thank you," Mimmo replied. He put his hat on the adjoining chair. "How you feeling, Bruno?"

Everybody in here spoke only in Sicilian, so they did, too.

"I'm all right," Gigenti said. "You?"

"Yeah, all right. Maybe you told Zamarella not to shoot my head?"

"Not that."

Mimmo frowned.

"I heard you got the syph," Gigenti said. "Syphilis. It rots your brain."

"Bruno, I ain't come here to talk about my health."

Gigenti stared at him. He never could figure Mimmo out other than he took more than he gave, like everybody who worked under Corini and Fortune.

"They told you I'm off Bebe, right?"

"Good. You fucked that up big."

With that, Mimmo went to stand. "My mistake—"

"Sit down, Mimmo. Sit." Gigenti hissed in pain as he waved. "Go ahead. Speak your mind."

"I don't like how it's playing," he said as he folded into the chair.

"I got nothing for you," Gigenti said.

"Maybe I got something for you. That's what I'm saying."

Gigenti sipped the bitter coffee. "Like what?"

"Like why Carlo won't let you sleep in the house," he replied. He saw Farcolini holding a nasty cat by the scruff and tossing it into the street, the cat being Gigenti.

"What do you know, Mimmo?" Even if the guy had a bug rooting around his brain, maybe he remembered something.

"Who told you Pellizzari was going to be in that hotel in Jersey City?"

The tip came from a low-level in the Hudson County DA's. Frankie Fortune got it and passed it on. "You know who. Let's not play games, Mimmo."

"So why does Pellizzari step into broad fuckin' daylight by himself?"

"Mim—"

He held up his hand. "Because he thought Anthony had men waiting to steal him out of there."

"Why would he think that? It don't make sense."

"'Cause he had in his hand a note saying so. The delivery boy gave it to him and then Pellizzari steps out, pop, and the cops find it."

"What note? I don't know nothing about a note." A note like that pins the hit on me. To Carlo, it means betrayal. "So why didn't I hear about this note?"

Mimmo shrugged.

"Who wrote it?"

"'Who wrote it?'" he repeated. "Come on, Bruno."

Fortune, Gigenti thought.

Mimmo said, "And the delivery boy is the same guy who busted your window."

"You know this kid?"

"It's not the kid," Mimmo said. "I'm you and I find out how one of your guys knows he's the Jersey bagman."

Gigenti tried, but Little Buff had fled, taking his wife and baby. Nobody could find him to bring his arm back in a rag and show it to the rest of the crew.

Mimmo said, "Somebody recruited your boy to rip off Anthony. Another fuckin' setup."

"The same guy."

"It wasn't me. It wasn't the kid with the groceries."

Gigenti nodded slowly.

"You see what Carlo thinks of this? You pin the Pellizzari hit on Anthony and then you swipe his feed? And then you take a shot at me. Jesus."

"Nobody is saying I put one in you—"

"Please, Bruno, all right? The cops, they got the slug out of Pellizzari's head. What happens if we give them the one from my shoulder?"

Zamarella and that fuckin' Carcano bolt-action rifle.

"All of this, it's an insult to Carlo, all of it," Mimmo said. "We look like fuckin' children."

Gigenti calculated, grimacing as he leaned in. "What do you want from me?"

Mimmo hadn't put it to words yet, but he knew what he'd lost and needed back.

"I want to walk down the street," he said. "I want people to know I count."

"You count?" Gigenti said.

Mimmo nodded firmly like he believed making his move meant turning back the clock and restoring his youth, giving him another shot at power he never had.

Today they were down at the Battery, Bell and Tyler, facing the brawny towers of Wall Street.

Hunched over a container of coffee to ward off a whipping wind, Tyler tried to make sense of it. "Gigenti challenged Farcolini and Farcolini put him in the hospital. So Corini is still in charge. They hit Baum and Fortune is taking over Marsala."

Bell nodded. "You got it."

"What's it mean?"

"Farcolini is pulling the strings," Bell said. "He knows if he stays in Havana it's the same as being here."

"What would you do?"

"If I'm you?" Bell had thought about that last night as he lay in bed, still in his slacks and shirt, suspenders hanging low, Imogene's new scent lingering. "How bad do you owe Farcolini for his help with the invasion of Sicily?"

"Dewey wants to be president," Tyler replied cryptically. "He'll never admit there was a deal to get Farcolini out of Sing Sing."

An ocean liner coming around the Battery blasted its horn. Tugs trailed and seagulls bobbed in the stiff breeze.

"Kick Farcolini out of Havana," Bell said. "Remind him the deal was Sicily, not 75 miles from Miami Beach."

Tyler agreed. "We've got to stop the flow of narcotics out of Cuba. For all intents and purposes, the heroin labs in Sicily might as well be on our doorstep." He looked at Bell. "You've got to get closer, Leo."

He shook his head. "Can't happen. They'll never accept me."

"What about your friend?"

"Charlie…"

"He's in thick now."

"Leave him be."

"Haven't you asked yourself what he was doing in Havana?"

"Helping Mimmo," Bell replied, tapping his shoulder where Mistretta took a bullet.

"He carried a suitcase full of cash to Farcolini. Your friend is supporting the drug operation that's destroying the youth of America."

"Sally?" Bell laughed. "That's bullshit."

"It's a natural progression. First, the envelopes hidden among groceries, then a suitcase…"

"If there was a suitcase—"

"There was."

"—he didn't know. Believe me. It's a game to him but he draws the line. Look, he wants to run the grocery store. That's his ambition. This thing with Corini, and Marsala now, it's a thrill, that's all. He's cherry and he likes it that way."

"Bagman. In on the Pellizzari hit. Trafficking in narcotics." Tyler counted on his fingers. "Cherry's been popped."

Bell said, "Marsala wants to take him to Hollywood. He'll be three-thousand miles away."

"Hollywood? He muscles Gigenti's crew and he gets a reward?"

"Maybe for you Marsala's a reward…"

Tyler stood, leaving the coffee container under the bench. "He's crazy, you know."

"Sal? No. No, he's—"

"Marsala."

"Crazy how?"

"Crazy as in insane," Tyler said. "Certifiable. The Army would've taken him with the leg. You think a limp mattered much in '42? The psychiatrist said no. Psychoneurosis is what they call it. Mental instability. Manic depression. Crazy."

Bell grew up with the rumor that Marsala had tried to kill himself when he was a kid, ending up with a fractured thighbone. But too crazy for the Army?

Tyler said, "Your friend has no idea what they have in store for him."

"He'll be all right," Bell said as he stood, his voice quivering with doubt.

"Benno's a born patsy, Leo. You know it."

CHAPTER THIRTY-TWO

The Nevada State Police found another contractor in the desert, a hole behind the ear, but only after he'd taken a first-class beating, tuned up with pipes and bats before mercy descended. That made four guys turned into carrion feed since September who had hired and purchased for the Sandpiper.

A prosecutor with the state attorney general's office called on Saul Geller, who kept a trailer at the far end of the hotel and casino's parking lot, clear of the dust if not of the pounding of frantic construction, in anticipation of a March 1 reopening. Geller shared it with Harry Milton, the cowboy hotel and club owner Baum had run out of town when East Coast money bought up property the 72-year-old Milton didn't know he was selling. To win him back, Geller gave Milton two points off the top and a title, figuring it'd be worth it if the locals thought one of their own was in charge. In turn, the widower named Palm Tree Enterprises his beneficiary, but only were he to die of natural causes.

"Now," said the prosecutor, R. W. Saturday, "I've lived here in southwestern Nevada all my life and I've never heard of four men in the same business who worked on the same job turning up dead in a matter of less than two months."

Geller sat behind the desk, Milton on the sofa. The furniture was rented and looked it. To add to the office's ragtag appeal,

Milton suggested keeping the blinds askew and a bottle on the desk.

"You understand that we need to study your records and see if you might've had any cause to be upset with these gentlemen," said Saturday, who was about Geller's age, maybe 35 years or so, but weathered like he spent more time chasing leads in the sun than at trial in a courthouse.

"We've had a terrible time locating Mr. Baum's records," Milton replied. "So if you have any luck finding them, we'd be grateful if you would share them with us."

"Mr. Saturday," Geller said, "we terminated all contracts as of December 1. The only firms working on the Sandpiper now were hired by Mr. Milton and myself."

"But you are aware that it's rumored the four contractors, the deceased contractors, had provided materials and supplies to your predecessor, had them removed from the property and resold to you at the same price."

"Not to us, R. W.," Milton said. "To Mr. Baum."

Geller said, "We have a private security firm on hand now and several licensed private investigators, all of whom are registered with your office. We don't anticipate any problems of that nature."

Saul Geller arrived in Nevada the day after Ziggy Baum was killed. Milton notified the Las Vegas *Evening Review-Journal* of their new partnership and the newspaper made sure to report Geller's reputation as a no-bullshit businessman, who also was son to one of Carlo Farcolini's trusted deputies. Within 24 hours, two envelopes turned up at the hotel, both addressed to Geller. One contained $31,000 in cash from Snowland Irrigation, the other a certified check for $82,000 from Lovelock Carting. More followed. Suddenly, companies wanted a clean slate.

Saturday nodded thoughtfully and tugged on his ear. "You expecting any trouble from Senator Dunney and his crowd?"

"The crime commission? Why should we?" Geller said. "Palm Tree Enterprises is in the entertainment business. We intend to comply to the letter of the law of the state of Nevada."

"Though you list Anthony Corini on your board of directors."

"Mr. Corini has a lot of influence on the East Coast," Geller said. "We'll draw our clientele from throughout the United States."

"Any chance he had something to do with those boys you brought in from New York? Your private security firm."

"None," Geller said. The muscle came from Gigenti's crew.

Milton said, "Hell, Mr. Baum wasn't doing great with local talent, was he?"

"If I didn't know you since I was a boy, Harry, I'd said maybe you had something to do with the hard time they gave Baum, seeing how he booted you out."

"Which ought to tell you I had nothing to do with killing them and dumping them where the coyotes could pick at them."

Geller said, "Mr. Saturday, if there's nothing else."

"As a matter of fact, there is," the prosecutor said. "What I'd like to know is…" He clapped his hands. "Where do I sign up?"

Milton pushed off the sofa. "Let's walk, R. W.," he said.

Ree's agent never sent her a script unless he was certain she was right for it. Mal Weisberg drove this one to Bel Air himself.

They sat under an umbrella by the pool, the lanky, silver-haired agent draping his jacket on the arm of the white, cast-iron chair. Ree sat across from him. She wore burnt-orange slacks and a white silk blouse open to her cleavage. Even without makeup, she was Weisberg's most beautiful client. And most troubled. In the movie business for more than 20 years, he'd never known someone who, at her core, didn't care what happened to her. She worked hard, conducted herself as a professional and was diligent about her appearance. He found her charming, sweet even, and knew she appreciated the job he did on her behalf. But it was all a guise. Inside she was empty, and as far as he was concerned, by choosing Bill Marsala as a lover, she proved she held herself in gutter regard.

The houseboy brought a pitcher of limeade, tall glasses and a small carafe of gin.

"Eleanor," he said after they toasted, "I have in my briefcase the most exciting script I've read since Huston wrote *The Maltese Falcon*."

As she added a generous splash of liquor to her drink, Ree smiled. Weisberg always claimed every script he presented was almost as good as Huston's.

"And this time I mean it," he added. He slid the script across the glass table.

"*Mikindani Bay*," she read aloud.

"It's in Tanganyika, but they're shooting in Mozambique, a Portuguese colony on the southeast coast of Africa. You'll be based in the capital."

"Africa," she said, thumbing through the pages.

"You're an adventuress and you tangle with a big-game hunter," Weisberg said. "You go into the wild, up river. There's action, romance, danger." He mentioned the director's name. A legend, a three-time Oscar winner. "He wants you."

"Who's playing Anton Victor?"

He told her. A huge star, maybe a few years past his prime, but box office gold and hearty enough for the lead role, for sure. She knew him, a nodding social acquaintance. The veteran actor had recently taken up with the widow of a silent screen star, which didn't make him seem any younger. But he was a pro and Ree knew a Metro picture with him as the lead had a chance to flow on time.

"How long?" she asked.

"Exteriors ought to take six to eight weeks," he replied.

Two months in Africa, she thought.

"You're guaranteed a nomination, Eleanor," Weisberg said. "This will make your career."

She reached for the carafe.

From the wings, Marsala watched Ronnie Oliver at the piano run the band through a couple of Basie standards. He was thinking, I'm here in Kansas City. We could've had Prez or Ben Webster on tenor, Walter Page on bass, Jo Jones on the skins. Instead we got refugees from a third-rate Philharmonic who play like it's criminal to spice the soup. The music's so stiff, I should goosestep on stage.

But Marsala came on light and the applause was nice, generous even, the nightclub just about full. The first number was a challenge for the band—"All or Nothing at All" up-tempo and in double-time; "Cugat without the congas" is how he put it to Ollie when they finalized the arrangement in LA—but it worked.

They went right into his most recent hit, that rollicking piece of fluff. The tenor murdered the solo, but the tune drew a surprising reception and Marsala thanked the crowd. "Hey, it's great to be back in KC, ladies and gentlemen. One heck of a swinging place," he said as he tugged the mic cable and moved downstage. "Now, here's a lovely number..."

A ballad from '43 and he nailed it. Women sighed, drifting back to their younger days when their men were overseas and only Bill Marsala gave them the warmth they needed.

From his perch, Marsala could feel their reaction. He had it tonight, his baritone smooth, his delivery poised and confident, his power within his control. He was embraced by the sound of his own voice and certain it was about the best goddamned place in the world to be.

Afterward, Rico Enna edged through well-wishers in the corridor and stuck his head in Marsala's dressing room, which was maybe the size of a service station toilet. "Nice, Bill," he said. He'd already contacted Frankie Fortune.

"Thank Ollie," Marsala replied as he tossed his sweat-soaked shirt in the trash bin. "His back must be killing him from carrying the band."

The dressing room reeked of menthol like a TB ward.

"Plane leaves in two," Enna said.

They arrived in Chicago at six in the morning. Breakfast, a couple of pills and Marsala slept until five in the evening. Saturday night at the Chez Paree and a crowd gathered, including press and boys from the Chicago crew who came backstage. Marsala was in a good mood. He liked joking with "the bent-nose squad," as he called them. He let them know he'd seen Farcolini, telling them Don Carlo was in the pink. "He'll outlive us all, believe me," Marsala said. Then Enna shooed them away. By the time the agent returned, Marsala had soured. "Fortune sent them," he complained.

"No, this is the place to be, Bill," Enna tried as Marsala spooned horseradish into a cup of hot tea. "Saturday night in Chi town."

Half the crowd was liquored by the time the band ended Basie's "Taxi War Dance." Marsala came on to modest applause and a couple of catcalls. In their cups, the crew was in a mocking mood; once their broads got to say hello and have a picture taken, the skinny kid from Narrows Gate meant no more to them than somebody else's pet. The Chicago musicians swung hard and during the opener, Marsala gestured for the trumpet player to grab another chorus. "Take a bow, fella," he said as they went into the pop fluff. Next, the ballad from '43 started gorgeous as Oliver flicked the intro sweet and the trombone put a cushion under Marsala's voice. But he could hear the tough crowd talking while he sang. He tried that old trick, singing softly to draw them in, but it didn't catch.

When the applause died, a guy yelled in falsetto, "Oh Bill, you slay me." Even the ex–bobby soxers sprinkled throughout the club laughed.

"Thanks, doll," Marsala replied. But the heckler's remark stuck and by the time the band settled into the second ballad of the set, the crowd was behaving as if the music belonged deep in the background. "Sssh" went some distressed Marsala fan at stage left and "Fuck you, lady" came the reply from a guy as Marsala was trying to work a lyric, the band sweet but not syrupy and the brass biting right. Polite applause at the song's end but he heard the clatter of silverware and china.

Then Marsala said, "This next one's from my new picture. It's a swell number—" From the back, a coarse call for Marsala's first hit in 1940. "Come on, fella," Marsala said, annoyed. "We're not in high school, are we?" The line fell flat and so did the new tune. Marsala signaled for "She's Funny That Way" and the piano intro brought a decent reception, but the singer, thrown off his game, entered a beat too soon, rushing the rhythm section.

At the side of the stage, Enna felt for Marsala. He sounded good: even now, listen to how he moved to the bridge, pulling it back so he could glide with the reeds. But the audience didn't give a shit. Big town, every headliner in the country played it, every night a show worth seeing, so Bill Marsala at the Chez Paree wasn't an event. He was something to do over dinner. Maybe they hoped Eleanor Ree would walk in.

"Thanks very much, Chicago," Marsala said when the tune ended. Maybe the crowd thought he was second-rate, just some jug-eared kid who became a star when the men were in Europe and the Pacific. But he had more to say, he was Bill Marsala, for Christ's sake, and fuck these nobodies who couldn't recognize talent. When he was behind the mic, he didn't need to bend to anybody.

In the audience, Big Mouth stood and again demanded the bittersweet ballad Marsala had struck gold with when he was a contract singer for that gruff, demanding trombonist who pushed him around, mocked his looks, scorned his popularity. "Sing it!" the guy shouted, hectoring Marsala like he was a performing chimp. "Come on, Billy boy! Sing it!"

"Listen, buddy," Marsala said, glaring at the back of the house. "Don't you get it? I hate that fuckin' song."

The liquor-soaked guys laughed, but Marsala heard a gasp from every woman in the room who had given her soul to him when she was a tenderhearted kid.

"Good times," Marsala added quickly as the uncomfortable rumble grew. "Great memories. But, oh that tune. Sometimes, you just want something different. Ollie, let's try one of our new arrangements for these wonderful people. Ladies and gentlemen, the Gershwin brothers gave us this beautiful number..."

The following night, a threat of a cold, cold rain turning to snow, a gale off Lake Michigan and fewer than 200 people came to the Chez Paree. Three of every four tables sat empty. Earlier, the

Sun-Times had reported Marsala told Chicago to buzz off. "The has-been hasn't got it," a columnist wrote, adding that he performed with "the desperation of a drowning man. The smart set will stay away in droves for tonight's sendoff, and no one doubts they'll do the same when his latest Hollywood bomb is released this week. As far as we're concerned, good riddance."

The Los Angeles *Daily News* ran the column. It usually cut the local mentions, but in this case, the editor bumped it to the top. The headline: "Marsala to Chicago: Buzz Off!"

Frankie Fortune was in Marsala's room at the Wilshire Towers when the singer arrived with Enna. The moment the door opened, he sprung from the darkness toward Marsala and grabbed him by the throat, pinning him against a wall. The singer's feet dangled.

"You told Chicago to fuck off? Who the fuck are you to tell anybody to fuck off?"

Fortune let him drop.

"Get up."

Marsala struggled to stand. The tumble jarred his bum leg.

Enna retreated to turn on a light, avoiding the luggage he'd carried in. Behind him, Terrasini's old room was empty, the furniture carted off and sold.

Fortune said, "Every time you open your mouth, Bebe, we get fucked. Every fuckin' time."

Marsala took out his handkerchief and wiped the spittle from his lips.

Enna said, "Frankie, what they reported, Bill didn't say it."

"Don't make excuses for this—"

"Frankie, the Chi crew was busting his balls, hecklers, and he said he hated a song, not the town."

"A song. What song?"

Enna gave him the title.

"He sings it every night," Fortune said. He looked at Marsala. "Every night."

"Sure," Marsala said. He knew what was coming even before he boarded the plane in Chicago. So far, he was getting off light.

"Frankie, he was on. A great show in KC, the second night in Chicago."

Fuming, Fortune told them to bring a big-name columnist to the apartment and erase the mess. "Make everything better. Do it now, before the three nights at the Palm Tree Lounge. You don't make the Gellers look like a couple of *ciuccios* for having you at their club. And get on your knees and beg until Hollywood forgives you for insulting Phil Klein. Dead, and everybody out here tells me he's still a better man than you."

"I'll make it right, Frankie."

Fortune jabbed a finger into Marsala's chest. "There's no next time, Bebe."

Marsala tried to turn away, but Fortune grabbed his chin and twisted.

"This is the last shot. Fuck this up and I put you down myself."

How do you like this shit? Fifty degrees in Narrows Gate the first week of February and there's a huge puddle outside Benno's like the second Hudson. Benno push-broomed it toward the sewer and the fuckin' thing came right back on its own. He stood there, scratching behind his ear.

Bell was sitting on the stoop next door. He'd decided there was no way to finesse his pal. "Tell me about the suitcase."

Benno leaned on the broom handle. He tipped his hat to the back of his head. "Who told you about the suitcase?"

"The suitcase, Sally."

He came closer. "You guys know?"

"What 'you guys'?"

"Your Army pals."

"I'm asking you. Me, you."

"They made Bebe pay tribute to Don Carlo," Benno told him.

"How much?"

"A lot of large."

"And you carried it to Havana."

Benno said, "Bebe carried it to Havana. I carried it to Bebe."

"Jesus, Sally—"

Benno saw Bell was giving him a face. "No good?"

"Where did they get that kind of cash?"

"These guys? They can find a couple hundred Gs in the sofa cushions."

An Oldsmobile blew by, sending a wave of murky water over the curb. Benno skipped to avoid it.

"Sal, this is no joke. They aren't doing you any favors."

Benno knew Bell had done some kind of arithmetic that let him see the next steps. Bell was good like that.

"Tell me," Benno said. "Make it plain."

"No more suitcases, Sal."

CHAPTER THIRTY-THREE

Eleanor Ree was with Marsala at the Wilshire Towers when Louella Parsons arrived, Christmas decorations still on the mantle and walls, the tinseled tree in the corner. The Negro cook Enna hired whipped up a simple luncheon of roast chicken with potatoes and parsnips. The scent welcoming her, the columnist asked Ree if she made the meal. In a simple pale-green one-piece, flats on for the moment, the actress joked they were all lucky she hadn't set foot in the kitchen.

"I thought we'd have Italian food, Bill," Parsons said as Ree served the meal.

Marsala took it as a dig but let it pass. "Linguine with garlic and oil is the best I can offer. My mother's gravy was always 'a little of this, a pinch of that.' For me, it never comes out right."

"Are you living here, Eleanor?"

She said she was still at her home in Bel Air.

"So Bill will move there?"

"We haven't discussed that yet," she answered, hitting her lines right. "It's possible, but of course not until the divorce is finalized."

Parsons took notes. "Bill, how is it coming along? Are you and Rosa on speaking terms?"

"Sure. We had a fine Christmas. You know, Louella, I grew up with Rosa. We were kids when we started together. She'll always be dear to me, and of course there's Bill Jr." He reached and clasped Ree's hand. "But with Eleanor, it's true love."

"And you feel the same?"

Ree said, "I do." She was jittery inside; the breakfast gin hadn't quieted her nerves. She was sure Parsons knew about *Mikindani Bay*, and Ree still hadn't told Marsala about the film.

"Louella, I'd like to explain what happened in Chicago. I made a boneheaded play, a real dumb remark, and it blew up in my face."

After he told her the story, he said, "If Phil had been there...I can't tell you how much I miss him. I was so angry when he died. Mad at him for leaving me like that—crazy, I know—and mad at myself for flying off the handle. I guess sometimes you don't know how special someone is until they're gone. His grandchildren will never go without, believe me. They'll know how much this town adored him."

Parsons looked up from her notes. "But you fired Phil Klein."

"Ten times and ten times I begged him to come back. No, nine times. I didn't get the chance to..." Feigning a tear, Marsala excused himself, returning to the table after hiding with the cook in the kitchen.

Chocolate mousse for dessert. Parsons asked, "Eleanor, what's your next project?"

"I'm sure you've heard rumors," Ree began, "but I haven't committed to anything. I need to discuss things with Bill. Now that his career is about to take off, I want to offer all the support I can give him."

"You sound like a new bride."

"You know me, Louella. I'm just a tobacco farmer's daughter from South Carolina. I want a family and a nice place for my husband to come home to. I love the pictures and my fans, but I've always known what's most important."

Marsala sipped his coffee, nodding his agreement.

"Will you travel with him?"

"When I can, but I think I'd better let him concentrate on his music," Ree replied. "Bill Marsala's still the champ, you know. It's so exciting."

Fortune read Parsons's column. Ree is the brains of the outfit, he thought. "Get him back on the radio now," he told Enna. "Don't wait for the Sandpiper."

"On record or a show?"

"Both."

The Palm Tree gigs in Miami went off without a hitch. Three nights, three home runs. Cy Geller and his wife led the applause, the old man sitting stork-like tall, cold judgment on his tanned face. The hated ballad from 1940 went over big, so did the jazz numbers: The local trumpeter, a Cuban, figured out that playing Sweets was the way to go. Ree flew in for the Saturday show and called in a big favor. America woke up on Monday to find a photo of Ree and Marsala with Ernest Hemingway between them, Papa saggy-eyed from drink and still weak from a flu he'd caught in Havana. "Heard they harassed you in my old hometown," Hemingway said of Chicago, within earshot of a reporter from *Life* magazine as the famous trio shared stone crabs. "They can be bastards, can't they?" The Miami papers tried to play the engagement cool—the fickle reporters didn't know which way to jump—but they admitted Bill Marsala knew how to please an audience.

The following week, Fortune flew with Marsala and Enna to the three-night engagement in Houston. Fortune came and went, camping out at another hotel, but he caught two shows. Another success, the locals friendly, and up in New York, Winchell wrote, "Oil Town gave Marsala's oh-so-lovely performance applause by the geyserful. Narrows Gate's favorite son will be lighting up Hollywood for 10 days before he returns to the main stem for two weeks at the Caribbean. Dollars to doughnuts sez it'll be New York's hottest ducat since he first conquered the Paramount."

"Who sucked his dick?" Fortune asked.

"We owe," Enna conceded.

Fortune, Marsala and Enna went on to Vegas.

Construction was back on schedule, Saul Geller told them. The first week of March was guaranteed. Enna promised his agency would turn out all its clients for the opening. "By the way," Fortune said to Marsala, "your name is off the lounge."

Marsala didn't respond. His throat was acting up, raw as a skinned knee. He feared the clits' return.

"I like you quiet," Fortune said as they returned to the trailer, an oven in the Nevada sun.

Marsala had two weeks until the engagement at the nightclub on Sunset Strip owned by Saul Geller's new partner, Harry Milton.

The weekly radio show was back on, Chesterfield as sponsor.

Ree's ex, Guy Simon, dropped by Marsala's apartment, bearing ideas for arrangements he'd sketched to turn the old hits new. The "Cugat without the congas" approach was too heavy-handed for the studio, he said, leather patches on his elbows, pipe in his fist. Referring to the charts he proposed, he said, "Bill, they'll hardly realize you're serving jazz. In the studio, you go whichever way you choose."

"Give it a shot," Marsala told him.

The singer wore a cashmere sweater over a turtleneck. Concerned about his pipes festering, he had Canter's send over chicken soup, which he sipped piping hot. Three days in a night-club with four days off was one thing. But he was facing 10 nights in a club, recording sessions and the radio show, which meant appearances on his guests' programs in return.

"I'll need funding, Bill," Simon said.

"Get in touch with Enna."

The next day, Enna called to say Simon's charts were brilliant. "Let him arrange the new sessions," he suggested.

Eleanor Ree was naked on his disheveled bed. "It's incest," Marsala replied.

She made a circle with her index finger near the side of her head.

Marsala laughed. "Sure," he said to Enna. "Hire him. What the fuck."

"You're nuts, too," Ree told him when he returned to bed.

"For you, baby."

The following morning, Marsala was up before noon. Showered, shaved, a little coffee and a soft-boiled egg he'd made while he called Ree just to hear her voice. Then he told the valet to bring around his car. He was off to visit Rosa and Bill Jr. He felt bright today. He was certain he could pull it off.

Nino Terrasini opened the door. He had Bill Jr. on his hip.

"Glug," said the boy, his chin glistening with spittle.

"Where's Rosa?" Marsala asked. He hadn't expected this.

"Out."

"And you're in, I suppose. Or are you just the babysitter?"

"Sitter. Still." He lifted Bill Jr. and passed him to his father.

The kid wailed and reached for Terrasini, who patted his cheek, kissed his forehead and walked into the sun, giving father and child a chance to settle down. When Terrasini returned, he found Marsala on the floor, stacking blocks for the boy to topple. Bill Jr. seemed content. Yesterday, Rosa had to use tweezers to get out an olive pit he'd jammed up his nose. "He's curious," she said.

"He sure is," Terrasini replied.

"You living here?" Marsala walked to the liquor cabinet, a hitch in his step.

Terrasini told him West Hollywood.

"I'm trying to figure out why you split," Marsala said, an inch or so of scotch in a tumbler.

"I didn't. You left."

"I left Rosa."

"And Phil."

Marsala said, "It would've blown over."

"Save it, Bebe. I know you and I knew Hennie. What else do I have to say?"

"You think what you want," he said. He swirled the glass, spinning the liquor and then polished off the drink. "I'm here to talk to Rosa."

"She's not here."

"Or she's hiding."

"You're kidding, right?"

"You tell her to hide from me?" Marsala said as he walked to the staircase. Terrasini heard him enter the master bedroom, the guest room and second guest room. Bathroom doors opened and closed. Coming back down the stairs, Marsala slid the empty glass on the bar and went into his office. He found it packed, the boxes stacked, the walls bare.

When he returned to the living room, Rosa stood at the front door holding a bag of groceries high against her beige coat.

Marsala said, "Hi Rose."

Terrasini retrieved the grocery bag.

Marsala went in to peck her cheek, but she turned and took off her coat, revealing a brown one-piece and alligator belt that matched her shoes. "What are you doing here?"

"I came to say hello," he replied. "To see how Bill Jr.'s doing. He looks terrific. You, too."

Rosa shut the closet door and walked past him to lift their son. The boy's expression didn't change, but he dropped his head on his mother's shoulder, looping his chubby arms around her neck.

She rocked back and forth as she spoke. "Please call before you come."

Terrasini watched from the kitchen doorway.

"Fair enough," Marsala replied.

"You can see Bill Jr. when you like, but just call. And don't bring her."

"Rosa—"

"If you don't mind, I've got things to do."

"Jesus, Rosa, we can't talk a little?"

She stared at him. "'We were only kids when we started dating,'" she said evenly, quoting Parsons's column. "Is that right, Bill?"

"Well, we were—"

"Now you've found true love."

"Rosa. I'm all jammed up," he said, palms open at his sides. "I didn't mean to say it wasn't swell, the times we—"

"Swell?" She nodded derisively. "Thanks. Now I know. Swell."

"I'm sorry," he said, stepping toward her. "Look, this is coming out all wrong. I wanted to say I'm sorry. I blew it, I know."

She ran her hand across the top of the baby's downy hair. "Is that it? Is that what you came to say?"

"I want you to come to the Strip, Rosa," Marsala said. "To see the show. Let bygones be bygones."

She looked at him, her expression blank with disbelief.

"You'll see some of the old crew. Frankie Fortune—"

"But not my uncle."

Marsala sighed. "No, not Mimmo."

She turned slightly, allowing her son to see his father's face. "Say good-bye to Daddy," she said.

"Rosa, come on now. I'm trying to do right here."

She didn't reply.

Resigned, Marsala said, "All right. Fine."

When he leaned in to kiss Bill Jr., he put his hand on Rosa's arm but withdrew it quickly when she stiffened.

"I'll walk you out," Terrasini said as Rosa passed him on her way to the kitchen.

When they reached Marsala's car, the singer said, "She'd kill me if she could."

"What's the point?" Terrasini said. "To her, you're already dead."

"I'm still the boy's father," Marsala replied, opening the door. "I've got rights."

"He's a good kid, Bebe. Don't make him a tennis ball."

"I came here—"

"For once in your life, do the decent thing. The thing that helps somebody besides you."

Marsala got behind the wheel and pulled the door shut. He stared as Terrasini went back inside. Ten minutes passed before he turned over the engine and drove off.

At work in his cabana office, Cy Geller summoned an armed guard and asked him to bring a phone. He called New York City. Though he doubted Corini, he respected protocol; he explained the situation and proposed a temporary solution, adding "with your approval, Anthony." Fifteen minutes later, Geller had Fortune on the line from Los Angeles.

Geller said, "Leave town. Anthony agrees."

"Leave town," Fortune repeated. "All right."

"Canada, perhaps."

Fortune didn't know a soul in the entire country.

Geller explained, and Frankie Fortune now considered Sen. Alvin Dunney and the crime commission a threat, though he knew that Corini, in his thuggish arrogance, viewed Dunney as a disposable clown.

"You'll be subpoenaed if he finds you," Geller said. "It's federal, so leave until the Los Angeles hearings are over."

"What about Bebe?"

"Anthony says you have a backup plan."

"I do," Fortune said. "But make the order come from Anthony."

Geller hesitated. Earlier in the week, he'd had a disquieting conversation with Bruno Gigenti, who he called at Don Carlo's request. He expected a tally of complaints about how he'd been treated in Havana and maybe a display of temper. Instead, Gigenti said he had proof he'd been set up.

Geller already knew this was true. Corini spoke of a note on a dead man's body that the police hadn't found. It was either delivered and retrieved or it never arrived. In either case, only the men who composed it could be certain it existed. For a moment, he thought of testing Fortune to see if he was an accomplice to the betrayal.

"Watch your back," Geller said instead.

"Yeah," Fortune replied, thinking the old Jew was still talking about Dunney.

This morning, as they sat together over coffee and crullers at the kitchen table, the radio told the Bells and the rest of the region that Sen. Alvin Dunney had formed a commission to investigate organized crime. He intended to hold public hearings in Los Angeles, Chicago, Miami and New York. The Bells stared at each other, simultaneously left their seats and padded to the hallway.

With his father at his side, Bell dialed Charlie Tyler at his hotel in Washington.

Drowsy, Tyler confirmed the report. The Dunney Commission would have subpoena power, he added. He refused to tell Bell whether he had been assigned to the investigation.

"Tyler's working for Dunney," Bell told his father when he put down the phone.

"Sal," Mr. Bell said.

Soon, Leo Bell turned up at Benno's, which wasn't yet open for customers.

"Leo!" Gemma cheered. She was spooning cured olives into a honey jar but stopped and waddled over to give Bell his kiss. Meanwhile, Benno's uncle, who was rinsing bay leaves one at a time, nodded and smiled.

"You see this?" Bell asked Benno, holding up the Friday morning newspaper.

Benno, who was trimming the escarole he'd picked up at the market, said, "Why do I got to read the *New York* fuckin' *Times* when I live in New Jersey?"

Bell pointed to the headline.

Benno scanned. "Yeah, so?"

"Some senator is investigating your pals."

"Good luck. Like he ain't already in our pocket."

"This guy's from South Carolina."

Benno looked at him, his expression saying if South Carolina is on Earth, Farcolini and Corini own its senator.

"Sal, I'm not fucking around. If this guy's got any juice, it's trouble. If you've got a record, Sal, or you ignore a subpoena or you lie under oath, you're fucked. They'll probably call Corini, Gigenti, Frankie Fortune, Mimmo—"

"Zamarella," Benno added, remembering Pellizzari's brains on his face.

"They can call anybody they want, Sally. They can call you."

"Me? What do they want me for?"

"They don't want you," Bell said, "but they want you to give up what you know."

Benno thought about it. Then he gestured for Bell to follow him into the back of the store. He tossed off his apron. "What do I know?" he said.

Bell stayed in the doorway. "You know what you know, Sal. Cut the shit."

"I'm saying who knows what I know? Corini, Frankie, Mimmo…"

"Dunney squeezes you to get to them, not vice versa," Bell said. "But then the papers say you're a mobster."

"For what? I brought food. The suitcase I gave to Bebe—"

Benno stopped. Looking over Bell's shoulder, he saw Mimmo weaving through the store.

Mimmo took the newspaper out of Bell's hand and tossed it on the table. It unfurled as he nudged past Bell to sit. As befuddled as he was angry, he said, "Ding, what's it mean?"

"You need a lawyer, Mimmo."

"A showboat from nowhere, this Dunney," he said.

"A showboat with subpoena power," Bell replied.

"Nobody's worried."

Good, Bell thought. Let the arrogant pricks all walk into the trap. Hoover allowed them to roam free. Dunney does this right and they'll die by their own hand.

Benno noted that Mimmo had put on about 20 pounds since he was ousted from Havana. He no longer patrolled the neighborhood and whatever good his evening strolls used to do for his constitution had been reversed. He was lumpy and gray with rings around his tired eyes that you could even see behind his sunglasses.

"You heard from Frankie?" Benno asked.

Mimmo said, "As a matter of fact, yes. Come with me."

Bell grabbed his hat from the table.

"Not you, Ding," Mimmo said.

"No, I'm coming." Bell followed them through the store and out onto Polk Street.

Boo Chiasso and Fat Tutti waited in the dull February sun and stared down Bell with his raincoat, tweed blazer, button-down shirt, baggy slacks, loafers, this guy thinking who he is.

"Fuck it," Mimmo said. "He wants to come, let him come."

The little caravan took off behind Mimmo—Benno and Bell, Chiasso and Fat Tutti. They went through the candy store, past the fountain, over dirty leftover snow. Benno and Bell went into Mimmo's house. Chiasso and Fat Tutti stayed outside, Chiasso snatching the newspaper full of Dunney and the commission out of Bell's hand like it was a weapon.

Mimmo stopped a few steps into the narrow kitchen, leaving Benno and Bell between the refrigerator and the back door.

"They told me to tell you you're going to Los Angeles," Mimmo said to Benno.

"Me?" Benno laughed. "When?"

"Now."

"Now now?"

Mimmo reached into a drawer, rooted around and pulled out a roll of cash. He peeled off $1,000 in fifties. "You'll need a car but we'll take care of that."

"What am I doing there?"

"You sit Bebe," Mimmo replied, as he pushed the cash into Benno's hand. "Frankie's got some other business."

"For how long?" Bell asked.

"We'll see."

Benno held up the money. "This ain't going to do it then. Give me the roll and I'll bring back change."

Mimmo hesitated. Then he peeled off a couple of bills for himself and passed the rest to Benno. "There's five Gs there."

"Mimmo..." Benno said. It was three at most.

Mimmo grabbed a pad and pencil off the counter and scribbled a phone number. "Call this when you get there."

"You're serious, huh? Go now?"

"Sally..."

When they crossed the backyard, Benno said, "You coming?"

Bell drew up. "To Hollywood?"

Benno tapped the fat roll in his pocket.

Bell used a pay phone in the lobby of the Avalon Theater to call Washington.

"Charlie, I'm going to Los Angeles."

Tyler hesitated. "Why?"

Bell explained.

"Why, that's fine," Tyler said. "The commission—"

"—is holding a hearing in Los Angeles," Bell interrupted. "Are you admitting you're working for Dunney?"

"All right, Leo. I am."

"You've told the commission what I told you?"

"Of course."

Bell calculated.

"Leo?"

"You want me to do legwork in LA?"

"That would be very helpful."

"Promise you won't subpoena Benno."

"Leo, I'm not in a position to do something like that."

Bell wondered who was in Tyler's office. "Benno doesn't know anything you don't already know."

"Leo, let's continue the discussion when you arrive in LA," Tyler said as he cut the connection. In his office, the towering Washington Monument in view, he looked at his visitor and said, "Our man on the inside. He'll be in Los Angeles."

"That's fine, indeed," said Alvin Dunney with an easy drawl. The senator was in his early 50s. He had a long face and the top of his head shone. The hair above his ears was cut short and graying.

"It's a sign," Tyler said, smiling. "Luck is mounting on our side."

"Which we'll need."

"Ironic," Tyler mused. "Our man is helping with Marsala."

Dunney nodded. On his thigh sat a fat file of information collected through interviews and wiretaps, as well as Tyler's study on organized crime he'd based on Landis's analysis of Hitler to support a conclusion he'd held before the process of gathering facts had finished.

"Do you plan on calling Marsala?" Tyler asked.

"Oh, not yet, I don't think," Dunney replied.

CHAPTER THIRTY-FOUR

They were walking through the busy terminal at Los Angeles Airport when Benno pointed. "I know that guy."

"That's not him," Bell said.

"It's him. The guy, he comes in, says 'half pound of prosciutto sliced thin.' Like who the fuck gets prosciutto thick?"

"He's a porter. I doubt the guy travels three-thousand miles for ham."

Benno stared across the terminal at the broom and barrel.

"Plus, I'm sure they got prosciutto in LA," Bell added.

They had sat apart for most of the flight because they both wanted windows to see the snow-covered checkerboard farms below, the winding rivers, mountains purple and majestic surrounding the vast desert where the newspapers said somebody was dumping guys who had fucked over the late Ziggy Baum. Benno wondered whether he'd spot a herd of wild horses trailed by some cowboys or a chuck wagon. Across the aisle, Bell was thinking the same thing. It was his first time on a plane, despite the Army. He'd never been west of Newark.

Veering toward a bank of phone booths, Benno dug out the phone number Mimmo gave him. He held the door so the light went on but Bell could listen in. The nickel dropped.

The stolen DeSoto was in the parking lot just like the voice said, key sitting on top of a tire. At the newsstand, Bell bought a map and, after he loaded the trunk, gave it to Benno. "Earning my keep," he said when he nestled behind the wheel.

Soon they got off Route 66, Benno craning and peering, his hat bobbing on the back of his head. They arrived at the Beverly Hills Hotel.

"Holy shit," Benno said.

"Ditto." Bell saw a paradise, palm trees spread against the sky and grass like they cut it with tiny scissors.

The guy behind the desk was waiting for them.

"Yes, sir, Mr. Benno. Mr. Spaletti informed us that you'd be arriving this evening," he said, using Fortune's real name. A Negro took their bags and they were escorted through a flowery garden to a bungalow painted pink on the outside. A sofa for Bell in the living room and Benno scoped out the bedroom.

The Negro hung around until Bell caught on and gave him a quarter. "Thank you, sir," the guy said without enthusiasm, like a quarter didn't mean shit.

"I'm calling Bebe," Benno said. He was stretched across the king-size bed, arms and legs spread like he was making a snow angel.

"Where?"

"At—" Benno sat up. "Shit. Fuckin' Mimmo. He didn't say." He reached for the phone.

"It's late back home," Bell said.

"Fuck him. He wakes up."

"No. I got an idea."

"How? You know the same nothing as me."

Bell returned with a map of the stars' homes. Marsala lived at the Wilshire Towers, which was pretty close by.

"How'd you get that?" Benno was halfway changed into blue sharkskin.

"The bellhop. Cost me another quarter."

"Let's go," Benno said.

"Could I say something?"

At the mirror, Benno was making his tie. "Say it going."

"We don't know he's there. If he's not, then it looks like you're not sitting on him right already if the guy at the desk tells him, 'Some guy was here…'"

"We check the restaurants."

"But we don't know which. Let's find out where he goes, who he sees, what's what."

Benno watched Bell through the mirror. "And?"

"I'm hungry and I need a bath."

Running his hand along his chin, Benno said, "Yeah, I could use another shave."

They were interrupted by a knock on the door. There in the hall was a dumpy guy in a floppy brown suit, matching hat and shoes beat to shit.

"Fortunato Spaletti?" he said.

"With one eye, I'm Spaletti?" Benno asked.

The guy reached into his breast pocket, pulled out some kind of paper and thrust it at Bell. "You're served," he said.

Benno watched him waddle away. "You're served what?"

"A subpoena." Bell scanned the document. "To appear before the Dunney Commission next week."

"You?"

"Not me," Bell replied. "Frankie."

Bell slid the subpoena onto an end table and then he went to the closet. A couple of suits were still there next to empty hangers and no luggage on the top shelf. Across the room, the drawers held a few shirts folded neat and some socks but were mostly empty. On top of the chest, a lone tie bar was in an ashtray.

"He took off," Bell said. "Now we know why."

"Unbelievable," Benno replied.

"Why? He's a stand-up guy? He can explain himself under oath?"

"No, I'm saying it's unbelievable they think you're Frankie Fortune. No offense, Leo. You ain't no mutt, but Jesus…"

In the morning, the *Los Angeles Times* told them Bebe was playing 10 nights at a club on the Sunset Strip beginning Friday and that he had a radio program this evening, *Chesterfield Presents Bill Marsala,* the cigarette getting top billing. Then Benno saw a copy of *Life* magazine with a photo of Marsala and Eleanor Ree. He chatted with the newsy. "She live around here?"

"I wouldn't know," the guy replied.

Benno bought *Life*, a box of Chiclets and said keep the change. "Bel Air," the guy replied, noting that Ree had lunch in the Polo Lounge now and then. Benno threw him a five-spot like Bebe would've.

They hurried breakfast, Benno insisting they get to work before sightseeing. Impressed with his friend's diligence, Bell drove along Sunset to Bellagio Road.

Benno opened the magazine, tore out a photo and held it by the windshield. "Start looking," he said.

Bell glanced at the picture. There was Ree, her arm around Bebe's waist, the guy beaming and her bare feet in the grass. The house stood behind them. Up this street, down that one, Benno looking left with his good eye, Bell looking right. "You notice something, Sal?"

"If you like perfect, this is the place."

"The street names," Bell said. "Perugia, Stradella, Cecina, Siena…"

Benno turned. "I would've thought the opposite."

Bell didn't tell him he saw Maureen O'Hara crossing a lawn. No sense him bringing up the Irish.

"Brake," Benno said suddenly.

And there it was: Eleanor Ree's.

Two cars were parked in the shade at the side of house. "We wait," Benno said.

"Where?" The streets were empty, not even a gum wrapper or bottle cap, never mind a car sitting at the curb.

Benno looked around for cover. Then he said, "Ah, fuck it." He stepped out and walked up the path to Ree's front door. Halfway, he turned and flicked his fingers, saying, "Come on, Leo."

Marsala kneeled on the sofa to look through the curtains. Coming up the path was a serious guy, tall with a dimpled chin and wire glasses and New Jersey written all over him. Somebody else was pounding the knocker.

Enna had already called to warn him. "There's a chance you could be compelled to appear."

But they wouldn't ship a process server across the country.

Maybe the guy is from Corini and Fortune, Don Carlo approving a hit after Chicago. Oh, Jesus. Would he do that now that I've made good with Klein's family, sweet-talked Parsons and *Life*? I tried to talk to Rosa and now I'm working my ass off earning. Jesus Christ.

Fearing the pounding would wake Miss Ree, the houseboy opened the door.

Panicking, Marsala heard the visitor ask for him by name.

"Who shall I say—sir—"

Marsala froze.

Benno turned into the living room. "Bebe!" he said, smiling, his arms flung wide.

The one-eyed kid from Narrows Gate. Marsala sagged in relief.

"Whoa. Look at you," Benno said.

Marsala wore a paisley silk robe that hung open to show his bony frame and fresh boxers. Black socks.

"Sal," he managed, his throat dry and aching. "What the hell are you doing here?"

"I'm in for Frankie, which should make you happy. He's dodging Dummy and the commission."

Bell appeared at the door.

"That's Leo from Polk Street, too," Benno said. "He's the driver. So, yeah, I'm promoted." He pointed at the singer, then at himself, back and forth. "Which means we don't fuck up. Am I right, Bebe?" Then Benno said Marsala owed him another suit. "You don't want some bum at your back."

Marsala laughed. "Sure, kid. A new suit. Why the hell not?"

Benno bought Bell a tie, saying, "Here you go, Sluggo" and Marsala laughed again, glad it wasn't Fortune holding the leash. At the Formosa Café, Benno ate inside while Bell headed off in search of a sausage-and-pepper sandwich. At the rehearsal hall, Benno went in but came out about 10 minutes later, saying, "You won't believe this but Eleanor Ree's husband, that bandleader Guy Simon, he's in there, and him and Bebe talk like it's nothing."

"Enjoy your lunch?" Bell asked, the sun bearing down on Santa Monica Boulevard.

"Yeah, it was swell. All the stars eat there. It's like the Warner Brothers cafeteria."

"You seen Porky Pig?"

"Porky—Wait. You ain't pissed off, are you?"

Bell stared down at his friend. "Nah," he said finally. "You're doing good. You're sitting on him right."

"Bebe's rehearsing with the band so now we got the afternoon off." He clapped Bell's arm. "What do you say we hit the pool?"

A long way from diving off the piers into the Hudson. At the Beverly Hills Hotel they bring you drinks; all Benno had to do was sign his name. "To the good life," he toasted.

At five o'clock, Bell chauffeured him to Bel Air to retrieve Eleanor Ree. He departed as Bell walked the path toward the house.

"Salvatore Benno," she said as she swept into her vestibule. Maybe she was only going to be on radio, but she was dressed to be seen. Shimmering hair, an emerald-green gown and shawl, heels that made her legs a miracle and glittering gold jewelry. The way she walked said, "I'm me, who the fuck are you?"

"Eleanor Ree. You know, you're kind of cute."

"Thank you, Mr. Benno."

He held out his arm and as the houseboy opened the door, she took it. Together, they stepped into the warm November twilight. Too bad Bell was already gone. What he could've told them on Polk Street!

He put her in Bebe's car. By the time he reached the driver's seat, she had a little silver flask in her hand.

"Do you enjoy a drink, Sal?" she asked.

The way she said it, Benno would've swilled iodine to please her. "I like a cold beer when it's hot," he replied, backing the car out.

"Sorry. No beer in here." She took a long swig.

"Gin," Benno said. "You ride the express, huh?"

"It does give the world a certain glow."

Benno had to get them onto Sunset Boulevard, then look for something called La Cienega. "You know your lines, Eleanor?"

"I most certainly do."

Bebe said the guest star was some comedian, but Ree was going to make a surprise appearance. Over lunch at Warners, Benno thought of asking him how come he never put Rosa on one of his programs, but he was having too much fun to throw Bebe into a mood.

"I'm thinking maybe America wants you tiptop."

Ree looked at him, his arm hanging out the window, flickering neon reflected on his glasses, wearing a grin she didn't think he could lose. I used to be that happy, she thought, that innocent. No, I wasn't. Not ever. She gave Benno the flask. "Save it for later."

"You bet," Benno said.

A messenger delivered a list of names from Tyler and Bell didn't recognize any of them, save Sigmund Baumstein, who was already dead, and Eugenio Zamarella, who probably made him so. From the phone booth off the hotel's Crystal Ballroom, active now with some sort of black-tie civic affair, Bell reported his ignorance of the West Coast mob.

Tyler replied, "With these men, you've got drug dealing and you've got the racing wire."

"I got nothing," Bell replied, "and if Fortune knew you were going to serve him, you've got a snitch."

Tyler admitted LA was empty of top crooks, who were now scattered across the country and beyond. They had three mugs who would testify in public, strictly low-level slime who were bartering to reduce their sentences. The commission was losing its momentum. Radio had intended to broadcast, but they withdrew. Even Hearst's papers, having demanded a national investigation, now mocked the commission's show in LA. "Second-rate doesn't play well here, Senator Dunney," some editor wrote. "We're a long way from South Carolina."

"Quit while you're behind and go where you can do some good," Bell said. "I mean, why cut the tail when you know where the head is?"

"We've got no jurisdiction in Cuba, Leo."

"Oh, really?" Bell replied. The papers said the Department of Justice told the U.S. drug companies to stop shipping product to the island until the Cuban government beefed up its activities against illegal narcotics, meaning Farcolini's operation. So far, the Cubans, with Senator Balboa as their spokesman, declared the embargo "an act of imperial aggression."

Bell added, "And I hope you've got better boys in Miami than the numb nuts you got out here."

"Go to the hearings," Tyler said. "See if you recognize anyone."

"No soap," he told him. "They spot me and I'm there for you or I'm there for Corini. Either way, I lose."

A big cheer rose from the crowd in the ballroom and flashbulbs popped as the guest of honor was handed his award. Bell saw the commotion as a sign he should leave. "Best I can do is read the papers," he said quickly.

"Leo, wait," Tyler said. "What would you suggest?"

Bell was standing in the booth, hunched below the overhead lamp. He leaned into the mouthpiece on the box. "Arrest Cy Geller. Take his passport. Make him testify in public."

"Is that—"

"And put a few fuckin' boats between Havana and Biscayne Bay."

"Pretty funny, Bebe," Benno said when Marsala, Ree and Rico Enna came down the corridor toward the parking lot. He'd watched the show from the back of the house, closing his eye when the distracting sights ruined his idea of a good radio program.

"That's praise enough for me, kid," Marsala replied. He had color in his cheeks and a bounce in his step. That fuckin' ascot again, though.

"And you should do comedy, Eleanor. I'm telling you—you're a riot."

For that, Sal Benno got a kiss on the cheek from Hollywood's hottest broad. *Madonna mio*, he'd be lying if he didn't admit little Sally wiggled down there.

In the skit, Bebe was in a restaurant with that jolly comedian—of course they were just standing at a couple of music stands reading their lines—and the waitress comes in. It's Ree, and to get a rise out of the crowd, they had her walk onstage to some guy making sounds like a horse clopping. She started to giggle two seconds into it, but she had the crowd in the palm of her hand with those eyes and that smile, mugging it when they made it like she spilled hot soup on Bebe.

When it ended and the applause wouldn't quit, Bebe said, "Eleanor Ree, ladies and gentlemen." Then he added, "I love you, baby." After Bebe sang that song with the pale moon that don't excite him, he said, "Bedtime, Bill Jr. Give Mommy a big kiss good night," and the crowd liked that fine.

Now he said, "Sal, no offense but we eat alone. Rico, buy the kid dinner. He's all right."

They stepped into the parking lot and a bunch of people, not just kids, rushed in for autographs.

Benno said to Enna, "I'm supposed to stick with him."

"*È bene*," Enna replied. "We know where he'll be."

"OK," Benno said, not exactly suspicious, but if this Enna was so good, they don't need me out there.

"Sal," Marsala said. "Come get me at one o'clock. Tomorrow."

For dinner, Enna chose the Polo Lounge at the Beverly Hills Hotel. Enna knew everybody in the joint and at his request, they seated them behind this thick, twisting tree. Bell thought the big gun from the talent agency didn't want to be seen with two guys from Narrows Gate, but he reconsidered when he realized that Enna was a street guy who had sanded the edges and learned legalese.

"You have to understand something," Enna said. "This is make or break for Bill Marsala."

Benno was working on a pretty decent–sized steak. "You mean with Corini and Farcolini," he said, his mouth full.

"His career. He blows it here and he loses Vegas. It's all over but the shouting."

"I don't get you. He's Bill Marsala, right?"

"Not for long if he doesn't pull this off. He's back doing cock-tail lounges along the Palisades. Kid, out here, if you're not com-ing, you're going."

Bell watched as Benno ran it through his head. He knew he was thinking, Wait. I saw Bebe at rehearsal with all those musi-cians ready to serve him and then Eleanor Ree dolled up and the people cheering on the radio...

Enna leaned in, the candlelight dancing under his chin. "Bill hasn't had a solid hit in years. The music in the can, people won't go for. His pictures bleed—to tell you the truth, Sal, I don't see he has a career in pictures. You heard 200 people showed up to see him in Chicago—in a room holds five times that many?" Enna shook his head. "It's not good."

"So," Benno said, "how do we help him?"

"Get him where he needs to go and tell him he's swell. Any bad news comes along, you intercept it. Make sure he rests. It's too bad he cleaned out Terrasini's room. You could've moved in."

Bell had a question for Enna. "Can I ask something?"

"Sure. Go right ahead."

"Can he do it?"

"Look, Bill Marsala has a million-dollar voice and a two-cent head," Enna replied. "Growing up in Narrows Gate, you guys know that. When he's singing and the crowd's cheering, the world's his oyster and he puts his crazy impulses aside. So, yeah, he can do it. Eleanor is a big plus. She's as nuts as him, but she stands up."

Benno still had Ree's flask in his pocket.

"The thing is to finish the record, knock 'em dead on the Strip, do the same in New York and open like gangbusters at the Sandpiper.

"So to answer your question, he keeps singing and everything's all right. He don't and we're all fucked."

"Not me," Benno said. "Not Leo."

"This thing blows and nobody's walking away, Sal. I know Anthony Corini since I was a kid. And I don't have to tell you about Bruno Gigenti and what he thinks. They don't lay out this much jingle and say, 'Fuck it. We gave it a shot.' Am I right?"

Benno shrugged, but he had to agree.

CHAPTER THIRTY-FIVE

Being that it was Friday, Mimmo went out looking for fish for lunch, maybe some nice *sarde a beccafico* or a thick piece of *tonno a la Siracusana*. But the motherless bastards in the old familiar restaurants in Narrows Gate looked at him like he stunk or with pity, maybe he was ready to be burnt up with the rags. Hungry, he started to wander, his mind out of focus with greater frequency now and he wound up on the tubes again, a crinkled old man sitting there bundled up in a topcoat, hat, scarf and sunglasses. This time he got off at Christopher Street and wound up on Mulberry, his nose leading him toward a first-class Sicilian meal.

And who should he see but Bruno Gigenti. The underboss limped, but with two young iron slabs on either side, he presented his power. The people out in the cold sun nodded at him, a few men raising a chilly finger to tap the brim of their caps. Scowling, Gigenti ignored them.

"Bruno," Mimmo said.

The young guys turned together to shield Gigenti's back.

"Bruno, *come va*?" he shouted, his hand in the air. "*Mangiamo il pranzo*, eh?"

Gigenti turned and elbowed between the two giants. "I told you I got nothing for you," he said in Sicilian.

"I'm saying let's eat lunch."

"With you? No."

The grin fell off Mimmo's face. "Why not me?"

430

Gigenti shot him a look long from his shoes to his hat that told him he was a sorry old nobody on Mulberry Street, too.

He wanted to reply sharp and hard, reminding Gigenti he owed him for word of Fortune's plan to embarrass him. But he couldn't summon an argument, couldn't operate his brain right, facts lost in a mist. Instead, he saw a *paesano* of maybe 20 years turning his back. "What did I do?" he asked.

The two young guys looked at each other, wry smiles on their lips.

"Go away, Mimmo," Gigenti said. "Do yourself a favor and go away."

They left him standing there, dumbstruck. He couldn't recall where he was or where he was supposed to go.

A big day, but you couldn't tell by Bebe. The same routine, except he spent last night at the Wilshire Towers, though first he had steaks on the grill at Ree's, button mushrooms in butter, a little vino and a couple of nightcaps. Bebe slept until noon, then he told Benno to have lunch sent over, so they ate, if you call chicken soup eating. Then Ree's ex, Guy Simon, came in, that pipe-sucking snob, and he showed Bebe some dots on lines, and he said, "It's golden, Bill."

"Wasn't golden at rehearsal."

"Entirely my fault," Simon said. "I've elongated the reeds."

Next came Bebe's rubdown, this big Russian broad or Hungary, and she beat the living shit out of him. Benno sat there on the sofa, wondering if he should go in the bedroom and wrestle her off him, but he came out oiled, pink as a baby, a towel around his waist. "Kid, you haven't lived," he said. "You want a go?"

"Fuck no," Benno told him. "I thought she was murdering you in there."

Out she came, her table tucked under her hammy arm. He said, "See you next week, Cuddles," reaching like he's ready to pinch her ass. She giggled.

And they drove over to the club, the mooks were sweeping, cocktail waitresses dragging as they put matchbooks in the ashtrays, the bar was getting stocked, and Bebe's piano player was making the band play this number and there's Ree's ex again, ol' King Shit. "You want to run it down, Bill?" Simon asked.

Bebe waved him off as he went to find his dressing room. "Sal, see if they can bring me some hot tea."

He put horseradish in it.

"Wake me up a half hour before the show," he said as he wrapped a towel around his neck. Pants off, he pulled over a chair, put his feet up, wriggled until he was comfortable. His hands on his chest, he was out, boom, snoozing in seconds.

Benno was thinking, This guy Enna, he don't know shit. He's got him on death row and meanwhile Bebe's like he's on a cruise ship, not a worry in the world.

He went outside to meet Bell.

"Been busy?" Benno asked.

"Homework." They were on Sunset, not too far from the nightclub, cars rolling by, and the moon low on the other end of the boulevard.

"Since last night?"

Bell said he drove over to see footprints in the sidewalk.

The morgue at the *Los Angeles Times* gave him information to wire back to Tyler in New York, but it wasn't more than any secretary could've located. The guys on his list were career criminals. They had records before their balls dropped. If the FBI didn't know them, Bell concluded, we're all in trouble. And the *Times* and the *Examiner* treated Dunney's hearing like something between a nuisance and a joke. Two days of bullshit, and the senator and his troupe packed up and were off to Chicago. Maybe they look hard enough they could find a couple of gangsters there.

"You talk to Imogene?" Benno had a suit bag over his shoulder, his finger crooked in the hanger head.

"I did."

"You miss her?"

"I miss her. I even miss the A&P. You?"

"I don't know." Benno kicked the sidewalk. "I sent my aunt some postcards. I wouldn't mind being home. But," he smiled as he looked at his friend, "this place is some fuckin' place, no?"

"If somebody else is paying, sure."

"Ain't that the truth."

"What's in the bag? You get another new suit?"

"No. It's Bebe's tux. Which I'd better get inside."

Benno told the guy at the door Bell was with him. The guy said, "Sure, Sal. Enjoy yourself."

Cy Geller and his wife were driving south along the Dixie Highway, returning home from their Friday night dinner at Chungking's. Egg drop soup, two egg rolls, chicken chow mein with crispy noodles and white rice and plenty of tea: the same order for years and the same $2 tip since the proprietor refused to charge the Gellers for the meal.

At Southwest 37th Avenue, Geller eased right, away from the flow of traffic. He entered a familiar street shrouded in darkness by mossy trees, gaslight flickering only every block or so.

When he crossed Florida Avenue, a black car darted into the intersection. Geller accelerated to avoid a crash but he was slammed hard. He and his wife bumped heads and his shoulder banged against the driver's side window.

After checking his wife, Geller gathered himself and stepped into the night air. The hulking men in the other vehicle were coming toward him, crossing broken glass in a manner Geller took as a threat. So did his armed guards, who arrived seconds later, having been caught at a red light on the highway.

One of the men in the dented car shouted, "What's wrong with you, you stupid old bastard—"

A guard's bullet caught the man in the neck, propelling him sideways. He fell to the street.

The guard pointed his gun at the second man, who raised his hands.

Geller looked at the man who'd been shot. He was crawling now, moonlight shining in the pool of blood that trailed him.

"What do you want to do?" Geller said to the second man.

"Well, I don't want to die," he replied with surprising composure.

A second guard drew next to Geller and tugged him toward his damaged car. The guard was to drive the Gellers to the marina, the procedure drawn up nearly a decade ago.

But then a police car turned off the Dixie Highway with a squeal and raced along 37th Avenue, and then another roaring squad car followed, red lights whirling. The cops leapt from their vehicles and began firing. Geller's first guard was hit, his body rattling even before he slammed the asphalt.

The second guard shoved Geller down into the backseat and fired. He clipped a cop near the shoulder. A barrage of bullets killed him seconds later. One bullet came through the rear window and passed through the front, raining glass on Mrs. Geller, who was lying across the seat, arms covering her head.

Geller was pulled from the car, then his wife, who was dizzy from the crash and the shock of violence. He was frisked, shackled and hurried to a squad car just as an ambulance arrived.

Geller watched as the medic treated the man who had been shot in the neck. Sitting on the curb, his friend talked to a policeman, who nodded but took no notes.

At the police station, Geller learned that the man who drove into him was a cop, and so was his wounded passenger. Geller was charged with failure to yield. He was told, to his surprise, that there was an outstanding warrant in his name in New York City for an alleged violation of the Sullivan Act 14 years earlier. Since Geller hadn't carried a weapon since the mid-'20s, this was unlikely. But when he was released in his own recognizance provided he surrender his passport, he understood—they were demanding he testify at the Dunney hearings in Miami.

Instructing Saul to help transfer his remaining assets to his mother, Cy Geller resigned from the board of Palm Tree Enterprises, liquidating his shares and moving the proceeds offshore. He intended to empty his safe and ship the money to Cuba, but when he tried to contact Don Carlo in Havana, he was told he had returned to Sicily. The embargo of pharmaceuticals and medical supplies by American companies, executed at the urging of Congress and the Department of Justice, had turned Cuban officials against Farcolini and his operation. Since he no longer trusted Corini or Fortune, the cash in the safe, Geller decided, would go to Bruno Gigenti, who would protect his son.

When they spoke by phone, Geller told him everything. "Corini and Fortune," he said. "It wasn't you, Bruno. I should have said something before Havana. To Carlo."

"What are you going to do?"

Geller paused to watch tiny lizards dart across his sunny veranda. "I'll have to testify or I'll be cited for contempt."

"That's no choice. Let me look into it."

Geller said, "We're dealing with men who saved the free world. They're on a mission. Organized crime, communism... The pendulum swings."

"Too bad it had to be you."

"In Miami, who else?"

Geller was no fatalist but the feds' play was inevitable. Were he on the other side, he would've done the same thing, though with less spectacle. The end game was underway, its result clear. He shook his head, he tsked his lips. If only he weren't in such top-notch shape.

"Where is everybody?" Bell asked as the house lights dimmed.

"Sssh" went Benno, giving him an elbow, too.

By "everybody," Bell meant Hollywood. He didn't see a single movie star, not one, not even Ree. Bell figured those guys over there were musicians, especially the Negroes, and maybe recording executives, given how Guy Simon was bullshitting them. Most of people in the bubbly crowd were women dolled up nice, coiffed and perfumed, their husbands dragged along, looking pretty dapper, too, like the California sun had given them good health. Benno asked the waitress who were the guys Simon was with. She said, "Harry Milton. The owner," and so Benno figured the Jew was Saul Geller and they were checking Bebe out for the Sandpiper.

Ronnie Oliver settled at the piano and the house band went into "C Jam Blues," a catchy Ellington number, and then a snappy

436

version of one of Bebe's old hits with the trumpet player, which put the crowd in a happy mood.

Bell whispered, "I thought he hated that trumpet guy—"

"Hey, I'm listening over here."

"I'm just asking—"

"Will you put a fuckin' plug in it, Leo? Sheesh…"

And now Bebe, the spotlight bold and bright. A single-note fanfare, and then the band suddenly stopped and only the bass player and the drummer, using brushes on the high hat, continued with a seductive little beat, setting Marsala up like a cool cat strutting down an alley.

"All of me," he sang. "Why not take all of me?"

Bobbing his head, crooning soft and low, Marsala came down the steps at the lip of the stage and approached the eager audience. As he sang, he strolled from table to table and looked each woman, one by one, right in the eye, a warm, welcoming smile on his lips.

"Take my heart, I'll never use it…"

He leaned down and cupped one woman under the chin. As she beamed, he went and clapped her husband on the back and started drifting toward the band, his swagger hiding his limp.

"You took the part that once was my heart…"

He was back on stage when he sang the next line and then the band burst in like thunder as he repeated the first verse, snapping his fingers. When the sax soloed, Marsala stepped back and stared at the guy like he was playing the greatest thing he ever heard and for the rest of the tune, it was like they were having a cozy duet.

When it was over, the couples near the stage gave Marsala a fierce ovation, a few of them standing in appreciation.

"Knockout," Benno said as Bebe nudged the spotlight toward the sax player.

The next night, the club was packed with celebrities and columnists and as Benno told Bell while Bebe napped, this was part of the singer's plan. On opening night, he let his fan club see that he was still their guy and the music business know he was onto something else. With Benno sitting around doing nothing, Enna spent the afternoon calling the critics who went to the show and then Bebe got on the line. "What did you think?" he'd ask and they'd tell him. Bebe made this gesture with his fingers, saying the guy on the other end was yapping like he knew, but his face said he was glad they were kissing his ass again. "Come back tonight, if you're free," he told them. "We're going to try a few new numbers." Bebe might be an empty skull half the time, but he was Sicilian, so he couldn't help but be smart once in a while, too.

Now it was maybe 10 minutes to showtime. Back in blue sharkskin, Benno was by himself, Bell having taken a pass, so he perched at the bar with Marsala fans. He was staring at Eleanor Ree. Fifteen, maybe 20 Hollywood broads in the place, dolled-up women he'd seen on the screen at the Avalon from the time he gave up Westerns and yet Ree was the one nobody could take their eyes off of. OK, she had the best seat in the house, right there where you couldn't miss her, Bebe seeing to that. But it was like some special light was shining on her or maybe it was inside of her shining out, the way she smiled playful, those cheekbones, those lips, the dimple in her chin. The couple with her, he's a big star from that picture she went to Spain and Paris for, and his wife is pretty and petite, but nobody's paying attention 'cause she's sitting next to Eleanor Ree, whose date is Rico Enna, that lucky fuck. For a moment, Benno thought, I should be sitting in that chair. But then he heard this voice saying, Are you fuckin' crazy? You're in

Hollywood. You, Salvatore Benno. The people from the covers of magazines are sitting so close you could flick their ears and you complain? You better stay out of the sun and stop with the rum coolers and Champagne, *ciuccio*.

Aware of the stakes, Ree smoked nervously, sipping a gin martini she would've loved to guzzle. The studio called this morning and asked if she'd sit with the star of the Hemingway picture. She knew Enna had already turned out the agency's clients for the show and as she looked discretely around the club, she knew about half of them had demanded their personal appearance fee to attend. Bill wouldn't be told. He didn't have to know anything that might blow him off the tightrope. She'd learned that when he was high, it was best to keep him up there. But if he failed tonight, in front of this crowd, if his voice frogged on him…

She felt a gentle hand on her shoulder and turned to find her agent. "Mal," she said, offering her cheek, her perfume.

Mal Weisberg kissed her, shook hands with the movie star and rapped Enna on the arm, as if to tell him poaching Ree wouldn't play.

"I'm in Bill's seat," Enna explained.

"I heard good things," Weisberg said to him, "and it's nice what you did for Klein's family. Better Bill's seen as a mensch. Mazel tov." He turned his attention to his client. "You I haven't heard from…"

"Oh I haven't had time to think, Mal."

"*Life* magazine. Lunch with Louella. You've been busy. I understand." He leaned in and whispered, "You haven't told him yet, have you?"

"You're right," she replied, glancing at Enna. "Next year at this time he'll be bigger than he's ever been."

Bebe had a late dinner with Ree on Rodeo Drive, but first he had to go home and take a shower and it was almost midnight before Benno dropped them off at a little French joint. Flushed with success, Bebe said, "Leave the car, Sal. Take a cab," but Benno said no and waited outside, his head bobbing as he sat behind the wheel, black coffee doing nothing to give him a boost.

After dropping them off at Ree's in Bel Air, Bebe dancing across the lawn, Benno drove back to Sunset Boulevard, parked Marsala's car in the Beverly Hills Hotel lot and dragged his ass to the bungalow. He put the key in gentle, figuring Bell was asleep.

But Bell was sitting on the sofa, dressed, some kind of odd expression on his face. Like he'd been crying.

"What?" said Benno, tossing his hat aside.

"Ah, Sal…My father died."

"Oh, Jesus, Leo. No…"

Bell stood and Benno gave him a big hug, Bell hugging back, grabbing at him.

"Leo, I'm so sorry. Jesus."

Dropping back to the sofa, Bell explained. Imogene called. His father had been taken to St. Patrick's in Narrows Gate. Chest pains, and some young nurse there who went to St. Claire's remembered she was dating a Bell, not a common name in the town, and by the time Imogene rushed down from school, his father was dead.

"I'm on the first flight out."

Benno paced. "This is a fuckin' shame. Your father was a great guy, Leo."

"He died alone. He did everything to set me right and I make it so he dies alone."

"Jesus, I really liked him. I feel awful."

"He's going to be buried as a Jew, Sal."

Benno stopped. "What's that mean? Wait—I know what it means. Leo. Leo."

"I'm doing it."

Benno boiled it down to one question. "Imogene?"

"And everybody," Bell added. "Like this day wasn't coming."

"Maybe you could do it in secret?" Benno suggested to Bell. "The burying…"

"No more secrets, Sal."

"Hey, I stand by you, Leo. I'm just saying. They got Jews in the A&P?"

"The least of my worries is losing my job."

Benno was going to tell him, if that happens, go to my uncle. You could fill in for me until I get back to the store, but he thought maybe Bell would take it wrong, Leo with his big ambitions.

"You're OK in school?"

Bell allowed himself a smile. "At CCNY, it might help."

"Imogene's family?"

Bell shrugged. "I can't see I'm wrong about her."

Bell's bags were packed, all his books put away.

"I'll take you to the airport," Benno said.

"Good, but let's go now. Since you got Bebe's car, I figure we should ditch the DeSoto. Reduce the risk you get nabbed with a stolen vehicle."

"But we're at the airport at four in the morning?"

"It's seven in New York. I can call my father's partner and get him working on the arrangements."

Benno thought he'd call his aunt and tell her to go see Leo, hold his hand, make sure nobody leaves him by himself.

Imogene O'Boyle was at the gate at LaGuardia and she kissed Bell's lips and held him tight as he started to well up again. "I love you, Leo. Look at me. I love you."

In the parking lot, he stopped and dropped his bag at his side. "I have something to say."

"I know. The police told Mary Frances." She was the St. Claire's graduate who worked at St. Patrick's. The upstairs tenant in Bell's brownstone had heard a crash, then he found Mr. Bell in the hallway, clutching his robe, gasping for air. He called the cops and when they entered the apartment, there was his Torah on the nightstand.

"Only Sal knows," he told her. "I hated keeping it from you."

"I'll say it again. I love you, Leo. Now let's go do what must be done."

She'd played it out during a sleepless night and today as she took two buses and a subway to Queens. Her father would come around; her mother probably not. If she married a Jew, she might find it hard to find a job at a Catholic hospital.

"They posted time of death as after midnight," she said.

"He'll be buried tomorrow." He told her about Eli Kreiner, who agreed to arrange the service and burial.

"I'll go with you, Leo."

Bell tossed his bag into his trunk, a rattle rising as his textbooks hit his toolbox.

"I have something else for you." She went on her toes and kissed his cheek. "That's from Sal. He said, 'Tell him it's a kiss from his brother.'"

Cy Geller knew the feds were in on it. How else can you reach a man who lives in a fortress with armed guards? The feds made it plain to City Hall: You fail to help us produce Geller and the mayor and chief of police will appear before the Dunney Commission. And that drug money Geller spread around town? Maybe they can explain exactly where it went.

So they called Geller and told him a witness had come forth, a man walking his dog on Florida Avenue on the night of the shoot-out, who said the undercover cops had rammed Geller on purpose and that the guard had fired to protect his injured boss. "Come down," they said, "let's make sure what he says makes sense."

A stupid story. A child could do better. But he agreed to go, calling in advance after leaving a note for his wife on his desk in the cabana. Rather than involve his guards, he took a taxi. On the way downtown, he stopped and posted a letter to his son in care of the Sandpiper.

Outside the police station, he paid the fare, giving his customary tip. As he left the vehicle, a dark-skinned man approached. He wore a pale lime suit, a yellow shirt and huaraches. "Mr. Geller?" he said.

Geller opened his arms wide.

The Cuban man shot Geller three times in the chest and then leaped into a car that had raced in, scraping against the curb. As the car sped away, the process server who'd been waiting for Geller leaped down the police station steps, followed by a stampede of cops, some of whom had their weapons drawn. By the time they reached Geller, he lay dying, blood oozing from his chest and bubbling along the corners of his mouth.

The process server called his boss at Justice, who contacted Washington. "How did it happen?" he was asked.

"Suicide," the lawyer said.

The gunman was back in Havana by nightfall, reporting to Farcolini's ally, Jorge Ortega.

The night before, Geller had called Ortega. "I can invoke my rights under the Fifth Amendment of the Constitution of the United States," he said. "But it will be seen as an admission of guilt. Jorge, I am not a young man. The future is the matter at hand."

"Come here," Ortega said, knowing Geller had a small, competent navy at his disposal. "I can assure you that you will be safe."

"Let's not postpone the inevitable," he replied. They had chased Farcolini back to Sicily by pressuring the Cuban government and its medical establishment. They could insist that he be returned to the United States by some similar embargo.

"If it has to be this way," Ortega said with a sigh. "I am terribly sorry."

"Jorge, there is another matter," Geller began. "I would like you to tell Don Carlo of a missing note, an implication, a betrayal."

CHAPTER THIRTY-SIX

Bell recognized no part of the ceremony, had never in his life heard El Maleh Rachamim, the memorial prayer familiar to Eli Kreiner and the congregation, all of whom waited as he, with Imogene at his side, followed the casket out into the gray morning. He wore a yarmulke and a sliver of black ribbon pinned to his lapel.

The Cypress Hill Cemetery isn't far from the temple, Kreiner told him last night. Nonsectarian, he added, which Bell took to mean that one day he might be buried somewhere near his father, who the rabbi praised as a man who did what he had to do to bring a new generation to America. He's forgiven, Bell told himself, not realizing Roman Catholicism had informed the thought.

He knew no one who approached now to shake his hand, men Kreiner introduced as their customers and vendors. They nodded respectfully at Imogene as Kreiner spoke to her father. Young women in black milled under the bleak sky. In his solitude, Bell studied the barren trees and the stout little birds that pecked at random seeds.

He felt a touch on his elbow. "My condolences, Leo."

Charlie Tyler removed his gloves to shake Bell's cold hand.

Too fatigued to be surprised, Bell accepted the courtesy. "Thanks for coming, Charlie."

"Of course," Tyler replied.

Bell gestured for Imogene.

"I'm sorry to meet you under these circumstances," Tyler said to her. "Leo, is there anything I can do?"

"No, I don't think so," Bell said, as Imogene took his arm in hers.

"Would you like me to come to the cemetery?" Agitated and uncomfortable, Tyler was unfocused and vague. His work for the Dunney Commission had him on edge.

Bell said no. "I'll be all right."

"Might I have a word then?"

Tyler started up the hill toward the avenue. Bell followed him as Imogene withdrew.

"I wasn't sure whether I should come to see you," he began. "I don't know if I should be here now."

"What do you need, Charlie?" Bell shivered. His topcoat and hat were in his car.

"Cy Geller is dead, Leo," he said. "Without his testimony, Miami's going to be a bust."

Bell nodded. Tyler's problems seemed a remnant of a distant time.

They stopped near a rusted hydrant. "We had the mayor in our scope, Leo, and the port director. Without the threat of Geller, we can't make the case."

"Charlie—"

"The target of the Dunney Commission isn't just organized crime. It's the politicians who support it. Our ports are under control of a criminal enterprise with the tacit approval of local and state government. This has to be stopped, Leo. Business demands it."

"Charlie," Bell said, frowning, "I'm burying my father here. Can't you under—"

Tyler clutched Bell's elbow. "We're picking up Benno."

Bell recoiled. He yanked his arm free.

"It's crucial, Leo. The suitcase he delivered to Farcolini—"

"Marsala delivered it. I told you that." Bell clenched his fists. "God damn you, Charlie."

"Leo, calm down," Tyler said quickly. "With Fortune missing, I need Benno to collaborate. Who gave it to him? Marsala can say he doesn't know. We can trace the money back to Corini—"

"You have got to be fuckin' kidding me."

"We can't fail in New York, Leo. Everything is riding on it."

Outside the temple, mourners were waiting for Bell to return. Idling motors purred, exhaust fumes rising through the chilled air. Imogene had begun to walk the incline.

"In other circumstances, I'm out of line, Leo. I know. But I've got to call in my chits. Benno's coming in."

"I don't owe you shit, Charlie."

"I've been making a future for you. It's not going to be easy in Justice for you—"

"Because I'm a Jew?"

Tyler wore a wry smile. "Everybody needs an advocate, Leo."

"Landis was yours and you threw him overboard."

Imogene said, "Leo, we'd better…"

"I'm sorry, Miss O'Boyle," Tyler said. "Here he is. All yours."

"Don't do it," Bell insisted.

"Leo…"

"Give me a week. A couple of days."

Tyler hesitated.

"Two days," Bell repeated.

"Think it through, Leo," he said, his gaze shifting to Imogene. "Look forward."

This time, the guest star on *Chesterfield Presents Bill Marsala* was a tap dancer. When Bebe told him, Benno thought, A tap dancer on the radio? That's as stupid as Edgar Bergen on the radio. But it turned out the guy sang, too, and there was a skit where he and Bebe were supposed to be carrying a refrigerator up some steep steps, and a pissy little dog tugs on Bebe's cuff, some guy going "woof woof," also there's this banana peel and the guest star was funny as hell. Also, the guy was colored, which Bebe didn't tell nobody and Benno wondered if all over America people thought he was great and as soon as they found out, they wouldn't no more. He'd been thinking about shit like that since Mr. Bell died and Leo went Jew.

Benno was standing in the same spot as last week, the audience spread out before him, the busy stage, and Enna was pacing behind him, wearing a path in the rug. After he sold some Chesterfields, Bebe said, "Ladies and gentlemen, here's one I think you know. We'd like to make it our next hit, so let's see if you enjoy it." Enna stopped and stepped up next to Benno close enough to pick his pocket.

Then came the saxophone player with that bluesy feel and Ollie played a few notes and the audience sighed. Sure, they recognized it: Marsala's first big hit from forever ago. Only modern, the band kicking in strong like Basie after a while, the thing swinging smooth.

Bebe smiled when he sang—which didn't make sense when you heard the lyric—but the whole house was smiling, too, and when it was over, they went nuttier than the people did in the nightclub. Enna went, "Yeah!" He punched the air and slapped Benno's arm, then gave him a big handshake.

In the parking lot, Enna said, "Bill, fabulous. Really fabulous."

Marsala was blasé, which is how he acted when he thought he was as great as the other guy was saying.

"Are you happy with yesterday's take?"

"I haven't listened to the acetate yet," Marsala replied as he signed autographs, giving them that automatic grin when he returned their pens.

"I want the record in the hands of the New York disc jockeys before you open there," Enna said.

Marsala nodded. "Let's get together in the morning."

"Your place?"

"Why not? We'll give Eleanor some peace."

Eleanor, Benno thought. Yesterday, he picked up Bebe to bring him to the recording studio, and she was on a towel in the grass next to her swimming pool. She'd started out in a two-piece bathing suit but then her top was untied and she was naked upstairs, more or less, and Benno thought if only that pain-in-the-ass houseboy would call her and up she'd jump. Which took his mind off Leo Bell for about 30 seconds.

He opened the car door and Marsala slid in back. A tap on the window glass and a little wave to his fans as Benno pulled away.

"Sal, drive by Canter's and pick up some chicken soup," he instructed.

"You want to shower first?"

"I'll do it at the nightclub."

"OK, Bebe."

In the dressing room, Marsala said, "Bring me a hot towel."

Benno found one and Marsala pressed it around his throat. Then he spooned down the chicken soup and then hot tea with the horseradish, which Benno tried at the Polo Lounge while the waiter watched. Never has a Sicilian drunk anything so bad, Benno was thinking, but then his nose caught on fire and then he could breathe so good he thought he could smell his aunt's cooking 3,000 miles away. Didn't do a thing for his throat, though.

Now Bebe took a piss, washed his hands like a surgeon and then he went to sleep on a couple of chairs.

After the show, Marsala, sagging, said he wanted to go to the Wilshire Towers.

"You all right, Bebe?" Benno asked.

"Just tired."

"I guess so," Benno said. "You recorded yesterday afternoon, then a show. The radio today, then a show."

Marsala had his eyes closed.

To the rearview mirror, Benno said, "Could be worse, though."

"Yeah? How, kid?"

"Like maybe you could be back on Polk Street, and you got a wife with jiggling arms, she smells like Lestoil and yesterday's scungilli and there's three crying babies and you're working at the shipyards."

Marsala opened his eyes. "Sal, did my mother tell you to say that?"

"Funny," Benno answered. "Just yesterday I was thinking about Hennie."

Wearily, the singer said, "Not a day goes by…"

"Yeah, but good or bad?"

"Both. But when it's bad, Sal, she's usually making a speech like that."

Benno apologized. Now he felt like shit. Bebe hadn't done nothing but treat him good, better than Fortune or Mimmo. He decided to drive to Wilshire Boulevard with his mouth shut.

"What's eating your ass?" Marsala asked. "The driver, right? His father dying."

"To tell you the truth, Bebe. He's not a driver. He's my friend since kindergarten at St. Francis." They cruised through a yellow light. "I think he's miserable."

"I'm sure he's miserable," Marsala replied. "You lose a broad, Sally, you go find another. But just you try to find another mother or dad."

I wouldn't know, Benno thought, since I ain't had neither.

Marsala leaned up and clapped him on the shoulder. "I'll tell you what, Sal…"

Corini made the call. Gigenti thought about it, agreed and now they were on the 86th-floor observation deck of the Empire State Building with the tourists. Corini wore a camel's hair coat, thick brown scarf and leather gloves against the ungodly March wind. In gray, Gigenti limped toward him, his face contorted by a fierce scowl.

"What?" Gigenti said.

"It's just you and me," Corini said in Sicilian.

Gigenti stared at him. "Bullshit. You got two men up here and I got two."

"I'm saying with Geller gone and Carlo back in Sicily, it's you and me."

Gigenti shrugged, his collar rising above his ears.

"You been served?"

Gigenti said no.

"I have. And the mayor and people on his staff."

"Your mayor," Gigenti said.

"They're putting me on the television."

Gigenti was unmoved. What did he care? Television, radio, the newspapers, magazines. They were none of his concern.

A little kid ran around them, chasing his father's hat as it tumbled in the wind.

"You talked to Ortega," Corini said. "You want Miami."

"I got Miami and now Ortega works for me."

"And you? Who do you work for, Bruno?"

When Gigenti didn't reply, Corini said, "I'm thinking you go to Sicily. See Carlo and get a reminder."

"I think maybe you leave the country this time."

"I'd say we both go," Corini said, "but I can't travel."

He could, but it wouldn't be easy, not with the two-bit feds sitting on him so tight he had to go to Jersey this morning, change cars and drivers on the plank road and double back for the meeting with Gigenti two miles from his apartment. They were treating him like a criminal.

Worse than the feds was Gigenti, who was taking everything he wanted like he was daring Corini to come at him with muscle.

Corini started to stroll, beckoning for Gigenti to follow. They walked through shadows into the dull rays of the midday sun, heading toward the reason he picked such a public spot.

"You see what Dunney did in Chicago?" Corini asked. "He embarrassed people—the mayor, aldermen, state senators."

"Yeah, but the money flows. Who gives a shit? Nobody I know runs for office."

"Bruno, we work with those people. Maybe you don't like it but it's what Carlo wants. And it's smart. We make them and they're in our fuckin' pocket from the start."

Gigenti laughed bitterly. "Like I can't buy in anytime I want."

They continued to the Fifth Avenue side of the building. On the East River, cargo ships crowded the harbor, tugs edging into position. The docks on both sides of the icy waterway flurried with activity: Cranes swung weighty pallets and trucks lined in jagged rows to move in and out. Forklifts scooted in search of freight while stevedores leaned into dollies stacked high with goods.

"Without the politicians, we lose that," Corini said, pointing east.

Undeterred, Gigenti said, "You through?"

"I'm asking you to go see Carlo," he repeated. "Find out what he wants with Cy gone and stay out of the country until Dunney blows over. Let your crew run the show."

The moment Geller asked him to provide protection for his son, Gigenti knew he had no need for concern. Corini's attempts to eliminate him—exposing him for the Pellizzari hit, setting him up for the robbery of the Jersey bagman, provoking him into winging Mimmo—had all failed. Now Don Carlo knew the truth.

"I'm not going nowhere," Gigenti replied. "You want somebody to see Carlo so bad, make Fortune go."

"I can't. He's up in Canada and the feds are watching."

"Then send a telegram," Gigenti said as he limped away.

"Don't make me an enemy, Bruno," Corini shouted in Sicilian, the wind scattering his words. "It's good for nobody."

Gigenti waved his hand, the gesture telling Corini to go to hell.

Mimmo was sitting all by himself at the Grotto, a table near the kitchen and everybody who walked by looked at him like they wished he would blow away. Twice, he got excited seeing somebody coming his way, maybe they'd join him for lunch. "Hey Lou-Lou," he'd start saying, his hand jumping into the air. "Hey, Pork." But they kept going, even Joey Flattop, who stole underwear off clotheslines as a kid and Mimmo cuffed him around, a favor to his late mother. Now a cop in Jersey City, Flattop made a U-turn, his shoes sliding on sawdust.

Mimmo stared down at his steak *pizzaiola*, Volpe giving him gristle. The vino was lukewarm, the bread ready to mold.

"Mimmo."

He looked up slow. For a few seconds, he'd forgotten his misery. He was picturing himself young in a white dinner jacket, a red carnation, working the room at the nightspot they burned down, the best job of his life. For a few years, he had class.

"You all right, Mimmo?"

He tried to focus.

"I'm Leo. Sal Benno's pal."

"*Che cosa volete?*"

Bell nodded toward the empty seat.

"Go ahead."

As Bell sat, Mimmo ignored his guest, cutting through the tough meat to fork a sliver into his mouth.

"Mimmo, I heard you've been served," Bell said, speaking low.

"Served? Served what?"

Bell looked at the plate. Jesus, he thought, there's one less dog in Narrows Gate. "The commission. Dunney."

"So what? It don't matter."

"Mimmo—"

"Think I give a shit what some senator wants?"

"Mimmo, you can play this guy."

He looked at Bell.

"This guy opens the door for you."

Intrigued, Mimmo put a finger across his lips. He whispered, "*Parli Siciliano.*"

Speaking Sicilian in the Grotto was like speaking English in the House of Lords, but Bell went with it. "They clear a path. You get my meaning, Mimmo?"

Sucking on his teeth, Mimmo nodded knowingly.

"You, you're a big fish," Bell continued, "but they want mayors and governors. They're going to go after them through Corini. Maybe a seat opens up."

Mimmo nodded to the Chianti in a basket, telling Bell to take a glass.

Bell obeyed as if he'd been given orders from a powerful boss. "Thank you."

"Why do you bring this to me?"

"You've been good to me, Mimmo."

Suddenly, he remembered Ding was a Jew. "Let me think about it," he replied.

"Take this phone number."

Mimmo palmed the slip of paper.

Dismissed, Bell kicked through sawdust and left the crowded restaurant.

Mimmo sat in silence, calculating. He snuck a look at the phone number he'd been given. His plan was soon lost to fantasy, but later he remembered Bell had stopped by, paid a tribute, showed courtesy. It felt good, up and down.

Like old times.

Moving by train from Calgary to Saskatoon and hopscotching Ontario for Quebec, Frankie Fortune tried to find a city where he felt he could disappear. At every stop, he called Geller's private number, the secure line in the cabana, and nobody answered. He was concerned. Once, twice, three times, he's not there is one thing. Every time is something else.

He read the Canadian newspapers to find out what happened, but all he learned was Dunney scored in Chicago, showing a couple of aldermen with their lips on the tit and putting a state senator in a jam. The local crew looked like slap-happy morons, colorful characters who stole milk bottles off the back steps instead of guys who put heads in a vise grip until they heard pop. Dunney set himself up by asking Giorgio Labbi about a bank job he pulled in '38, and Gigi Lips said, "Sure, but I spent the dough in Marshall Field's. Everybody made out." Fortune wondered if the crew showed up in black shirts and white ties, chalk stripe jackets with wide lapels, like the mugs in the movies.

Now he was in Toronto, a big city that was too close to the border for his taste, but at least they spoke English. He took a room at a hotel in Yorkville, expecting Germans like the ones in the section with the same name in New York, and made himself a promise he'd stay out of the Italian neighborhood in Scarborough, which sounded about as Italian to him as white toast.

The local broads worked out OK, but pretty soon he couldn't take Canada any more. He had the feeling the bartenders and waiters and bellhops and barbers and taxi drivers and the guys at the newsstands who smiled and said "Good day" and "How are you enjoying your visit, sir?" and "How is our country treating you, sir?" would just as soon put an ice pick in his American spine if they could get away with it. He went for a walk in a park and saw a bunch of guys playing hockey and sure enough, they started beating the shit out of each other. These nice people, the streets so clean you can eat off them, the cops patrolling on foot and nodding hello, and what the fuck is Celsius? He was a nobody here.

So he gave up, went to dinner over in Scarborough and talked in Sicilian to the maître d' and the waiter, who had a goddamned Canadian accent. He nestled in a corner, kept his eye on the door and ordered chicken cacciatore and a bottle of black-cock Chianti, which was the best meal he had since he was sent to Hollywood.

He was thinking about dessert, maybe a little *cucidati*, and at that moment what should happen but Bebe comes on the jukebox singing that piece of garbage song even Hennie would've hated.

Fuckin' Bebe.

Crooking his finger, Fortune called the waiter over. "Don't you have any of your own singers up here?"

"Sir?"

"I mean, who's the Bill Marsala of Canada?" he asked.

The waiter looked down. "I don't understand, sir."

"I'm asking if you have your own Bill Marsala. Some Canadian singer who's Sicilian and the broads go moist over."

"Sir, I'd have to say Bill Marsala is our Bill Marsala. He's quite popular."

Convinced the waiter was holding back, Fortune said, "Get the fuck out of here."

The check paid, he bundled up to find a taxi. First, he'd have to confront the wind that had people walking tilted over, their scarves flapping like flags on a pole, if it stopped they'd land on their faces. I've got to get back to New York, he thought, his hands buried in his pockets. Something's happening, and I've got to—

And then Eugenio Zamarella came out of the shadows and he put the tip of his .45 behind Fortune's ear, telling him to move onto the side street.

Fortune thought, I'm not dead yet. There's a chance. "Who sent you?" Fortune asked as they walked into the driving wind.

Zamarella had on that kind of stocking cap that shows only the eyes and mouth. "Corini gave you up." They turned the corner. "Over there," Zamarella said, shoving Fortune toward a dark alcove between buildings.

"Corini gave me up?" Fortune asked as he backpedaled, hands at his sides.

"*Arrivederci*, Frank—"

Suddenly, Zamarella gagged, a stiletto jutting from his throat. With a flick of his wrist, Fortune hit his mark from a dozen feet out.

As Zamarella fell to his knees, his gun discharged, missing Fortune's shoes by inches.

A Scarborough beat cop saw the muzzle flash from the avenue and had his weapon drawn as he reached the crosswalk. To his surprise, he saw a man on his back, a gun in his hand, looking at the sky.

"You," the cop shouted. "Right there. Drop your weapon."

Zamarella rolled awkwardly to his side and pulled the trigger. His shot missed the cop.

The cop returned fire, hitting the masked killer in the chest, the lining of his coat spitting out as he collapsed.

Fortune ran off, clinging to shadows.

Racing in, the cop then saw the knife protruding from the dead man's throat.

Later, the Royal Canadian Mounted Police told the cop's supervisor that Eugenio Zamarella, a reputed member of the legendary Carlo Farcolini gang, was suspected in the for-hire murders of at least 15 people in the United States. They congratulated the cop, telling him, in their own way, that he'd taken out the garbage.

While they were glad-handing each other back at the precinct, Zamarella's gruesome mug shot in the *Daily Star*, Frankie Fortune crossed the border at Niagara Falls, saying good riddance to Canada.

CHAPTER THIRTY-SEVEN

Mimmo came along Polk Street from the candy store, walking in slow motion, a midmorning stroll, then he paused like he can't believe what he's seeing, maybe that merciless joker up there in his head was playing games again.

"What are you doing here?"

"I work here," Benno said. He was cranking the awning down, shaking out old leaves and other muck from the long winter.

"You're supposed to be with Bebe."

"Bebe don't need me. You got Enna, who follows him like a dog. You did good, Mimmo. You straightened Bebe out good."

Shuffling to stay warm, Mimmo nodded. "Tell me about Ding. You still think he's a stand-up guy?"

"Why not?"

"Why not? Twenty-something years in the neighborhood and he don't tell nobody who he is."

"We know who he is, but now he's a Jew. Like Cary Grant."

Mimmo stopped. "Cary Grant?"

"Cary Grant."

"Cary fuckin' Grant?"

"So help me," Benno said, holding up his hand. "So how about you put out the word: Leave Leo alone or else."

Puffing up, Mimmo nodded thoughtfully. "I could clear his path."

Changing the subject, Benno said, "Mimmo, tell me. What's gonna happen? I mean, say, Don Carlo can't come back, already Cy Geller's dead, Frankie's on the lam, who knows what's going on with Gigenti and I heard the radio says this commission wants Corini's ass. For Christ's sake, you're all we got."

Mimmo liked that. He nodded slowly. Then he stroked his chin. Then he walked away, unsure of where he was going.

Benno sighed in relief. He went back to cleaning the awning, knowing he kissed Mimmo's ass for a while, like Leo asked. But, Jesus, the day they let Mimmo run the thing is the day we shut off the lights.

Bill Marsala stopped in the Hampshire House corridor when he heard rummaging in Ree's room. Certain it was Fortune or one of his men, he considered an escape down the corridor toward the elevator.

The door swung open.

"Bill!" Eleanor Ree jumped into his arms. She kissed him frantically, happily. Squeezing him tight, she wrapped her leg around his calf and felt the winter's chill on his clothes.

"What are you doing in New York?" he said. Smiling bright, he tossed his hat and scarf aside. "I had no idea."

"I wanted to surprise you. I did, didn't I? I surprised you."

Two upright steamer trunks were tucked against the far wall, tugging the curtains on the windows onto Central Park. "How long do you plan on staying?" he joked.

"I want to look my best every night." She wore slacks and a pearl silk blouse. Her hair was back under a kerchief.

He said, "You look fabulous now, baby."

She grabbed his hand and yanked him toward her bedroom.

Marsala let his topcoat fall to the carpet and to hell with his aching throat and the worries.

Bell entered Benno's as the shop set to close. Aunt Gemma put down the broom, hurried over to kiss him and started crying. Then Sal's uncle walked over sad-eyed, shook his hand, but then cupped his cheeks too as he offered his condolences.

"You go to see Bebe?" Gemma asked in English.

"Indeed we do. At a nightclub."

"With your girlfriend?"

"I want her to meet you, Aunt Gemma. I swear you'll love her."

Gemma smiled. "Maybe she has a friend for Salvatore?"

Bell crossed his fingers.

Then Benno appeared wearing a suit Bebe bought him, its smoke gray double-breasted jacket cut trim with an expertise Albino the Tailor couldn't match.

"You ready?" he asked.

"Ready," Bell replied, winking at Gemma.

Benno waved as they exited.

Engine purring, they turned onto Observer Road, driving alongside the Lackawanna yards. Benno said, "I was thinking of introducing Nina to Bebe."

"Sure, but go easy on the 'Bebe said this' and 'Me and Bebe did that' tonight. Maybe it's better Nina gets to tell her story this time."

"How about Corini?"

Bell looked at him. "She wants to meet Anthony Corini? This is a good kid, Sally. Going to the Caribbean, seeing Bebe, that's enough. She's dazzled."

"You sure? I take it she sees me ordinary."

"Be ordinary. Don't be selling Bebe, Eleanor, Hollywood."

"I got to say hello to Corini."

"Maybe you nod, huh?"

A night wind whistled through the car's windows. "Your in-laws are set for Sunday," Benno said. "The cover, drinks, the meals—they're on the arm."

"Thank Bebe for me, OK?"

"I meant to ask. What did they say when you told them?"

"Mr. O'Boyle said he's been working with Jews his whole life and they're no cheaper than anybody else."

"And Imogene's mom?"

"She said, 'Jesus, Mary and Joseph!' She's been crying in church since, wearing down her rosary beads. She's got me shooting dice with Pontius Pilate."

"At least she ain't asked if you got horns," Benno said.

St. Claire's was across the boulevard. Bell could see the girls in silhouette as they waited in the vestibule.

Anthony Corini and his wife were in a prime spot—since he owned the Caribbean that stood to reason—and Rico Enna sat with them, smiling but torturing his napkin. Actors from Broadway and radio circulated, prizefighters, too. Winchell held court and there was this kind of electricity in the air, Imogene and Nina gawking, the nightclub packed like the A train at rush hour, even the balcony. Maybe everybody knew Bebe was in a spot and they saw a chance at a bargain double bill. Tonight, Marsala sings, Marsala loses his temper and throws a punch. Marsala entertains, Marsala explodes. Though Benno would've bet if Bebe exploded, it would be with sadness, not anger.

Poor Bebe.

Then Benno felt a hand on his shoulder and he got a kiss on his cheek. There's Eleanor Ree in this unbelievable blue dress, cleavage you could wriggle in nice. "Sal, aren't you going to introduce me to your friends?"

Bell stood up. Oh yes, this was the most beautiful woman in the world. "Hello," he managed.

"Are you the lucky girl who's with Sal?" she said to Imogene, who, mouth open, pointed to Nina.

"Take good care of him," Ree said. "He's a keeper." And then she was over there with Vincenzo the Fireman and Hennie's two sisters and if that ain't a smart move I don't know what is.

"Told you," Benno said. "She loves me."

Ronnie Oliver brought the band to the stage, the combo in tuxedos. They gave the audience some Basie so they would settle down and then came one of the tunes from Bebe's long ago done with pep. Benno snapped his fingers on the two and four, and he wasn't the only one.

The music went quiet and then only the bass pumped.

Spotlight.

Bebe.

The crowd cheered him good and solid; here and there, people rose to their feet. Bebe had a bounce in his step, the California sparkle, his blue eyes twinkling in the spotlight. He went right into "All of Me," Billie Holiday style, crooning along with the bass, keeping his voice steady and low.

Then "Sweet Lorraine," but when they came to the tricky bridge, Bebe let the trumpet take it. Holding the mic down by his thigh, he did a little dance spin to hide a cough. But then the ballads went beautifully. Imogene leaned against Bell and Benno and Nina exchanged this cute look. Maybe a little heat was building between them. Taking a chance, Benno reached for Nina's hand and she surrendered. And when Bebe went into the "Casablanca" song, Nina snuggled against him. From across the room, Ree gave Benno a smile he knew he'd never forget.

"Ladies and gentlemen, I can't tell you how good it is to be back home," Marsala told the audience. "New York City. Bright lights, big town. Our town." He took a sip from a teacup and returned it to the velvet-topped stool they had there for him. "Memories, huh? So many beautiful memories."

The saxophone player came in low and bluesy. Marsala said, "They tell me you like this one. I do, too." And then, he sang that old familiar tune Ree's ex rearranged and it went over like milk chocolate, the audience on their feet when it was over. "Thanks, folks. A hell of ride. Thank you."

Then came the Cuban-style number and halfway through Bebe waved and said, "Good night" with a big smile and blew everybody a kiss. The band kept playing as he left the stage.

"He cut it short, Sal?" Bell said across the table.

Benno watched as Enna excused himself and walked calmly through the cheering crowd to the dressing room. Then Benno did the same, telling Nina he'd be right back. Like Enna, he kept his expression cool, like he didn't suspect nothing, and he didn't look at Corini neither.

"Lightheaded," Marsala said as Enna settled him into the dressing room's armchair. "I couldn't work through it."

Benno stood by the door. He heard the band at work, keeping the crowd entertained.

"No encore?" Enna said, a note of hope in his voice.

"No can do." Marsala coughed into his handkerchief. "I hope I'm not coming down with a flu."

Enna folded his arms. "I'd better let Ollie know."

Marsala nodded. "Apologize to Anthony. Tell him we'll slay 'em double tomorrow."

Benno stepped aside as Enna hurried out.

Marsala coughed again. He looked into his handkerchief, then held it up for Benno to see. It was dotted with blood.

"Sal," he said, "can you get me home?"

"Sure. You want Eleanor, Bebe?"

"Let's do this on the QT," Marsala said as he stood, his face pale under the stage makeup.

Benno held out an arm. "Lean on me."

The doorman flagged a cab. Benno hurried the singer to its backseat.

Thirty-five minutes later, Benno returned to the club to find Bell and the girls nursing coffee. Most of the crowd was gone, including Corini and his wife.

"Where have you been?" Bell asked as Benno sat.

He looked across the room at Enna and gave his head a little shake.

Bell said, "They want the table for the next show?"

"There's no next show," Benno replied.

The suite at the Hampshire House was vast and empty. The scent of chicken soup lingered in the air and Marsala, in his silk pajamas and robe, rubbed his neck with a mentholated balm. He felt like shit.

And then she arrived.

Thank God she arrived.

"You were wonderful, Bill," she said as she tossed her coat on the sofa.

"No, I had to call it a night," he replied as he came to kiss her cheek. "Could you tell?"

"Not really. Not until Rico said you were fighting a cold," she said as she continued to undress. "With all the travel you've been up to, it's no wonder."

By now, she was out of her dress and in her bra, slip and stockings, her shoes kicked across the bedroom. "You want a drink?" she asked.

"I can't, baby. The pipes are acting up."

Ree hurried across the living room. "You sounded fine."

"For half a set, sure."

"No one minded."

"The folks who turned out for the second show might."

"They love you, Bill. They'll understand. Ordinary people catch colds, too."

He perched on the sofa's arm, a slipper dangling on the end of his foot, lit cigarette between his fingers. "How was my father?"

"He only mentioned Rosa twice. But he apologized immediately. Bill, he's a sweet old man. Your Aunt Dee's quite the character."

"Did you talk to Winchell?"

She topped off the glass with a splash of quinine. "He talked to me. Does that count?"

Marsala watched as she came toward him. She put the cold glass against his lips. He took a sip.

"Finally," she purred. "Solitude."

He stood. "What's with the steamer trunks, Eleanor?" he asked.

"Bill. Not now."

"The trunks, El."

She kissed his lips and took his hand. "I have to go. A job."

"Where?"

"Far away, Bill. It's killing me."

He looked deep into her eyes. "Where, baby?"

"Africa. Southeast Africa."

The news sent a charge from his head to his heels. "When were you going to tell me?"

"I still don't want to tell you, Bill. Don't make me. Not tonight." She pressed against him and hung her arms around his neck, the hissing drink now behind him.

"For how long?"

"Are you angry, Bill?"

He wasn't. He was melting in sorrow, the world slipping away. "How long am I going to be without you?"

She said, "We'll have Thanksgiving in London. And a long Christmas break in Rome."

"You'll be away a few months," he said.

She stepped back. "It can't be. I couldn't bear it."

Marsala crushed out the cigarette and without thinking, lit another. Panic rising, he began to pace. "Baby, you've opened a trapdoor. That's one heck of a surprise. A real doozy."

"I wanted to tell you, but only when you were back on top. And you are, Bill. You're on top."

He blew smoke toward the ceiling.

"You'll knock them dead at the Caribbean. You'll have another number-one hit, and it'll be jazz like you wanted. Then onto Vegas. Bill, it's happening for you and I'm delighted."

"But what's it mean without you?"

"Without me? Like I won't be thinking of you every crazy minute we're apart." She intercepted him and grabbed his chin.

"Look at me. I love you. I'm over the moon for you. Do you have any idea how proud I was tonight?"

She was inches away yet Marsala already felt abandoned.

Afterward, his body sated but his mind alive, he took two sleeping pills and nested next to her warm, naked body. When he woke up many hours later, she was gone.

"I love you always," said the note pinned to the door. "Always and forever."

He cleared his aching throat. To the empty room, he said angrily, "What does she think I am? A child? 'Always and forever'? What the fuck is that?"

Robe flowing behind him, he stormed into the kitchen, turned the flame on under the teapot and called Enna, who was in a deep sleep. "Find Mal Weisberg and get me everything on the picture," he demanded, his voice coarse. "I want the name of every grip, every crane operator, every caterer, every fuckin' Ubangi in that jungle."

Rubbing his forehead, Enna said, "Yes, Bill."

"Do it now."

"All right—"

Marsala slammed down the phone.

Boo Chiasso wasn't much for subways, but he did all right. He left Gigenti's storefront on Mulberry Street, got on the BMT and arrived near Rockefeller Center, where the Dunney Commission had its New York headquarters. Head high, shoulders squared, he bowled through the business crowd, went through a gold revolving door and entered the RCA Building. He was sent upstairs to

see a man named Tyler, who introduced himself as an investiga-
tor for the Department of Justice.

The room was barely big enough to hold a desk and some
chairs. Keeping his coat on, Chiasso sat facing cooing pigeons
on the ledge and musty blinds sloping at the jamb. The windows
were filthy.

"How can I help you, Mr. Chiasso?"

"I need immunity," he replied, crossing his long legs.

"From what?"

"You know what. It's a matter of time."

"Well then, why don't we serve you here and now? You can
tell your story under oath."

"I haven't killed nobody," Boo Chiasso lied.

"I don't know if that's true. With narcotics, you can't ever say."

"I'm not involved in drugs."

"Mr. Chiasso, please. We're extremely busy here."

Tyler knew who Chiasso was. Domenico Mistretta told him
when he came in and laid out his entire operation. In his lucid
moments, the man the crew called Mimmo was a fountain of useful information. As Senator Dunney himself said, "Thank heav-
ens for a man with a perceived grievance."

"Everybody you call ends up dead," Chiasso said.

"Not everybody." Tyler opened a folder. "But I'd contend that
the Department of Justice isn't to blame."

"Oh yeah," he snorted. "Some coincidence."

"What do you have for us, Mr. Chiasso?"

"Immunity," he repeated.

Tyler sighed. "Mr. Chiasso..."

"Maybe I could tell you who took out Fredo Pellizzari."
Chiasso withdrew his cigarettes from his coat pocket. When
he brought one to his lips, Tyler offered him a light. "It was

the same guy who hit Mimmo," Chiasso said as he settled back.

"Mimmo. Would that would be your boss, Domenico Mistretta?"

"Not no more he ain't."

"Ah."

"I'll give you the gunman for immunity."

Tyler already knew Eugenio Zamarella was the hitter on Pellizzari and Mistretta. The bullet Bell turned over matched the one that passed through Pellizzari's head; both were a match to Zamarella's Carcano bolt-action rifle, found under the floorboards in his bedroom out in Rego Park.

"Mr. Chiasso, you've misread the scope of the investigation. Our purpose is to understand the tie-ups between the rackets, business and politics."

"Who can help you do that?"

"It's an open hearing. The witness list is a matter of public record. Does it lead you to believe we're investigating the murder of your friends and associates?"

"Mimmo's on the list," Chiasso said.

"As is Anthony Corini."

"So maybe you *are* looking at murder."

"You'll have to do better than Gus Uccello in the 1920s. Are you suggesting you have recent information that implicates Mr. Corini?"

"In murder? Let me think about that."

Tyler stood and looked out the window. He began counting the water towers on the East Side roofs, a trick he used to maintain his silence. Next, he'd try to recall the home addresses of the 57 men and one woman on the witness list, more than half of whom, if you included attorneys with clients in government, were associated with the city of New York.

"Maybe if you asked me a question," Chiasso said finally.

"Who ordered the hit on Mr. Pellizzari?"

"I heard it was Corini."

"But you don't have firsthand knowledge."

"I wasn't there, if that's you're asking me."

"Then it's hearsay, Mr. Chiasso. We'll need something of substance before we can negotiate. For example, your organization's money—"

Chiasso scoffed. "My organization."

"—money comes from various enterprises throughout the county—kickbacks, the numbers racket, horse racing, nightclubs, prostitution, narcotics. Then it goes out. To whom?"

"I'm in New Jersey," Chiasso said. "What goes on in New York City I wouldn't know."

"You're saying Mr. Corini knows."

"He talks to politicians all the time."

Tyler nodded. He sat on the window ledge, his back to the city. "But on occasion, you've been given responsibility for the distribution of funds outside New Jersey. Am I correct?"

"I'm not sure. What do you want to know?"

"Tell me about the money that was sent to Havana for Carlo Farcolini."

"They did that?"

"We have a witness, Mr. Chiasso. Where did the money come from?"

Chiasso stood, dusted his coat and went for his hat. "No immunity and I say Cy Geller was probably responsible. Maybe Ziggy Baum, too. The Jews."

"So you do know."

"No immunity and I say Cy Geller and Ziggy Baum."

Tyler walked to the office door. "Did you get what they sent you for?" he asked.

"I seen what I seen."

"Extend our greetings to Mr. Gigenti," said Tyler as he reached for the knob.

In the early morning's silvery light, Benno was driving his uncle's jalopy and next to him was Bebe, baggy-eyed and droopy in his gorgeous camel's hair coat, paisley ascot and burgundy scarf. Maybe an hour ago, Benno came into the store straight from the fruit and fish run. As he dropped a crate, the phone rang.

Bebe, whispering scared. "Sal…"

Alarmed, Benno said, "Bebe, what? What happened?"

"Let's ride, Sal," Bebe replied. "Please."

"OK, Bebe," Benno said.

Jesus, Benno thought as he barreled through the tunnel, this guy's got nobody.

Now he was back on the Jersey side, River Road going north toward the George Washington Bridge, Bebe over there like he was drying up. When Marsala rolled down the windows to flick out his cigarette, the Hudson came in smelling like oil and raw sewage.

"Drink that soup, Bebe," Benno said. He'd asked his aunt to come down and fill up a thermos.

"I'm good, kid," he whispered.

"Then sleep, why don't you?" Though he was zipping along on a swerving road, trucks in the next lane and behind him, too, Benno started to wriggle out of his leather jacket for Marsala to use as a blanket.

"No, no, Sal. I'm fine."

"Hey, Bebe. Not for nothing, but Eleanor loves you. The way she looks at you. *Madonna mio.* Guys would kill for that look."

Marsala managed a lifeless smile. He was sure the clits were back but this time he couldn't run, not with Corini breathing on him, despite rumors of a downfall via the Dunney Commission. Marsala knew he was being judged and couldn't understand why: He could earn at the Sandpiper in Vegas—the reviews from Los Angeles, the hit record, the radio show's popularity and now the residence at Corini's own joint proved he could. He was on the straight and narrow, true to Eleanor, respectful to Rosa, a good father, a good Joe to reporters and columnists. Perplexed and with no one to talk to, his depression deepened. He got it into his head that Corini was calculating whether he should be allowed to live. Frankie Fortune, who was supposed to be guiding his career, had disappeared. They killed Ziggy Baum, who dropped the ball. Mimmo they threw in the gutter. The guys in charge of me, Marsala thought, go down.

This he had to face without Eleanor. Already his life was reduced to meaningless routine. His anger spent, he concealed his anguish and gave a professional performance, and then retreated to the hotel for a restless sleep, the pills failing to combat the sense the bed was a sad, lonely place. He woke up before dawn with his throat red and raw. He vomited, nerves overcoming reason. He was lost, aware he couldn't face the world alone. He needed somebody to tell him he was all right.

"Maybe you should pick a fight with some guy," Benno suggested. "Get the blood going. Let's call your old trumpet noodge."

Passing under the bridge, Bebe said, "Sal, do me a favor, make a left here, go around a circle there, take a quiet side street." Soon Benno pulled into a cemetery.

Bebe told him to keep going. "Park over there," he said, pointing.

They got out of the car and Benno walked with Marsala across the spotty grass, the tree branches a web of gnarled fingers, everything foreboding, tombstones, dead flowers, silence save the crunch of the turf underfoot. Then there it was. Rosiglino, it said in big stone letters above the bronze door, Bebe's original name, the mausoleum the size of a garage, fancy columns and compassionate angels with half-moon wings.

Benno stopped, but Marsala continued like he was going inside the tomb. He put his bare hands on the door. After a moment, he began to whimper. "Mama. Help me, Mama."

Benno shivered.

"Mama," Marsala said, "tell me what to do."

Benno expected Marsala to faint, but the singer blessed himself and bowed his head in prayer.

Benno did, too.

His eyes ringed red, Marsala came down the path.

"What did Hennie tell you?" Benno asked.

Marsala shook his head. "She's not talking to me."

"Ah, Bebe. Don't say that. She was proud of you."

"Kid, if I couldn't sing she would've thrown me in the gutter."

Benno didn't say nothing because everybody in Narrows Gate knew that was true.

Bell was rattling around the house, his father's scent still in the air. Crates he'd brought from the A&P were scattered across the landing. He had so much to do but soon he didn't do anything but stand and stare, thinking himself a poor excuse for a son. He'd done that for days.

He was so deep in his thoughts that he missed the doorbell the first time it rang. Then it called again repeatedly, as if it were stuck. Pulling back the curtains, he looked into the darkness and turned on the porch light. There was Tyler in a suit, no topcoat, meaning he'd just got out of his car right in the middle of Narrows Gate where everyone could see.

"Leo," he said as he rushed in, pulling along the night air. "I haven't heard from you."

"Shouldn't you be preparing your witnesses?" The hearings across the river started on Monday.

"Where have you been?"

Bell walked toward the parlor and sat in his father's seat, sinking into the cushion. "Nowhere but here, Charlie."

The floor of the fireplace was littered with cold ash.

Tyler remained standing. "I'm going to talk to Salvatore Benno."

"No," Bell said. "I gave you Mimmo. That's enough."

"I wasn't asking your permission, Leo."

Bell saw desperation. "Marsala took the bag to Cuba. Get Mimmo to tell you he gave it to a messenger to take to Bebe."

"Mistretta says he doesn't remember."

"OK. Tell him that's what happened. Make him remember."

"What did Benno say? Will he testify?"

"I didn't ask him."

Tyler started to pace. Suddenly, he threw up his hands in frustration. "Fuck it. I'm calling him."

"You'll be blown to shit if you do."

Tyler stared down at Bell. "Meaning?"

"Maybe somebody calls Winchell. Somebody tells him the commission can't work a half-wit like Mimmo to get what it needs. Maybe somebody calls Hearst and tells him you guys are protecting Bebe."

"You'd do that?"

Bell shrugged. "I gave you Mimmo. My conscience is clear."

"You'd put yourself on the wrong side?"

"If you ever had a friend, you'd know there's only one side." Bell put his hands on his thighs and hoisted off the sofa.

"You've killed yourself, Leo. I hope you know that. You're dead in Washington."

"Charlie, I was already dead. You guys haven't kept your word yet." With a flick of a finger, he signaled to Tyler to follow him to the door. As he leaned against the newel-post, he saw his father's hat hanging on the rack next to his well-worn vicuña coat.

"Call Bebe," Bell said. "You've got a question about the suit-case, call Bebe."

"Then it's a circus." Tyler was sweating.

"All right. It's a circus."

CHAPTER THIRTY-EIGHT

Under the television cameras and the glaring lights, the Senate Criminal Investigation Committee hearings at the U.S. Courthouse in Foley Square proceeded with dry determination. The committee's slow-talking chief counsel set out to introduce into the record names of the organization's members who operated in and around New York City. As Alvin Dunney and five fellow senators watched from their perch, witnesses testified to a relationship with Anthony Corini, who existed at "the axis of commerce and criminality," according to one senator, a Democrat from Rhode Island. Witnesses included the chairman of the association that operated several racetracks in the area; a former union organizer who had a scar that ran under an eye and across his nose; a cop from upstate whose wife saved $180,000 on his weekly salary of $142; and a businessman from Queens who was described as "influential in Republican circles"—causing the senators from Vermont and Michigan to recuse themselves while he was on the stand. The man from Queens testified that the mayor's office had recommended several companies Corini owned either directly or by proxy, but otherwise the morning was a dud. When a dozing man in the back of the crowded courtroom let out a roaring snore, Dunney laid on the drawl to say, "I know how you feel, sir. We will try to make this afternoon a little more to your liking."

After a break for lunch, they brought in Mimmo. "Where's the television?" he said, though the bright lights bounced off his sunglasses.

The attorney Corini sent went "Ssh."

"Go fuck yourself," Mimmo told him as he found his seat.

"I'm Domenico Mistretta," he said after he was sworn in. "I got a house in Narrows Gate and I got another house down the shore in Deal."

"What do you do for a living, Mr. Mistretta?" asked Sam Bamberger, the beagle-eyed chief counsel.

"I run the Blue Onyx Lounge."

"Given your real-estate holdings, would I be safe in assuming the Blue Onyx Lounge is a profitable enterprise?"

Mimmo said, "It's so good somebody might burn it down."

"Sir?"

"Why don't you come and see for yourself? On the house."

A ripple of laughter. Dunney smiled, too.

"Senator, I know what you really want—"

"I'm not a senator, sir—"

"Which one's the senator?" Mimmo asked his attorney.

"Up there," he said, pointing to the platform, where shoulder-to-shoulder lawmakers and staff were flanked by the U.S. and the state of New York flags. Two stenographers' fingers danced across their machines.

"Who's Dunney?"

Each senator had a nameplate.

"I'm Senator Dunney, Mr. Mistretta." The collar of Dunney's shirt seemed too large; anticipating photos, he wore a new necktie.

Mimmo said, "You want to know how I make my money."

"That is correct," Dunney replied. "Among other things."

"Ask."

Bamberger said, "Mr. Mistretta…"

"Ask," Mimmo repeated. "I got nothing to hide."

Dunney looked at Mistretta and saw a man teetering toward caricature. In Chicago, the clowns won. He wasn't going to let it happen here. "How do you make your money, Mr. Mistretta?"

"I gamble and I gamble good."

"Is that all?"

"That's enough."

Again, laughter from the gallery. The press, lubricated at lunch, scribbled furiously.

Referring to notes on a yellow pad, Bamberger asked, "Is it not true that you are one of the owners of the Cangemi Linen Supply Company?"

"True. The laundry. Yes."

"Can you tell us the other owners' names, Mr. Mistretta?"

Suddenly, Mimmo's mind went blank. The other owners' names?

"I bet boxing," he said finally. "Prizefighting." He tapped the side of his head. "I know a good boy when I see him."

"Yes sir. Regarding Cangemi—"

"I like the ponies, too," he continued. "I got a system and it don't fail."

Bamberger turned to the panel. Dunney nodded discretely.

"A system?" Dunney said.

"Bet across the board. A long shot shows and you do better than a big favorite running strong." A wink was hidden by his dark lens. "You come to the track with me, Senator, I'll show you."

"I just might do that."

Laughter.

"Mr. Mistretta, what we're trying to ascertain is who are your associates in the linen supply company," Dunney said.

"Anthony can tell you," Mimmo replied. "He knows."

"Anthony Corini," Bamberger said.

"That's him."

Satisfied, Bamberger moved on. "Mr. Mistretta, you also have a stake in several restaurants in the area."

"Yeah," he nodded. "Frankie's joints."

"This would be Frankie Fortune. Fortunato Spaletti."

"Frankie Fortune."

"You are close to Mr. Fortune, are you not?"

He leaned close to the microphone. "I know Frankie since we were kids."

"How did you meet?"

"At the reformatory in Chemung."

For the next several minutes, Mimmo was walked through his history. Alert again, he replied carefully, avoiding incriminating himself. The chief counsel helped. He didn't want the man who was giving testimony that would implicate Corini to be exposed as anything more than a corrupt nightclub owner who had interests in businesses that laundered money from the Farcolini crew's illegal activities. Nor would he want it known that the witness suffered from an advanced case of syphilis.

"Does Mr. Corini have a stake in these restaurants as well?"

"As well as who? Bruno?" Mimmo shook his head. "Bruno's not interested in lounges and laundries and restaurants. Bruno likes the gutter."

"Excuse me?" Dunney said.

"Bruno likes the gutter. What, you think Zamarella could decide who he wants to hit?"

"Mr. Mistretta," Bamberger said, "are you telling the commission that Bruno Gigenti ordered Mr. Zamarella to kill?"

"Absolutely."

The press looked at each other as they hurried their notes. Mimmo's attorney struggled to protest.

"Quiet," Dunney said. "Let the man have his say."

Bamberger wanted to move on, but Dunney waved him off. "Mr. Mistretta, you know this as a fact?"

"Come on, Senator. Who don't know this? You think Zamarella wakes up and thinks, 'Today, I'll shoot Ziggy'? What do you think he was up in Canada for? Sightseeing?" Mimmo waved a hand dismissively. "Ah, this guy didn't piss without Bruno saying go."

"Senator, may we have a short recess?" said Mimmo's lawyer, red-faced. "I need—"

"Sit," Dunney said.

Bamberger pressed. "Mr. Mistretta, about the restaurants—"

Mimmo pointed a thumb to reporters' row. "Ask them. They'll tell you. Bruno likes the gutter."

The senator from Rhode Island whispered to Dunney, who nodded.

"Mr. Mistretta," Dunney said, "I think we have a sense of your activities and your relationship with Mr. Anthony Corini. I thank you very much for your time and your frank—"

"Wait a second," Mimmo said. "Ain't you going to ask me about Bebe?"

"I'm sorry, sir…"

"Bebe. Bill Marsala. I know things about him, too."

Bamberger sagged at the new detour. He hadn't yet asked Mistretta about the cement companies, carting businesses, trucking firms, garbage haulers and talent agencies from which Corini,

Fortunato Spaletti, Mistretta and others were paid salaries that seemed impossible given the firms' revenues.

"Bill Marsala the singer?" Dunney asked, feigning surprise.

"Bill Marsala the singer. We call him Bebe. Short for ball buster."

"I see."

"Oh no, no, you don't." Mimmo wagged a finger. "This guy, Mister Hollywood Big Shot, he's...*Que cosa fastidiosa.*"

"I'm sorry—"

"You know. A regular pain in the ass."

"All right, then."

Mimmo sat back triumphant.

Marsala woke from his pre-show nap at the Caribbean to find Enna with a hangdog look, holding a newspaper behind his back. And there was Benno, the Sicilian Speedy Alka-Seltzer, drooping like somebody let the air out.

"What?" Marsala cleared his aching throat and threw off the towel around his neck. "What is it?"

"Bill," said Enna.

"Bebe," said Benno.

Marsala shot up in the chair. "Eleanor?"

"No, no, Bill."

"Better give him the paper, Rico," Benno said as he leaned against the dressing room door.

Marsala stood and, though he wasn't wearing pants, wriggled quickly into his loafers. He held out his hand and Enna surrendered the *Daily News.*

"Marsala's Uncle Sings" screamed the headline. Underneath, it read, "Mob Turncoat Rats Out Corini, Gigenti." The rest of the front page was covered with a big photo of Mimmo, in his sunglasses, coming down the courthouse steps, uniformed cops on either side. He looked like a vulture that'd just finished a satisfying meal.

Benno watched as Marsala opened to page three to follow the story. He read it, then sat and read it again, bobbing his head as he scanned the text.

"It doesn't say what he told them about me," Marsala said finally.

"I don't believe he said anything, Bill."

Marsala read a quote. "'I know things about him.'"

"But they didn't follow up. Bill, they're not interested in you. They want the mayor. Congressmen."

"And Corini," Benno said. "Mimmo was ready to fuck him good."

"Maybe they talked to him afterwards. In chambers," Marsala said.

"I don't believe so, Bill."

"What does Corini say?"

"I don't know. I couldn't reach him."

"Isn't he here?"

Enna shook his head.

Marsala leapt from the chair. "Don't you know what that means? I'm fucked. Corini's washing his hands of me. That's it."

"Bebe, don't get fucked up over this," Benno said. "One, you got a show and two, how can Mr. Corini be in public with you after Mimmo and this Dunney son of a bitch?"

Marsala's eyes darted from Benno to Enna, Enna to Benno. "Did he send a message, at least?"

Enna said no.

"He knows something. Mimmo talked to them."

"Bill, it doesn't make sense. The—"

"Of course, it does. Of course." He grimaced as he coughed. "Look what they asked him: What does Corini own? Then Mimmo tells them Corini owns Marsala."

Enna said, "They aren't after you. The politicians and Anthony and Don Carlo's operation, but not you. Bill, listen to me, you go out there tonight and you kick ass. There's not a soul in that audience who isn't behind you."

"They don't give a fuck about all this," Benno added. "You're their guy." He felt for the singer, whose panic was mounting.

Eyes wide, Marsala flung the *News* on the dressing room floor and kicked it into the air.

"That's it, Bebe. Get mad."

"Bill, when Dunney and the commission leave town, you'll still be here at the Caribbean. Knockin' them dead with your number-one hit record."

"Hey, Bebe," Benno said, "you're from Polk Street. Tell them where they can stick it."

Marsala stared at Benno. Then he relaxed and let out a chuckle. "You're right, kid." He turned to Enna. "You know something, Ricky? This kid knows. He knows." The singer went to the mirror and began to unbutton his shirt. "Ricky, do me a favor and get them to give you some hot tea."

Enna nodded and left the dressing room. As soon as Benno closed the door, Marsala spun and said, "What can you find out, kid?"

"Maybe you could get your father to talk to Mimmo. But I think you've got to say 'Fuck it.'"

"Can you call Corini?"

"Looks desperate. He knows I'll be doing it for you, no?"

"There's got to—"

"You know, your voice sounds worser by the minute, Bebe. You OK?"

"My throat's raw."

"No shit."

"But this thing. Sal, this thing…These guys want to fuck me. They want to fuck me."

"What guys? The feds? They want information. You know how cops work. They squeeze you until you give up a guy they're after. You don't, *then* they fuck you."

Benno pointed Marsala toward a chair and sat across from him. "Maybe you could tell your buddy Winchell that Mimmo's got the syph and remind him he's Rosa's uncle, not yours. Tell them the Mistrettas hate you and that explains everything."

"You tell him."

"Me? You want me to talk to Walter Winchell?" Benno laughed. "Holy shit, Bebe."

"It's easy, kid."

"For you, maybe. Look, call him on the QT. Tell him. It's the truth, ain't it?"

Marsala nodded. "Maybe you're right."

"Of course I'm right. Fight back, Bebe." Benno stood and tapped Marsala on his bony knee. "I'll see you after the show."

"Sal. Thank you."

He meant it sincerely and Benno knew it. As he went to find a good spot in the balcony where he could mind his own business, Benno worried. Leo was right. They're going to pressure Bebe unbelievable. And right now, Bebe's got one thing—his career—and they can take it. They can take it like that. Benno snapped his fingers. Like that.

Marsala cut the set short again, his voice faltering, and Ronnie Oliver signaled the band to cover the raspy notes. Even when he was on target, he sounded like he did on that piece-of-shit pop tune, like some ordinary guy. Benno knew Bebe was distracted— he hardly spoke to the audience; none of this, "We're on a hell of ride, folks" and "Ain't life grand?" The capacity crowd knew, too, and an uncomfortable murmur rippled around the room. Say something, Bebe, Benno thought. They love you, they want you to do good. Explain. Mimmo's got a worm in his melon and you feel bad for Rosa and Bill Jr.—they're embarrassed by her uncle's behavior. Make it water off a duck's back.

But from the back of the house, it looked to Benno like Bebe was going to forget the words to songs he's been singing for about a decade, his eyes blank, his mind racing like a squirrel. He did a pretty good job on the new hit, but then he rushed through the Cuban "All or Nothing at All."

Marsala waved, blew a kiss and he was gone.

Benno scuttled between tables to the dressing room while Oliver and the band continued the song. When he knocked the code and Enna sprung open the door, he saw the mirror was in pieces on the floor and so was the teacup and saucer, the *Daily News* a soggy mess, like somebody put it down after a bad dog.

"Sal, get the car," Enna instructed as Marsala toweled off.

Slipping into his coat, Benno waited, knowing Marsala's habits. The singer quickly took off his tux and though he was rushing, his face frozen hard in anger, he folded his slacks and carefully placed them on the hanger and then the jacket and into the suit bag they went. Benno grabbed it, crunching glass underfoot.

"I'll be around back," he said to Enna. He opened the door and found a cop standing there and a guy in a suit and topcoat, his face red from the harsh night wind.

The guy stepped in. "Mr. Marsala," he said, "my name is Charles Tyler and I represent the Department of Justice."

"Good for you," Marsala said as he continued to dress.

"Senator Dunney would like to speak to you."

Marsala stopped.

Enna said, "Can't this wait? Mr. Marsala isn't feeling—"

"When?" Marsala asked, looking over his agent's shoulder.

"Tonight."

"Where?"

Tyler told him the commission had offices at Rockefeller Center.

"They'll recognize me," Marsala said.

"We'll address that."

Benno knew Tyler was the guy Leo worked for in the Army and the son of a bitch who wanted him in front of Dunney because of the fuckin' suitcase.

"Give the guy a break, huh?" he said. "Ain't it bad enough you put him in the papers with crazy Mimmo?"

"Sal, let it go," Marsala said in Sicilian. He looked at Tyler. "What's your plan?"

"After midnight, through the garage, up a private elevator. In and out."

Marsala knotted his tie. "And if I say no?"

Tyler took a subpoena out of his inside pocket. "You'll precede Mr. Corini on the stand. Or you'll be cited for contempt of Congress."

"You must be desperate," Marsala said, as offhandedly as he could muster.

"Actually, we had a very good day, Mr. Marsala."

A light rain had begun to fall and the windshield wipers on Bruno Gigenti's car pumped erratically as his driver waited on Mulberry.

The door to the club opened and a guard nodded, his hat dotted with moisture. Gigenti emerged, sliding quickly into the backseat.

"Williamsburg Bridge," he said, sounding like he'd gargled broken glass.

"South Street OK, Boss?"

Gigenti grunted.

"Broadway to Myrtle?"

"I'll think about it," he replied.

Soon they were coming off Bushwick Avenue, a left here, another left, a turn against the traffic light. Gigenti's house was on the right.

"*Arresto,*" said Gigenti, who had been thinking in Sicilian.

The car skidded on the damp street.

Gigenti stepped out. Turning up his collar, he started toward his home, his head down.

When he looked up, he saw, coming toward him out of the cold mist, a man in shirt sleeves, a tie and slacks, no coat, no hat, his hands high, palms open.

Frankie Fortune.

Gigenti produced a .38 Special and without breaking stride, he pointed it at Fortune's face, the hammer already cocked.

On the other side of the street, a man stepped to his porch, a rifle raised and aimed at Fortune's head.

"*Sono venuto a chiedere scusa,*" Fortune said so everyone could hear.

Gigenti kept walking. "Apologize?" he said in English. "Beginning when?"

"You win, Bruno." Rain soaked through Fortune's shirt. "It's over. You win."

"I win." He said it plainly, a fact.

"Let me straighten out this mess."

"What mess? There's no mess."

They were a few feet apart now and the .38 Special was still fixed on the center of Fortune's flawless face.

"Mimmo."

"He's a dead man."

"As a token of my esteem, Bruno. As an admission of my guilt."

"And then what?" Gigenti asked.

"Anthony."

"Ah," Gigenti said as he put the cold nozzle of his gun against Fortune's forehead.

"You don't want him talking to the commission," Fortune said as he pulled down his hands. "He's not Mimmo, but…"

"But what?" Gigenti still didn't know why he shouldn't kill Fortune right here and now.

"They won't think he's insane, Bruno."

"Like Mimmo."

"Like Mimmo."

"Maybe I put one in your brain and Anthony understands everything."

"Not in front of your house, Bruno," Fortune said, shivering.

Gigenti slowly released the hammer. "Maybe Anthony's not the problem."

"Dunney," Fortune nodded. He let out a long sigh of relief. "Let me offer you a solution there, too. Another thing that won't touch you."

CHAPTER THIRTY-NINE

There wasn't much in the apartment under the viaduct, but as he packed away his books and started to take down the travel-magazine photos Imogene pinned to the wall, Bell felt a rush of sentimentality. It had been their little haven, a broke-down sanctuary, and he was swept by vivid memories not only of their lovemaking but the conversations afterward, the tenderness, jokes she'd made or how she'd put on his shirt when she ran to the rusty bathroom down the hall and he sat on the bed waiting for her return. There was no need for the apartment now—his father gone, he and Imogene were free to be together at his home—but in his mind, here was where they fell in love.

Lost in his reverie, at first Bell didn't hear the thud on the steps and the groan of the old wood. When he did, he was annoyed that Tyler found it.

Bell opened the door. "Charlie, goddamn—"

It wasn't Tyler. It was Boo Chiasso, his face all shadows and angles, his wide shoulders filling the landing. He pushed back his hat and took a long, deep breath.

"Did something happen to Sal?" Bell asked.

Chiasso dug into his topcoat pocket like he was feeling for his cigarettes. Seconds later, he had a .45 in his fist.

"Back up," he said. "Get back in the room."

"Boo?"

"Move, Ding."

Bell retreated, hands up, palms open.

Chiasso nudged him and Bell banged into the bed.

"Sit down," Chiasso said.

"You'd better think this through."

Chiasso raised the gun and brought the butt down above Bell's forehead. A gash opened, blood spurted and Bell collapsed, slamming against the edge of the bare mattress and bouncing to the floor.

Coming to two or three minutes later, Bell blinked and felt for the blood on his face before he rolled over. He struggled to the old chair in the corner, knocking aside a crate half-filled with books.

Chiasso sat across from Bell on the mattress. "Fuckin' cozy in here," he said, looking around.

Bell felt his brain pounding under the wound. When he bent to retrieve his glasses, blood spurted again. Chiasso had gotten him good.

"What's going on?" Bell asked again.

"You talk to the feds."

Bell dabbed at the gash in his head. "You mean the guy who tried to serve me in Beverly Hills?"

"The guy who came to see you at your old man's house," Chiasso replied. "This guy we know. He's with the commission and he talks to you."

"Tyler," Bell said. "We were in the Army together."

"You told him about the thing."

"What thing?"

"Don't be an asshole, Ding. The thing. *Our* thing."

Bell said, "I don't know the thing. I don't know shit."

"You know Benno and Benno tells you. And you, being a Jew, sold us out."

Bell glared at him, but he had no play. Chiasso was squared on the bed, the gun on his thigh, finger on the trigger. The nozzle was aimed at Bell's stomach.

"What do you need, Boo? What Tyler knows?"

"Too late to deal, Ding." He stared hard and cold.

Fat Tutti made the call. "We got trouble," he said.

Mimmo had been dead asleep. He had clouds in his head, half his mind in outer space. But then he remembered: He'd made his move and to hell with all of them that treated him like he was some stain, and Bebe, a first-class bum.

"Mimmo. You there?" Tutti said.

"Carlo?" The boss was calling to tell him he was right to stand up, Gigenti and that smug fuck Corini fuckin' up the entire enterprise.

"Mimmo, it's Tutti, for Christ's sake." He was out of breath standing still. "We got trouble."

Fat Tutti? "What time is it?" He groped the nightstand for his dark glasses.

"Mimmo, the feds are in the store."

"The candy store?" he asked as he sat up. Little tufts of gray hair peeked above the rim of his undershirt, his comb-over sticking this way and that. He swung his legs over the side of the bed. "Those motherfuckers. You're at the store?"

"I'm at the store," Tutti told him.

"I'll be right there. Don't do nothing."

He dressed as fast as he could. His wife, they could drop the atom bomb in Narrows Gate, she wouldn't hear it while she slept. He grabbed his hat and was out the front door, he didn't even brush his teeth.

He noticed the darkness first, the streetlamp in front of his house all of a sudden broken. And then the black town car at the curb, the engine running.

"Hello, Mimmo," said Frankie Fortune. He was standing right next to him on the stoop, his back against the sandy stone.

Mimmo sank. "They brought you back for this?"

"For what, Mimmo?" he asked as he nudged him down the steps toward the car.

They couldn't give me one fuckin' day to enjoy what I done, Mimmo thought. They couldn't let me see myself a man again. "One question."

Looking left, right, Fortune said, "Go ahead."

"Why did you burn down the Saint Tropez? The Saint Tropez was better than that dump. The Lakeside, it was a dump."

"All right, Mimmo," Fortune said as he felt the stiletto under his sleeve.

The meeting began at three in the morning, New York City slowing down and Rockefeller Center dead, the ice rink shuttered, gold Prometheus floating in darkness. Benno brought Enna's car to the garage entrance like Tyler told them. Enna sat in the front seat with him, Bebe in back with a jowly, white-haired lawyer nobody introduced Benno to, but his name was Leland Archibald. Everybody was quiet like they were in church waiting for Mass to begin, Bebe's eyes drifting. The muscles in his jaw twitched.

At the bottom of the ramp, Benno pulled over.

They all got out, the underground garage murky, cold and damp. A guy from Justice in a trench coat flipped his identification.

"Stick around," Enna said to Benno.

Good luck, Bebe, Benno wanted to shout, but he was already on his way, following the fed, the ancient lawyer's leather briefcase swaying in his hand.

"Rico," Benno said. He continued in Sicilian. "Is he the guy?"

"The lawyer?" Enna replied in Sicilian, too. He'd hired Archibald on the advice of the president of the talent agency. "He's connected in Washington."

Which Benno knew was no answer.

Enna hustled to catch up and joined the group in the elevator.

Just before Tyler closed the doors, Marsala looked up and gave Benno a small, sickly smile, the kind that could break your heart if you gave a shit.

Benno put a "go get 'em" thumb in the air. He ached for Bebe, the skinny son of a bitch being way over his head with these Dunneys and Archibalds.

Tyler had commandeered a boardroom high up in the night sky, its glass wall showing streetlamps and brake lights below and stars over Narrows Gate. Photos of the construction of Rockefeller Center lined the other wood-paneled walls, elected officials and financiers in hardhats. A dozen high-back chairs surrounded the long table that dominated the room. Dunney was seated in one at the table's center, the lawyer Bamberger at his side, their backs to the view, papers strewn here and there. In the corner, close to the door, was a joyless stenographer.

Even before he removed his coat, Archibald protested. "We were to understand this was an informal meeting."

Bamberger said, "A transcript will serve to protect both of us."

Marsala saw that the two Washington lawyers knew each other.

"Mr. Marsala," said Dunney as he rose from his chair and walked to greet the singer. "My wife is one of your greatest fans."

"Tell her I said thank you, Senator."

Archibald had warned him about Dunney. "Don't be fooled by the drawl and the country bumpkin routine," the patrician lawyer said. "He's smart and ambitious. Don't let him see you as an enemy."

Dunney said, "You understand why we have to speak, Mr. Marsala, after the today's debacle…"

"I feel like I should apologize." Marsala folded his coat over a chair's back. "I'm sure you know by now that Mistretta is my wife Rosa's uncle. I'm not a big hit over in that family these days."

"But he put on quite a show, did he not?" Dunney said as he returned to his seat.

Archibald sat next to Marsala. "Was it necessary for your Mr. Tyler to threaten to call my client to testify in public?"

"It certainly could come to that," Dunney said. "But if I had my druthers, I'd hope we'd have a productive conversation tonight and eliminate that possibility."

"That's why I'm here, Senator," Marsala said. "I think if you ask Mrs. Roosevelt and President Truman, they'll tell you I've served my country whenever they've asked."

"Very good," Bamberger said as he rubbed his tired eyes. "Now, if we may begin…"

Archibald said, "I suggest we define the scope and boundaries of the conversation the senator mentioned. As Mr. Marsala has indicated, he's eager to cooperate, but—"

Bamberger said, "I can assure you that we have had no testimony, public or otherwise, that suggests Mr. Marsala is engaged in the kind of activities we're investigating."

Marsala sighed in relief, but Archibald said, "That doesn't address the issue of immunity."

"We're not after Mr. Marsala," Dunney said. "I don't think I could return to South Carolina if I did damage to his career."

"How can I help you, Senator?" Marsala said.

Bamberger replied. "Is there anything about your relationship with Carlo Farcolini you think we need to understand?"

"He was a friend of my father's. When I was a kid, I broke my leg and he gave me a radio. He liked the way I sang, I guess, so he stood by me. I don't know. Maybe he feels responsible for me—you know, the radio, music…"

"And Anthony Corini?"

"If you're in show business, you play his clubs. Look, if you want to ask me whether I'm in bed with their organization, I'll tell you. The answer is no. But I've known those guys since I was a kid singing in saloons. The 'bent-nose squad,' I call them. You don't pick your audience, Senator, and they like nightclubs." He shrugged and put up his hands. "What are you going to do?"

"When is the last time you spoke to Mr. Corini?" Bamberger asked.

"I haven't talked to Corini in a while. I saw him the other night at the Caribbean, but we didn't speak."

"Did you know Cy Geller?"

Marsala shook his head. "I met him once or twice, but I wouldn't say I knew him."

"Fortunato Spaletti?"

"Frankie Fortune, sure. He ran a few clubs and restaurants. A couple weeks ago, we met for brunch in Beverly Hills."

"Was he responsible for your career prior to his disappearance?"

Marsala bristled. "Buddy, nobody's responsible for my career but me."

Archibald tapped the singer's wrist. He'd warned Marsala not to antagonize Sam Bamberger.

"The mistakes I've made," Marsala added quickly, "they're all mine."

"But Mr. Spaletti accompanied you to Los Angeles for the purpose of expediting your relationship with Mr. Enna and the Sandpiper resort, did he not?"

"Phil Klein died and the agency asked me to accept Rico. Fine. That's the business. I needed a change." Marsala looked at Dunney. "My career was on a respirator. Your wife can tell you that, Senator."

Dunney smiled and nodded, but his eyes remained fixed on his notes.

"Returning to Carlo Farcolini for a moment," Bamberger said. "When was the last time you saw him?"

"In Havana, not too long ago. I was booked for a show at the...Rico?"

"El Malecón," the agent said. All night, Enna had watched Marsala swing from panic to defiance and back again without logic or reason. The pulsing veins at the singer's temple told Enna he was growing angry again despite Archibald's counsel.

"Who was present at the show?"

"A lot of people. But Corini was there. Frankie was there. Farcolini."

"Representatives from the Cuban government, would you say?"

"I don't know those guys. They could walk in here now and I still wouldn't."

"That would include Fulgencio Balboa—"

"Who?"

Archibald said, "How can it be relevant whether General Balboa attended a performance by my client?"

The question hung in the air as the steno machine clacked. Bamberger waited while Marsala sipped lukewarm water.

Enna leaned in to whisper to Archibald, who said, "Senator, Mr. Marsala may need to rest his voice for a few minutes."

Dunney nodded. "That's fine."

Without a flicker of concern, Bamberger said, "Tell me when you're ready."

Marsala stared at the commission's attorney. Dunney's prodding he could take—the guy was a senator, for Christ's sake. But the lawyer was a hack in a cheap suit. Nobody gave a fuck what he thought.

"Let's go," Marsala said.

Archibald said, "A short recess, gentlemen." Though the lawyer cared little for popular music, he was aware of Marsala's legendary arrogance. Left unabated, it was a vehicle to self-destruction. "Perhaps you could find some hot tea."

Marsala interrupted. He didn't want no favors from that bum Bamberger. "No, I'm fine. Let's go."

Bamberger said, "Did you meet privately with Mr. Farcolini?"

"It would have been an insult if I didn't. I told you. He was like an uncle to me."

"What did you discuss?"

"He asked about my old man. He mentioned my mother. To tell you the truth, he wasn't excited about my divorce."

"Anything else?"

"I don't know. General chitchat. People like to talk to celebrities. Right, Senator?"

"I'm not a celebrity, Mr. Marsala."

The singer chuckled. "Lately you've been getting more ink than me."

"Did Mr. Farcolini express his gratitude to you?" Bamberger asked.

"For what? Singing? It's a job. If they meet the fee, that's gratitude enough."

"For the suitcase you delivered to him."

Marsala was jolted. "Suitcase?"

"You carried a suitcase to Havana. It wasn't with your baggage when you returned."

Archibald turned to look at his client.

"I'm trying to remember," Marsala said. "I had my own luggage, the same kind I always travel with."

Bamberger slid a manila envelope from under his notes, opened it and slid a photo across the table. Before Archibald could intercept, Marsala grabbed it.

"Is that not a photo of you carrying a black suitcase onto the flight from Miami to Havana?"

"Yes. That's me," Marsala said.

"In the second photo, are you not leaving the plane in Havana with the same suitcase?"

"Yes," he repeated.

From his post at the double doors, Tyler studied the singer's changing expression, his scowl vanishing as he shifted in the chair. Tyler had taken the photo in Havana. The picture and many others he'd snapped were proof Marsala made the delivery.

"Did you look inside the suitcase, Mr. Marsala?"

"I couldn't, Mr. Bamberger. It was locked."

"It was locked?"

"Yes, sir. As I recall, the suitcase was locked." Marsala inched toward the table and folded his hands together as if in prayer. As his defiance withered, he felt a rush of panic. His throat began to constrict. He grabbed the water glass.

"Who unlocked it?"

"Frankie. Frankie Fortune."

"In your presence?"

Marsala nodded.

"What was in the suitcase, Mr. Marsala?"

"I didn't know until it was open."

"Mr. Marsala," Dunney said, "please answer Mr. Bamberger's question."

"Money," he said. "A lot of money."

"Would you risk a guess at how much?"

"Sam," Archibald scolded. "Your point is made."

"Mr. Archibald," Dunney said, "I'm sure we would like to know what constitutes 'a lot of money' to a man of Mr. Marsala's considerable achievements."

"I—Thousands. Could've been a hundred thousand. Maybe more."

"In excess of one hundred thousand dollars?" Bamberger asked.

"Yes."

"Perhaps two hundred thousand? Three hundred thousand?"

Marsala nodded compliantly. "Could've been. Yes."

"I see." Bamberger waited while the singer sipped water again and cleared his throat. "I may have asked you this already. Was Mr. Fortune in attendance when the money was presented to Mr. Farcolini?"

"He was, yes," Marsala nodded. "He gave it to him."

"And who asked you to carry such a large sum of money to Mr. Farcolini?"

Archibald interrupted. "Sam, Mr. Marsala made it clear he didn't know what was in the suitcase. Please."

"Mr. Marsala."

"Salvatore Benno," Marsala said. "He brought the suitcase to my room at the Hampshire House."

"Salvatore Benno," Bamberger repeated. The name meant nothing to him.

"The Jersey bagman," Marsala continued. "He's in Mimmo's crew. They call him the Delivery Boy."

Enna stood and walked toward the door. Asking Tyler to step aside, he reached for the knob. "Tea," Enna whispered, pointing to his own throat.

Tyler let him pass.

"Did Mr. Benno tell you what was in the suitcase?"

"No."

"Did he tell you where the money came from?"

Archibald said, "Mr. Marsala already told you he was unaware—"

"After the suitcase was opened, did you tell Mr. Benno what was in it?"

"Yes."

"What did he say?"

"Nothing that I can recall," Marsala said.

"Was he surprised?"

"Not really."

"Is it your opinion he knew what was in the suitcase?"

"He might've. There must have been a reason why he insisted that I carry it."

It took Enna a while to find the public elevator. He asked the sleepy operator if he could be taken directly to the garage. No, he was told, so he walked out of the RCA Building into the cold and hurried down the ramp, and there was Benno, leaning against the car, arms folded, his eyelids closed like he was asleep standing up.

He moved when he heard Enna's shoes on the concrete.

Enna said, "Get out of here, Sal."

"Why? What happened to—"

"Give me the keys and get out of here."

"I don't understand. What's happen—"

"He gave you up. He told them you knew he was carrying 500 large to Don Carlo."

"Bullshit."

"I know the suitcase was lock—"

"No, I mean bullshit that Bebe gave me up."

"Sal," Enna moaned. "Sally…"

Benno stared at him as knowledge took hold. "Am I fucked?"

"Maybe. I don't know. But get out of here so they don't pull you in tonight."

Benno reached into his pocket and turned over the car keys. "Fuckin' Bebe," he said, shaking his head. He hustled toward the ramp.

"All right, Mr. Marsala," Senator Dunney said. "I think we have an understanding of how the operation worked."

Marsala sat back. "Does that mean I won't have to testify in public?"

"I can't say for certain," he replied. "But you've done yourself some good here tonight."

"Senator, if you call me to appear, my career will be over."

"I'm sure I don't know if that might be true. Allow us to review our notes. We'll let you know." Dunney turned to Bamberger. "Sam?"

The attorney made a dismissive gesture.

"That seems unnecessarily cruel, Senator," Archibald said. "As my client told you, he's at a crucial stage in his career."

Dunney said, "Mr. Archibald, it's a little late for speechifying, so I'll let you calculate how crucial our investigation is to the free flow of legitimate commerce and the termination of the narcotics trade that so richly profits Mr. Marsala's friends."

"No one doubts the legitimacy of your efforts, Senator," Archibald replied.

"Well, thank you for the endorsement," Dunney said as he stood. "Mr. Marsala, I hope the next time we speak will be under more amiable circumstances."

Tyler held open the door as the senator departed.

"What's it mean?" Marsala whispered. "Are we done?"

Archibald held up a finger. He said, "Sam?"

Bamberger didn't respond.

"Sam."

"He pushed it down, Leland," Bamberger said. "To a delivery boy. Meaning he's still in the middle."

"He can't tell you what he doesn't know."

"We'll see," Bamberger replied.

Marsala said, "Ask the kid." He was standing now, his palms on the table. "He'll tell you."

Bamberger looked at Marsala. "The commission is more likely to ask you."

The singer trembled. "Oh, Jesus. How rough do you guys have to play? It's four in the morning and I'm doing what you asked."

"Don't leave town," Bamberger said as he went back to his notes.

"I was going to London."

"I don't think that's a good idea."

Archibald said, "Bill—"

"I need to travel," Marsala protested. "It's part of the job."

"Leland," Bamberger said, "tell Mr. Marsala we can seize his passport. Tell him we can stop him at the airport with the press in tow. Or tell him he ought to continue to cooperate."

"You want my career. That's it, right? You want to take my career."

Bamberger sighed wearily. "Mr. Marsala, you may be surprised to learn that there are a great many things in this world more important than your career."

"Not to me, fella."

"No," Bamberger said. "Apparently not."

Having no way to get home until morning and stunned by his own stupidity, Benno walked all the way down to the Washington Market. Amid the hustling vendors and shouting drivers, he warmed his hands near a garbage can fire and waited for his bumbling cousin, who now could be considered the smartest American-born Benno, seeing as he didn't put his faith in a life-long shit heel like Bebe Marsala.

They got back to Narrows Gate around 8 o'clock, Benno insisting on driving and for good measure, he told his cousin to sit in the back and shut up. When they caught a red light coming out of the Holland Tunnel, he turned to apologize. "It ain't your fault I'm a fuckin' dope," he was going to say, but his cousin was asleep, his head nestled among the lettuce and escarole.

He pulled the truck in front of the store. His uncle came out, looked up and down Polk Street and beckoned Benno inside.

There was Imogene O'Boyle with his aunt, who was rubbing little circles on her back.

"Sal, have you seen Leo?" Imogene asked.

"I been out all night. No."

"Sal, I'm worried. We were supposed to meet. Leo wouldn't stand me up."

"No, I know that. You checked his house?"

She nodded. "I went to the apartment, too."

"By yourself?" It was dangerous under the viaduct at night.

"He said he might clean it out. But there was no answer."

"What about school? Maybe he falls asleep in the library, he's behind in his studies because of me and his father."

"Sal, something's wrong. You said you were out all night—"

"No, I was with Bebe." Benno thought for a moment. "I got an idea," he told her, trying to hide his concern. "Don't worry about nothing."

He gave her a hug, kissed her on the side of the head and then he left the store to go see Mimmo.

CHAPTER FORTY

And there was Frankie Fortune in Mimmo's usual spot in the candy store, reading the bad news in the morning paper, his handsome face saggy and worn, the California tan all gone. His suit was wrinkled.

Meanwhile, Tutti was drinking coffee from a container. He hoisted out of a chair when Benno entered.

"Where's Leo, Frankie?" Benno asked.

Fortune said, "Maybe he's at the fuckin' synagogue."

There was nobody behind the counter and there weren't any kids wasting time on the funnies and pinball before school.

Fat Tutti locked the door.

"Now I know it's you," Benno told him. "What a dumb play."

Fortune said, "Sit down, Sal."

"I like it fine where I am."

"Suit yourself," Fortune replied. Then he looked at Tutti, who grabbed Benno by the shoulders and jammed him into a rail-back chair.

Benno adjusted his glasses. "Something's grinding you down, Frankie. You need a vacation and I don't mean Canada."

Fat Tutti smacked Benno so hard his hat flew off.

Fortune said, "You want to see Ding, you'll keep your mouth shut."

Benno stared across the table.

"Your buddy's a Jew rat bastard, Sal. The government comes to his house."

"You know that, huh?"

"And so I say you're a rat bastard, too." Fortune pointed at him.

"Me?" Benno raised his voice in frustration. "The feds are squeezing Bebe about the suitcase he gave you in Cuba and I'm in the middle."

"He gave *me*? If that's so, I should be on the witness list."

"For one, you was on the witness list in Hollywood and two, you ain't on it in New York because we ain't rolled on you, Leo and me. Jesus, Frankie. What the fuck is wrong with you?"

Benno was furious, but what could he do? He slugs everybody and Bell pays. "You know something? The guy nobody can trust, Frankie, is you. You turned me into a bagman. You put me next to Pellizzari when he got popped. You left me in Hollywood when the feds came and you took the suitcase from Bebe."

"Yeah, but it was you who embarrassed Bruno in his neighborhood, breaking his fuckin' window over a few Gs. You put yourself on the map." Fortune made a big deal out of closing the newspaper. "So you've got to pay."

Here it comes, Benno thought.

"Anthony's been good to you. Am I right?"

"Well, I don't see he tried to get me killed or nothing."

"You're his guy?"

Benno laughed. "I don't think he remembers me if I sat on him."

"Don't be modest, Sal."

"Leo, Frankie. How do I get Leo?"

"Easy. You take out Dunney."

Benno snapped back. "What?"

"You put down Dunney."

"Says who?"

"Who's testifying on the television next week?"

"Mr. Corini wants Dunney hit?" Benno shook his head. "That don't make sense."

"Nobody sees it coming."

"What, I walk into the courthouse—"

"Dunney's on the six o'clock back to Washington tonight out of Pennsylvania Station. He's in a crowd, people rushing home, maybe he's got somebody at his back, maybe he don't. You put one behind his ear and Tutti pulls you out of the madhouse. You're back on Polk Street before nobody knows you were there."

"I'm hitting Dunney with Tutti?" Scowling, he turned, looked up at the big fat bodyguard and said, "This is a good idea?"

Tutti made a circle in the air, telling him to face Fortune.

"Otherwise, Ding goes off the viaduct," Fortune said. "Two hundred feet and he lands on his head. Suicide. He's so confused—his father's dead, and now he's a Jew."

Benno thought, Who's got more to live for than Leo? Imogene, school, a chance to get away from these mooks.

"Give me what you got in your pockets," Benno said.

"Nobody's paying you, Sal. Getting Ding—that's the pay out."

"You putting your money with me says I'm coming home. Tutti shoots me in the noodle in the train station and the money goes to the cops. I know the game, Frankie. You couldn't bear it."

When Fortune turned over $800, Benno said, "The other pocket." He wound up with $2,200 and change.

"I ain't using my uncle's gun," he said.

"Tutti takes care of that." Then Fortune made this gesture with his chin that told Benno he could stand. "Don't be cute, Sal. Dunney lives and Ding dies. *Semplice.*"

Simple for you, Benno thought as he retrieved his fallen hat.

Fortune ambled behind the soda fountain to use the mirror. He looked at Tutti. "Cool him down," he said as he turned on the water to wash his face.

Tutti jostled Benno toward the back room and a wooden storage unit maybe six feet high and wide enough for cartons of ice cream, soda, some hamburger and franks, like one of those Hollywood saunas in reverse. As Tutti shoved him, Benno figured the icebox couldn't be much colder than it was outside, and Fortune don't want him frozen stiff if he was killing Dunney. Benno saw that maybe the icebox could buy him time to figure out how to help Leo, given that Fortune had already let him know they had him down by the viaduct, no doubt with Boo, that Frankenstein-looking fuck.

Tutti pulled back the handle. The heavy door swung open with a groan. "In," he said.

A blast of cold air smacked Benno in the face. Through the fog he saw, tucked in a corner, Mimmo, his hat up on his head, his sunglasses at a strange angle, his throat slit from ear to ear, brown blood stains all down the front of his shirt.

"Here you go, Sal," Tutti said, grabbing Benno's arm.

Fat Tutti shoved him toward the body and then he yanked the door tight, padlocked it, too.

After a while, Benno turned sideways. To a freezing corpse, he said, "What'd you think was going to happen, Mimmo?" He figured the guy was lucky they couldn't kill him twice.

The calls began arriving at Ree's hotel in Lourenço Marques, Mozambique, shortly after noon. The operator, who spoke English with a Portuguese accent, did as she was instructed: She told Marsala Miss Ree was at work in the jungle where she could not be reached for several days. On the fifth try, Marsala offered her $1,000 to "drive a Jeep, ride a camel, do whatever the hell it is you people do and tell her I need to speak to her *now*." The man sounded so desperate that she almost put the call through to the actress's room upstairs, where she was resting after a hectic morning.

Ree's agent sent a cable that arrived last night as she, along with the picture's male lead, the female costar and the director, returned from dinner. "Bill implicated at Senate hearing. Trouble ahead. Will advise ASAP. Mal."

Not a half hour earlier, the director, a grizzled Hollywood veteran who'd relish his time on the veld, said, "Ree, I need you happy and carefree. Your smile brings this picture to life."

Which was true. Earlier, the blonde female costar, whose character was as prim and dour as Ree's was salty and bright, said, "You wouldn't consider trading parts, would you?"

The male lead grabbed a handful of Ree's ass. "Rehearsal, my dear," he said with a trademark wicked grin.

Then the cable.

"Oh, Bill," she said as she retired to her room and began to undress. She thought to call him in New York but fatigued from travel, she fell asleep.

The next morning was dedicated to an early safari across the border in Tanganyika. She thought of Marsala the moment she awoke and was eager to reach him. But as she was about to shower, a knock on her door brought another cable from Weisberg. "Bill dropped by Chesterfield. Record deal gone. Tour? Stand by. Avoid press. Mal."

She couldn't understand if Weisberg was telling her not to read the papers or to dodge calls from reporters. She wondered if Bill was screaming at the Hampshire Hotel staff or curled up on the carpet in a fetal position. Looking at the liquor cabinet, she almost broke the promise she'd made herself not to drink before noon.

"I heard your singer's past is catching up to him," said the male lead as they boarded a Jeep for the trip to the heliport. "Don't worry. There's enough out here to keep you occupied." By 10 o'clock—two in the morning back in New York—they were spying on a pride of lions in the bush, the females lounging in shade trees. Two hours later, a herd of zebras galloped across the plain perhaps 200 yards from where the cast and crew enjoyed lunch. The sky was endless, a perfect baby blue.

Marsala told no one he was fleeing to Los Angeles. Enna, who cat-napped in his office, found out when he arrived at the Hampshire House. From the lobby, he telephoned his boss at the agency and then called Corini, who told him to come to his apartment on Central Park West.

Corini met him at the elevator, closing his apartment door behind him like he had guests. Annoyed, he resembled an older version of the thug he'd once been.

"What did he say?" he snapped.

"I haven't spoken to him since he left New York."

"Rico, what the fuck did he say to Dunney?"

"He said you run nightclubs."

"What about Carlo?"

"He's like an uncle."

"You're saying he didn't sing?"

"He gave up Benno."

"Who?"

"The delivery boy. The kid who got your money back."

Corini shook his head slowly and made a face like he could spit.

Enna said, "I'll book Joey Aaron at the club. All right?" The comedian ran around like a 2-year-old on sugar, made like a walrus with chopsticks in his mouth, told a few moss-covered jokes and sang a couple of tunes. Obnoxious, but he went over.

"Tell the press Bebe was fired."

"We could put it on his sore throat," the agent suggested.

"Fired," he said angrily. "And you dump him face-to-face. Then you go see Geller's son at the Sandpiper and come up with another singer for the resort."

Enna waited for further instruction. Hearing none, he said, "Good luck on Monday, Anthony."

Corini shook the agent's hand, then he pressed the elevator button. "Those Washington bastards are going to find out I ain't Mimmo or Bebe. They won't lay a glove on me."

In the lobby, the doorman flagged Enna a cab cruising the sunny, frigid avenue.

"LaGuardia Field," he told the driver. He was thinking Corini was underestimating his opponents.

They let Benno out of the icebox at noon. Fat Tutti told him to call his aunt and say he's all right and if he wants to sleep, sleep. But you ain't leaving and we're pulling out at 4 o'clock.

"What, no lunch?" Benno said as he sat on cartons of Butterfingers in the storeroom. "Go to my uncle's and—"

"Shut up, Sal," Tutti told him.

Benno smiled. If he was hungry, it meant Fat Tutti was starving, the guy ate enough for six. "Tell me you ain't in the mood for a little calabrese, a nice piece of provolone, some olives, hot peppers…"

Instead, Tutti had Nunzie deliver two of those Irish pizzas. "No thanks," Benno said, turning away. He had himself some M&Ms.

At twilight, they went toward a cloud gray Pontiac.

"Drive," Tutti said.

"No." He pointed to his glass eye. "I want you on my good side."

"Sal…" Then Tutti said, "Fuck it. Let's go and get this done."

Benno jumped in the passenger seat and Fat Tutti, his stomach pressed against the wheel, steered north behind St. Matty's and toward the viaduct. Benno looked out the window and sure enough, he saw a light shining in the top floor of Bell's flop, meaning somebody was home and it wasn't Imogene O'Boyle.

"You got the gun, Tutti?"

Heavy traffic funneling toward the Lincoln Tunnel made them crawl. "Don't you ever shut up, Sal?"

"I ain't said nothing since we left the house."

They inched ahead, Tutti's bumper ready to kiss the car in front, brake lights flashing like it's code.

"What happens we miss the train?" Benno asked.

"We got plenty of time."

"Says you. I see three hundred cars squeezing into one hole up there."

"Sal, I'm telling you to shut the fuck up."

"Maybe you should throw me out of the car."

Tutti said, "If I had my way, you'd be dead, fuckin' Ding, too, and for good measure I burn down your uncle's fuckin' store." He looked at Benno. "How's that?"

"Typical."

A car on Benno's blind side tried to inch ahead, but Tutti cut him off cold.

"I know you maybe fifteen years, Tutti, and I ain't heard you say so much. Maybe this thing's got you in knots like Frankie. Or maybe you're jealous you ain't the Jersey bagman. Corini don't know you from Tonto."

"Jealous of you when maybe there won't be no you by tomorrow?" Fat Tutti snorted. "Grow the fuck up."

Tutti made a sharp, hard move with the wheel. Now the mouth of the tunnel was straight ahead.

Benno curled around in the seat like he was going to nap, his back to the overheated big man, Pennsylvania Station maybe 20 minutes away.

Tutti pulled the Pontiac into a carriageway hectic with taxis and impatient drivers waiting for family and friends, gasoline fumes rising.

Benno said, "You can't park here."

"I'm dropping you off."

"That's the plan?"

Tutti nodded. "I'm coming in on the Thirty-Third Street side."

"I got to pop Dunney, find you—"

"I'll find you."

"—find you and then we run through this gigantic fuckin' station, upstairs like a mountain and cross traffic to the car so we can drive back to the tunnel?"

"Right."

"That's nuts."

"If you do it like you're supposed to, Sal. If not, good that you're fucked. You deserve it." Fat Tutti put his hand inside his coat.

"Hold on," Benno said, nodding.

514

Up ahead, two cops bundled against the wind patrolled the carriageway, their nightsticks swinging and slapping their gloved hands as they chatted.

"Pull over to the left," Benno said. "There's a couple of cars with the engine ain't running."

"I'm dropping you off," he repeated.

"Give me a second to get my head straight, OK Tutti? This is big."

Fat Tutti huffed ugly, but he put the car in first and drove across the narrow alley, passing under a footbridge to a waiting room.

Benno took a deep breath. "Give me the piece," he said, thinking of Leo Bell.

Tutti looked into the rearview and seeing the cops moving away, he dug again into an inner pocket and gave a .38 to Benno.

"A Snubbie?" he said as he counted the rounds.

"It does the job," Fat Tutti said. "Believe me."

He snapped the cylinder back into place. "Let's go over it one more time."

"Sal, get the fuck out of the car."

"I line up like I'm waiting for the six o'clock to Washington and here comes Dunney and I pop him and then the cops take me out. I'm dead and Leo dies."

"Sal—"

"Me and Leo die."

"Goddamn it, Sal—"

Benno jammed the nozzle of the gun against the top of Fat Tutti's mammoth thigh and pulled the trigger, sending a bullet deep into fat and flesh.

Tutti cried out. He looked at Benno, stunned. For good measure, Benno reached across and shot him in the other leg, this time inside the thigh. Fat Tutti slammed against the door in pain but like the first shot, nobody heard nothing, all those cars and mounds of seared skin acting like mufflers. And here comes the blood.

Benno twisted the rearview mirror until he saw the cops turn the corner. Even though people were pouring out of the station and hopping into cars and cabs, passing headlights sweeping over him, he put the nozzle of the gun under Fat Tutti's chin.

"You notice you ain't dead, right?" Benno said. "But only if Leo's OK. You understand me? Something happens to him and you're next."

"You're fucked, Sal," Fat Tutti managed, his face red and contorted. "Ooh, you are fucked."

"We'll see." He took the car keys and then he stepped into the cold. Turning down the collar of his coat and adjusting his hat, he went toward the station, squeezing between two taxis. Bending like he was tying his shoe, he buried the .38 in a back pocket and hoped he didn't have none of Fat Tutti's blood on his clothes or face or nothing.

All of a sudden, standing in the middle of a million people rushing for trains or hustling to quit the station, Benno realized he didn't know what Alvin Dunney looked like. He sped through the crowd sideways and made his way over to the newsstand.

"Which way is the train to Washington?" he asked the newsy, who pointed.

Benno ran like he was escaping a fire.

The train wasn't supposed to leave for 15 minutes, but already people were going toward the tracks. The loudspeaker said this train was boarding, that train was boarding, but no cops were charging through the station looking for him, at least not yet. He would've sworn he felt the trains rumbling under the marble floor as he studied every face, turning his head so his good eye led.

Then Sal Benno saw him. Just like a regular guy, the senator was joining the shuffling line.

Benno walked over, took a breath and said to himself, OK. Here we go. He opened his mouth. "Senator—"

Dunney smiled polite but he turned away. He was talking to Bebe's lawyer, Archibald.

"Senator—"

"Sal Benno," said the guy behind Dunney. He was blond and tall and he looked like what they used to put on Army recruiting posters.

Dunney kept going.

The guy said, "It is inappropriate—"

"You're Tyler," Benno said, "Leo's guy." He stepped in front of him, blocking his path.

"Mr. Benno—"

"They got Leo. Frankie Fortune's got Leo." Benno tried to stay calm, but he could hear panic in his own voice.

Tyler stared at him. "I can't help you, Mr. Benno."

"I said they got Leo. They'll kill him."

"Excuse me. I've a train to catch."

"Tyler. Come on. Jesus."

Dunney and the white-haired lawyer went toward the darkness. Tyler followed.

CHAPTER FORTY-ONE

As she helped him into his jacket, the stewardess whispered, "Mr. Marsala, the captain said there are reporters on the ground."

"Thanks, doll," he managed with a listless smile, his voice a weary rasp. She'd nursed him through his panic attack over the Midwest and helped him clean up after he vomited the lunch she'd served. Now he tried to slip her a $50 bill, but she said no. Holding his elbow, she led him to the door as the propellers sputtered to a halt and the chocks were set in place.

The press boys started in even before he was halfway down the steps into the Southern California sun. He made like he couldn't hear them, cupping a hand to his ear. What he needed to do more than anything was talk to Eleanor and even if it cost $10Gs in dimes, he was going to call her in Mozambique from the first phone booth he saw.

She was going to say, "Don't worry, Bill. It'll be all right, sure it will. I'm devoted to you. You're somebody."

"Bill, have you heard the news?" a reporter asked. Flashbulbs popped as Marsala reached the tarmac.

"I've got nothing for you, fellas," he said, elbowing past pencils and notepads.

"Bill, do you think it's fair that you've been dropped by Chesterfield?"

Another reporter said, "And the record label?"

Each sentence landed like a slap. Lightheaded, he tried to grip his composure as he entered the terminal. "Fellas, look. I'm having trouble with my throat and—"

"Is that why you were fired by the Caribbean?"

"Bill, what's Eleanor's reaction to all this?"

"Is it true you'll be called to testify in public before the Senate commission?"

"Come on now, fellas. You know that Domenico Mistretta is my ex-wife's uncle. I'm in the middle of something here."

They trailed him as he headed toward baggage claim.

"It's all a big misunderstanding," he added.

A reporter tugged at his sleeve.

"Hands off the threads, asshole," Marsala snapped, yanking his arm free. A photographer caught the skirmish.

Out of the corner of his eye, Marsala saw a sign for a men's room. He veered toward it and washed his haggard face with frightening vigor. Then he ducked into a stall, locked the door and started to sob.

Three hours later, Eleanor still hadn't returned his calls—she's in the jungle with the men, said an operator at the Lourenço Marques Hotel. "Yes, they have walkie-talkies, but…No sir, we can't send one of our people to Tanganyika. It is quite a distance. Sir—I'm sorry, sir."

Marsala sent six cables within 90 minutes. "Where are you? Call your Bill in Beverly Hills. Pronto," Slowly and painfully, the messages withered to, "Baby, please. Baby."

Enna's wife said the agent was on his way to Los Angeles. The head of programming at the radio network wouldn't take Marsala's calls nor would the representative at the sponsor, Chesterfield. Same with the record company: Marsala's a pariah. The singer paced the apartment, rubbing his temples, patting his stomach as it gnawed, sweating as the walls closed in. He called Mal Weisberg, Eleanor's agent.

"If you love her, Bill—"

This time, Marsala hung up.

He sat on the bed, then stood seconds later. Sat, stood. A shower, but his mind kept misfiring and when he closed his eyes against the soap's sting, he saw his mother's disapproving scowl. Pacing in his bathrobe and slippers, he wandered into Nino Terrasini's old room and he had an idea. It was desperate, but what else could he do?

Certain he was unfit to drive, he told the concierge to call a taxi.

She came to the door in a fog of a mother's well-earned sleep, tying a terry cloth robe, her hair pinned under a scarf. Alarmed, she said, "Bill, what happen—"

"Let me in," he said as the taxi pulled away.

"I don't think so," said Rosa Mistretta Rosiglino.

"Please, baby. I'm in trouble."

Clutching the old robe at the collar, she stepped back and stared at him: crisp gray suit, white shirt without a tie, his hair perfect but his expression dripping dread.

"All right. For a few minutes. You can see Bill Jr."

He limped into the living room. As she shut the door, he said, "Is Nino here?"

"Bill, it's past midnight."

"Is he here?"

She reached for the door again.

"No, no. I'm sorry. Rosa. Jesus. It's all gone wrong. It's…It's all gone wrong."

"Sit down, Bill. I'll put on some coffee—"

"Mimmo screwed me," he said. "Why did he do that?"

"He didn't say anything. He's confused, he's sick."

"What he's done, Rosa. God almighty, what he's done."

"But the radio says he did it because I told him to. Did you say that, Bill?"

"No. I said he was angry with me because of you. Listen, he's killed me, baby. I'm dead. Look at me, I'm dead." He started to pace again. "The radio show, the record deal. The Sandpiper, I'll bet. Mayer won't have me at Metro."

She thought he might burst. "Bill, you'd better calm down. Bill."

"I'll need an operation for my throat. Who knows how it will turn out?"

"Bill. Pull yourself together. This is no good."

He retreated, dropped onto the sofa and buried his face in his hands. "How did it go off track?"

"You're asking the wrong girl, Bill."

He looked up. His eyes moist, he sighed. "All at once. Everything. Gone in a flash."

She said, "Stay here a minute. I'll get coffee."

She went into the kitchen, and, while she rattled the espresso pot and let the water flow, she dialed Terrasini. She whispered, "Bill's here. He's in rough shape." As the coffee brewed, she returned to the living room. Marsala was staring at his reflection in the mirror above the mantle.

"Where is Miss Ree?" she asked from a distance.

"In Africa."

"Fucking some big-game hunter?"

Without turning, he said, "You too, huh, Rosa?"

At least, I'm warm here, Benno thought as he crouched under the stairs of Bell's flop. Every now and then, he'd hear thudding footsteps, a floor high above him moaning and squeaking. Boo

Chiasso, he knew, and he wondered what the cops did with Fat Tutti and his ventilated legs.

Earlier, after coming back to Narrows Gate by the Port Authority bus, he tried to pull down the fire-escape ladder on Bell's flop, using the Siamese pump as a stepstool, but it wouldn't budge from rust. Then he figured cement-head Chiasso might hear and here I am out on a shelf in the freezing cold and dark and Chiasso shoots me and I go down looking like just another shit-for-brains Sicilian crook. They kill Leo, too, and that's that.

So he waited, amazed that his temper let him think so he could cook up a scheme.

And then it happened, just like he imagined.

A car came up slow, its headlights going dim. It bounced over the curb and crunched pebbles and broken glass where the sidewalk used to be. The engine coughed as it shut down and the emergency brake growled when it was set. The door opened and closed.

Benno inched like a crab, the Snubbie drawn. He heard footsteps outside. Then the building's door opened cautious and the wintry night came in along with Frankie Fortune, who looked up into the blackness at the top of the steps. Before Fortune knew what happened, Benno sprang and had the gun jammed into the bone under his eye.

"Hands," Benno whispered, "or I'll shoot you like Tutti."

Fortune felt the nozzle dig into his skin.

"Drop the blade. Frankie."

The stiletto fell to the floor.

"You'd better hope Leo is alive," Benno said.

He pushed Fortune up the stairs, matching each step he took, holding the banister with his left hand and jabbing Fortune's spine with the gun. At the landing, Fortune turned to negotiate, but Benno sent him along, knowing Chiasso was listening, the old stairs announcing an arrival.

"Leo!" Benno shouted. "Boo, I'm coming to kill you, you ugly son of a bitch."

The wood buckled and creaked, the banister wobbled and finally Benno could see a strip of light under the door. He was sure Chiasso was right there, ready to shoot.

"Here I come!" Benno screamed.

The door swung open and Boo Chiasso appeared, firing rapidly, each round ripping into Fortune's torso. As Fortune slumped, Benno shot over him, hitting Chiasso square in the face. In agony, Chiasso fell to his knees and hunched over. What the hell, I've gone this far and Benno stepped up and shot him through the top of the head. Nobody was going to fuck with them no more.

Leo was tied to the bed, a bloody towel gagging his mouth.

Benno knelt to help. But his hands started shaking and he couldn't get the cord untied. Bell mumbled until Benno understood. He removed the gag.

"Sally, what the fuck?" he said.

"You're telling me. Look at me. I'm dancing over here."

"Get my arms." Bell was soaked in sweat. Blood had caked on his forehead.

Finally, Benno took apart the knot that had Bell's right wrist tied to the springs. Then the left hand was freed and soon Bell was untied and standing.

"Your coconut…"

Bell said, "Boo liked to dent it. Three times." He reached and rubbed the bumps on his head. "What do we do now?"

"I'm tired of thinking," Benno replied between gasps. "What'd you got?"

Over by the sloppy pile of books was some bedding. Bell lifted a pillowcase, took the gun from Benno and wiped it down. He climbed over Chiasso, put Fortune's fingers around the grip, then let the .38 tumble down the stairs.

"I hope that works," Benno said.

"It'd better," said Bell as he rubbed his wrists. "Let's get out of here."

"Don't make me forget Frankie's knife."

Bell hustled into his topcoat.

Out in the icy air, a car or two roared up the viaduct, but underneath it was as dark as a cave. Breath pluming, Benno said, "Imogene said you didn't bring your car."

"I'm not using it anymore. I'm giving it back to Tyler."

"Tyler," Benno said. "That fuck."

"Jesus, Sally, what did I miss?"

Terrasini got there as fast as he could. "He's in rough shape," Rosa said and that meant Bebe could hurt himself. Though what could he do that would be worse than what's already happened, according to the papers? To get back to where he used to be, he'd have to start below the bottom and with the clits on his throat and no war where all the boys are gone. He's no longer just a skinny kid from Narrows Gate, New Jersey, with a silky baritone, gosh and golly, his blue eyes twinkling. Hennie isn't around to steamroll everybody and Don Carlo won't help. The recording industry won't touch him, radio neither or the movies.

Terrasini knocked gently, not to wake Bill Jr., and peeked in before entering. Marsala was pacing the living room.

"Bebe?"

Marsala hugged him desperately. Terrasini, who'd seen him on his knees and in the clouds, thought, He's gone. Bring the straitjacket. Bebe Marsala's cracked. "Can you pull yourself together, Bebe?" Terrasini said. He steered Marsala to the sofa and eased down at his side.

Rosa sat across from them on the edge of the chair, arms folded, concerned though there wasn't a drop of pity in her dark eyes.

"Corini will tell them everything," Marsala said.

"What's everything?" Terrasini asked. "We know Don Carlo since we're kids. He liked the way you sing."

"I'm blowing back fifteen percent—"

"To a talent agent. What he does, that's your concern?"

"Nino, they got me delivering a half million dollars to him in Cuba."

Terrasini looked across at Rosa.

Of course, they did, she thought.

"Frankie Fortune told Carlo it was from me. In gratitude. Corini will tell the commission the same thing."

Rosa said, "You don't have a half million dollars to give away. If they check the bank, they'd know that."

"Rosa, honey, they'll say this is money you don't put in the bank," Marsala said. "I saw how the commission works. They've got the big hammer and let me tell you—they know how to use it."

Terrasini offered his former boss a tiny cup with hot espresso and a splash of sambuca. Marsala declined.

"You got somewhere to go?" Terrasini asked.

"I can't leave the country."

"Yeah, but you got friends."

"Who do I know who isn't in show business? Or Carlo's crew?"

Rosa shook her head.

"Bebe, when's the last time you slept?" Terrasini asked.

"I—I don't know. I spent last night with Dunney and his snakes."

In Sicilian, Terrasini said, "You need a fresh head."

"*Ho bisogno di nuova vita.*"

"I didn't say a new life. A good night's sleep is all you need."

"Bill," Rosa said, "go home. Tomorrow you get a new agent."

"Who'll represent a bum who has no deal and no future?"

"Bill, self-pity's never gotten you anywhere," Rosa said as she stood.

Terrasini stood, too. "Come on. I'll drive you home."

Marsala looked up. "For old-time's sake?" he said bitterly.

"Sure, Bebe. For old-time's sake."

Marsala slumped toward the door. He said, "I fucked up good, huh, Rosa?"

"You sure did, Bill. First class all the way."

Terrasini scolded her with his eyes. Then he reminded himself that this was Marsala's way—he makes like a puppy dog so you feel sorry for him and forget how he stomped on everything decent and common, and then when he sings, it touches you and you forgive him for all he's done.

"Come on, Bebe," he said as he opened the door.

"Good-bye, Bill," Rosa said as they walked toward Terrasini's car. She watched as they drove away.

Some crew they got in the back room at Benno's at four in the morning: Benno and Bell, Benno's aunt and uncle, and there's Imogene in her nurse's uniform with the white hose and the only Italian sergeant on the Narrows Gate force, Enzo Paolo, who knew everybody on Polk Street since they was born. Meanwhile, the knuckleheaded cousin is in the truck and maybe this time he drives backward through the tunnel or he forgets the peppers.

Benno thought, Ain't this something? A meeting on Polk Street and no Mimmo, no Frankie Fortune. No Boo Chiasso or Fat Tutti.

"You need a Jew lawyer," Paolo said in Sicilian. "Oh, sorry, Ding."

Bell shrugged. Since he wasn't dead from Boo Chiasso hitting his head, he was in a forgiving mood. At first, he tried to talk Benno out of telling Paolo. "Why own up?" Bell had asked. "To gauge if the story plays," Benno said and Bell thought, Well…

"Why do I need a lawyer, Enzo?"

Imogene interrupted. "Sal. English, please."

"Sure, sorry." He returned to Paolo, over there half in his blue uniform, half in his pajamas. "I'm saying Fat Tutti puts a gun on me and Fortune says I should kill Dunney or Boo throws Leo off the viaduct. Tutti is going walk me through Pennsylvania Station with a gun at my spine to see I do it. So first I clip him and then I come and get Leo."

Brown-skinned, silver-haired now and chiseled around the jaw, Paolo was doing his best to say nothing. He nibbled a cannoli Gemma threw in front of him, which kept his mouth occupied.

"I guess Fortune heard about Tutti with the legs, so he comes to kill Leo like he said he would and Boo shoots him, thinking, I don't know, it's the feds, maybe. Fortune got off a few rounds, I guess and by the time I get there, everybody's dead. Except Leo. Boo, that ugly bastard, trussed him like a pig and he don't feed him."

Paolo said, "'Fortune got off a few rounds.' The knife man had a gun."

Benno shrugged.

The cop looked at the powdered sugar on his fingertips. "Also maybe you can explain Mimmo in the trunk of Tutti's car you were in. His throat slit."

Gemma gasped. Imogene clung to Bell.

"You say something about a knife man, Enzo?" Benno asked.

Bell said, "They were killing each other and Sal found me after he escaped Tutti. Cut and dried."

Paolo said, "Tutti claims you held him up for twenty-two hundred bucks, Sal."

"At Pennsylvania Station?"

"That's what he says."

"Boy, that's thanks for you. He threatens me, so I shoot him in the legs instead of the brain. Maybe he likes it better you got Fortune and Boo killing each other like *selvaggi*."

"Savages," Bell said sideways.

"I mean, if I'm this big-time armed robber, why do I call the cops and say, 'Go find dead Frankie Fortune and Boo.' Huh?"

"Where's the gun you shot Tutti with? He says it was a snub nose .38."

"I threw it in the Hudson. Why do I need a gun?"

"In the Hudson. For Christ's sake, Sally."

"Hey, how am I supposed to think clear? I got Frankie making me kill senators, and they're holding Leo and I'm walking through New York City carrying a piece and maybe it's hot 'cause Zamarella used it or somebody. I'm over by Port Authority anyway, so I walk to the piers…"

Benno gave the whole speech with his shoulders up around his ears, his hands waving.

"Do you remember which pier?" Paolo asked.

Benno said no.

Bell said, "Enzo, I wonder how many Snubbies you'll find on the bottom of the river."

"You know what they wanted to do, don't you?" Benno said. "If I hit Dunney, it's like Corini ordered it. Which means Frankie threw in with Gigenti, who wants to run the crew and to hell with show business and politics."

Paolo nodded. Bruno Gigenti did like the old ways. In Sicilian, Paolo said, "Maybe Gigenti respects you now. Could be he forgives you busting his window and scaring one of his boys."

"You heard about that, huh?" He wagged a finger and in English said, "Don't try to trap me, Enzo. I don't want Gigenti's respect or Dunney's or nobody but the people sitting here in this room. I'm out. Period."

Bell thought that was pretty good, so he stood to go, walking over to get a hug from Gemma. He figured he'd take a nice long shower, spend a little quality time with Imogene and then he'd call his father's partner Eli Kreiner and get Salvatore Benno the best Jew lawyer he could find. Then he'd go back to meandering around the brownstone and trying to figure out what to do with the rest of his life.

"Anything to add, Ding?" Paolo asked.

Bell said, "No." But he thought, God bless reasonable doubt.

CHAPTER FORTY-TWO

Terrasini walked Marsala into the Wilshire Towers. The young UCLA student who served as the night doorman had his nose in a textbook. He said "Nino!" like a cheer, but then soured and said, "Mr. Marsala, I have a telegram for you." Whenever Marsala came in liquored up, the singer liked to bust the kid's balls for sport.

Terrasini handed it to his old boss as they went into the elevator.

"More gloom and doom," Marsala said, shaking the yellow envelope.

"How do you know? You don't know…"

"Believe me, buster. I know."

They rode up in sullen silence.

Inside the apartment, the air stale with cigarettes, Terrasini lit a flame under the teakettle.

The singer went to the sofa and, much as he'd done at Rosa's, melted into the cushion. He stared nowhere, his face hollow and gray. There was a sudden rap on the door, but Marsala didn't turn. When Terrasini asked him if he should open it, Marsala shrugged. The way it was going, it was the feds, handcuffs out, a photographer right behind them.

But it was Rico Enna, topcoat over his arm, briefcase in his fist. "Nino," he said, in a way Terrasini knew he'd brought more bad news.

"Bill." He entered, dropping his coat on a chair. "I'm sorry I didn't get to travel with you."

Marsala didn't reply.

"How are you feeling, Bill?"

"Like the world wants me to get off."

The kettle whistle blew and Terrasini left for the kitchen.

"You saw Anthony, right?" Marsala asked. "What did he say?"

Enna said, "Joey Aaron's filling in. You need to rest."

"The Sandpiper, too?"

"A good, long rest, Bill. Take care of your pipes."

Terrasini put the steeping tea in front of Marsala and clapped him on the shoulder. "I'll call you tomorrow."

He figured he'd hurry back to Rosa's and make sure she's all right. No matter what Bebe had done, he was Bill Jr.'s father. She still cared, if only for that.

"Buck up, Bebe," Terrasini added with a forced smile. "This bout has a lot of rounds left."

Marsala nodded, blue eyes vacant.

On the way to the door, Terrasini stopped at the phonograph. He figured, OK, a little music and Bebe will see life still has its richness whether he's up or way down.

The LP on the turntable was one of Marsala's favorites, music they'd studied together. Terrasini turned it on and by the time Billie Holiday was crooning cool and mellow over chugging rhythms, he was down the hall.

"Lady Day," Enna said as the door swung shut. "What's the telegram, Bill?"

"Can they send a subpoena by cable?"

Marsala ran his thumb under the envelope flap. Enna watched the singer read.

"Oh, yeah." Marsala let the telegram float to the floor. "Oh, yeah."

Enna retrieved it.

"Dear, dear Bill. Sing your song. You know who you are. Wish I could say more, but I've a duty to this little family we've made here. I won't forget you. Love, Eleanor."

"Bill, I'm sorry," Enna said. "Damn."

"A Dear John letter all the way from Africa."

Lady Day's song ended. A slow ballad began with Lester Young playing a beautiful breathy intro.

"You want a drink, Bill?"

Marsala didn't respond.

Billie Holiday entered golden. "In my solitude, you haunt me…"

Marsala stood.

"I'll get it, Bill."

Enna went to the bar.

Prez kept blowing as Lady Day sang, "In my solitude, you taunt me with memories that never die."

The ice bucket was empty, so Enna went into the kitchen and filled a tumbler with cubes from the refrigerator.

When he returned, he saw sheer curtains fluttering.

"…I'm filled with despair…"

Marsala had climbed over the rail and set his heels on the balcony's thin concrete lip 22 stories above Wilshire Boulevard.

When he was a kid, he threw himself off a ledge near Elysian Fields, landing on River Road in front of a truck, his femur fractured, the bone jutting out of his thigh. His mother came to the hospital and hugged him tight, crying until she ran out of tears.

Now there was nobody.

Enna dropped the glass. "Bill. Jesus!"

Marsala looked at Los Angeles spread out before him, the hills, lights in the distance. From here, he could see all the way to Narrows Gate a long, long time ago.

"…I know that I'll soon go mad. In my solitude…"

They thought I was kidding when I jumped off that ledge, Marsala thought. When I took the mirror glass to my wrist. When I shot that gun in Madrid.

Buddy, there comes a time you look into that void and you're certain you'll never escape it. You hear it calling your name…

As Enna lunged, Marsala leaned into the night sky and let go.

Terrasini was about to slide into his car when he heard a loud, grotesque thud behind him. Before he turned, he knew what it was.

Marsala's fallen body was fractured and twisted. Blood was flowing across the asphalt. Terrasini looked up along the tower.

The kid behind the desk ran out and then spun away in disgust.

"He fell," Terrasini said, backing away. "He was feeling sick, he went for air and he fell."

Jumping in the car, he pulled out of the lot and raced toward La Cienega and the 101 to Rosa.

Upstairs, his mind spinning, Enna told himself to calm down, to gather his thoughts. He called the police. "There's been an accident." Then he called his boss at the talent agency in New York and asked him to call Corini. He didn't want the cops to find Corini's number on Marsala's phone.

Then he took the elevator down to Bebe's body. A janitor stood next to the UCLA kid and Jesus, Marsala was in a sickening pose and all that blood and already a smell.

"He leaned over," Enna said. "He must've been tired and he fell." Enna repeated his story to the beat cops who didn't give a shit. But the dispatcher knew they had a mess on their hands and the call went all the way up to the captain, who contacted Hearst.

Rosa's phone rang just as Terrasini arrived.

Next, Louella Parsons called Lourenço Marques, Mozambique, and was told Eleanor Ree was in Tanganyika and would not return for hours. Then she woke up Mal Weisberg and Ree's agent was the first one to use the word despondent. Recalling when Marsala was raked across his wrist by mirror glass, Parsons asked if the singer was despondent enough to commit suicide. Weisberg replied, "Eleanor will be devastated. She loved him. I hope she can muster the courage to continue."

At the Hay-Adams Hotel in Washington, D.C., Charlie Tyler was jarred from sleep by what he thought was his wake-up call. But it was a colleague at the Department of Justice. Standing at the bedside in his boxers and undershirt, Tyler said, "It doesn't matter. The hearing won't be postponed." They were already sitting on the news of Mistretta's murder.

Up early, Imogene O'Boyle turned on the radio in Bell's kitchen while she made herself a cup of Nescafé. A minute later, she was nudging Leo awake.

"Bill Marsala is dead," she said.

Bell sprung up. "Dead?"

"The radio says he fell off the balcony at this apartment in Beverly Hills."

He killed himself, Bell thought. He scrambled out of bed and dressed hurriedly.

"Sal?" Imogene asked.

"Better we should tell him."

Sitting in the back room at the store not quite heated by the Franklin stove, dragging around the peppers and eggs he made himself, Benno was trying to figure exactly when Gigenti's men would invade. He was already confused in his thinking, unable to separate what happened from what he said happened. Plus he shot two people and who on Polk Street would buy that Boo Chiasso shot Frankie Fortune—true—and Fortune shot Boo—not true—and then there's that rat fuck Mimmo. Leo was looking for a lawyer and there goes the $2,200 in Benno's pocket, plus the rest he skimmed over the years.

Suddenly, screaming police cars blew by, sirens and lights, and then Bell and Imogene walked in, even though Benno's wasn't open yet.

"Sal…"

Benno looked up at Bell, whose face was red from the cold. "Now what?"

"You put on the radio?"

"The truck don't have a radio. You know that."

"It's Bebe. He's gone. Off the balcony."

Benno shot out of the seat. "He killed himself?"

"That's what I'm thinking."

"Holy shit."

"I know."

"Holy shit," Benno repeated as he sat slowly. Then he stood again. "You think somebody threw him off the balcony? You know, they got some of Ziggy's guys still and maybe Zamarella's guys."

"Sal, you know Bebe. You heard what he did at Elysian Fields when he was a kid."

"Bebe. Jesus. I guess after Mimmo, then he rats me out to the commission and Corini can't like that."

"Eleanor, too. You think she's carrying his picture around Africa?"

"You know he's got clits on his pipes, right?" Benno asked.

Imogene blinked.

"They say he fell," Bell shrugged.

"Fuckin' Bebe," said Benno.

EPILOGUE

It had been a difficult weekend for Anthony Corini. Bruno Gigenti moved a new crew into the candy store in Narrows Gate, declaring ownership. From his leather wing chair in his apartment on Central Park West, Corini took it as intended: Your boy Fortune is dead. Mimmo, too. The muscle Chiasso. Your advisor Cy Geller. Farcolini is in Sicily and I own the Cubans. Your bet on Marsala marks you stupid. And now your politicians are dumping you. I'm taking everything. You are finished.

Still, Corini came to the courthouse cocky and defiant, and in no time the heat of the blinding television lights melted away the veneer of respectability he'd spent years maintaining. As he positioned himself at the table facing the commission, ignoring huge cameras on rolling stilts and stepping over cables, he told himself to remember that politicians were like entertainers. They liked to put on a show. You remind them they're in charge of nothing and they fall apart like children who dropped their candy.

As instructed, he stood, looked around the crowded courtroom, raised his right hand and bellowed, "I do." Then he sat next to his white-bread attorney, a heavy hitter Farcolini used for his deportation negotiations, who was on a first-name basis with Dewey.

"The television isn't the same as radio," the lawyer advised.

"It's radio with pictures," Corini snapped.

"Actually," the lawyer said, "it's not. It's a microscope."

Mr. Corini replied, "Good. Anybody who looks is gonna see who runs who."

"You'll be judged," the lawyer continued.

"By who?" Corini said with a sneer.

Sworn in, Corini sat for an hour as Sam Bamberger read his police record, slowly and methodically showing him to be a violent street punk who'd become "the Jukebox King" and, in time, successor to Carlo Farcolini, the organization's deported and disgraced head. Every legitimate enterprise Corini was associated with was shown to be a front for organized crime activities.

Corini simmered. He was amused. Openly annoyed. Bored. He yawned. He examined his hat. He studied his fingernails, unaware that, as Bamberger continued in dry monotone—a voice so hypnotic and lacking in emotion that no sensible person could doubt everything he said—the camera was fixed on him. It captured Corini as a man capable of the allegations made against him now and during last week's hearings.

Finally, Bamberger addressed Corini. "The commission would now like to ask you a few questions."

Corini replied, "It's about time."

Bamberger began each query with "Isn't it a fact that…" or "Would it not be true to suggest…" which made them difficult for Corini to rebut. "It's not a fact," he said at one point. "It's a fact because you say it's a fact?" He was reduced to a litany of denials and claims of a faulty memory. Bamberger treated him like a common criminal.

Bamberger turned over the questioning to the senator from Rhode Island, who wore a sun visor against the hot television lights. He proceeded to interrogate Corini about his relationship with two dozen politicians, most of whom were associated with Tammany Hall and all of whom visited him at his apartment on Central Park West. Photographs taken at restaurants, nightclubs, ballgames and the track were introduced into the record and shown on television. Corini thought he'd regained his footing as the attention turned to these assemblymen, mayors, councilmen. "We shared a few cocktails," he said. "Like you do with friends."

"On what do you base these friendships?" Rhode Island asked.

"Just like you, Senator. I can do for them, they can do for me."

"Please tell the commission, what is it that you do for these men, Mr. Corini?"

"I've been around a long time," he replied. "I know a lot of people." Looking at the senator's nameplate, he added, "Even in Rhode Island."

Uncomfortable laughter rippled in the courtroom. Reporters looked at each other. Corini's remark sounded like a threat.

"Mr. Corini," Dunney said as he tapped the gavel. He was convinced Bill Marsala's death was murder, as Mistretta's had been. His triumph tainted, he wanted to expose Corini for the base criminal he'd always been. "Mr. Corini, did you offer your services to any war effort?"

"No," Corini replied.

"Can you tell us what you have done for your country?"

"Paid my taxes," he said, sitting upright and hanging his elbow on the back of the chair.

"We'll discuss that assertion with you in executive session, Mr. Corini," Dunney replied, jotting a note.

"Anything you want to ask me, you ask me here. In public."

"I'm sorry to inform you of this fact, Mr. Corini, but here you don't make the rules. Here you are no better than any other citizen of this country, many of whom fought and had family and friends who died in its service."

And with that, Corini collected his hat and coat and walked out. Bamberger's shouts of contempt of Congress trailed him into the corridor, where photographers waited.

On the advice of his attorney, Corini returned the following morning, his voice hoarse, his eyes showing signs of a flu. He was prepared to cooperate, he said, if he was afforded the same level of respect as any other taxpayer. But it was too late. He'd proven himself a creep, a thug, a gangster. Any politician—and the former mayor of New York was the next witness to testify under the unforgiving lights—linked to him was scarred by the association. The *Daily News* reported that he was the first mobster to be rubbed out by television.

Rosa called Vincenzo as soon as Nino told her about her husband's suicide. "He was taking the air and fell," she said to her father-in-law. Then she asked her father and sister Bev in Bayonne to go stay with him until she flew in with Bill Jr. She took charge of the funeral arrangements, greeting old friends at Kalm's and withstanding the pity in the sad eyes of the thousands of fans who were ushered in to touch the closed coffin, a few sobbing like they lost a lover, a brother, a trusted friend.

Despite the spectacle, she couldn't avoid sentimentality. She no longer loved him, not after he'd captured her heart and then betrayed her. But it had been a hell of a ride, as he would've said, and there were memories. As she explored them, she found herself feeling terribly sorry for him. He'd suffered his whole life, never having enough to satisfy his need for the sort of unattainable perfection Hennie demanded. Everything threatened him;

everything conspired to make him unworthy. The applause wasn't enough, the acclaim, money, the fans, women. Fear and anxiety came in waves, happiness out of an eyedropper. If only he could've taken a step back to see what he'd done: for a while, this skinny little kid from Narrows Gate made it to the top of the world. If only he could've been happy with the music, his family, Bill Jr. Then nobody could've touched him.

Marsala's short, remarkable life was celebrated to an overflow crowd at St. Matthew's. A tenor from the Metropolitan Opera came over and sang "Ave Maria," the Sicilians in attendance nodding respectfully. They'd already started scheming how to get Polk Street renamed Marsala Way; you could make good money off tourists with a thing like that. The radio played Marsala music nonstop. Everyone all over Narrows Gate could hear it floating across the river from New York City. Maybe they were listening to it all over the country, that voice, the tenderness, romance, the spunk and maybe they couldn't help but think, Gee, I wonder what Bill Marsala would've become when he grew into a man and sang about what he'd learned of heartache, loneliness and the bitter nectar of life and love. They didn't know his head was never coming out of his ass, that Hennie had beat him down for good, that his demons taunted him even when he was filled with joy. The fans listened to the testimonials, remembered the comfort he brought during the war and they thought he was bound to do more, to give more, to continue to add sparkle to life. They didn't know.

The press made a big deal out of who hadn't attended the services—Anthony Corini, Bruno Gigenti, Alvin Dunney and Eleanor Ree, who got as far as London, where she was photographed in tears, though with her eyes behind dark glasses, who can say? Many celebrities attended; most politicians didn't.

Neither did Louis B. Mayer, who had someone send flowers. Guy Simon came across country, feeling guilty that he'd convinced Marsala to eat horseradish for his throat. A childish prank, compensation for losing Ree to an inferior intellectual. But a good one, was it not?

Terrasini cried, remembering Bebe as a gutsy kid desperate to sing, desperate for applause. You did good, Bebe, he thought. Jesus, Bebe, don't you know you did good?

Marsala was buried in the crypt with his mother where, Benno told Bell, she could bust his balls for all eternity.

The next day, Rosa held a wake for Mimmo and nobody outside the Mistretta family came and half of them stayed away. "Don't even think about it," Bell warned Benno, who was curious to see how Mimmo looked defrosted.

Benno was dying to go settle up with Gigenti's men at the candy store, but Paolo the cop said no, the Jew lawyer said no. Bell said, "Game's over, Sal. They're through with you." It came to Benno that he'd done Gigenti a favor, clearing the last scraps off the plate, and maybe they should leave it at that.

Where could Anthony Corini go? Sicily was out; by now, Carlo Farcolini knew that he had been manipulated by his former trusted associate into believing Bruno Gigenti had provoked the petty violence among the New York–area leadership. Corini wouldn't last one hour if he traveled to his native land.

Canada? No. Since the death of Eugenio Zamarella, the authorities were eager to take down other U.S. gangsters. It produced a stirring of national pride: in New York, Chicago, New Orleans, Miami, Los Angeles, crime reigned, but not here, they said, ignoring the links between U.S. crews and operations in Toronto, Hamilton, Montreal and Vancouver.

Argentina? Gigenti had made a fortune in South America, money he used to secure the services of his street gangs while he watched Corini's plans crumble. The organization Gigenti grew in Rosaria still prospered.

Cuba? Impossible.

But Corini had to leave the country. He faced a contempt of Congress charge for his evasion during the Dunney hearings and his remark about his taxes had provoked an investigation by the Internal Revenue Service. His friends in business and entertainment were now loyal to Gigenti, who reluctantly acknowledged that owning a town like Las Vegas had its advantages. Even Saul Geller, who now occupied his father's seat and Ziggy Baum's, refused his calls.

In New York, he couldn't walk down the street, couldn't order a sandwich in a coffee shop. People who once bowed and stepped aside now looked at him like he was something stuck to the bottom of their shoes.

He would go to England, he decided. It would take a while to establish himself, but he'd open a club and book talent. The musicians who came overseas wouldn't care that he no longer had Farcolini's power behind him. He'd pay good wages. The plan Cy Geller proposed for Vegas and the organization's nightclubs— maybe it would play in the UK. Maybe Corini could find a singer like Bebe he could groom. He took an atlas off his shelf. Surely there was somebody in London, Birmingham, Manchester, Dublin or Glasgow who could profit from his support.

His wife, humiliated by his performance on TV, declined to go along with his latest scheme. For the past decade, she'd allowed herself to believe that he was a legitimate businessman and that the politicians, industry leaders and their wives were their friends.

His passport was registered under his real name. He decided he would take a train to Boston and fly across the ocean from there.

There was no one to say good-bye to.

He packed one valise. He sewed $42,000 into its lining and in his coat another $16,000. He still had almost $3 million in offshore accounts. He'd instructed his attorney to sell his investments and settle with the IRS.

Suitcase at his side, standing in moonlight, he looked around the vast, immaculate Central Park West apartment. A long way from a stone house outside Canicatti, Sicily. A long way from that rat trap in East Harlem.

He pressed the elevator button but he heard nothing in response: no whoosh of the lift in its cradle, no rattling chains.

"Even the fuckin' elevator operator," Corini muttered as he walked to the stairs.

When he arrived at the lobby, 12 flights later, the attendant's desk was empty. The bellman was gone.

Corini headed to the revolving doors.

"Anthony."

Corini turned.

Bruno Gigenti raised a pistol and pulled the trigger.

As Corini crawled toward the door, Gigenti stood over him and fired five more shots into his body, the last into the back of his head, blood spatter leaping to the gunman's face and onto his gritted teeth.

Back in his club on Mulberry Street, Gigenti dictated a message to Don Carlo in Sicily to confirm that the task he'd approved had been done.

Six days later, a cable arrived. "Thank you, my dear friend," wrote Farcolini in Sicilian.

Benno and Bell were dressed up to go to the Avalon to see some picture and maybe go to the Grotto for *zuppa di vongole*. They had to drive to Jersey City to retrieve Nina and Imogene, which made no sense since the movie theater was about three blocks from where they started. Benno was behind the wheel of Tyler's car, a gift from Bell to Vito and Gemma.

Bell said, "I've been thinking. I think we should open a Benno's uptown."

Benno laughed. "For the Irish? For what, cabbage and boiled fuckin' meat?"

"Your uncle says they come to the store and buy regular."

True, Benno thought. But like little kids confronting the ocean.

"I'll run it for you," Bell added.

"You? A Jew runs a Sicilian food store for the Irish. That's some thinking, Leo."

"We'll call it Benno and Bell's."

"You serious?"

"Next we open one in Kearny out by Imogene's."

They rattled up the plank road.

Bell said, "I'm going to major in business and I'll do the books. Plus I know produce and we can bring in Vernon Buie to help."

"The colored gimp from the A&P? The guy shot in the war, he cleans the chickens?"

"He's solid, up and down," Bell replied.

Benno was thinking all those taps to the head Boo Chiasso gave him had sent Bell to Wackyland.

"What happened to Poland? To seeing the world?"

"First, I settle down."

"With Imogene."

"Sure. Of course," Bell replied. "Besides, the world ain't going anywhere."

ABOUT THE AUTHOR

Jim Fusilli serves as the rock and pop music critic of the *Wall Street Journal*. He is the author of six books: *Closing Time*; *A Well-Known Secret*; *Tribeca Blues*; *Hard, Hard City*, *Mystery Ink* magazine's 2004 Novel of the Year; *Pet Sounds*; and *Marley Z and the Bloodstained Violin*. He served as the editor of, and contributed chapters to, the award-winning serial thrillers *The Chopin Manuscript* and *The Copper Bracelet*. He developed Narrows Gate as a setting in numerous published short stories. "Chellini's Solution," which appeared in the 2007 edition of the *Best American Mystery Stories*, features Narrows Gate in the years following World War II. "Digby, Attorney at Law" portrays the fictional city in the early 1960s. "Digby" was nominated for the Edgar and Macavity awards in 2010. Fusilli lives in New York City with his wife, the former Diane Holuk, a senior public relations executive. Their daughter Cara is a graduate of the New School.